AYWARD
PASS
THIMBLETON

CLIFFS OF WAYWARD

CLIFFS OF WAYWARD

VERONICA KING

INIMITABLE
BOOKS
UNFORGETTABLE STORIES

Published by Inimitable Books, LLC
www.inimitablebooksllc.com

Library of Congress Cataloguing-in-Publication Data is available.

First edition, 2025
Cover design by Keylin Rivers

ISBN 978-1-958607-15-2 (hardcover)
10 9 8 7 6 5 4 3 2 1

To the readers who are wrestling with their sense of self: growth is messy, but growth means change.

ALSO BY VERONICA KING

Down the Well

Enchanted Glass: An Inimitable Lenormand

From the Diary of Agnes Jaeger:
The Secrets of Silver Leaf Academy

TRIGGER WARNING

Typical fantasy violence, light body horror, instance of roofieing, derealization (feeling as though reality is unreliable), implied past sexual assault/sexual abuse

PART ONE

ONE

Splintered wood scraped against Lore's fingertips as she picked up another piece of debris. Lore fought back images of blue magic being cast and the haunting, lifeless eyes of the then-reanimated Grayshade's corpse. She didn't remember all this wreckage during their fight with Crinkle. *Had it really only been two weeks ago?*

Lore let out a sigh, and her thoughts wandered while she collected broken pieces of Charmsend in her arms. Memories softly kissed her mind like ocean waves lapping against a sandy beach. It felt like just the other day, when Lore had pulled herself from the depths of the orange brick well and was welcomed by empty streets that carried music, laughter, and the savory scent of fried foods. No street in Charmsend held those same sentiments today. She continued to pick up the rubble while the recollection of meeting Mathilde and getting dragged into solving a town murder mystery caused a smile to grace her cheeks.

She looked around at the folk of Charmsend gathering up the rubble. It was here, the aftermath of their battle. Some animals walked 'round with wheelbarrows, collecting fragments of stone, wood planks, and ash. Others hammered iron into lumber fresh from the forest as they fixed buildings and market shop fronts. Lore's eyes scanned the square. And some stood around patches of frozen ground with fire-lit sticks, hoping the heat would melt the magic-imbued ice.

Then Lore's fingertips met a cool chill. Looking down, she saw a piece of fragmented ice from one of Crinkle's spells. The sensation sparked the memory of the pale blue light that radiated from the ethereal stag. Mist fell from its mighty body the way a gentle waterfall flows into a small stream. She recalled how small she felt in front of the herculean and ghostly animal. The memory caused a feeling of smallness to wash over her.

When she knelt down to add another piece to the stack she was carrying, the weight felt as if the larger moon tumbled from the Thimbleton sky and landed squarely on her shoulders. Her collection was so heavy, Lore worried her arms would fall off. She reached for another piece of rubble mindlessly, but the sensation of her finger grazing fur brought her back to the present moment.

Amber eyes fixed on her own. Killmoore's head tilted to the side as he studied her furrowed eyebrows and glassy gaze. "Everything okay, Lore?"

She ran her tongue over her teeth as she tried to put together the words to describe her heavy state of mind. *If only I could blame it on the weight of the new set of antlers.*

After a beat of silence, the fox stepped closer to her and put a rust-orange arm around her shoulders. "Don't worry. We'll get you home," he assured, leading her to a less crowded spot. "Mathilde is gonna bring it up tonight to her sisters over dinner."

Lore nodded as she leaned against the cold iron lamp post. She didn't have the energy to correct the bounty hunter. Besides, what would he think if she told him the true fear stirring within her? The doubt itself whispered to her, the sound of her own voice. *What if what waited for her back 'home' was worse than being the only human in a strange land? Even if it was a human with antlers.*

Killmoore set the pile of debris he was carrying onto the ground and shoved his hands into the pockets of his once-regal blue coat. It was now more or less tattered rags. She looked the bounty hunter up and down. His words from when she awoke after the battle danced their way across her consciousness and through to her ears as if she were hearing the words for the first time again.

"The well is impassable. But my dear friends, nothing is impossible."

Lore pushed the memory aside. Her eyes slid past her ginger friend and settled on Mathilde, picking up far more than she could reasonably carry—buckets of nails and scrap pieces of two-by-fours. "Do you really believe what you said?" Lore asked aloud, her attention still focused on the gray mouse.

"You'll have to be more specific. I say a lot of things," Killmoore laughed as he pulled a scrap of paper from his pocket. The sound of him un-crumpling the onion-skin-thin parchment took her attention away from Mathilde. The setting sun was still strong enough that Lore could see the faint image of the deep blue-green jewel she knew hung around the fox's neck, hiding under his shirt.

"You sure you don't want to cash in that bounty first?" Lore asked with a rasped laugh.

His gaze held hers, no smile spread on his face at her humor. "I'm not too worried. From what the bat said, the way to send you home is in the general area of the Romplands, so I'll get my bounty."

The flurry of hushed conversations under the cover of night, safely inside the sleeping yellow manor, had blurred together. A fuzzy concept of a plan for the four of them had been hashed out—and *re*-hashed out—so many times that they all seemed to become one heavy burden. *Bad enough to make my stomach ache.* Because while Mathilde was excited for the journey, Lore couldn't help but think she was being selfish for stealing the mouse away from her sisters after reuniting them.

Her memories of Charmsend melted away to make room for the fragmented images of Lore's life from before. The old woman who appeared in the puddles of water before Crinkle had banished her, Killmoore, and Mathilde from Charmsend.

The woman's snow-colored hair fell around her face like wispy clouds. And then there was a young man with inky black hair, who had a smile that made starlight seem dim. *What if they weren't real? What if it was my mind seeing what I wanted to see?* She had not remembered the walls of a house, nor a smell that would have been paired with it.

Her focus drifted back to the townsfolk. Though their square lay in ruins, they had each other to lean on. They had homes and lives to return to.

"What if…" she mumbled. "What if I don't have a home to go back to?"

Killmoore folded the paper and placed it back in his pocket. His snout twitched, and he scratched his white-tipped triangular ears. "You've got to have a home." A subtle fog escaped with his words as Killmoore's warm breath met the crisp air. "At the very least, you surely have a family to return to. Others of yer kind who've been searchin' for you."

He sounded sure of his words, but Lore wasn't entirely convinced.

"What if they aren't looking for me, though?"

A distant look overcame her friend's face, but then a sincere smile spread across his features. Big enough to show the yellowing of his sharp teeth. "Well, I know I'd be out there lookin' for you. And I know I'm not the only one who feels that way." He nodded toward Mathilde, who was now sitting on the load she'd been carrying.

The sun continued to sink behind the tree line that hugged Charmsend's borders. The lanterns lit themselves, and Lore felt a gentle pat from cold metal against her back.

"Good evening, Grian." Her voice was distant, as if it were off chasing lost pieces of herself instead of picking up the pieces in front of her.

"Grian! Glad to see you've got your spark back," Mathilde called as the mouse waved, approaching the two.

The gray mouse stood with her hands on her hips. "Why do you both look like the backside of a Grayshade?"

"You know the kindest greetings. I'm surprised you don't have more friends," Killmoore teased back.

Lore softly smiled. "Looks like most of the mess is cleaned up."

Mathilde adjusted the end of her jacket that wrapped around her wrist. "Yeah, that's why I think tonight will be good." She sounded so sure that it rubbed off on Lore. Even if it only stuck for a moment.

Maybe Killmoore is right. I have *to have a home to go back to.*

Mathilde held a flat hand to the side of her snout, as if her sisters on the other side of the square would hear her whispers. "I'm excited for my first real adventure." Though her voice was quiet, the excitement hung in the air around the trio. Wrapping them in warmth. That or it was just Grian's fire radiation from above, spilling heat over them.

Lore rolled her eyes and smirked. Leave it to Mathilde to not consider unmasking and defeating a corrupt wielder who also killed her father as *not* a real adventure.

"I'm pretty sure getting closure by the death of your father's killer *was* 'an adventure,'" Lore pointed out.

Mathilde's nose twitched as she waved a hand. "That all happened *here*. Adventure involves leaving home." The mouse looked Lore up and down. "It's in every story ever."

Regardless of how the mouse defined adventure, Lore felt a bit of hope again, even if it was hollow and fragile. At least it was there, and that has to count for something.

Mathilde looked down the cobblestone path that would lead them to her home.

The smaller of the two moons peeked over the prickled treetops that poked the darkening horizon.

Killmoore picked up the small pile of rubble from earlier. "Right, well, I'm off to go put these in a barrel. I'll meet you both back at the house." He didn't wait for a response as he quickly shifted past Mathilde.

The mouse shook her head and turned. Her eyes followed him.

Lore followed Mathilde's gaze to Killmoore, who was talking to Tansy over a bright green wheelbarrow. He had sat the debris inside, and was leaning close to the vixen.

Mathilde impatiently tapped her foot.

"It's okay. Let's go and get some things packed before our big announcement at dinner," Lore chimed. "He said he'd meet us there."

Mathilde let out a groan and stomped her feet as she followed Lore down the alley.

The breeze nipped at their noses, and Lore felt a rush of relief when the yellow manor came into view. The old iron gate snapped closed behind them, latching shut. Their feet rhythmically hopped up the steps and across the creaking porch.

Mathilde opened the oak door that was only recently put back on its hinges, and inside they went.

The house was silent. Only the faint orange flicker from the hearth illuminated the inside.

"Well, it won't be long before my sisters and Merlin return for the night," Mathilde huffed. "I hid some clothes that Dina was getting rid of, and I tossed them under your bed for this quest."

Lore nodded. "Thank you, Mathilde."

The gray mouse stretched her two arms above her head as she walked to the rickety stairwell. "We may be going on a long trip to the Romplands, but I won't let anything bad happen to you. It'd be a shame if you got lost or injured on the journey meant to send you home, Lore."

Lore faltered as she walked to the stairs. She stood in the dimly lit room and slowly turned in a circle, taking in all the details of the home. The glass mushrooms on the mantle holding each other's nubs and dancing slowly above the flames that swayed like golden tendrils. The heavy curtains that kissed the hardwood floors, the fabric glossy and slick. She recalled how the cloth had felt in her hand as she slipped out the window under the staircase.

That moment felt like it was only moments ago.

The cozy kitchen, with its small table and endless chairs placed around it. Lore had come to enjoy eating a warm meal elbow-to-elbow with the mice sisters.

I'll miss this when I leave. I'll miss them.

The smell of applewood from the hearth filled her lungs as she took another deep breath in. Her hand glided over the dark polished banister as she ascended to the top floor of the home. No matter how hard she tried, she couldn't force her mind to remember each and every characteristic of this place. The yellow manor in Charmsend wasn't something she could pack up in a suitcase to take with her, nor were her friends. The breath from earlier poured out in a sigh. For all its grandeur, what she would miss most was the way the floorboards creaked when she walked on them. It was a strange sense of comfort.

Lore turned back to Mathilde and could see the faint line of a smirk on her furry face as she leaped up the stairwell, skipping every other step.

She entered what became her room in the short time she had been in Charmsend. The flowers were closed and didn't move an inch since she had entered. They were asleep, and she was looking forward to some good rest. Who knew when she'd be able to sleep in a comfortable bed once they left? She collapsed on the bed and stared at the ceiling. Would tonight be the last time she looked at it? Who knew?

It all depended on Minifred.

Lore slid off the bed and onto the floor with a huff. It groaned from her weight. She blindly reached under the bed until her hand bumped into the crumpled paper bag. She pulled it out. On the front was a silhouette of a cat, printed in vivid pink ink. Dina's was written in an arch across the top in the fanciest handwriting Lore had ever seen. She smiled. The calico cat had become a familiar face she was happy to see around.

She opened the bag, and inside, she saw a pile of unfolded clothes that appeared to be tossed in at a moment's notice. That, or Mathilde had run home with the bag, shaking the ever-loving hell out of it. Lore dumped them on the floor and began sorting through them. First, she took all the bottoms—pants, skirts, whatever she could find—and put them on the bed. That left everything else to still comb through. The charm of her bracelet jingled against the silver band as she worked.

For all their talks, no one had given Lore a straight answer on the expected weather, or what to pack. Lore paused, looking at the articles of clothes that seemed to sprout from the floor like daisies in spring. They are animals—*I guess they don't need to wear clothes. They probably just do it as a courtesy.*

She set the silk shirts to the side. Unless they were going to a fancy party no one had told her about, they didn't seem very practical. She let another blouse slip from her fingertips into the growing garden of discarded clothes. But just in case, she'd bring along one of the nice tops and a skirt.

Did this cat own anything *other* than silk?

Toward the bottom, she found a wool-knit sweater. It was cream-colored and went well with the two pairs of pants Lore had put on the bed. She gathered the three articles of clothing and folded them on top of her green flannel. The one thing she felt connected to, even though she couldn't remember why. She heard the oak door shut on the level below, and anxiety gnawed at her gut.

Lore felt frozen by the bedside of folded clothes. Her eyes drifted to the borrowed sweater. *I hope it'll stretch over the antlers.* Lore let a sigh escape the tight cavity of her chest. One thought lingered, a buzzing thought that couldn't be quelled by practicing steady breath. *I hope they take the news of my impending goodbye well.*

Her excitement and nerves wrestled in the pit of her stomach as she reached for her door. The thought of starting the journey to go home was like sucking on a sweet and sour candy, though she wasn't sure about the specific flavor. It was exciting, but also leaving the safety she'd found here was daunting. *And who knew wherever home was?*

Lore's eyes drifted down to her lap as she picked at her fingernails. She could still feel the awkward staring contest between the two sisters, even though neither mouse was looking at her.

The talking had lasted long beyond dinner, and they still didn't seem to be getting anywhere. Not even after Lore tried her best to explain the slapdash details of their plan. She had hoped Merlin would help her make the case to the eldest mouse. Lore started, "So, we'll head west—"

It was Killmoore who had chimed in. "South, Lore. The Romplands are south. Mythvale is west."

Lore felt heat rise to her cheeks and her eyes couldn't meet the judgemental raised brow of Minifred. The human looked at the bat. *I swore he had said something about going west.* Lore continued like that for a few painful minutes. Trying to blend a coherent plan from the days of chatter that overlapped like a fever dream.

Mathilde cleared her throat and had her hands spread flat on the table, her brows furrowed, and the defiance radiated off her the way a flower's aroma tickled your nose on a damp spring day. Her demeanor didn't tickle, though. It hit you suddenly like a bag of bricks to the gut.

Lore gulped.

Killmoore's foot tapped her under the table, grabbing her attention.

She looked back up, unsure if it was a "it's okay, we'll figure it out" message, or if it was "this is an accident waiting to happen" message. The scene felt unnervingly familiar, but she couldn't place where the discomfort was coming from, and it was eating her from the inside. Like a worm that would chew its way through the juiciest fruit from its tree.

"Lore needs to go home, and you can't stop us from leaving," Mathilde said in a controlled tone that contradicted the frazzled look in her eye.

Minifred casually took a sip of her drink and fixed a pointed gaze on her youngest sister. "I never said Lore couldn't go." Her slender, long fingers curled around the mug that rested in her grasp. "I said that she and Killmoore are more than free to leave." Her eyes looked Lore up and down before fluttering back to Mathilde. "If that's what she wants. But I've never heard her state that she wanted to return home."

Lore felt like stones were piling up in her throat. She couldn't speak, even though she wanted to. *I do wanna go home. Even though it's a gamble on what I'll be returning to—I want to.* Her leg shook under the table as the silence weighed on her shoulders, still unable to find her words.

"Of course she wants to go home," Mathilde spat.

A spoon dropped on the table from one of Mathilde's other sisters. The group's eyes bounced back and forth between the oldest and youngest of them as they waited to see what happened next.

"You can't speak for her, Mathilde," Minifred chided, her expression softening as she looked at Lore. "Who's to say you aren't forcing desires onto her just so you can leave and go on an adventure you aren't ready for?" The eldest sister's words were a sharp accusation.

Mathilde slammed her fists on the table. "I made a promise!" She was determined to keep her word.

Lore nodded slowly. "I *do* want to go home," she finally whispered.

The sisters either chose to ignore her words, or they were so wrapped up in their own quarrel that they would talk over anyone right now.

"And how would you know if I were ready or not? That's not a call you can make, Minifred." Mathilde's scowl tightened. "You aren't our mother."

A harsh statement wrapped in a pretty envelope—licked with anger and sealed with venom before delivery.

Minifred deflated. Quiet hurt leaked from the corners of her eyes as her clenched hands lay folded in her lap.

The tension from the atmosphere trickled into Lore's spine, forcing her to sit straighter. Her heart raced like a starved hunting dog chasing after its prey. She shoved the chair back away from the table—away from the argument in front of her. But her body felt frozen to the chair as everyone's eyes fell on her. Like they suddenly remembered that the human existed again. "I want to go home," she muttered, slightly louder than last time, looking at the ground.

Minifred composed herself. "An understandable want," she said out of the corner of her mouth. "But Mathilde is forbidden to go. No offense, but I'm not going to entrust the safety of my sister to a human who doesn't know Thimbleton. Even if she *has* grown antlers."

"We have a plan!" Mathilde argued.

Lore locked eyes with Killmoore, then her gaze shot to Merlin. They all seemed to be thinking the same thing. So many talks of what *could* be done played in Lore's mind. *Which plan had they actually settled on?*

Killmoore cleared his throat. "I have been thinking that maybe we should try to restore Lore's memories before we search for a way to send her home."

Where did that come from?

"Wouldn't she get her memories upon returning home?" Mathilde pointed out.

"It's not guaranteed," Merlin added, speaking for the first time, tapping his chin. "That's actually clever thinking on the fox's part."

Lore saw Killmoore bristle in his seat, but the fox stayed silent.

She swallowed hard. "Do any of us even know how to restore my memories?" She paused as silence crept across their kitchen table discussion. "At least Merlin knows a general location that could send me home."

Minifred scoffed. "That's still not a *plan*."

"Do you even know of a way to restore my memories, Killmoore?"

The fox scratched the scruff behind his neck. "Well, let's say I know a place a bit north that keeps a bunch of ancient knowledge and magic."

"How far north?" Mathilde asked with sparkles in her eyes, like a flurry of glittering snowflakes.

"The Wayward Mountains," Killmoore replied. "I know a village at the base of the mountain we could stay at. Cloch Chruinn."

Minifred crossed her arms. "Gannon talked about the mountains, said they're dangerous." She paused, eyeing Mathilde. "I don't think it'd be smart for a novice adventurer to go on such a hazardous first *quest*."

Killmoore scratched behind his ear. "Well, there're the myths of fog beasts, yes."

Minifred raised a brow. "And bandits."

Killmoore leaned back in his chair. "Bandits are everywhere."

The eldest mouse sister was unamused. "The aviary of mad corvids."

The fox's face hardened. "Now, you know that's an unjust stereotype."

"Not to mention the terrain," she added.

Killmoore drummed his digits on the tabletop. "Thimbleton's diverse landscape is absolutely beautiful this time of year."

Lore felt her spine stiffen as Minifred locked onto her.

Rather predator-like for a mouse.

"You heard the fox." Minifred's tone hardened. "How do you plan to deal with all that, human?"

Lore felt the heat rise in her cheeks. *I don't have an answer.* She couldn't tell if it was the weight of her absolute ignorance about the world beyond Charmsend or the pull of the antlers atop her head, but the human couldn't look up. She sat, not a word falling from her mouth. The silence gnawed at her ears.

Merlin cleared his throat as he set his silverware across his plate. "I plan to accompany the youngsters on their first official quest."

Minifred shot a sideways glance at him. "You think I'd trust you with my sister just because you're our dead father's friend?"

Lore watched the fox's face curl with a delighted smirk at Minifred's skepticism. The bat bobbed his head as he reached into his coat pocket and pulled out a wooden pipe. Lore chewed the inside of her cheek as she noted how ridiculously small and fragile Merlin looked sitting in Gannon's seat at the dinner table. *Minifred may think the same.*

"I think you are a good sister," the bat continued, his voice steady as he reached in his other pocket for a pouch that smelled of freshly peeled bark and rich earth. Merlin packed the front of the vessel with the ground herb and, with a flick of his right wrist, a small flame glided from his fingertip to the packed pipe, lighting it. The bat quickly blew out the flame and took a deep inhale.

The table, all aside from Killmoore, leaned forward in their seats, waiting to hear what the great Wielder would say.

Merlin's mouth gaped slightly, and smoke fell from the opening like a dragon preparing to ignite a mighty breath of fire. "I think Mathilde's gumption is to be admired."

The mouse in question beamed. As she opened her mouth to rub it in her sister's face, Merlin's voice hummed out a rather long breath.

"However..." he said, keeping them all in suspense.

Minifred perked up at the promise of him taking her side. "Go on."

The Wielder stood up from his seat and walked over to the hearth, setting his back to the group. His gaze focused on the glimmering flames that grew as he neared them, as if they were happy to be greeted by the caster. "However, it's naive to think there won't be danger. It is not a simple trip to the Wayward Mountains."

He took another breath in from the pipe before the smoke poured out once more. "I know two things to be certain. First, the fox has a point. It'd be safer to restore Lore's memories before sending her home. Second, Gannon would have encouraged Mathilde's curiosity and need for exploration, but he would have wanted her to be..."

He paused and spun on his heels, facing the group once more. "Well, I think any father would want his daughter to be protected on her adventures." He gestured to nothing in the air with his pipe. "So, if I go, you can rest assured that your younger sister is protected by someone seasoned in the adventuring department, and is skilled at wielding Thimbleton's wild magic. This way, Mathilde will be able to see the world outside of Charmsend. *Safely.*"

Minifred absorbed his words, her fingers dancing on her chin as she thought. "I suppose I've never been able to stop Mathilde before with her goings about. She is constantly pushing the boundaries I set for her." Her tone gentled. "At least if you are there, I will know she is in the hands of someone who ventured side by side with our father."

Mathilde mouthed a silent *thank you* to Merlin, who nodded with a smile and a wink.

Killmoore leaned back in his chair, his ears flattened. A huff escaped from his mouth, but he didn't speak.

"Wonderful. We leave at dawn," Merlin chimed as he turned again to face the lively, welcoming blaze of the hearth.

Lore swallowed hard, and it felt like she was pushing sand down her already dry throat.

Now that the issue had been decided, dinner proceeded as normal—as it did any other night since she had fallen into Charmsend. The sisters talked and lamented childhood nursery rhymes until the flames in the hearth dwindled. Merlin had seated himself in the alligator-sized armchair and dozed off shortly after the song about a chipmunk who stole one of the Great Owl's feathers.

The only sound in Lore's ears that didn't blur into the background was Killmoore walking out of the house. His footsteps were heavy on the floorboards, and he closed the large oak door silently behind him. She looked over her shoulder and saw the bounty hunter walk into the night. The gleam of his ax in the moon's milky light was all she could see before he—and it—was engulfed by the darkness.

"He'll be back tomorrow," Mathilde said, her voice ringing with excitement. There was a sparkle in her green eyes—shining in anticipation of her very first grand adventure—an adventure for her memories.

Lore reached down and fiddled with her bracelet. The silver was cool against her fingertips. Most likely the first of many adventures, if Mathilde had it her way.

Lore smiled softly and nodded. "You're probably right." She shifted in her seat as the sisters continued their talk. Her back ached, and she could no longer stay awake with the repeated readjusting. She got up and made her way to the staircase, thoughts swirling in her head like an early spring storm.

What were the conversations at her family's dinner table? Her breath was shallow as her mind tried to paint a picture of the faint faces that would resurface from time to time—dreaming up scenarios of what things may be like when she returned home. The smiles she'd be greeted with and what meal they would all share. Even if she still had her doubts, why not try to spin those scary 'what ifs' into what if her home was filled with love and good food, just like the yellow manor?

Lore opened the door to her room and left it cracked open as she stood there for a moment, watching the night wind shake the treetops along the walkway lining the house's garden gate. But the warm light from the street lamps didn't waver. If anything, it burned stronger. She didn't close the curtains before crawling into the comfort of the bed. Instead, she continued staring at the orange glow in the cold, late autumn night.

I will be like Grian's flame, she told herself as her eyelids started drooping. *I won't be smothered when the wind comes for my spark.*

TWO

Bird chatter did not awake Lore like some idyllic movie. Nor was she roused from her rest by the subtle sound of the sister's morning babbles that happened over cups filled to the brim with steaming tea. No, her eyes shot open because she heard a ruckus on the other side of the flower covered wall.

Lore wiped the dreams from her eyes and narrowed her gaze at the cracked door. She waited to see a sleepy mouse silhouette pass by, but saw a quick figure dash down the steps. Silently, she slid from between the bedsheets and walked over to the door. Though she was light on her feet, her breathing was heavy.

Her hands gripped the door as she slowly cracked it a bit more, so the opening was big enough for her to shift between. As she did, a piece of chipped wood caught her nightshirt, and she felt like someone had drawn a stinging line on her skin beneath the top.

She clenched her jaw, wiggled the cloth free with her right hand, and slowly descended the staircase. Her eyes scanned the living room and kitchen below. Nothing seemed out of the ordinary. The hearth had glowing embers in it, and the silver light of the early hours radiated from behind the thick curtains.

Lore walked towards the round kitchen table. Her fingers traced the natural knots of the wood mindlessly as she searched for something that wasn't supposed to be there.

Then her eyes locked on Gannon's bedroom door. It was *open*.

She tilted her head and meandered over to investigate. The last time that happened, an intruder had torn apart the room.

Would that happen twice?

Merlin's voice filled the silence behind her. "I wasn't expecting you to be the first to rise."

Lore turned to see the bat at the bottom of the stairs. "Weren't you sleeping in the chair?"

He smirked. "Well, yes, I was." He moved to the kitchen and conjured water for the teapot. "But I do believe I said said we'd be leaving at dawn, didn't I?"

Lore stretched her arms above her head and let out a sleepy yawn. "Yeah, I guess you're right."

Merlin said nothing as he got the mismatched teacups down from the cupboard.

"Merlin," Lore said as she walked over and leaned her body on the back of a chair.

"Hm?" He lit a burner with a spark from his fingertip.

Her eyes were trying to peer into the bat's head. "Did you see anyone in the house a few moments ago?"

"You're the first one I've seen this morning," he admitted, then turned to lock eyes with her.

Lore pulled out the seat and sat down as he slid the mug with a daffodil on it across the table. It greeted her like a ray of sunshine. She wrapped her fingers around the cup.

"What kinda of tea are we feeling before our big quest?" Merlin asked, rummaging through the cabinets. He pulled out an assortment of dried herbs in glass jars down and placed them on the counter. "Peppermint with a touch of lemon balm," the bat answered, proving his earlier question had been rhetorical.

The kettle puffed out steam and shrills as Merlin moved the pot off the burner and carried it to pour into Lore's cup. He dropped a mesh ball filled with herbs in the cup.

"Thank you."

The old bat nodded along and waved his index finger in a circle. Blue flames sparkled around it.

Lore leaned back in the chair and cupped the mug in her hands. She enjoyed the warmth and silence of the morning hours. Lore blew on the cup and took a sip. *The perfect temperature.* Her eyes drifted back to Merlin, who was busy preparing breakfast.

"You certain you didn't see anything?" she pressed.

The bat stopped quartering onions and mincing garlic. He turned to face Lore again and grinned. "I didn't, and if I am honest…" There was a brief pause. "I don't think you did either."

Lore sat the mug on the table, squinting at the caster. "Excuse me?"

Merlin laughed. "I'm sorry. What I meant was you're probably just tired and didn't get restful sleep."

Lore leaned back in her seat, still unsure what to think of the caster's words. She was tired, though. She felt her eyelids getting heavy.

Merlin turned to finish chopping the onions he planned on frying with eggs. "Why don't you go up and sleep in a bit longer? We won't leave for another half hour or so."

Lore drummed her fingers on the stained wood table top. She didn't want to, but she knew Merlin was right. She took another sip of tea, savoring the cool mint sensation across her taste buds. As the tang of lemon tickled the back of her throat, she pushed the cup forward and her chair backward and let out a drawn-out yawn.

"I guess even a twenty-minute nap wouldn't hurt," she admitted, and her arms felt like she had twenty-pound weights strapped around them. She walked to the staircase, barely able to hold her eyes open, but somehow, thanks to Lady Luck, she managed to crawl back in between the bedsheets, which were somehow still warm. It was if she had never left them in the first place.

The voices echoing in the streets below roused Lore from her bed. She rubbed the sleep from her eyes and tried to push away the odd familiarity of the morning. *I feel like I've done this already.*

She slid out of bed, and the dusty pink flowers spread on the wall in full bloom as the pale yellow sunlight poured in. Lore pulled the brown paper bag out from under the bed and looked inside it. Making sure that the clothes in it were the ones she had picked out. She looked to where the stacked pile of clothes she didn't want. They were almost as high as the little wooden table beside the bed.

Her eyes drifted to the family portrait on the nightstand. "You'd be excited for her, I'm sure," Lore said to the faded photograph of the alligator she never knew. She left the paper bag by the door and then went to make the bed.

One last time, she told herself as she pulled the sheets up. Then she grabbed the two ends of the quilted comforter and gave the blanket a big flap so it'd cover the bed. As the quilt fell onto the bed, Lore swore she saw a raven-haired man standing on the other side. He had a smile on his face, and somehow it made her feel at ease. Before she could ask the ghost about her past, he was gone. Just as suddenly as he had appeared.

She sat on the foot of the bed fidgeting with her bracelet, as the murmurs of the sisters at the kitchen table rose through the floorboards. Memories of the raven-haired man were fuzzy like T.V. static, and though she couldn't fully make out what he looked like, Lore knew that he must have been important to her.

Her eyes drifted to the green flannel that hung on the doorknob. She took a deep breath. Today is the first step to what could be a long journey home. *But I will get home.* Lore stood up and walked over to retrieve her flannel, sliding it on in one fluid motion. Next, she picked up the brown paper bag with the 'Dina's' logo. She chewed the inside of her cheek and pulled the door closed behind her, not bothering to look back.

Lore didn't miss a beat going down the steps, and Mathilde turned to her from the kitchen table.

Her eyes sparkled like a kid who got the birthday gift of their dreams. "Mornin', Lore!"

Lore smiled and walked over to greet the mice. "Morning, ladies," she said, clutching the brown bag to her chest.

"Where's your suitcase?" Maybel asked.

Her match kicked her under the table.

Minifred sighed. "She didn't come to Thimbleton with her belongings packed neatly in a suitcase."

"Oh, it's okay," Lore said. "This bag should be fine. It's just clothes."

Merlin turned with a plate of scrambled eggs and roasted veggies. "Oh, nonsense," he said as he pushed up his sleeves. With a wave of his hand, the paper bubbled until Lore felt smooth leather against her.

Looking down, she saw it was a brown carry-on.

"There," he said with a smile. "Much better for dealing with the harsher elements of the northern region."

"You are wearing more than that, aren't you?" Minifred asked with a brow raised, looking Lore up and down.

The boots she wore had seen more than a thousand miles, and the pants had a small hole at the knee. The wool sweater felt like a cloud had fallen onto her shoulders and taken a shirt shape.

"This should be warm enough," Lore assured as she pulled a chair out. "I feel like I'm sweating a little bit already, to be honest." She scooted her seat close to the table between Minifred and Maybel.

The mice continued to shovel the breakfast down their gullets, and Minifred sipped on her tea and looked out the window. The sun was just rising. Beautiful golden rays flooded over the valley and peeked through the single-pane glass windows of the buildings of Charmsend.

Mathilde's fork clanged against a clean plate. "We have Merlin. He can summon fire, so I don't think the cold will be a problem."

Merlin smiled warmly at Mathilde's adoration. "Well, we should be off after Lore finishes." He looked at the human, who was daintily picking over her breakfast. "We don't want the sun to get too high in the sky before we part, lest we want to sleep in the woods."

Lore noted the twinkle in the eye of someone who slept in the woods for many years as she took a bite of her scrambled eggs. She squinted and Mathilde's sisters buzzed with questions.

"How many animalfolk do you think you'll come across?"

"Do you think she'll see a mountain lion?"

"Do you think they'll be victims of highway robbery?"

"Do you think—"

Minifred's teacup slammed down onto the table. "Enough!"

Eager to escape, Lore finished shoveling the last bit of eggs onto her spoon and into her cheeks before shooting up to place the plate in the deep kitchen sink. She slid the newly morphed leather bag's strap over her shoulder, and it fit snugly across her chest. She shoved the collar of her flannel back under the flap. "Ready," she said.

As Lore and Merlin watched Mathilde hug her sisters goodbye, her stomach churned, probably from eating too quickly. She felt a grumble in her gut travel upward and let out a loud belch. Lore rubbed her cramping stomach and groaned in a strained voice, "Excuse me."

"Uh—very well then." Merlin interrupted. "We are off, and though the space between us will be large, we'll keep you close in our thoughts, and us in yours."

Lore watched as Minifred wiped a tear as Mathilde pulled away from her hug. Her hands gripped the straps of her own satchel.

"Be safe." Minifred's voice wavered as the door closed behind them.

The air caressed the apples of Lore's cheeks with a frosted kiss. Kill-moore was pacing back and forth on the sidewalk in front of the house.

"You're late," he said flatly, as he snapped a pocket watch shut.

"Oh, we'll still make good time!" Mathilde beamed as she skipped down the stairs. "Cheer up, ya grumpy fox." She playfully punched his arm—a standard greeting between them.

Killmoore's ears lay flat as he dusted where she had hit him. "Where is our carriage? We were supposed to leave twenty minutes ago."

Merlin scratched his head. "I thought I told Sable to drop it off here before daybreak." The bat shook his head and pushed up his billowing sleeves. "Maybe she thought I meant the square?" he mused aloud while his fingers rubbed his chin.

Killmoore's foot started tapping. "Well, let's not waste anymore time. The square it is."

Lore felt her stomach gurgling again, but that annoyance didn't stop her from hearing the panic in the bounty hunter's voice. She had only heard the smooth-talking silver-tongued fox hold panic in his voice like that once before.

Her mind flashed back to the contorted hovel Crinkle had called home. Lyudmilla burst into the room after them. The way he tried to warn her to run. The memory dissipated, and her jaw tightened.

"You are being a bit of a drama queen, dontcha think?" Merlin's voice was light, but weights laced the question, weaving in and out between each word.

"It's okay, Killmoore." She rested her hand on his shoulder gently. "If I'm honest, I'm nervous about traveling, too." Lore chewed the inside of her cheek as she tried to decide what was more nerve-wracking. Traveling to the Wayward Mountains or restoring her memories. After all, what if it was everything she never wanted? And not remembering anything would be better?

The fox's amber eyes glimmered with appreciation, and he gestured with his hands vaguely. "See, someone gets it."

Merlin's lips pursed, and his tongue made a popping sound, but said nothing else.

Lore's brow furrowed as she looked over the gray mouse's expression. She wasn't crossing her arms in anger. Instead, the tips of her ears slightly drooped. Lore's mouth gaped open as she searched for words to pry open Mathilde as if the mouse were a locked box, but the key that would have been Lore's words wasn't forming.

Perhaps she's just disappointed about running an errand in order to go on this 'amazing adventure.'

Lore's gaze then met Killmoore's, who rolled his eyes. "Come on," he grumbled as he stomped toward the town square, which was just a short walk north of the yellow manor. "Let's get this over with."

Mathilde and Lore trailed behind him, but the fox was walking at such a rushed pace they had to book it to catch up with him. Merlin easily walked beside them.

Mathilde kicked a stray pebble. "Well, this isn't how I was expecting things to start," the mouse groaned as the group headed toward town.

Lore patted her friend on the back. "Not everything happens like it does in books."

"Lore is right, Mathilde," Merlin chimed in. "There were plenty of... detours that happened when your dad and our bunch were on the road."

Before Mathilde could add another complaint, Lore noted that the usual crowd was out this morning. Nothing had changed aside from the jackets getting thicker, and the knitted scarfs that wrapped around their necks. Colors varied from rich reds to brilliant blues. Lore's feet kept pace with Mathilde's scamper as the three finally caught up to Killmoore.

"Well, where is she?" Mathilde asked, her eyes scanned for the docile hedgehog in the crowd. Her foot tapped impatiently on the stone ground.

"It appears we aren't the only ones leaving." Killmoore nudged Lore and gestured to a cart just on the other side of the square. It was parked by a pop-up shop that had strips of dried meat hanging by some twine from its freshly repaired roof. Lyudmilla was loading up the back of the cart with a few bags of jerky.

The trio made their way over, leaving Merlin to have a magical chat with Sable. Lore tilted her head at the creature strapped to the front of the cart. It looked to be a wooden toy horse. However, it wasn't dull and lifeless, like an opened holiday present. Its coal-colored eyes shimmered as it let out a mechanical whinny.

"Looks like you are prepared for a long journey." Mathilde gestured to all the burlap sacks in the back of the cart.

Lyudmilla's pale eyes drifted to the calico cat sitting at the reins. Dina had a small mirror in her hand as she touched up her ruby-red lipstick. Her eyes caught the onlookers in the reflection. She snapped the small mirror closed and shoved it into a bag she had on her lap. Then, as she fluffed her tail, her lips curled into a sly smile. "Darling, I told you, I only packed the necessities."

Lyudmilla tossed her double-handed ax into the bed of the cart, making it rock.

"I don't think fifteen bags of clothes are necessities, but okay." The white wolf walked to the wooden wind-up toy horse and began turning the key on its back.

"Where are you gonna go?" Mathilde asked as she pressed her small foot against the wooden wheel of the cart.

"West," Lyudmilla said flatly. "We're going west."

"Why?" Lore found herself sounding like a sad toddler who didn't understand why that mommy and daddy were getting a divorce.

Lyudmilla grumbled something as she climbed up to sit beside the calico, and Dina waved a hand as if the answer were obvious.

"There's nothing for us here." Her eyes flickered like a bonfire in the early morning sun. "We're chasin' a fresh start."

"We're chasing Lore a way home," Mathilde said, her chest puffed with pride.

The cat grinned from her seat in the wagon. "Well, hopefully she'll fit back into the human world. I've never read anything about a human having antlers." Dina gestured with a playful laugh at the antlers protruding from Lore's hair.

Killmoore let out an uneven breath. "Hope it's the start you both want it to be." Tension still coated his voice, but he seemed genuine.

"Thanks, fox." Lyudmilla snapped the reins, and the horse began pulling the cart. The sound of metal ticking tickled Lore's ears, the wind up key spun, and the metal of the toy horse's hooves hit the ground. The sounds together could have been the start of a melody.

Lore shifted her weight from side to side, her stomach still bubbling, and watched as the carriage disappeared from sight.

Killmoore turned, finding a bench to sit on.

Mathilde furrowed her brow. "What are you doing?"

"Sitting."

The mouse's ears folded down at the tip. "What happened to finding our carriage?"

The bounty hunter twiddled his thumbs. "I just need a minute, okay?"

Mathilde shot Lore a look, waiting for her to say something.

Lore's stomach gurgled as it turned over again. She grabbed her stomach and muttered, "I think a brief sit would do me some good, too."

Mathilde huffed and stomped her foot. "Do I have to do everything?" Before either the fox or the human could answer, she turned on her heel. "Stay put so I know where to find you after I sniff out Sable. Maybe Merlin already found her."

Lore shook her head at her friend's words. Killmoore was eerily silent. The only noise he made was the *tap tap tap* of his fingers on the bench.

"How long do you think it'll take to reach the mountains?"

"If we left now?" Killmoore's voice was as tight as a rubber band being stretched to its limit. "Little over two days, possibly three, depending on how the roads are."

Lore nodded, taking in his words. "You mean it will depend on how often our toy horse stops and needs to be rewound?"

The fox scoffed. "I was thinking more along the lines of if we are safe from bandits, but if that bat is even an ounce as great as he thinks he is..."

He paused for Lore to agree, but she was too focused on her stomach gurgles to be peppering him with questions about his not-so-subtle distaste for Merlin.

"Anyway, if he's such a magnificent wielder, staying safe shouldn't be a problem."

Lore let out a sigh and reached for the antlers atop her head. They had soft velvet growing, and rubbing the texture quickly became a way for her to soothe herself. "So, what made you think of retrieving my memories before sending me home?"

When the fox didn't respond, Lore nudged his shoulder. "Killmoore?"

He shook his head like he broke free from a trance. "Right, sorry." The fox tapped his digits on the bench. "What would home be if you couldn't remember anything?"

Lore raised a brow.

The bounty hunter explained, "Listen, it was just a thought that *boom—*" He waved his hands around his head. "Popped in my mind, and I thought it'd be worth putting out there."

"So, there's a potion store up north that sells memory-restoring tonics?" Lore asked.

Killmoore let out a heavy sigh. "I've been to where we are going, and the item we're after is protected, but—"

Their attention snapped toward a new sound.

"Hey!" Mathilde called as a large smile was brandished on her face. Merlin followed not far behind her. "We got it!"

Lore looked past Merlin, expecting a wooden horse to be following to pull their coach, but all she saw was the bat carrying a pumpkin-sized turnip in his arms.

How was a vegetable going to help?

The bat gingerly placed the turnip with dirt still speckled across its flesh onto the ground in front of the bench. "I present to you..." He paused for dramatics and took a deep bow. "Our ride." Merlin said it as if he were presenting the trio with a dragon sporting a saddle fit to ride in the skies over Thimbleton.

Did they even have *dragons here?*

Killmoore's face was so stiff that if he were lying on the ground, Lore could have mistaken him for a corpse. "What," he pointed, "is *that*?" The last two words he said with a seething annoyance.

Merlin only laughed, which made Killmoore's eyes narrow, and Lore swore one twitched.

"Keep your tail screwed on." Mathilde chimed, patting the fox's back.

"Mmhm," Merlin hummed as he pushed up his sleeves once more. He started waving his hands.

"You aren't conducting a grand orchestra," the fox mumbled loud enough for Lore to pick up on.

Glowing golden embers seemed to gather around his palms, and he whispered some unrecognizable tongue. Before Killmoore could air another grievance, the turnip trembled, then bounced.

The bat's whispers grew louder, and his eyes gleamed.

Folks in the square stopped and stared at the unusual event, some with fear on their face as if this were the Crinkle battle all over again.

The root vegetable continued to rattle, and then suddenly, it stopped. Underneath, the ground shook as the turnip grew until it was the large enough for a giant's salad plate. The light green stems stretched and curled under the tuber itself. The purple around the top of the vegetable faded, looking more like spilled dark wine rather than a turnip top. And the stems arched around the turnip leaves that were unfurling, wide and flat. The dark green appendages pressed into the ground, lifting the turnip up away from the stone.

Lastly, an invisible knife carved hole for the door.

Merlin walked around the turnip with a smile the size of a crescent moon. He reached for Lore's hand. "Carriage for three."

Lore tilted her head. "Where are we gonna sit?"

The bat laughed. "Oh, of course, how silly of me."

Lore's eyes drifted to Killmoore, who looked unimpressed by the display, then to Mathilde, who seemed to have galaxies full of adoration in her eyes.

She took Merlin's balmy hand, and two steps unfolded from the turnip. They were bone white, and as Lore stepped onto the first one, the cutouts for the windows fell and hit the stone path with a thud. She watched two benches emerge from the turnip walls. The smells of mustard and dirt wrapped her in a cloak of earthy scents.

Lore felt like two triangle eyes were looking at her and waiting for her to step through. As she did, the tips of her antlers caught on the vegetable's flesh.

Killmoore entered and huffed. "Where is the coach box?"

Merlin helped Mathilde up the steps and smirked. "No need."

The fox rolled his eyes. "If horsepower won't pull the turnip, then how will we get to the Wayward Mountains?" He crossed his arms. "Or do we need to split up and go find you a horse, too?"

The caster shook his head and patted the side of the turnip. "Still runs off my magic, just with more style than a wooden and metal toy."

Killmoore pinched the fur between his eyes and reluctantly climbed into the root vegetable and slumped beside Lore. "Whatever, let's just get on the road already."

Mathilde leaned forward and mused, "It's just like a standard coach, but this is better."

The bounty hunter brooded and looked out the window, avoiding any eye contact. "More like a magic fancy cage."

Merlin said nothing as he held the smile on his face and took a seat beside Mathilde, and with a snap of his fingers, the self-driving turnip began walking. It was clunky at first. The way it walked felt like they were experiencing firsthand what it was like being a baby deer. By the time they passed Dina's bar, which was now rebranded as TANSY'S, the ride was smoother. The change of ownership seemed to happen overnight.

I wonder what design Tansy will pick for the paper bags.

It wasn't long before they passed the bones of what was Crinkle's dwelling. The sight of the abandoned house only worsened Lore's aching gut. The feeling lingered even as they entered the Twisted Wood.

Like the mangled treetops above her, Lore was also knitted tightly with nerves. The fog swirled and Lore could feel the icy breath of the Grayshade who had attacked her, Mathilde, and Crinkle on the way to the Iron Rose Greenhouse.

Lore's mind reached for the memory of the ghostly stag that aided her in the fight against Crinkle. The image of Crinkle fading to dust and the darkness that Lore drowned in after.

Out the window, she saw in the distance a figure walking toward them. Their steps were clumsy, and it made her racing thoughts halt all at once. She looked at her travel companions. Killmoore's hair bristled, and he already had a hand on the hilt of his ax.

She gulped, preoccupied with a single thought in her mind.

I thought Merlin and the Grayshades were the only ones able to survive in the merciless Twisted Wood.

THREE

The heaviness of suspense tangled itself in the air and, paired with the thick fog, made the silence among the four sitting in the turnip all the more uncomfortable. Soon, the sound of scratching footsteps echoed in the coach. Merlin's hands radiated a dim copper glow. Lore caught herself in the reflection of Killmoore's polished ax blades as the cloaked figure loomed closer and closer. Soon, they heard unsteady breathing, and then Lore saw it.

An inky black feather floated to the ground like a spinning maple seed. She squinted, and as the figure came around the turnip, she saw a long black beak protruding from the dark cloak as the figure ran a feathery wing along the outside of the turnip coach.

Mathilde jerked towards Merlin, but the cloaked avian's focus was fixed on Lore. *Perhaps he was inspecting the enchanted carriage.* Lore's eyes darted back to Mathilde as she shifted her weight from side to side under the crow's gaze. *The crow was about as tall as Killmoore.*

She watched as the whites of Mathilde's eyes grew, but Mathilde sharpened her gaze when they made eye contact. *Is she putting on a brave face for me? Or did she finally just swallow her fear?*

Then the beak of the stranger leaned forward a bit. The mouse's nose twitched as she sniffed the air.

"Who are you?" Mathilde demanded.

The bird threw its head back and let out a caw-like cackle while long, dark feathers gripped the window. The cloak hood fell from the bird's head and gathered around its neck. "Sometimes," it said as long jet-black feathers that resembled fingers pitter-pattered on the coach, "I wonder the same thing," he drawled.

Lore raised a brow and noted that Killmoore tightened his grip on the ax hilt.

"What's your business then?" Lore asked.

The crow moved quickly over to the window Lore was sitting by and peered through it. For a moment, she wondered if she should have sat across from Merlin instead.

His wing tips gripped the base of the triangular window. "You want to have a gander at ol' Crosby's collection."

Lore noted the slender crack that ran up the right side of his beak and continued along his face up to his right eye. It didn't change the intensity of the unyielding yellow orbs that flickered over her.

"Crosby?" Merlin said as his hand dimmed.

Does that mean the crow is harmless?

The crow cocked its head to the side rather unnaturally and let out a random squawk.

The abrupt noise startled Lore, but she didn't move a muscle. Lore watched as Mathilde's ears folded downward, and the burnt orange fur stood on Killmoore's neck.

A peculiar creature.

It was at this point Lore heard a rat-a-tat-tat on the roof of the turnip.

Merlin's gaze grew narrower and narrower on the crow.

Did he hear it, too?

Crosby craned his head in through the carriage window and proudly announced, "Crosby G. Carver. Collector of the shiny sparklies and seller to the highest bidder."

With each word, the crow leaned closer and closer to Lore's face until she smelled a strong musk coming off his breath.

Mathilde's forehead wrinkle pulled tight. "What shinies do you sell?"

Crosby let out a high-pitched giggle and backed away from the carriage with no pattern to his steps. Then, with a brash squawk, he flapped his cloak open for the world to see his glory. Merlin quickly covered Mathilde's eyes.

His glory being all his shinies he's collected, of course. The crow was fully dressed, albeit he looked like he could visit a tailor for some mending. Lore leaned forward to exit the turnip.

Killmoore lunged to keep the door closed, but Lore just smiled as she saw an array of random pocket watches, rings, stones, and abandoned broken pieces of metal. Some stray pieces of metal were twisted into a spiral, others bent in random places. Lore pushed past the fox in the close quarters of the turnip.

"Lore, we don't know this crow," Killmoore spat under his breath, grabbing her forearm as she placed a foot on the step of the carriage.

She shook her arm free and made her way toward the salescrow. *He is such an odd character, besides he could have something useful for the journey...right?*

"But Crosby knows you." The crow's head tilted so that one bright yellow eye was able to fixate on the fox and human. His inky, dark feathered wings rubbed against each other like he was some plotting villain in a child's fairytale.

Merlin freed Mathilde's eyes and folded his hands into his lap. "I actually agree with the fox on this, Lore." He glanced down to Mathilde, as if to tell her as well. "Best stay in the carriage."

Lore scanned the sparkling lost treasures against the blue-black fabric of the crow's cloak. Her eyes fell on a pocket watch that looked like dragon scales had been carved onto its silver surface. "You've got quite the collection, Mr. Carver."

Her fingers grazed her chin as she played with her thoughts. She leaned forward until her nose was a mere inch or two away from all the lost treasures safely fastened to the inside fabric that looked like a starless night sky.

"Crosby, call Crosby, call Crosby," the crow cawed.

Lore giggled to herself. "Well, Crosby..." Lore stared at the treasures as she straightened out her back and rested her hands on her hips. "You have many fine pieces in your inventory."

The sounds of wings flapping above her trickled down the air like soft raindrops. Almost like the pitter-patter on top of the carriage when the traveling sales crow first showed up but, soft enough that she didn't pay them any mind.

The crow's head bobbed up and down as if he were jumping on each word that fell from Lore's lips.

"However, I don't have any taels to buy from you. But there is a town a bit further up." She pointed toward where they came from.

"*LORE!*" Merlin's face immediately pulled tight once the bat realized just how shocked he sounded.

"No taels needed, lass. Crosby does the bartering as well." His words were offset by squawks between them.

Lore smiled. "Of course, silly me." The sounds in the treetop above her of brittle branches snapping, muffled chatter, and clicks had sent a shiver of goosebumps up her arms.

The crow pulled the midnight fabric back around him like a cocoon and stepped towards Lore.

The chill from his peculiar movements traveled to her stomach.

He circled around her before rubbing a few feathers against his glossy black beak. "Interesting," he said in an almost sing-songy tune. "Oh, interesting indeed." The melody of soft coos rained from above, and though Lore wanted to look up, her gut told her not to.

So, she bit her bottom lip and kept her gaze on the mangled tree trunk in front of her. The hair on the back of her neck felt like it was being tickled by a feather Crosby had plucked from himself.

Once the crow was in front of her again, Lore backed up. Her eyes fell onto two glossy feathers, holding a pair of silver spurs between them. "I've no need for those?" Lore said, the words sounding more like a question as they left her lips. *Not exactly a useful item we'll need on this journey.*

Crosby's scarred eye twitched as he shuffled closer to her and whispered, "But you will."

She stumbled backwards until her hand grazed the smooth surface of the turnip. She felt Killmoore's hand pull her back up into the coach. The fox closed the door and took the window seat Lore was previously sitting in. Directly across from Mathilde. The human had a moment of relief being back inside the enchanted turnip, but it didn't last long as Crosby was peering back through the window again. Lore was thankful that in that moment Killmoore was the shield between her and the mad crow.

"Well, if it's all the same to you, Mr. Carver, we will be on our way." the fox's eyes flickered over to Merlin, who was carefully observing the interaction. "We are already behind schedule." Killmoore grumbled.

Crosby leaned in the triangular window once more. His neck hooked inside the carriage. "You must listen to Crosby, Human," the crow squealed, unafraid or simply foolish to be so close to Killmoore, who was still armed with sharpened blades.

Lore didn't know which. No matter the answer, it didn't stop yellow-glinted eyes from piercing Lore like a freshly sharpened knife.

"Crosby will see you again, human," the crow squawked, then gave frantic flap of his wing.

With their focus on the wandering salescrow, and the overwhelming sound of claws digging into the turnip's flesh, no one noticed the slip of a shadow of a smaller bird inside the carriage.

Merlin clapped his hands once, prompting the enchanted vegetable to pick itself back up and continue its path through the Twisted Wood. But the carriage wasn't moving as smoothly or quickly as before.

A glance outside the window revealed Crosby was hooked into the turnip. Lore looked at Merlin, who seemed strained against the crow's unassuming strength. Her stomach jumped as the back of the carriage was lifted, and the sound of the bird's wings beating filled the coach.

Her heart raced wildly. "Merlin, can't you make this thing go?!"

"I'm trying!" The bat called his hands glowing amber.

"Crosby will see you again, human." the roughness of his squalls itched against Lore's skin as the words hit her ears.

"Yeah, yeah," Killmoore said with a huff as he pushed the crow away from the window. *I guess sometimes magic isn't as strong of a solution compared to simpler, brutish, actions.*

Though the carriage now moved quickly, it was not fast enough to escape Crosby's last words. Still, she leaned back and let a sigh escape. As the breath left her lungs, she noticed her wrist felt a bit lighter.

Her bracelet was gone.

She peeked out the window, expecting to see the crow walking towards Charmsend, but what she saw left her stunned.

In the mangled woven treetops above Crosby, there were dozens of carrier crows. Some had letters in their beaks, others carried broken metal shards or gemstones. One landed in front of him and dropped something at Crosby's feet, causing a little dust cloud to erupt. Then, the normal-sized carrier crow joined the others in the trees above.

What really made Lore's stomach churn, though, were the crows that carried stray eyeballs or other severed appendages in their beaks. If that wasn't the worst of it, Crosby's head tilted, his yellow eyes locked onto her.

Though she knew she was safe in the coach, she could feel the hair on her neck stand up as if the crow were behind her again. Then he gave a little wave goodbye, causing the silver chain's links to shimmer in the faint sunlight.

Did Crosby really have a carrier crow steal my bracelet?

Lore snapped her neck back into the coach. Her chest felt heavy with confusion. *Were all those carrier crows there the whole time?* The silence was almost as thick as the grime that had been on Crinkle's walls. *Did Crosby have magic that cloaked the other crows until he wanted me to see we were completely surrounded by the murder?*

Then, the soft sheen of silver caught her eye. The pair of spurs lay between her boots. Lore felt like her bones were rattling, and as Killmoore reached down to pick them up, her mind felt clouded with the complexity of what just unfolded, and how quickly it happened.

It didn't last as Mathilde's voice cracked, breaking the stillness. "I can't believe it."

Killmoore slid his axes back into their holsters. "I know. Seems the weirdos don't wait till dark to come out anymore."

Mathilde gripped the edge of her seat. "Are you kidding me?!" her eyes buzzed with intrigue, and she threw her arms above her head. "He was so interesting. Imagine the stories he has to tell."

Merlin leaned back. "I suppose they would be fascinating." He stretched out his arms, his leathery wings catching the setting sunlight. "But who's to say the crow is a reliable narrator?"

As Mathilde speculated on what kind of stories Crosby could share, Lore looked back out the triangular window at the landscape. Expecting to be met with the same gloomy grays and dead trees she had come to know. What her eyes caught was something most unexpected. Even more unexpected than a trinket crow salesman in the middle of nowhere.

Merlin described what her eyes had seen. "In some places, the ground had patches of moss, like freshly-installed green carpet. In others, the tree bark appeared to be a rich shade of brown, and the branches above held lush green leaves. I hoped I would be able to see the day that the Emerald Pass began healing itself."

As the turnip continued on the set path, the trend of the forest patching itself with random bursts of emerald greens that were sprouting once more, interlocking with the twisted trees.

The sound of water sloshing grew louder and louder until the group saw a series of small rivers interlocking among one another, like an intricate braid by the forest's design.

At its center, Lore noticed some standing stones that were moss-touched as the moons rose above the treetops. Dim yellow orbs lit up, revealing more than just one set of standing stones.

"I didn't think it would take long for the Great Hare to get to work healing the forest once the corruption of Crinkle's magic stopped bleeding outward, but I wasn't expecting anything this fast," Merlin muttered. "Truly amazing, and we are among the first to see it."

Lore was familiar with the frost phantom of the Stag. *That's right, there are four great guardians of Thimbleton.* Lore cleared her throat, recalling the song that she saw Lyudmilla sing at Gannon's grave. *The Hare must be the guardian of this region of the island, the guardian that some bandit thought he could kill.*

The enchanted turnip slowed as water rushed against its dark green leafy feet. Lore noticed the knots and notches in the stones, and at the very center, she saw a stone statue of a very large rabbit standing on its hind legs, sniffing the air.

Though one of its ears was missing, and a paw had also been lost to time, its glittering green gemstone eyes pierced through the dim forest.

"Wonder what this means for the Grayshade," Killmoore mused in a raspy voice.

Merlin didn't look at the fox as he stayed fixated on the stone statue Lore had noticed. "I suppose maybe they are healing somewhere, too."

Mathilde slid Gannon's verdant bound journal out of her satchel and a freshly sharpened lead pencil was held tightly between her slender fingers as she opened it and started writing on the next blank page.

"Before it was the Twisted Wood, this forest used to be known as the Emerald Pass," Merlin said, his voice steady.

"Yes, Gannon had written it all down. I have read it," Mathilde said as her hand was still scribbling notes on the blank page of the journal. "Gannon made predictions in his journal," the mouse explained. "Predictions, theories, and observations."

Merlin raised a brow and looked at the gray mouse. His gilded eyes glistened. "Ah, I didn't realize you had already read through all his writings in such a short time." The bat paused a beat. "Has Lore and Killmoore heard it, though?"

Killmoore let out a groan as his eyes stayed fixed and alert to the moving environment outside the turnip.

Lore shrugged. "Wouldn't hurt to know."

"This region was once said to be the burrow of the Great Hare. The valley was rich with life and vegetation." The bat's voice rang with the familiar tone he had the night the trio was brought to his house in the Twisted Wood. "Naturally settlers moved in and called the valley home."

Lore tilted her head. "Well, that was a short story."

Merlin shrugged. "That's because for years, the Forest lived in a peaceful state, and the magic flowed freely. It was able to grow much like those who visited. It was only when Crinkle's magic corrupted the well that the rot spread to the rest of the wood."

The bat paused and leveled his tone back out in such a way that didn't make him sound bonkers. "And you know the rest from there. The creatures that called the burrow home transformed into the Grayshade thanks to the corrupted magic."

"So you saw it before? Before it became the Twisted Wood?" Lore asked the caster.

"Well, of course," Merlin said.

Mathilde flipped another page in her adoptive father's journal. "Gannon did, too. He has it all written down here."

Merlin turned his body to face Mathilde more as he leaned over to see what she was writing, and he wondered aloud, "I always had wondered what secrets and deep thoughts your father had shared with those pages."

FOUR

When the carriage stopped, Lore admired the ribbons of the orange setting sunlight that flickered farewell through the canopy.

"This will do," Merlin said plainly.

While the bat and the mouse stretched their legs, murmuring about the growing green of the forest, Lore stayed by Killmoore. He was being pretty quiet, even taking into consideration his bounty hunter job.

"Tael for your thoughts," Lore gently pressed.

The fox's eyes were fixated on the forest repairing itself outside the window. "Just makes me think of the first time I walked through this wood." He took a moment to pause. "When I entered, it was twisted, haunted, and dead."

Lore nodded with understanding, though her eyes rolled at the sensation of her antlers scraping against the soft white of the turnip above her. "It's almost like the forest is healing itself after a great fire."

Killmoore nodded, then his snout twitched. "Do you think we are capable of such growth after our own personal burnings?"

Lore stiffened at the fox's question while he brushed past her out of the carriage. *Clearly, he didn't want any sort of answer.*

Lore followed behind, the scent of rain washing over her. She inhaled deeply, and a strange sensation of having felt this before fluttered in her stomach. Faint images of herself running through sheets of rain popped into her mind, and the haunting sound of her own laughter echoed in her ears.

"Lore!" Mathilde's excitement pulled the human away from her wandering mind.

"Hm?"

"Isn't it beautiful?" The mouse said spinning, gesturing to the tree's bursting in hues of green.

Lore nodded, and looked past the mouse, her gaze set on Merlin and Killmoore. The two were clearly bickering, though, about what she couldn't hear. Not over Mathilde's shrill rambling. Naturally, Lore walked over to the other two members of her party. "Hey," she said, "What's going on over here?"

Merlin seemed pleased to see her, and Killmoore sighed, "Nothing."

"Well," Merlin began, "I wouldn't call it nothing."

The bounty hunter forced a laugh. "I'll be back. I just need to take a walk to clear my head." Lore and Mathilde watched as their friend turned to leave.

"We'll come with you." Mathilde insisted.

"No." Killmoore didn't even turn his head to speak to them.

"Well, just me then." Mathilde pressed.

The mouse went to follow the fox, but Lore reached a hand out to grab her shoulder. "Sometimes it's best to give folks space when they need it," Lore said, mulling over the question Killmoore had asked her before he left the carriage. *Do you think we are capable of such growth after our own personal burnings?*

"No matter," Merlin chimed as he ignited a fire.

Mathilde sat by the warm red and orange tendrils, her ears almost encompassing her figure in a sort of hug.

"You know," Merlin said, a bit of excitement leaking into his voice, "Mathilde, perhaps you could read a passage from your father's book. What were my old friend's theories on what killed the Emerald Pass in the first place?"

Lore watched Mathilde carefully. The mouse's large green eyes had their sparkle back. It seemed the bat did know how to cheer her up. While Mathilde dug around in her bag for Gannon's little green book,

Lore found herself looking in the direction that their friend had left for their little walk. The orange ribbon of light was quickly becoming a distant memory as darkness filled in the openings of the trees.

He'll be back, Lore assured herself. After all, she wasn't sure of the dangers that could be hiding among the trees. And the last time she, the fox, and the mouse were in a forest together, they had agreed there was safety in numbers.

While Mathilde flipped through some pages, Lore rubbed her neck. This little act of self-care had become a nightly routine. Thanks to the extra weight of her antlers and the strain they put on her muscles.

"Here." Mathilde lit up. "Gannon's official theory has to do with how Crinkle's greed had corrupted the magic of the wishing well."

"Interesting," Merlin said under his breath.

"Says here that because Crinkle had done a good job of isolating the village and part of the Emerald Pass, that the magic that ran through to the Infinite Run became infected by the corruption from Charmsend's natural magic spring. The result was a gradual decay."

She turned a page and continued reading. "The spirits of the forest that used to help lost travelers were also affected. They were overcome with such hunger that they started turning on the very travelers they used to help. And when travelers stopped coming through, they feasted on each other." Mathilde shuddered when she closed the book. "How grim our lives were, and we didn't even know it," the mouse murmured, as if to herself.

"Did I miss story time?" a familiar voice asked in disappointment.

Merlin narrowed his gaze on Killmoore. "That's what happens when you go on *spontaneous* walks. You miss the good parts."

The fox scoffed. "*Good* parts," Killmoore repeated.

Lore pushed her way into the back and forth. "Actually, story time is still happening, and it's your turn to tell one." Her brow raised, daring Killmoore to challenge her on it.

The bounty hunter's ears flattened. "Fine."

Lore watched while the fox tried to settle in beside the campfire.

He cleared his throat. "So, I know a bit about the town we are heading toward."

"Well, I'd hope so." Merlin sounded a bit annoyed.

"I believe it's my turn to speak right now, ember hands," Killmoore said with a snarl.

That wasn't like him either, Lore noted.

"As I was saying, in the town of Cloch Chruinn. Houses of every color of the rainbow line bronzed streets, so polished that you could see your reflection in them. Lanterns hanging outside of homes and businesses are lit with magic fire. The flames dance between hues of blue and spritely violet." Killmoore paused for a beat, looking around the fire to make sure we were paying attention. He cleared his throat before speaking again. "The town is at the base of the Wayward Mountains, and the mountains are what many spirits of nature call home."

"What'd it look like?" Mathilde asked.

"Like a shadow of many animals meshed into one body," the fox said with a wave of his hand. "Anyway, the town itself is as vibrant as a gem mine. The folk there are as warm as this fire, too. From the bears who protect the village from the magical creatures of the mountain to the peaceful frogs that laze in cool waters the locals know as fairy pools."

"So you spent some time there, bounty hunter?" Merlin asked.

Killmoore's eyes narrowed. "Something like that." The fox pinched the fur between his eyes. "'Cause the villagers will do anything to keep peace, there's a festival held every year with one special spirit. Anyway, during the turn of the seasons, the night of the last harvest, the townsfolk gather in the streets with a collective offering for the spirit. The shadowy sprite would come into town. The entity was known to stir mischief. It was part of the festival, actually, but once the offering vanished, the race was on."

Lore noted the subtle smile the fox wore as he told the tale. "Race?"

"Whoever caught the spirit got a wish," the fox explained.

"How would you catch a spirit like that?" Mathilde asked in earnest.

"You gotta be clever," Killmoore said with a laugh.

Lore moved her hands across her neck and upper shoulders, silently cursing the weight of her deer-like burden. "If you caught the creature, what would you wish for?" Her question was not really directed at anyone in particular.

The bat was the first to answer. "I actually may have to think this one over."

"Would it be possible to wish the dead back to life?" Mathilde's voice wavered.

Killmoore's face softened. "Mathilde, some things are beyond the reach of magic."

Cool air kissed Lore's cheeks. The whistling of the wind was the only sound hanging in the air between them.

FIVE

Lore rolled up the wool-lined sleeping sacks Merlin had packed. The embers of the campfire died in the morning light that trickled through the foliage above them. The smoke spiraled into the air, and Killmoore poured some more water over the red-hot coals. They were about five or six miles from the center of the forest, at the roughest estimate.

The Infinite Run shrine, dedicated to the Great Hare, and the growth continued to spread even through the night. Mathilde was crouched close to the ground, drawing a pink flower that caught her eye when she woke. How long she had been awake, exactly, Lore wasn't sure, but she could tell the small mouse was taking in every detail. From the way the petals had a subtle glow in the frigid morning dew, to the amount of veins on the leaf that hung onto its tall slender stem, and writing it down in her father's journal.

Lore helped Killmoore load up the boot of the coach while Merlin tended to the tendrils that acted as the carriage's legs. It appeared that the leaves had been a bit torn up as they crossed a briar patch last night.

"Cloch Chruinn shouldn't be much further," Killmoore said as he latched the boot shut.

"Is that the village at the foot of the mountain?" Lore perked up. "The one you were telling tales about by the fire last night?"

The fox beamed. "Sure is."

His tale of Cloch Chruinn replayed in Lore's head like it was her favorite movie scene. The lighting was soft and orange from the fire's flames.

Lore pictured the way Killmoore's eyes lit up when he spoke of his favorite bakery in the town, owned by a stoat who made the best sweets. He had fondly recalled that he often shared a slice of sponge cake with his mom, topped with the biggest blackberries you'd ever seen.

The dramatic huff that Merlin released as she stood up brought Lore back from the happy memory. *A memory I'll cherish even when I'm back home.*

"These old bones of mine," the bat groaned as he stretched, letting his wings open to their full span.

Lore buttoned the thick flannel over the wool sweater Dina had given to Mathilde to give to her. The northern air was cooler, even more than she anticipated.

Mathilde scampered over to the coach, proudly waving the book in the air. "It's finished, and it's perfect!"

Killmoore's nose scrunched as he looked at the sloppy drawing. The lines waved where they should have been sharp and crisp. The stem looked like it had thorns when the flower had no thorns at all. "Are you sure we saw the same flower?" the fox teased.

Mathilde's face fell as she looked at her drawing. "Whaddya mean?"

Merlin walked over and looked intently at the pencil drawing. "Don't listen to him. I say it looks identical."

Lore smirked. "You know, Mathilde, you could press the flower."

The mouse tilted her head at the idea. "Press it?"

"Yeah." Lore walked over and picked the flower from the ground, and her eyes fell on the pink-petaled flowers that had popped up on the forest floor on the other side of a small glen. Decorating the ground like little blush sprinkles. She then took the flower to Mathilde. She placed the flower beside the mouse's amateur illustration. Then her hands closed the book. "Sit on this during the ride."

Mathilde smiled from ear to ear. "How'd you know this?"

Lore paused for a moment. "Ya know, I'm not sure."

Was this something I used to do? Who taught me to do that? That older woman? My grandma? Will I get to see her again?

She walked back to the turnip and stepped in to take her seat.

Killmoore followed behind her.

The enchanted coach was moving at quite a fast pace through the Emerald Pass, but then it came to a sudden stop. Not daring to move another leaf forward on the path. Silence defended the coach as Lore exchanged confused looks with her traveling companions.

"I guess that means we're here?" Mathilde finally asked.

Merlin let out a breath. "It would appear so."

The four looked at the village that lay in the shadow of the looming Wayward cliffs. Shades of gray painted the town of Cloch Chruinn. A settlement that Killmoore had described with such wonder and awe. The fox stepped down from the turnip carriage and stared at the busted-up welcome sign that was missing more than three of its letters. Mathilde slipped out behind him, Lore followed, and Merlin lingered in the doorframe of the transformed vegetable. His eyes fixated on the three.

Lore noted that Mathilde crossed her arms against the frigid harsh air that blew down from the Mountain. But was it really from the cold, or did the mouse feel disappointed the town wasn't like the image she had in her mind?

"Killmoore, this is everything opposite of what you said it would be." Her voice was quieter than usual. Lore chewed the inside of her cheek, and the fox stood there fixed on the ghost of a town. Lore watched his amber eyes. They were hollow as they searched for any sign of familiarity.

Just how long had he been gone from this place?

Lore fidgeted with the buttons of her flannel. "It's okay, Mathilde." *What else do I say? What else* could *I say?*

Merlin clicked his tongue behind them, still lingering on the door of the coach. "Foxes are known to embellish the truth."

Right now, he isn't the same bat dancing across a tabletop in a creepy forest.

Mathilde's brow furrowed, and Killmoore's breath hitched.

Noted.

"It was the way I said it was when I left." His voice lacked his usual moxie. "I-I..." Killmoore stumbled over his words.

Lore turned to look at Merlin momentarily, and though a fire felt like it was bubbling up inside her, her face was relaxed and calm. Lore readjusted her view to be settled on the mouse. Completely ignoring the Wielder's comment, Lore knelt down so she was at eye level with her friend. Keeping her demeanor calm so that it even matched her voice. "You know, Mathilde..." Lore's soft smile melted away at the mouse's look of confusion. Like snow-covered boots by a roaring fire. "Not everything stands the test of time. Not a stone of Thimbleton's earth, and certainly not something as temporary as a village or its folk."

The fox gulped hard. Lore looked at him, and a shadow washed over his face.

"It's okay, Killmoore," Mathilde said as she went over to grab his hand. "Lore's right."

Lore sighed a breath of relief, but it didn't stop the eerie feeling she had that Merlin's gold-flecked eyes were currently boring into the back of her head.

The fox looked like he wanted to say something, but all that he mustered out was, "Sorry your first adventure isn't as fun and lively as you thought it'd be, Mathilde." Killmoore stomped to the boot of the turnip coach, past Merlin's curious eyes. "I'll walk from here, thanks."

Merlin shrugged. "No worries. It's a small town. The carriage can follow behind." The bat hopped down from the frame of the coach door and started rummaging around in the boot with Killmoore. "Just think of it as an auto-pilot feature."

Lore briskly walked over as Merlin handed her a small bag to clip around her waist. "Don't forget your satchel in the coach," he reminded her flatly.

The bag weighed as if it held nothing, but a silver light dribbled from loose leather seams.

Lore clipped the small bag to her pant loop. "What is it exactly?"

"Something I hope you won't have to use," the bat said, the tips of his pointed ears folded over as he walked away.

Does he know about something we don't?

Lore raised a brow as her hand fell, barely touching the leather pouch that was now strapped to her side. Her eyes looked into Killmoore's gloomy gaze.

"You ok?"

The fox's hair bristled as if he were just shocked by an electrical outlet. "Yeah." He ran a paw through the tufts of orange fur between his ears. "Why do you ask?" He slid on his backpack, closing the boot shut with a thud.

Lore crossed her arms. "You just seem..." She rocked on her heels, searching for the right word. "Off?"

His paws gripped around the leather straps of the bag as he snapped them against his body. "Don't know what ya mean," he said smoothly, pushing past her. "Only thing off 'round here is this rinky dink town."

Lore pursed her lips and followed close behind the fox.

Merlin led them through the village of Cloch Chruinn. The streets were mucked with grime and soot. Buildings were cramped close together and were as gray as ash from a roaring blaze. Roofs were sunken in, others didn't have a functioning roof at all. And window shutters were snapped closed.

Though Lore felt like eyes were peering through their cracks, unsure of what to make of the strangers. She straightened her back with false confidence. *Wouldn't be the first time I was a stranger in town.* The thought stomped through her mind like the turnip carriage that followed.

The group continued on foot, unsure if there would be a soul to greet them. The path led to a circle at what seemed to be the heart of Cloch Chruinn. Lore only assumed it to be so, due to the other paths that also led to the spot they were standing in. Lore shifted her weight from side to side as Merlin and Mathilde knocked on doors.

No one greeted them, no one except the rigid statue perched upon a tree stump. Green flecks that appeared as bark were signs of bronze oxidation. The statue had been there for a long time, and a pool of water lay motionless beneath the circular disk the stump sat upon.

Lore wondered if taels thrown in, but she couldn't move to check.

She felt as if the creature were watching her.

The sculpture was so lifelike that she swore she saw its golden eyes blink at her. Long ears stretched up to the sky like a hare's. The arms were skinny and held close to its body. Its face rimmed with tufts of raven-colored fur. Small wings that didn't look strong enough to carry the creature's lower goat-like behind protruded from its back. Lore felt her hands twitch as the sculpted golden eyes pierced through her. She felt as if she were being pulled under ice-cold water.

Her mind raced as her breathing quickened. I've seen those eyes before. The shadowy tendrils of the fateful night she fell, or rather was pulled, down the well surfaced in her mind. She scratched at her forearm as if the creature that brought her here still had a grip on her. She shuddered and then she realized it was Killmoore's hand that had been placed upon her.

"Lore?" His voice was steady as he looked her over. "Are you okay?"

Her eyes snapped to him. "Fine." Her single-word answer was stiff. "Do you know anything about this statue?"

"It's the mischievous spirit I was telling yins about last night."

Lore pursed her lips. *Should I tell him?* This was the first stop on their journey. Maybe the dots she was connecting would rain out their big adventure. *That wouldn't be fair to Mathilde.* A disgruntled voice broke Lore away from her internal push and pull.

The fox's snout jerked toward the quarrel. Lore took one more look over the statue that seemed fixed on the twitching muscles in her hands, and the way her jaw tensed. *Damn, creepy statue.*

Lore and Killmoore walked towards the chaos, where Merlin and Mathilde stood arguing with a badger.

"Hello," Lore said as she stood beside Mathilde. "What seems to be the problem?"

Killmoore stood behind her, almost hunched out of sight. Saying absolutely nothing.

"This bat thinks he's gonna go up the mountain!" the badger said, as he pointed a sharpened claw in Merlin's face.

The caster seemed bored with the whole interaction.

"Why can't we go up the mountain?" Lore studied the features of the badger. His underbite. His disheveled hair.

"No one goes up the mountain." He crossed his stout arms and spat in front of Merlin's feet. "Least not anymore."

Merlin rolled his eyes. "Now you're just being rude."

The badger's face settled into a glare. "The mountain that's overrun with bandits, angry spirits, and ghosts of monks."

"Ghost monks?" Killmoore asked. "That's odd."

The badger scowled. "Dontcha know bad stuff comes in threes?"

The fox rolled his eyes. "The expression is, *everything* comes in threes."

Merlin's hands moved to his hips, drawing attention back to himself. "You know I am a Wielder. I think we'd be just fine."

The badger snorted, and his laugh sounded like the rumble of a hungry stomach. "There ain't been one of those 'round 'ere in ages."

Before Merlin could get another word in edgewise, a delicate voice was carried on the stagnant air. "Oh, I thought I told you to invite them, not rile them up!"

Another badger approached. She was in a thick green sweater and what appeared to be a long wool-lined skirt. A bright green bandana, the only vivid thing Lore has seen thus far, wrapped around her head. She looked like the sweetest little old grandma.

"Hope he hasn't left a sour taste in yer' mouths. I'm Molly, and this is my husband, Seán." An arm looped through her husband's. "Forgive him. He's grown grouchy with age."

Her husband let out a huff, but added nothing to her statements.

Merlin nodded and held his hands up, gesturing to the empty streets. "You're the first we've seen."

Mathilde smiled. "You said something about inviting us somewhere?"

Molly's honeyed eyes dripped with joy. "We own the Bumble Inn," She gestured down the road. "Just a little beyond that way."

Killmoore shifted his weight from side to side, still trying to be invisible behind Lore.

"What's the fox's problem?" Seán grumbled.

Mathilde cocked a brow and leaned back, looking Killmoore up and down. "He's just—"

"A bit shy," Lore interrupted her.

Mathilde locked eyes with her friend, confusion written all over her face. If there was one thing Killmoore was, it wasn't shy. She raised both eyebrows and tried to signal she'd tell Mathilde later. Luckily, the gray mouse dropped the issue.

"I suppose one night wouldn't hurt." Merlin chimed.

"Well, come on then," Molly called, as she began pulling on Seán's arm with a smile. "The inn is this way."

"Of course," Merlin's tone fell a bit more hushed as he eyed them like a stern parent. Silently, he let them know to be on their best behavior.

Mathilde shoved her hands in her pockets. "We'll talk later." She peeked behind Lore, her big green eyes fixed on the bounty hunter.

"Come on then," Merlin called as he continued following the old badger couple.

Mathilde scurried to catch up while Lore and her fox companion kept up a steady pace behind the others and *slowly* passed the statue of the phantom sprite, expecting its glittering golden eyes to follow them. The sculpture was still, as fashioned metal should be.

"You gotta tell me what's going on," Lore whispered, even though their hosts, Mathilde, and Merlin were too far ahead to hear her.

Killmoore kept his gaze on the road ahead. "You tell me what's going on with you first."

Lore clenched her jaw. "Why do you have to be like that?"

The edges of his lips curled into a smile. "Very pot calling the kettle black, isn't it?"

Molly really wasn't lying when she said their inn was just down the way. It wasn't far. In fact, when Lore looked over her shoulder, she could still see the haunting statue in the heart of Cloch Chruinn. A gust of wind blew, and the inn's faded wooden sign swung in the air gently, creaking against the breeze.

"Come in, come in," she cheered as she opened the door.

Seán went in first and groaned as he thudded a spiral-bound book onto the welcome desk.

The adventurers filed in. The Bumble Inn was small and cozy. Lore saw a stairwell that climbed up to another level. It appeared like a normal house. A normal house that they converted to a bed-and-breakfast.

"It's been so long since we've had visitors," Molly said as she handed Merlin a pen to fill out the sign-in sheet. "This little Inn of ours used to host all sorts of events." Molly rested her chin in her hands, her eyes glittered like topaz gems. "My favorite was the matchmaking events."

"Molly loves love," her husband grumbled.

Lore was listening, but she also noticed a large spider that was working hard to expand its web in a nook where the ceiling met the wall in the far corner.

"We'll only be here for one night," Merlin said as he scratched in everyone's name.

A deep and phlegm-filled cough traveled down the stairs. Merlin held the pen steady above the paper. "Well, sounds like you have had someone staying here," he said with a passing laugh as he looked at Killmoore, who was still shielding his face with the help of Lore's stature.

"Hey, is it one or two 'L's?"

"Two." The fox's voice was lower than usual.

The sound of labored coughing traveled down the steps again.

Seán's face softened as he muttered. "I'll go check on 'em."

Merlin's eyes lingered on the grouchy badger who was now climbing the old, faded blue staircase.

"Is it possible that I have my own room?" Merlin asked as he slid the book back to Molly.

The badger placed the book back in a drawer. "We can room you separately, but the single bedroom is a bit smaller."

Killmoore let out a sigh of relief.

"Not a problem at all." Merlin sounded very certain.

Mathilde tilted her head. "Wouldn't it be cheaper to room together?"

Merlin's eyes flickered as he laughed. "Well, when you're as old as me, it's worth it to pay a little extra to sleep separately from the rowdy youth."

Mathilde pursed her lips, then shrugged.

Lore eyed the gray mouse. *No witty response?* Lore's own thoughts were like walking a tightrope. On one side, she had the 'off' feeling from Killmoore pulling at her, and now, the other side was concerned for Mathilde just taking everything Merlin said at face value. *And somehow, I'll have to find a way to maintain this balancing act for the rest of the trip.* Anxiety rippled in her stomach, creating waves of apprehension.

Molly kindly smiled. "That'll be five hundred and eighty-four taels."

Killmoore sounded like he had choked on his own saliva.

Merlin rubbed his chin, mulling it over, when more coughs fell through the floorboards above them and echoed in the lobby of the Inn. "Who is that?" Merlin pressed.

"Oh you know," Molly said, her anxious tone contradicting the smile on her face. "Customer confidentiality and all that."

"Well, if there is sickness here, that means that my companions and I will be exposed to it." He looked over Mathilde, Lore, and Killmoore briefly. "Then I am afraid we may have to find another inn."

Tears welled in the badger's eyes. "*Please.* We need the taels."

Merlin walked around the desk and took Molly's hands in his. His sparkling curiosity faded into soft sincerity. "Who's upstairs?"

Tears fell down Molly's striped face. "My grandchild. Terrible case of fluid lung."

Merlin rubbed the tops of Molly's clawed hands with his thumbs. "Tell ya what," he said, his voice hushed and gentle. "I'll make a deal with you. I'll heal your grandchild, and we will pay two hundred taels for the two rooms."

She wiped her face, her eyes puffy. "You're a healer?" she said through an unsteady breath. "We used to have one in the village, but they took her a long time ago."

Killmoore rested a hand on Lore's shoulder as he peered around the human. "Who took the healer?" he asked.

His voice still sounded like it was dragging against a gravel road. Was he trying to disguise his voice?

The Bumble Inn owner wailed and fell into Merlin's arms for a hug. "Mordred," she sniffled. "He used to be the guard, but one day he went up the mountain and returned a very different bear."

The shrill cries continued, and Mathilde joined Merlin, rubbing a comforting hand on the badger's back. Lore heard heavy footsteps above.

Sure enough, Seán was flying down the steps, even with his slight hobble. "Whaddya do to my Molly?" he growled.

Merlin and Mathilde backed away from Molly as her husband wrapped his arms around her. She looked at him with those sweet honey eyes. "The bat is a healer, Seán."

The grouchy badger said nothing, just looked at Merlin skeptically. "Is that true?" His words were strained. The hopeful thought that he had stumbled across a healer seemed frightening to him.

Lore understood, though. Hope could be a scary feeling indeed, rather than fear of the hope being all for nothing.

Merlin nodded. "I've been a practitioner since I was very young. I started building this muscle when I was just a pup on the edges of the Fire Fields of the south."

Seán began nodding slowly, taking in the words Merlin had said. "Forgive me for my rudeness earlier, but would you be willing to cast a healing spell?"

Merlin nodded. "I already offered a deal to your wife. We are just waiting on the answer." His words were careful.

Molly wiped her face again. "Yes, that is beyond worth it if you can heal wee Crispin."

Merlin rubbed his hands together. "Perfect. Will you show me to young Crispin's quarters?"

"Aye." Seán led Merlin up the stairs, then added, "He has been sick for some time now."

Molly brushed off imaginary dust from her skirt. "The other room is on this floor. Follow me, please." She walked around the group and unlocked a door that had peeling navy paint. At one time, the Bumble Inn was probably every possible shade of orange there was. Now, it was in need of more than a few touch-ups. Molly pushed the door open and a full bed was revealed. It was a few feet away from a large window that looked out onto the street.

Gonna be hell for all three of us to squeeze into a single bed. The trio passed the old badger entering the room. "Enjoy your room. I'll be on the second level if you need anything." With that, she latched the door closed. Luckily, on a wall that faced the visible bed was a frame for a bunk bed. On both sides of the bunk, that was centered on the wall, were black and white photos. Lore walked over, running her fingers along the dust-covered frames.

"When was the last time you think they cleaned this place?" she thought aloud.

Mathilde took a deep breath in as she launched herself on the single bed. Dust particles flew into the air like a dirty snow globe that was just shaken. "More importantly," the mouse chimed, "who's gonna get the bunks, and who's gonna get the single bed?"

Killmoore walked over to Lore and slid his bag off his shoulder and plopped it onto the bottom bunk. "Doesn't matter to me." He shrugged, sitting himself on the bed beside his belongings.

Mathilde grinned and rushed to claim the top bunk.

"I call dibs on the top then," she cheered as she scaled the short ladder.

Lore shook her head with a soft smile. *Of course.*

Lore focused her attention back to the faded photos on the wall, adjusting her fingers beneath the strap of the leather bag that was wrapped around her chest, that was once a mere paper bag.

The image that really caught her eye was the one with the faded green frame. It was a large group of folk, all gathered in front of the phantom sprite's shrine. They wore smiles on their faces and had sticks topped with candied apples in their hands. She saw almost every animal she would expect to see around the mountains. Bear, fox, stout, and lynx, among many others. All were festive and cheerful. Lore could still make out the autumnal patterns on their knit sweaters. She heard a hard swallow from beside her and noticed Killmoore looking at the same photo.

"Notice any familiar faces from your frequent visits here?" she asked.

Killmoore crossed his arms. "Can't say I do." Something about his tone made her gaze linger on him.

The opaque light from the larger and slower of the two moons poured through the giant window.

Mathilde was busy on the top bunk unpacking her belongings. Sorting them and packing back up what she didn't need. She wrapped herself in a faint velvet blanket and stood up. Her ears barely grazed the ceiling. "Oh, yeah!" she declared. "We were going to talk about Killmoore's sudden social anxiety."

The fox's expression stiffened. "Tomorrow. I'm tired now." He then collapsed on the bed, letting out a huff.

Mathilde scrunched her face. "How can you be *tired*?"

Lore smirked and flapped the single bed's comforter a bit more, making sure to get all the dust off of it. Then she shoved the leather bag under her pillow. The small pouch attached to her waist pocket glimmered in the silver moonlight. Her hand hovered above it as she debated on if she wanted to remove it for sleep.

She chewed the inside of her cheeks as she slid between the covers and sheets of the squeaky twin bed. "Mathilde, we could have walked for the past two days and somehow you'd still have the energy to pull an all-nighter."

Mathilde threw her arms up in the air, the blanket falling from her shoulders. "Can you blame me? We are in a creepy little town that probably has mysteries all of its own and we are just passing through?!"

Lore shook her head with a smile as she laid back on the pillow, looking up at the room's yellow-stained ceiling.

"Do you know what that means?!"

Lore shrugged, not bothering to look over. "We should call it a night?"

Mathilde's face was painted with shock. "Are you *kidding* me?! We only have one night to figure out this town's story."

"Go to bed," Lore said with a laugh as she rolled on her side, looking out into the empty night streets.

"But don't you want to know who Mordred is?" the mouse squeaked.

"He sounds like a typical apple that rotted," Lore said, closing her eyes. Pretending that Mathilde would do the same.

"Killmoore, how 'bout you?"

He snored loudly, emphasizing just how much he didn't want to talk.

Lore's stomach turned. *I hope he's okay.* Yeah, the fox was allowed to not want to talk, but this wasn't that. *He's hiding something.*

Lore pulled the blankets up to her chin, something that Merlin would surely pick at until whatever 'it' was festered.

I can't let that happen.

Her eyes stayed fixed on the fox who, to her, was obviously pretending to sleep.

Mathilde sunk behind the wood planks. "Good idea, Killmoore. We can nap and strike up a midnight adventure through the haunted streets of Cloch Chruinn!" she declared, before curling up with a yawn.

Lore's heart softened for Mathilde. I know she's excited about being out of Charmsend, but why isn't she reading the room?

Lore shrugged off any remaining annoyance and sunk deeper into the comforter of the bed as Mathilde did the same.

I wonder how long it'll be before she submits to sleep. Or how long it will be before we're suddenly awakened because 'adventure calls.'

The warmth of the blanket engulfed Lore as she fought her thoughts that were threatening to swallow her whole.

Try to put yourself in her shoes.

Lore's grip on the blanket tightened as she pulled it up towards her chin. Her eyes shot open and met the wallpaper of the room.

I guess I am kinda like her. Thimbleton is a whole new world to me—literally. But I constantly feel as though I have to rush to return to a place that my mind's eye can barely remember well enough to paint a picture.

She rolled over, looking at the sleeping mouse, observing the way the blanket rose and fell with each breath.

I wish I could find even a sixteenth of the excitement Mathilde can.

Lore rolled on her back and looked up at the ceiling, her hands folded over her chest. *But for now, we rest.*

Lore's eyes became heavy and the only sound was the faint coughs from the floor above, that seemed to get fainter and fainter as sleep embraced her.

SIX

Lore tossed and turned as whispers stirred in her ear. She shot up and saw a figure crouched by the door. The moon's light had moved on the other side of the buildings and street. Leaving the room dimmer. She didn't miss a beat as she reached for her leather bag under her pillow. She held her breath as she chucked the bag at the figure's head.

Killmoore grumbled and pushed the bag across the floor. "Damn it, Lore," he muttered, rubbing the back of his head.

Lore huffed and crossed her arms. "Don't wanna get things thrown at you? Then don't be a suspicious figure in the night."

"Shh," he scolded as he waved her to come over.

She rolled her eyes, though she doubted he saw that. She tiptoed beside him and gestured to the glass he had pressed against the door.

"What are you doing?" her whisper was stern.

He shushed her again and held his ear up to the glass. Lore crossed her arms, pouting. Not only was the bed more uncomfortable than it was dusty, but now she was awake when she didn't want to be because someone wanted to be nosey.

"Listen," the fox mouthed, flicking his amber gaze towards the door.

She leaned against it, expecting she'd hear a trivial quarrel between the old married couple.

"We'll be gone in a few hours," Merlin's voice was hushed, but Lore knew it was his because of the quickness of his words. He always seemed to be in some sort of hurry.

"I'm sorry to rush you out, but if they find out we had customers, they'll take nearly all of it."

There was silence, then the bat began again. "What exactly should me and my party expect when traveling up the mountain?"

"Depends on where your destination is." Seán's voice was hard to miss—his low, dragging tone.

"A legendary library."

The badger let out a quiet whistle. "Well, you may come 'cross Mordred's grunts then. Nasty thieves. Took all they could from this town and continue to dig at an empty mine."

"Why don't you leave?" Merlin asked—an earnest question. Lore wondered the same.

"They took so much that we can't afford a new start, we can barely afford to feed ourselves. Most of the town has died. I heard rumors of what the more southern towns are calling us."

"What's that?"

"The blanch." The sadness in Seán's voice made Lore pull away from the glass cup. Her sad eyes looked at the bounty hunter.

"We have to help," Lore whispered.

Killmoore shook his head. "Sometimes certain things can't be helped."

Lore's eyes narrowed. "Bullshit."

Killmoore shuddered. "Oh, come on now Lore, don't bring a bull's shit into this."

She shook her head. "You know what I mean."

He looked away from her. His hand reached for an ax. "We'll be leaving soon. You should rest a bit longer while you can."

Lore crossed her arms. "You've been acting weird since we left Mathilde's house."

"Lore, please." The glowing amber of his eyes begged her not to press.

"The Killmoore I met in that abandoned cabin didn't leave Charmsend when a mystery reared its head."

The fox said nothing and went to sit on the bottom bunk. He took a stone out and began sharpening his blade. "Rest while you can. We don't know what will be in store for us as we try to reach answers about retrieving your memories and how to send you home."

Lore chewed the inside of her cheek. It was clear she wasn't going to get any answers. At least, not right now. She huffed as she crawled back into the bed. Cocooning herself inside the blanket that smelled of mothballs. She forced her eyes closed. Lore tried to distance herself from her thoughts about Killmoore, and soon she was falling back into a deep sleep, listening to the sound of the stone dragging against his blade.

The darkness of her mind swirled around her. Smoky tendrils hugged Lore like an old friend greeting her. She tossed and turned in her sleep as they beckoned her to join them.

She opened her eyes, and the dreamworld greeted her vision with a soft haze. As she rose to her feet, she felt like she was floating. She heard whispers coming from behind her, whispers that sounded like two or three voices meshed together. When she turned, a ghostly yellow butterfly flew around her in a circle, then fluttered off into the shadowy abyss of her mind, taking the whispers with it.

"Come back," she heard herself call, though she didn't recall opening her mouth.

She raced after the yellow phantom butterfly and she heard laughter roll off its small wings. Lore felt like she was moving through thick mud, but she swore she was moving as fast as her legs would take her. Then, the butterfly started sparking, and Lore smelled the slight scent of smoke.

More sparks danced on the insect's wings before exploding entirely, as if it were a firework, but from the fallout were golden lines that painted a scene.

A memory?

Lore watched as the lines showed a young girl and an aged woman in a garden together. Butterflies flitted around them and yellow flowers danced off in the distance.

Tears formed in the corners of her eyes, cold like ice, as they made their way down Lore's cheeks. She watched as the older woman handed the young girl a golden flower, and then the girl snapped a book around the flower. They laughed, and the older woman sat the book on the ground, and the little girl excitedly sat on it. The yellow lines from the exploding butterfly faded, but Lore caught sight of the older woman handing the girl a teacup and pouring some tea from a pot.

A picnic in a wildflower field? With my grandma? It has to be, right?

As the lines continued to fade, the sound of porcelain shattered. And Lore watched as the older woman picked up the pieces to the broken pot. Then the dream eased its grip off her, and the sound of glass bottles being shattered against the wall of Lore's consciousness awakened her.

Her heart was racing, and she tried to steady her breath. Her eyes darted around the room. It was empty. She could find no trace of Killmoore nor Mathilde.

Lore swung her legs over the side of the bed, her muscles still trembling. Her gaze slowly raised to look at the ratted curtains. With a shrug, she got up and brushed them open with one fluid swoop of her hand. Then on the other side of the glass window, she only found strangers that were out and about, but when they finally spotted her they just stared at the only human in Thimbleton.

Lore's face flushed red, and she felt like she was some strange zoo exhibit. Ignoring the jelly like state now forming in her bones, she snapped the blinds closed. She could see the shadows of the animals move through the finger sized holes in the fabric. The frustration of not understanding what her dreams meant, paired with the lingering smell of whisky, really soured her mood.

She jumped at the sound of the door creaking open.

"Have a nasty dream?" Mathilde asked, leaving the door wide open.

"Something like that," Lore growled.

"It's a good thing we are leaving. You sound as grouchy as Seán." Mathilde quickly closed the door, not giving Lore a chance to retort.

The human snatched her leather bag off the floor and then peeked between the threadbare curtain. She saw Merlin and Killmoore preparing the turnip outside. She let the tattered fabric flutter close as she sat on the foot of the bed, lacing up her boots. The smell of whisky made its way up her nostrils.

Where was that smell coming from? Lore heaved a tired breath. She finished the last knot on her boots and then stomped out of the room, yanking the door shut behind her, not caring to take in the details to save for a memory later. Lore couldn't seem to shake off the 'woke up on the wrong side of the bed' feeling.

Molly met her at the welcome desk. "Hope your stay was good."

Lore let her face relax a bit. "Any rest that's not on the cold ground is a good one," she lied, knowing full well she would have rather slept in the woolen sack under a sky full of star clusters.

Molly nodded and Lore halted as she turned on her heel. She leaned an elbow back on the desk to whisper to the owner. "I'd let Seán know that whisky this early could turn future customers away." She joked, of course, though a small part of her was serious.

Molly tilted her head, confused. "Oh sweetheart, we are a dry Inn. 'Ave been for years," she assured.

The door swung open abruptly, and a shrill voice stabbed Lore's ears. "Molly!" The exclamation was followed by a louder and coarser complaint. "Could you be any *more* obnoxious?"

She spun on her heels and struggled to keep her balance, courtesy of her antlers. Lore locked eyes with a lynx whose cold gaze felt like a remnant of Crinkle's magic. "Who are you exactly?"

Lore squared her shoulders. Now with her composure regained, she realized how big the antlers helped her feel. "I'm just leaving." She brushed past the lynx and his bow wearing cat companion.

"Thought their kind was dead," the cat announced.

Lore tried to mask the puzzled look on her face with a smile. *Don't let them know it got to you.* As she opened the door to leave the Bumble Inn, she realized she hadn't heard anymore coughing.

Merlin must have been able to make good on his promise.

That thought alone put a genuine warmth in her chest even as cold air met her.

Sure, the cat and lynx seemed to be rough around the edges, but she supposed you'd find people like that anywhere you go. Even in magical worlds down wishing wells.

There was a light mist that was kissing Lore's face, but she didn't mind. The turnip would shield them if the mist turned into a downpour.

Mathilde scampered over to meet Lore in the road. "Did Molly tell you the story, too?" Her voice was the epitome of excitement, as usual.

"No?" Lore shrugged. "Two other guests came in and interrupted us."

"Great, then I'll get to tell you," Mathilde said, very pleased. She took Lore's hand and led her to the enchanted coach.

Killmoore gave Lore a nod from outside the window as he locked up the boot on the back of the carriage, and Merlin hopped up the two steps to claim his seat across from Lore.

Mathilde sat beside her, her arms hugging one leg close to her body, while the other one dangled off the seat. "So," the mouse began with a hum as Killmoore closed the hip level door to the turnip behind him. "There is a harvest phantom from the Otherworld."

Merlin clapped his hands twice, prompting the turnip to stand. Its vine-like limbs were stronger from a night's rest. It began walking, and rain pelted the top of the vegetable's wine colored roof.

"And every year the spirit requires a part of the harvest to be shared with it," Mathilde continued.

"What work does it put in?" Lore asked as her eyes followed along the lifeless buildings out the window. As Mathilde was going to answer, a strange groan erupted from the turnip. Then the coach suddenly halted and thudded against the ground. The first thing Lore observed was the annoyed glance Killmoore shot in Merlin's direction.

"What in Stag's breath is this?!" Merlin barked as he pushed the door open. "Did your magic finally run out?" Killmoore groaned.

Merlin was quick to fire back. "Listen fox, I know you know that's not how magic works here."

Lore watched as Killmoore rolled his eyes.

"So, what's the problem, Merlin?" Mathilde asked in earnest.

The bat peeked his head through one of the triangle cut windows. "I think it's the lousy rain."

"The turnip doesn't want to walk because it's raining?" Lore asked, disbelief clinging to her voice.

Merlin's face was flat. "Yes."

"So now what?" the bounty hunter scoffed. "You gonna conjure an umbrella for the carriage so we can get to the library?"

The bat rolled his eyes. "No."

"Are we gonna stay another night?" the mouse's voice pierced the tension between their companions.

"At least until the rain lets up some."

The mouse's nose twitched, and her eyes gleamed. "Silver linings in the clouds, I guess."

Lore softened at Mathilde's ability to always find that lining.

"We get to explore more of Cloch Chruinn," she practically cheered.

Killmoore sunk further into his seat. "*Great,*" he mocked while crossing his arms. "Just what we need."

Lore noted her friend's ever growing odd behavior, but assured Mathilde, "Sounds like a great idea."

"The innkeeper is gonna see this little bump in the road as confirmation that we shouldn't travel up the mountain." Killmoore brooded.

"May as well head back to the Inn," Merlin added, ignoring the fox's gripe. "I'd imagine our rooms would still be available."

"What do you mean 'not available'?!" Merlin wailed.

Molly gave a nervous laugh. "I'm sorry, we only have the one room now."

"Oh c'mon, Merlin." Mathilde tried to soothe the bat. "What's one night with us?"

"We had two guests arrive this morning." Molly looked at Lore. "They came right as you were leaving," the badger explained.

Lore observed the way her worry lines deepened at the mention of the pair, but only nodded her head. "That's right," she agreed, trying to calm the anxious badger. Lore looked down at Merlin. "One night won't kill ya."

On cue, the lynx and cat walked down the stairs, carrying on about 'what they'd do with their share.'

While everyone shuffled into the room on the first floor, Lore noticed Killmoore frozen at the entrance, his gaze lost in the mirror behind the check-in desk.

"Hey," Lore whispered softly. "Killmoore, this way," she urged.

The fox shook himself free from whatever thoughts were binding him.

"You look like you saw a ghost," Lore teased.

He swallowed hard. "Yeah, you could say that."

SEVEN

Lore sat at the foot of the bed where she had slept the night prior. The smokey tendrils of a dream she could barely recall now reached for her, but her mind was too preoccupied with her friends.

Mathilde was ogling out the window at the rain and the occasional passerby. Her questions pelted the group like the rain hitting the window.

"Where do you think they're going?"

"Do you think they know anything about the Keeper's Library?"

"Where are they even going in such a ghost town?"

Merlin was tapping the nightstand. "You've always got so many questions, Mathilde."

"Ain't that the truth," Lore teased, earning an exasperated groan from her fox friend.

"Perhaps you kids should go search for answers then."

Lore's eyes shot to Mathilde, who had already scampered to the door. "Merlin's right, let's go."

Killmoore didn't move from the bottom bunk.

"Uh, Killmoore, c'mon," Mathilde called. "Unless you want to stay here with only Merlin for company."

"*Fine*," the fox groaned as he stood up.

"Oh yes, I'll hold down the fort," Merlin mused.

Lore tilted her head a little so her antlers didn't brush the top of the door frame. "I'm sure we won't be gone long," she said confidently as she pulled the door shut behind her.

Molly was missing from the common area of the inn. *Odd.* The thought left Lore's mind as quickly as it entered.

"Lore," Killmoore grumbled, chasing after Mathilde. "C'mon."

The human shook her head and followed behind the fox.

When rain greeted her face, she couldn't help but smile. *Leave it to Mathilde to lead us on a chase for nothing in the pouring rain.*

Lore wasn't expecting the search for all the mouse's answers to her random questions to have herself and Killmoore sitting at the fountain with a painfully familiar mountain spirit looking down on her.

She tried to ease herself by focusing on what Killmoore was doing.

"Take a picture," the fox snapped. "It'll last longer."

Lore rolled her eyes. "What crawled up your rear and died?"

"Patience," Killmoore answered with a flip of his hand.

Lore snorted.

"Now I thought them were deer antlers, not *pig* antlers."

Lore gripped the flat stone of the bench they were sitting on. "You are being so catty today."

"Shh," Killmoore said, and pointed to Mathilde, who had successfully flagged down a villager. "Watch."

Lore observed as the stout didn't have any answers to any of the questions Mathilde had come up with between their room at the Inn and Cloch Chruinn's square.

Mathilde walked back to her friends. "I feel like no one here actually knows what's going on with this place."

Without missing a beat, Killmoore answered while looking at his nails. "Or they just don't trust an outsider."

Mathilde pouted.

"Oh c'mon," Killmoore teased. "Don't pout. We humored you and the bat got the room to himself for a while."

Lore jumped in. "And all Killmoore and I got was rained on."

Mathilde was still mulling over an answer when a shrill voice pierced the air.

"Oh, great," Killmoore groaned. "*Those* two."

Lore grimaced. "I get a weird feeling around them." It wasn't anything specific, just a gut feeling. *Can I trust my gut? Or is my intuition off since I don't even know myself?*

Mathilde shook her head. "You two just need to be more friendly." Then she scampered towards the lynx and cat.

Killmoore shot up instantly. "Mathilde, no!" he growled.

Lore didn't think twice. If Killmoore sensed danger, she trusted him. He'd saved her ass back at Crinkle's, after all. And he had good instincts during that final battle.

"Excuse me, can you help me? We're," Mathilde gestured to their group, "looking for a library in the mountains."

The cat grinned and shifted his weight side to side with excitement. "Yeah, runt. And we're looking for the mountain spirit."

The mouse's face fell flat. "Ah well, you see—"

"Listen, mouse, we know you ain't from round here. And it's best you just scamper home now," the cat spat while crossing their arms.

"Can't scamper home. Kinda on a quest," Mathilde answered flatly, her tail flicking back and forth with annoyance.

"*You?!*" the cat cackled.

The lynx remained eerily quiet.

"What kinda quest? Finding the biggest cheese chunk," the cat continued to poke.

It made an anger settle in Lore's stomach and the quiet buildings that decorated the sidelines of the street blurred.

Killmoore stood by Mathilde and cut in sternly. "Let's go."

"You look familiar, fox," the lynx's voice drug on the ground.

Killmoore rested a hand on Mathilde's shoulder. "I think I'd remember someone whose breath smelled like the rear end of a skunk."

Lore felt a surge of ice in her veins.

The lynx revealed a set of blades. "That mouth always was what got you into trouble."

Clearly, Killmoore knew them, but what was more pressing was the sound of Killmoore's axes clinking against swords.

"Get Mathilde and go," he urged, his feet firm on the stone against the larger lynx that looked over him.

"Don't try to be the hero," Mathilde spat.

Lore felt like the tips of her fingers were running along a sheet of ice. Then, looking down, she realized... it was because she *was* holding just that. She marched past Killmoore and Mathilde, and did the only thing that felt natural in the moment. The second the ice left her grasp is when the cold ran through her body.

They were hurting my friends.

Under the cold weight, the lynx and cat were picking themselves up.

They come here to bully villagers.

"What are you?" the cat asked in disbelief.

They deserve to know fear.

Lore wasn't focused on answering questions—only protecting her friends. With a wave of her hand, a sharp icicle took the form of a spear from the rain crashing around them. "I'm the one who's going to run you out of town," she barked through gritted teeth. She felt a righteous fury ring on each syllable.

"Lore," Killmoore said gently.

Lore leveled the icy spear at the throat of the lynx. "Give me a reason why I shouldn't."

"This isn't you," Killmoore's voice tried to reason with her.

"Because Mordred would kill you," the lynx seethed, answering at the same time.

Lore felt a cold breeze rush behind her, and a blue haze clouded her vision. "Doubt it." She pushed the tip of the spear against the lynx, drawing blood.

"You're just a human," the cat stammered out.

Lore felt her heart race. *Am I* just *a human? What makes a human so different from an animal?*

She felt Mathilde's embrace around her waist and Killmoore's grip on her arm.

Their warmth thawed her wrath.

The sheer blue haze from her vision was gone. She dropped the spear and cleared her throat. "Go."

The sounds of ice cracking under the footsteps of the two felines as they ran sent chills down Lore's spine.

"Lore," Mathilde said. "What was *that*?"

"A change in weather," Lore said, gesturing to the slowing of the rain. "Maybe it's the stroke of luck we needed." *I did the right thing.* The thought was as shaky as her breath. She was trying to reassure herself more than her friends. "I did the 'right' thing," Lore added, watching the feline's shadows fade in the distance.

Killmoore pulled her and Mathilde into a hug. "I'm afraid to see the problems up the mountain that doing the 'right' thing has caused."

"Killmoore, we couldn't have let Lore kill them," Mathilde insisted.

Would I have killed them? Am I a killer?

"Let's go rest," Killmoore said as his grip loosened. "No one says a word to the bat," he insisted.

Lore raised a brow. She didn't question the fox. Though she did question Mathilde's ability to keep something that 'exciting' to herself.

The heaviness from Lore's antlers made her head tilt from side to side. The motion was churning nausea in her gut. Recovering from whatever had awakened in her moments ago. She knelt down on the ground, her head still throbbing.

She heard her friends' footsteps, then felt their touch on her back.

"Lore," Mathilde whispered, "are you okay?"

Lore peeked through her parted fingers and saw the mouse knelt down in front of her.

"We're here for you," Killmoore murmured, while giving her back a gentle pat.

Lore's focus shifted from the comfort her friends were giving her to the fountain behind Mathilde.

Something wasn't right.

A frigid wind billowed through the streets, the eerie feeling that had clung to Lore, and shadowy tendrils writhed against the statue that stood at the center of the fountain. She felt a rush of frost enter her lungs as the creature's golden gaze fell onto her.

"No," Killmoore said breathlessly. "It can't be. After all this time?"

Lore felt an icy pull coming from her chest, urging her to follow the creature. Her gut told her not to, but after what happened, could she really do that?

Can I trust myself?

The shadows dripped from the statue, taking the form of the creature cast in bronze behind it.

A shudder from the growing chill in the air made the entity bolt.

Then, Mathilde's hand gripped Lore's as she pulled the human behind her and called to Killmoore, "You said in your little story if we catch it we get a wish?!"

Killmoore's voice called behind the two. "Yes!"

"Let's catch us a mountain spirit," Mathilde declared, her voice filled with her usual gusto.

I may not be able to trust myself, but I can try to trust her optimism.

What Lore *couldn't* trust was the chill growing deep within her bones.

EIGHT

Lore's vision on the moving shadow narrowed. The way it quickly maneuvered around forgotten junk of back alleys wasn't by any means a surprise, but it was annoying. *Can't we just have a* break*?* Lore chewed on the thought as Mathilde trudged ahead of her. She didn't realize how much stamina or speed the small mouse had. "So, how many times has someone caught this thing before?" Lore huffed.

"From my knowledge, twice," Killmoore called.

Every step against the pavement sent an ache up her legs. "Only *twice?!*" She wailed as they turned a sharp corner.

"Unfortunately."

"Should we split up?" Mathilde shouted from the front.

Lore's lungs shriveled at the thought.

"Worth a shot," Killmoore yelled.

This has been the worst day ever. And I think I've had some pretty bad days here.

The creature vanished into shadow and Mathilde hung right, Killmoore took the left, and Lore continued on the path ahead of her.

The air tasted like copper as she heaved a stinging breath. She squinted, trying to locate the mountain spirit. "I hope Mathilde and Killmoore are having better luck," she mumbled.

Suddenly, a dull ache radiated through her shin. Next thing she knew, the cobblestones bit at her pant legs and elbows. Lore sat on the chilled ground while snowflakes drifted down into her hair. She reached up to rub the soft velvet of her antlers and let out a shaky breath. *It's a dead end.*

With her nerves tying her gut into knots, she stood, trying to ignore the tenderness in her legs. She grumbled something inaudible and turned, only to be struck by gleaming golden eyes.

She reached a hand out instinctively not knowing, if she could actually grab shadow. The creature's arm felt cold in her grasp. But she did have a hold of it.

"I've got you," Lore huffed. "I believe I get a wish now."

The rabbit-eared creature seemed to grin at her.

For a moment, she tried to think hard of what should be her wish, but quickly realized she also didn't know if there was a window of time before the creature would vanish once again.

Lore blurted, "I wish for my memory back."

The entity winked its golden eye and yanked its arm free. With a snap of its finger, Lore felt light-headed. Her vision spun, and the creature dissipated into the air.

Then she could only see darkness behind her eyelids, then it turned to a stage where she watched herself in a clearing run towards a shadow. The shadow was on a blue wishing well.

The memory shifted from Lore watching herself to her facing the creature at the well. Within another breath, she was pulled under and the rush of frigid water filled her ears. Panic tightened around her heart.

This isn't happening. This can't happen again.

She tried to tell herself as the memory spat her consciousness back out on the familiar streets of Charmsend.

"Lore!" she heard Mathilde's voice ring through the empty streets of a day already past.

She shook her head.

"C'mon now," she heard Killmoore mumble. "Snap out of it."

Lore gasped as she left the memory threatening to drown her.

Mathilde and Killmoore knelt beside her, tentatively patting her back and grabbing her arms to help her stand.

"What happened?" Mathilde asked, quickly followed by, "Your eyes were frosted over again." The corner of her eyes watered with worry.

Lore sighed as her friends helped her stand. "I caught it."

Killmoore let go of her as if he'd been burned, his face frozen with anxiety. "What did you wish for?"

"I wished for my memory back. But it only gave me a single one."

Mathilde gasped, followed up with, "And?"

"I did remember something." The trio began to weave their way back to the main road. "I remember how I got to Thimbleton."

"How?" Mathilde pushed.

"That creature—" Devastating pain cut her off. It felt like ice shards were sawing through her leg bones. She dropped to the ground, wailing.

"Lore!" Mathilde cried.

"No!" Killmoore shouted, holding the mouse back. "Her eyes are frost-touched again! You could get hurt, Mathilde."

Lore couldn't see her friends. The pain that sliced up her legs made it hard to focus on their voices. She couldn't help it.

"Hurt."

Lore could make out the word, but she couldn't be certain who was saying it. Or what had come before it.

"Find help," the voice urged.

The skin on her calves felt like it was stretching to the point of breaking. As if her calves had become balloons that were being pumped with too much air. Lore wailed as she reached to grasp the afflicted area. Her touch felt like fire that was going to make the thin layer pop.

She pulled her knees up to her chest as hot tears licked her cheeks.

"Inconsolable," a voice stated.

"Don't know," another said.

"This...bad," one more added.

The last thing Lore recalled was the sound of the voices of the ink haired man, and the old woman melted together and in unison agreeing upon "leave now."

Lore's eyes fluttered open, and her head had a dull throb. The pale winter sunlight trickled through the bare branches above her. *What hap-*

pened? The comforting scent of campfire smoke circled her. Lore propped herself up. It appeared her companions had left her alone. *But why?* Lore was almost standing up when her legs shuddered with agony. Then her antlers caught some stray shrubs that were near her. She let out a groan.

Flashes of being curled up on the streets of Cloch Chruinn played in her mind. She tried to tug her antlers free, but another sharp chill shot through her legs. She shuddered, and her stomach growled. *When was the last time I ate?*

Lore's gaze fell upon some blackberries, a bit overripe on the vine—but how bad could they be? Lore reached out, careful not to prick her finger as she plucked a berry from the vine, and gave her head another shake, which released her from the bramble's grasp. She plopped back down and picked a few more berries. *At least it's something.* She held one up to her lips, ready to accept whatever bitter taste waited for her. Opening her mouth, she popped the berry in and shuddered at the slimy texture that greeted her pallet.

She waited to see how long before the bitter-ripe taste left her mouth. It was her, the campfire, and a gentle, chilled breeze.

"Hey," Mathilde sounded surprised as she scampered to the human's side. "You're awake?!"

Lore raised a brow. "How long have you been there?"

"Just got back. I didn't go far. Just to get some water," the mouse said, waving the silver canteen.

"Where's Merlin and Killmoore?"

Mathilde sat down next to her. "They're getting something for the pain."

Lore nodded slowly and brought another berry up to her mouth. "Where are we?"

The mouse's ears fluttered.

Mathilde is attempting to hide her excitement.

"We're a little up the mountain!" She squeaked.

Lore looked down to her hands. The memory of holding a sheet of ice chilled her fingertips. She quickly buried her hands in her crossed legs, as if that little bit of warmth would thaw out the feeling.

"What happened to the others?" Lore paused for a moment, then added. "In the village?"

Mathilde shrugged. "I'm not really sure. Merlin wanted to get outta there fast."

Lore nodded absent-mindedly. I wanted to help the village. What if I made things worse?

"You were crying out in your sleep," Mathilde's voice was a whisper, but it got Lore's attention. "Merlin said he could heal you, and something about needing to find a ghost pipe first, but Killmoore said that don't grow up here and muttered something about willow bark."

Lore brought another berry to her lips, only for Mathilde to swat it away. "Hey!"

"I never got to tell you the story that Molly shared with me."

"Right." Lore's response was distant. She had a small tug inside her chest. *Did I get to say goodbye to Molly?*

"Well, the statue in town," Mathilde began.

Lore felt another ripple of pain in both legs.

"Yeah?" Lore hesitated as her memory thawed. "The one I caught?"

Mathilde nodded. "The creature spat on them because the harvest season is over."

Lore scrunched her face. "So, you're telling me I ate some magical entity's spit?"

Mathilde shook her head. "I'm telling you it's bad luck."

"Can you tell me what happened?" Lore pressed.

"I think it's best we wait for everyone else."

Lore rolled her eyes. "C'mon, Mathilde. What else am I supposed to eat here?"

Another breeze blew, and Lore made the mistake of stretching her legs. A cold, numbing sensation knotted in her calves. She squeezed her eyes shut and wailed in pain. She grasped at her legs and a rustle of leaves got Mathilde's attention. The ache subsided just as quickly as it came.

Lore directed her gaze to Mathilde, who was welcoming back Merlin.

An *empty-handed* Merlin.

Lore tried to stand once again and from her knees down she felt as fragile as ice.

"Lore," Merlin said, "you should sit back down."

"What happened?" Lore demanded.

Another ache shot up her calves, that made her drop to the ground.

"It normally takes a fawn a day to walk," Merlin muttered.

"A *what*?" Lore spat through gritted teeth, trying to hide how bad the pain was.

"There, there," Mathilde said as she rubbed circles on Lore's back.

Lore's eyes drifted past Merlin, and she saw Killmoore rush from the tree line.

"Here," he gasped as he fell to the ground beside her, "eat this."

She chewed chunks of shaved tree bark. The texture was smooth, but the taste was more bitter than the overripe berries. As she ate the bark, Killmoore and Mathilde helped her sit down on her sleeping sack.

Her calves didn't tighten in pain. Now, there was only a dull ache. She reached down and massaged her calves. She sighed as she rolled up her pant leg.

Was it frostbite?

Her heart felt like it skipped a beat at what she saw. A pit in her stomach opened.

No.

"It's gonna be okay, Lore," Killmoore assured.

Lore felt herself embrace the worst-case scenario. She ran her fingers over the flat, tawny fur in disbelief. *What silver lining was there when you have* deer *legs?*

NINE

Cleaning up camp the following morning should have been as easy as sweeping cookie crumbs off a hardwood floor. But with her new legs feeling like jelly, Lore struggled to help the entire morning.

Cleaning up camp the following morning should have been as easy as sweeping cookie crumbs off a hardwood floor. But with her new legs feeling like jelly, Lore struggled to help the entire morning.

"It's okay," Mathilde assured as she insisted Lore not gather the sleeping sacks.

"You'll need your energy for the hike up the mountain," Killmoore said as she tried to help smother the fire. "Right now, our only focus is getting to the library."

Would the library have any books on humans turning into animals?

"Hike?" Lore asked. "What happened to the carriage?"

Merlin sighed as he buried the pumpkin sized turnip in the ground. "She gave us all she had. Now, as Sable would say," the bat cleared his throat and did his best impression of the hedgehog, "return it to the earth."

Lore plopped to the ground. Feeling useless ate her alive as she waited for everyone else to complete the camp clean up. The worst part was her new legs rendered her unable to help. She battled herself as she trekked through the briars, shrubs, and various stones that warped around a once well-trodden path.

"Here," Mathilde said, handing Lore a long stick. "To help," the mouse insisted. "And look, I found one for me, too."

"Thank you," the human mouthed as she gingerly took the walking stick from the mouse.

Lore took another step. This time, she leaned some of her weight on the stick, and it made the walk more bearable.

"What are we looking for, Killmoore?" Lore called, scanning the landscape, but saw nothing more than a few trees and spoiled mountain berries.

"A ferry," Killmoore said flatly.

"I thought the mountain was singular. Why are there two peaks?"

Mathilde gave an understanding nod. "Common confusion, but what actually happened was years and years and years of erosion from a very persistent river. Some say it was the murderous sprites that swam in the deep all those eons ago that chipped away at the earth and stone. Until one day they were so starved they died themselves. Returning to the bottom of the river. Their bones carried to the silver shores of the northernmost rim of Thimbleton."

"Whatever the reason, it's a ferry that floats over a chasm of death and watery graves," Killmoore said, his voice pointed.

Lore wanted to come up with a clever and witty response, but she didn't have enough strength for sarcasm. She took a misstep, but luckily, the walking stick helped her catch her balance again. *I finally get used to the inconvenience of antlers and now this?*

"There it is!" Mathilde's shriek stole Lore's attention from her self-loathing. The mouse pointed as she peeked over the top of a shrub.

Lore noted a rickety dock kissing the edge of the mountain face in the distance. The joy of the discovery was fleeting as they spotted two animals in mismatched armor, flanking the entrance.

"So, how do we want to approach this?" Merlin asked.

"Cautiously," Killmoore said flatly.

They looked back only to see Mathilde heading towards the guards.

Of course she couldn't wait, Lore thought as she marched after the mouse, pain accompanying each step.

"Good morning, gentle folk!" Mathilde called and waved a hand, trying to seem as nonthreatening as possible. When Lore caught up to Mathilde's side, her eyes fluttered over the small vessel that appeared to have large ink spilled feathers protruding from its hull. She shifted her gaze and was greeted with a smile that made her teeth ache.

"A human?" the toad whispered. "When did a human fall from the sky?"

The frog smacked its stouter counterpart upside the head. "That's human-ish. Normal humans don't got antlers." It cleared its throat to repeat the question. "When did a human-*ish* thing fall from the sky?"

Lore wanted to bang her head off of a tree. *Thing?!*

"An interesting story, but what I am more curious about is getting across that crevice of unpleasantries." Mathilde began to steer the conversation.

The frog leaned on his sharpened spear. "Sorry. Can't let ya pass unless ya pay the toll."

"How much?" Lore asked.

Merlin and Killmoore had caught up to her and Mathilde.

"Well now, that there's more of yins, let's see," the toad hummed. "Carry the two and that leaves the total at..." The small stout amphibian paused, making faces as he mentally checked his math. "Eight hundred taels."

"Eight *hundred*?!" Mathilde gasped.

I know I'm no expert in Thimbleton economics, but that seems excessive. "What jacked the price that high?" Lore asked.

The toad and frog looked at each other with blank faces as if the answer were obvious and shared a laugh. Then the frog gestured to Lore. "Yous a human, it's a risk takin' you on our ship. Gonna need fair compensation 'case you go 'n decide to do what humans do."

Lore felt her cheeks warm against the snowflakes that twirled down from the clouded sky. "And what do humans do?" she asked through gritted teeth as she leaned on the walking stick.

Mathilde's ears flattened, and her eyes narrowed as she echoed Lore's sentiment. "Yeah, what do humans do exactly?"

The amphibians shrugged. "You knows...wrecks things."

"Ruins and destroys," the frog nodded.

Lore's jaw ached from the tension, but it couldn't be helped. *So it wasn't just Charmsend who believed the made up human malarky.*

"Human superstitions aside, what sorta arithmetic are you going by, anyway?" Killmoore pressed. "Eight hundred is unreasonable."

"The math works for him." The oversized armor rattled over the frog's chest as his low voice continued, "'Sides, we just follow orders, and what Mordred says is what gets done."

Lore took note of the anxiety that rang from the frog's mouth. *They're afraid of the bear.*

The toad nodded along with the frog's words. "Mordred is gonna make the mountain glorious again." Then the helmet, better suited for a bear, almost fell from the toad's head when he looked up in admiration at the frog. "Mordred's words are the law here."

Everyone but Lore's face became plastered in confusion. She raised a skeptical brow. *Crinkle thought he made the rules, too.*

Arms crossed, Mathilde asked, "Who gave Mordred that sorta power?"

Killmoore's eyes were as wide as two dishes meant for an alligator.

Lore swore the color faded from his face.

"Mathilde," he scolded.

She shrugged innocently, and Merlin explained, "We've heard the name, but nothing detailing who Mordred is."

The toad let out a long croak. "He got that power by rallying the folk. He's promised a brighter future." The frog hit the top of his helmet with the spear, making the metal clang.

I may not remember much from my world, but I have a feeling those promises never bode well for society.

"What was that for?" the toad groaned.

"Quiet," the frog spat, then turned his gaze to the group. "If you want to cross, it gon' be a thousand tael."

Merlin stamped his foot with annoyance. "How did two hundred tael just get added? You said eight hundred."

"Well, askin' questions ya shouldn't be gets another couple hundred tacked on," the frog explained casually as if his logic made any sort of sense.

Merlin looked at Lore, and she shrugged off his unspoken question. "Perhaps there's another way."

The toad looked at his friend. "Well, we *were* wanting someone to fetch us some lucky things." His statement was so smooth and cool that Lore could have slipped on the words.

The frog drummed his long, thin fingers against his chin. A finger pad got stuck every so often. "We's were wanting those things, yes…"

Mathilde had a spark in her eyes. "Where are these things?" She asked so sweetly it would have won over grumpy Seán from the Bumble Inn.

The frog smacked his wet lips and leaned down as if Mordred were somewhere within earshot. "Tell ya what," he began, "If you all bring us back the horseshoe of the Midnight Stallion—"

"Don't forget the cauldron," the toad whispered with an aching want.

"I haven't!" his taller, greener companion snapped. "And fetch us the cauldron of the phantom, we will take yins 'cross the river."

Mathilde nodded along, absorbing each word. "Do you have a lead on where these items would be?"

The toad began to tremble, the loose armor trembled with him. "Tell 'em where it's at," he muttered to the frog.

The taller of the two guards rolled his eyes. "It's just up that path there." He pointed a long, slender arm in the direction they were originally heading in. "There's an old abandoned house that's said to have both treasures on the property."

"Why haven't you gone to get it yourself?" Killmoore pressed.

The frog's eyes bugged a bit. "Hey? Do I know you?" He asked as he leaned over Mathilde, eyeing the fox.

"I haven't seen you a day in my life." The exhaustion was evident in the fox's voice.

"Something like Ar—" the toad grumbled.

"I think you're confusing me with someone else," Killmoore insisted, taking a step back.

Merlin cut in, "What's the deal with the old house?"

The toad looked at the frog, as if he couldn't bear to say it.

"It's supposedly haunted, and those who have gone to get the treasures before have yet to come back."

Lore folded her arms over her chest. "You think it's haunted?"

"It's *known* to be haunted, human," the toad declared with a shaking finger pointed at Lore.

"How do you know the previous parties didn't just give up and turn back to go home when they couldn't find your so-called 'lucky things'?"

The toad stopped for a moment and adjusted the belt around his waist that was sagging from the heavy club he had strapped to it.

"We'll get your desired lucky things," Mathilde said with confidence, like she was already holding them behind her.

A smile spread across the frog's flat face, and the toad called, "Good luck to ye!" as they headed toward the old, abandoned house.

"A horseshoe and a cauldron," Lore repeated.

"It's not just *any* horseshoe," Mathilde corrected. "It's the Midnight Stallion's horseshoe."

Lore pursed her lips. "Do any of us know anything about these items?"

Killmoore let out a throaty grunt. "The *Midnight Stallion's* shoe gets hung above the threshold to catch all the good luck."

Lore raised a brow. "Okay, and what's the deal with the cauldron?"

"It's said that anyone who cooks with it, will never prepare a bad meal," the fox answered.

Lore ran her hands down her face. *Good food was nice, but this was ridiculous.* "We're going to fetch a horseshoe they want for decor, and a cauldron they think will make their cooking better?"

"Diplomacy can have its drawbacks," Merlin murmured, his face featured an unreadable expression.

The group walked up the winding, narrow path. With each step, Lore could hear the crunch of loose pebbles beneath her. Her feet ached in her boots, and her stomach had wished for a bigger breakfast that morning, but she wasn't going to complain.

Meanwhile, Mathilde was busy filling the brooding silence with declarations of wonder.

"Being this close to the clouds," she would say, reaching up as if she could pluck away a piece of the marshmallow like fluff, "makes me want to have a s'more."

No matter how much Killmoore grumbled or Merlin added nothing to the conversations Mathilde was trying to stir, she kept talking. Talking about how amazing everything was. All Lore could think about, though, was if Mathilde just liked hearing herself talk, or if it was a way to comfort herself in the face of the unknown. Just like how she carries that little green book like a shield.

How hard could retrieving a horseshoe and an old cauldron be?

"What do you think the traditional desserts are at this time of year?" The gray mouse asked, continually trying to get some response out of her traveling companions.

"What do you think made the leader of the city guard go rogue when he ascended the mountain?" She followed up with, "Do you think we'll meet the reason at this abandoned house?"

Killmoore tried to answer at least one of the questions. "Apples are a popular ingredient when the weather turns cold." The fox moved some low-hanging branches out of the way as they passed. "Apple cake," he hummed behind them. "Apple bread." The bounty hunter's tail swishing back and forth tattled on him. Revealing just how excited the fox was to talk about local desserts. "Apple pie, you name it."

"They all sound delicious!" Mathilde chimed, pleased she finally found a talking point that landed.

A stone wall that looked like it had erupted from the earth long ago hugged the rocky path's left side. Mathilde ran a hand along it. "How long ago do you think this was built?"

"A very, very, very long time ago," Merlin said with his eyes forward. The moons now peeked over the clouds. Their crescent shapes looked like a mirroring lopsided smile.

Lore reached out and let her fingers run along the soft moss. Then her fingers hit the smooth damp surface of the gray stone. Her legs still throbbed with pain, but she felt like this was becoming her new normal.

Calling it her 'new normal' didn't make her antlers any less of an inconvenience, so she doubted calling her leg pain that would help her either. *But what else am I gonna tell myself?*

"Who do you think built it?" The mouse asked again.

"Someone who passed to the Otherworld long before our time." Merlin's voice was still flat. It was clear now nothing was going to break the bat's annoyance.

Killmoore let out a yawn. "I can't believe how quick the day went."

"Well, you know, shorter days, longer nights. It is that time of the seasons," Merlin added.

Lore's finger slipped into a crevice as her hands continued to glide on the wall, and soon the stone wall was all that stood between them and the abandoned house. It sat in the middle of an open, albeit overgrown field. There was a barn whose siding had looked blown off from a windstorm, or just ripped away from something as mundane as decay. It was an old, faded house that made Lore wish for one of Sable's warm hugs.

She had given so many after the battle with Crinkle. Sable's hugs were as magical as her gardening. When she wrapped her arms around you, it was like she was covering a seedling with warm dirt, full of nutrients and love.

Or perhaps a hug from the old woman I sometimes recall. Would her hugs be warm like Sable's?

The glass windows of this property's greenhouse were busted out in some places. Prickly things had protruded out from them and curled around what was left of the structure.

Lore's fingers wrapped themselves around the iron gate that was connected to the stone wall. Its top reached high and arched over to the other side, descending into the soil again and connecting to the rest of the stone wall. There was no fancy design like at Iron Rose, just the sharp triangular ends of the iron pointed to the darkening sky.

She didn't know if it was there for looks, or to keep folk out, or worse, to keep folk in. Her thoughts drifted back to Mathilde's questions from earlier. Lore pursed her lips as she watched her three friends open the gate without thinking twice if the reason that made the bear from Cloch Chruinn go rogue was inside that ghost house.

She shrugged and followed after them. "Wait for me!" she called as she hobbled after them, and muttered about her now apparent reliance on the walking stick.

"I'll check the greenhouse. Who knows what could be hidden in there," Merlin said, with a casual hand gesture.

Mathilde grabbed Killmoore's arm before he had a chance to speak. "And we will check the barn."

The fox smirked. "Ah, cause where else would a horseshoe be?" He allowed himself to be dragged away by the mouse, who was talking a mile a minute.

Lore looked at the old house. Its paint was dull, chipped away at by time. The shutters that were still on the building were clinging on for dear life thanks to one of the rusted nails.

Lore noticed a bench to the right of the entrance. She peered through the broken door and saw an empty house with broken glass and furniture scattered throughout. *Yikes. Looks like a war zone in there.* She sat on the bench. It felt a lot more stable than the house looked. Lore leaned her head back, closing her eyes as she stretched. Her thoughts wandered to the village of Cloch Chruinn. She wondered if there were ever rambunctious teens who ventured up here to snoop around.

"You must be new here."

The words tickled her skin like a feather.

TEN

Lore felt as if she could have turned her head any quicker than it would have snapped off.

Looking back at her was a creature about the size of Mathilde. Long ears that were black as night stretched from its head. Short, slender arms that hung close to a furry body that was the color of soot and charred things. Thin, small dragonfly-like wings protruded from the creature's back. Looking like they wouldn't be able to carry the weight of the figure from the waist down. As if it could tell what Lore was thinking, the creature rose in the air, hovering above the dead ground, then began kicking its legs. Its goat hooves occasionally clicked against one another.

She met its golden glittering eyes that were large and round like an owl's. Its short, dog-like muzzle revealed a smile.

Her hand shot to her bracelet. "It was you," Lore muttered.

"I've done many things, and have many forms. You'll have to be more specific," the individual said, as if pointing out an obvious detail. When Lore glanced at her wrist or looked at the empty buildings on the property, she still felt the creature's golden eyes studying her every move.

Lore felt the cool silver between her fingers as the memory played again and again of the small shadow taking it from her. She could see a field of daffodils behind her, and the raven haired man too. The memory of the mountain spirit had returned to her.

"I see reuniting you with a single memory," the figure pointed a long pencil thin finger at her legs, "has caused quite the reaction."

Her brows pulled together. "What do you know?"

"If I didn't take that bracelet, you wouldn't be here." The creature scratched its shadowy, wispy fur.

"So, why am I here?" Lore pushed, ignoring the bone chilling pain that shot down her shins in that moment.

The creature looked to the empty fields and run-down buildings on the property. Its gaze fixed on the sky. "Why do the moons rise together?"

Lore crossed her arms. "Answering a question with a question isn't actually giving an explanation for anything."

The creature smiled and revealed pointed teeth. "Well, do you know why they rise together?"

"No."

The figure nodded its head. "And I don't know why you are here, either. Sometimes things just happen."

Lore sat with that for a moment. This whole time she told herself there was a reason, Being brought here with her memories a hazy mess. Growing animal parts. It all had to have a purpose. Lore's hands began to tremble, and she felt a warm padded paw like hand take hers.

"They happen because it's by design," the creature reassured. "But by whom I'm unsure of."

Lore huffed. "Well, who told you to take the bracelet from me?"

"Oh, I took it because it was shiny." Gilded ringed eyes widened at the thought of sparkling silver and gold. "I have a habit of collecting such items. But someone wove into the great quilt that I'd be there that day, and do what I am known for, and take your shiny."

"You're referring to fate?" Lore laughed in disbelief. So, it doesn't matter. *Nothing matters because fate is here to fix the game for us.*

The melody the creature began humming drew her away from her cynical spiral. Somewhere in the deep darkened spots of her memory, she could hear the faint singing voice of an older woman. "How—" she could barely ask her question, "how do you know that song?"

The figure gave a wide smile. "They used to sing it for me, you know?"

"Who?"

"The town at the base of the mountain." The little beast sounded annoyed, as if Lore should have known. "You caught me there," it added.

"Well, why are you up here?" She tried to keep her tone steady. "Why are you all alone?"

"I used to live here, you know." It looked at the dead grass beneath its goat-like hooves.

Lore glanced over her shoulder at the abandoned house. "In this house?" She asked, her voice riddled with curiosity.

"On this plane," the creature said sadly, then followed with, "Why are you here?"

Lore looked around the property, unable to hear her friends, though theoretically they weren't that far away. "Well, it's quite the complicated story, you see."

The creature's eyes shone like polished amber that would dangle from the ears of wealthy court ladies. "I'm quite fond of fascinating tales."

"To put it shortly, there's two guards who watch over the floating ferry a ways down. And instead of paying their outrageous toll, we agreed that we'd fetch them some 'lucky' treasures."

The creature giggled. It sounded like a laugh that belonged to a mischievous child. "What did they desire that could be found up here?"

"A horseshoe from the Midnight Stallion, and a cauldron that is said that whomever cooks with it will always make the perfect meal."

The creature's puckish laugh faded as it had a bit of a realization. "Those items belonged to me," it said, locking eyes with Lore.

"May we take them?" She asked.

The creature said nothing, but Lore could tell the gears were moving.

"You can have the cauldron. It's in the house." The small figure pointed to the dilapidated cabin behind them. "The village hasn't had any good crops to share, so I've nothing to cook, anyway."

Lore felt sad for the little imp. It must have been so lonely up here on this frigid mountain all alone and unable to prepare food, or look forward to festivals.

"Thank you," she said, offering her hand out to the creature.

"The shoe is going to be a bit different," it said as it hopped off the bench, ignoring Lore's gesture. "I can't just give that away." The creature turned to face her again. This time, it spoke with its knobby hands on its goat-like hips. "You'll be taken on a ride, human."

Lore tilted her head, unsure of what the imp had meant by earning it. "Literally or figuratively?" *Is it going to test me somehow?*

The creature shuffled to a blackberry patch behind the bench she failed to notice before. The shadowy imp reached down and plucked one. "Care to have one, human?" it asked.

"No thanks." Her tone was short as her eyes darted from the creature to the barn, the barn to the creature, and over her shoulder to the busted greenhouse. No sign of her friends. *Curious.*

The creature cleared its throat, and when she returned her gaze to the small imp, it spewed spit over the blackberries, making them shrivel and become befouled. She shuddered at the confirmation that she had indeed eaten some magical entity's spit earlier.

"Why waste them?" Her voice echoed, as if the somber property were an empty room. The creature said nothing. Lore looked back up to the sky and noticed how high the two moons were. The smaller one was a crescent smile, the larger one beamed with silver light. Its silver glowing circlets created an ache in her.

She missed her bracelet. Lore had a hard time grasping at the idea that time had moved so quickly as she kept company with the mysterious creature. She turned to ask if it knew how quickly daylight had drained away, but the small figure was already gone.

Lore chewed on her lip and stood up.

It didn't even say goodbye. She felt strangely sad the creature didn't bid her farewell.

"Lore!" Mathilde called, waving her arms, "We've been looking for you for hours!"

Killmoore's face was painted with worry. "Where'd ya go off to?"

"I was just here." Lore pointed to the bench, and noted the over ripened blackberries that ran along the rotted wood of the house.

"I walked past that wooden bench three times and didn't see you," Merlin said, eyeing her up and down.

She took a step backward. "Did you guys find anything?"

"Not a trace of a shoe in the barn," Mathilde sighed, her ears dropping low like melting icicles.

"Nothing of importance in the greenhouse," Merlin added.

Lore smiled. "Well, I know where the cauldron is."

"How'd ya find that out?" Killmoore asked, leaning on the door frame.

"A friendly face." Lore smiled as she walked into the dark house. The scent of musk filled her nose, along with the scent of rotting wood.

The inside was as you'd expect. Dank, dim, and overall disarray. Lore tried to step lightly, trying not to make falling through decaying boards a habit. Lore tapped her walking stick across the old floor, testing its strength. She stepped over the broken picture frames. Behind the broken glass pane was a black and white faded image. Lore didn't stop to look over any minor details on the folk in the photo. Mathilde's pitter-patter against the groaning wood echoed behind Lore as she found herself in the kitchen. *Where else would an enchanted cauldron be?*

Lore could hear Mathilde asking Merlin questions that he probably didn't have any answers to.

"Why do you think the owners left?"

"We'll probably never know," he said as he squinted at dusted spines of books that somehow managed to stay on the living room bookshelf.

"Do you think maybe their great-great-great grandchild will come on an adventure to reclaim what was an inheritance for them?"

Merlin grumbled something Lore's ears couldn't quite make out.

She huffed and knelt down and rummaged through the cabinets. She was here on a mission. She needed to get that cauldron. Perhaps finding the cauldron would be proof enough that she deserved the shoe of the Midnight Stallion.

As she pushed aside old bakeware, her fingers were unfortunately met with the sticky webs of unseen spiders. She lifted corroded pots and old mason jars whose lids were painted orange with years of rust. They were filled with some mysterious dark liquid. She didn't want to break the jars by accident as she continued her search through the dim room, so she pulled the mason jars out, and set them gently on the peeling square linoleum floors.

For all I know, it's beyond spoiled and would reek of death. Or worse, the backside of a Grayshade. The haunting smell of musk, skunk, and ammonia swirled in the air around her, creating a cloud of every nose's nightmare. She shuddered at the thoughts.

Killmoore leaned in the kitchen's entrance. "So, who was this friendly face, exactly?"

"Just that," Lore said. She didn't want to reveal anything about the creature in case it was some sort of test. *I want to stay in its good graces,* she told herself as she stood to search the cabinets above the counter. She started humming, hoping it would distract herself from Killmoore's fixed stare boring into her.

It didn't.

He moved towards her, light on his feet, not making one board creak. The fox leaned on the counter, watching the human rummage through the old glassware. "You're keeping secrets." His closeness startled her, causing her antlers to graze the open cabinet doors.

Lore's brow furrowed. "Pot calling the kettle, eh?" She didn't bother looking at him. She knew his ears would be flat, and his whiskers twitching with irritation at her words. The silence between them grew so thick that it pushed Killmoore from the kitchen and back into the living room where Mathilde was busy showing him all the little knickknacks she found hiding under the flipped couch and behind a few books.

Lore released a breath and rested both hands on the grimy counter top. It was so muck-covered she couldn't even tell what color it was supposed to be. She let out a groan and wiped her hands on her pants. *Where else to look?*

Her eyes scanned the rest of the small kitchen, but there was nothing that caught her eye. Nothing that screamed a magical cauldron is here, but something did whisper to her. There was an old ratted floor mat in front of a hideous yellow stove that looked like it hadn't been used in ages. She kicked a corner up with her boot. Sure enough, there was a trapdoor.

Worth a look, she told herself as she threw the hatch open. The sound beckoned the ever-curious Mathilde inside. Her nose was in the air and her eyes were closed. She stopped by Lore's side, and her eyes went wide with wonder.

"Well, don't think for one minute you're going down there by yourself!" the mouse declared as she flipped the hatch open and years of sealed stagnant air escaped. Lore didn't want to think of all the things that could have died down there to make it smell so much like a rotting corpse, but if this was the hill Mathilde wanted to die on, she wouldn't be the one to fight her over it.

Mathilde craned her head into the hole to try to get a better look.

Meanwhile, Lore sat on the edge of the trapdoor, letting her legs dangle free in the dark hole. She fought away the thoughts of the darkness taking form and grabbing her by her ankles, pulling her down entirely. Mathilde gave her a smile and leaped right down, either too brave for her own good or she was just that foolhardy. Lore allowed her body to fall in after her companion disappeared from sight. A shooting pain traveled up her legs and made her knees ache when she hit the earth. She leaned on the walking stick to take some of the weight off her joints. She looked above at the little square of dim light and saw Killmoore's face peering in.

"Lore! Mathilde!" He called, a bit more frantic than he usually spoke.

"Killmoore!" she called back. "It's pitch black down here. I can barely see a thing!" Lore cupped her hands around her mouth. "Get Merlin!"

The fox's head disappeared from sight, and Lore felt like the shadows were creeping in on her. She hugged herself before the darkness had a chance to take form.

"Mathilde?" She called out, hoping to hear something back.

"Lore! It's amazing!" the red-clad mouse's voice echoed off the surrounding walls.

It made the humans' skin crawl, and as Mathilde's words continued to reverberate, they blended with each other and create new words entirely.

Words like 'Hazel Borough,' 'graduation,' and 'job' floated around Lore's mind.

She brought her hands to her aching skull. The pain started at the base of her neck and traveled through her head like a slow, radiant heat. More words kept adding themself to the invisible tornado of unknown terms. They swirled around her. Swallowing her up and at this point Lore felt like they were stealing away her oxygen.

The voices were unknown to her but one was a woman who sounded like she had a terribly bad smoker's cough. She said things like 'worthless' and 'too stupid to understand.' The other was a man's voice that sounded gentle and youthful. He said things like 'best friend' and 'you're such a fire flower.'

Before any more words could drill into her head, Merlin's hand was waving in front of her eyes, the other was engulfed in a bursting red flame. "Lore?" he asked gently. "Lore, are you okay?"

Her eyes fluttered as she pulled herself away from the pain, away from the aches in her skull, and she tried to focus more on a familiar face. The return of brief moments of her life should give her hope. All Lore felt was an anguish settle into her gut.

Do I doubt these memories because I don't want the little glimpses to be true? Or because they might be hallucinations? How can I trust myself?

Merlin's ears stood tall and alert as Lore took his hand, and he led her to where Mathilde was. There were walls not only packed with glass food but also an assortment of books and journals left in nothing more than busted up old milk crates. The kind a man in a white suit would leave on your doorstep in some suburban fantasy.

Mathilde was flipping through one of the journals. "These are so fascinating." She spoke as if Lore wasn't suffering in silence. Lore felt a bit of anger rise within her, but with Killmoore's hand resting on her shoulder, it didn't stay lit long.

"I bet they are," he added, though his voice was a bit flat.

"The owners of this property were once said to be descendants of the Otherfolk," her voice was dripping with awe.

"Oh," Killmoore huffed as he looked at the rows and rows of glass jars. "Everyone's got one great-great aunt that's supposedly Otherfolk."

Lore looked down to Merlin, who still held her hand, "Otherfolk?" Her question made her sound more dumbfounded than she would have liked, but it couldn't be helped.

Mathilde snapped the book shut and shoved it in her satchel. "The Otherfolk are said to be from the Otherworld. And they're rumored to be magical." Her words were laced with such adoration that they felt like a ribbon being wrapped around a gift for a loved one.

"Merlin can do magic? Does that make him a descendant of these Otherfolk?"

Merlin gave a quiet laugh. "No, no," he replied. "The Otherfolk have a more primordial magic; it doesn't have to be gifted to them by a greater being." He was silent for a moment, his eyes glazed over with an emotion Lore wasn't sure how to pin down. "They're just born with it, and the really powerful ones can shapeshift."

Killmoore's claws clinked on the glasses as he looked over dates of which the food was canned.

"I didn't know you were that desperate for food," Mathilde joked as she walked over to where the fox stood.

"It's what's behind them that I'm more interested in," his voice hushed as he removed more and more cans.

When the final jar in the way was removed from the shelf, Killmoore's eyes narrowed on a mark carved into the dirt wall. Mathilde gasped as her jaw hit the floor, and by now, Lore was leaning over his shoulder and Merlin held a light up to it.

It was not an intricate knot by any means, but it was one Lore had seen before. She had seen it on the lighter Dina had given Mathilde. On Petra's necklace, and on the first page of Gannon's little book.

But what was it doing here?

So far away from Charmsend?

"Well, let's see what's behind it!" Lore chimed as she reached a hand forward to be the first to dig away at the dry earth.

Killmoore pushed her arm away. "We don't know what digging behind it will do."

Mathilde pursed her lips. "Yeah, but what if the cauldron is behind it?"

Killmoore huffed, "Or what if that seal is the only thing keeping the house up in one piece?" He looked over to Merlin for support. "Come on, we saw before we came in how this place was barely hanging on by a nail."

Merlin rested a hand on his chin and began slowly pacing back and forth. His leathery wings dragging on the soft dirt floor. The light coming and going with him. Until he stopped. "Okay, okay. I *do* know some nature magic."

Lore studied the puzzled look on Killmoore's face.

"You're a fire wielder," he said dryly.

"Don't think too hard about it, okay?" Merlin began talking again before anyone had the chance to disagree. "I know I'll be able to act quick enough if the house collapses onto us."

Killmoore bit the bottom of his lip. "Fine," he scoffed.

Lore and Mathilde wasted no time digging away and sure enough, Lore's fingers grazed the cool cast iron.

"It's here!" she couldn't hide the excitement in her voice.

She and Mathilde pulled the cauldron from the wall, and the dirt fell in where the large pot once was.

Then, the house creaked above them, and Killmoore leaped instinctively on top of Lore and Mathilde, knocking them to the ground.

Luckily, that's all the house did was creak. Merlin offered a hand up to Lore, and Killmoore looked a bit embarrassed.

"All's well that ends well," Lore said softly, nudging her fist against his arm. He gave her a soft smile.

Mathilde dusted herself off. "How do we get back up?" She questioned aloud, looking toward the square hole in the ceiling on the other side of the root cellar.

Lore picked up the cauldron and noticed a latch on the wall closest to them. She rested its handle on the notch atop her trusted stick.

"Here," she said, gesturing with her foot.

Killmoore wasted no time opening it—or *trying* to. It probably needed a good oiling. Merlin cracked open a jar of muck and let it ooze down the handle. It smelled like putrid olives and the sourness made Lore's eyes water. It did the trick, though, the handle clunk and the door opened, revealing a small path that led out the side of the sloping hill the house was situated on.

When they emerged, they saw they were on the backside of the home.

"Well, at least we got one treasure. Those pesky amphibians can just deal with it." Mathilde said as she placed her hands on her hips.

A heavy wind stirred in the treetops surrounding the home and its empty property. The haunting whistle sounds added to the chill in the air. Lore swore she heard a faint whinny, but before she could brush it off as some mere trick of the gale, thunderous hooves stamped the earth. When Lore turned, she came face to face with a stallion whose coat seemed blacker than the night sky and eyes blazed gold with the fires of the burning star. She wanted to take a gulp, but her throat felt like it was trying to swallow glass shards.

Before any of them could react, the mighty horse galloped over to Lore and swiped her up with a swoop of his neck.

"The Midnight Stallion!" Mathilde yelled.

As her head bounced on the stallion's rear, she saw her friends getting smaller and smaller in the distance. The galloping made her legs ache even more. The fire that Merlin hurled was no use against the horse's speed. It's as though the beast was the frigid winter wind personified. Her heart was thudding hard against her chest, almost with the rhythm of the stallion's hooves beating against the ground.

A vigorous rush of air whipped Lore's long brown braid wildly. She tried her best to grip the stallion's bareback, but her fingers kept slipping against slick black fur. "Slow down!" she screamed, but all that did was give the horse a reason to bray.

The beast seemed happy with itself. Lore looked at the trees passing in a blur.

She couldn't just continue this ride from hell, backwards, and on her stomach at that. *I need to do something.* She tried to steady herself, and as Lore had accepted the possibility of meeting the hard cold ground from falling off the horse's back, she pushed herself upright and her arms searched blindly behind her. The creature was refusing to slow down. She needed to get hold of its mane.

The Midnight Stallion's powerful body came to an abrupt stop, and Lore's back thudded against the beast's stout neck. As she wasted no time trying to turn herself forward, the onyx black horse jerked hard and made a mad dash. The beast had taken sharp lefts and rights. It took everything Lore had to bob and weave away from low-hanging branches. It made little difference as her antlers still struck the low hanging shrubbery.

Her thoughts were racing, but not fast enough to keep up with the stallion. She balled the long strands of silky, black hair in her fists, making bits of silver dust fall from the animal's mane. She swore she heard the creature belt out a laugh. An eerily human laugh.

Whether by Lady Luck's design or mere coincidence, the silver glittering rays of the moon caught the spurs on Lore's boots. *That's right. That loony crow merchant gave her these.* Her legs wrapped tightly around the horse's ribs, her deer-like calves protested, but her nerves hung onto the last strand of keeping it together as she dug the spurs into the horse's side.

The Midnight Stallion let out a wretched scream, and the environment around Lore became less like a photo that was out of focus and more crisp and clear.

She wondered if the others could catch up. She thought about ways to get off the frightening ride, but the thought at the forefront of her mind was, *Will the silver spurs help put this hellish joyride to an end?*

Hours had felt like they passed, and the more Lore dug her heels into the stallion's side, the farther it felt like the horse was taking her away from the abandoned property. As if it was just mere moments ago that the creature had scooped Lore up. Another loud whinny echoed in the frigid air, a little puff of heat escaped the beast's mouth. It twisted and turned, doing its best to shake her free.

Confusing, really.

Why gather me up only to buck me off?

The sudden and sharp movements of the creature made her stomach twinge with nausea. The rocky landscape of the mighty mountain was all but a blur still racing past her. No matter how many times she dug her heels in, it only seemed to anger the hellish creature more than tame it.

With all the questions she had, all the questions that were unanswered, one thing was clear. She wasn't going to escape the hellish ride anytime soon. It wasn't until Lore found herself slumped over the horse's thick neck that the beast had slowed down to a steady trot. The gentle sound of moving water tickled her ears.

Her eyes drifted below as the horse's hooves waded through a clear brook. The orange light of dawn colored the water shades of pinks and peaches. Lore pushed herself upright and braced herself for the horse to dash suddenly, but it didn't happen. Her eyes fell onto the old manor where she had started.

The open iron gate welcomed them. The sight of Mathilde rushing down the dirt path to her was a welcoming sight for her weary eyes.

Her stomach twisted and her calves ached.

How long have I been gone? Hours? Hopefully not a full day.

"Lore!" the mouse called, waving her hands.

Killmoore followed close behind, certainly unsure of what the steed's next move would be.

With a gentle bray, the horse halted, and Lore wasted no time slipping off its back. It turned, closed its starlight-lit eyes, and bowed to her, making strands of its silver-speckled mane fall between its eyes.

"The crowned one returns," the horse uttered. Its deep but familiar voice sent a shiver through her bones.

The sun peeked over the horizon, casting a shadow from behind the house. The animal's silhouette highlighted that its ears now looked more rabbit-like than those of a horse. It rose and shook a leg, freeing a shoe.

It glittered in the fleeing moonlight. As Lore gently brushed dirt from the shoe, it radiated warmth in her hands.

Lore looked behind her and saw Merlin standing in the doorway of the battered house. Even the magnificent Wielder seemed to be ensnared by the commanding presence of the beast.

"Come again?" Mathilde said as she took a step backwards from the horse, bumping into Killmoore as she did so.

The stallion's eyes shot open, swirling galaxies shone from them. "Secrets of time undone and spells that were spun."

Lore's hands trembled and suddenly the weight of the horse shoe seemed to be a bit much.

"Meet the shadow, not the shell, after the final farewell," it continued.

As the sun rose higher in the sky, Lore noticed the *odd* silhouette of the not-quite horse. As it sank into the shadows of the surrounding tree line, relief washed over her. She could have waited there the rest of the day, the anticipation of the creature's return made her sick. But they didn't have the luxury of time.

It wasn't even five minutes since the creature returned to the shadows of the mountain and Merlin was ready to leave. The bat shooed the three down the path. His leathery wings flapped in the crisp morning air, rather frantically. "Come now," Merlin urged. "We've got what we need, no reason to linger."

Lore wasn't sure if it was because of the wild ride she had or if it was just her imagination, but the fearless wielder seemed to be frightened.

ELEVEN

The horseshoe and cauldron made a thud as they hit the ground in front of the amphibians, who were shaking in their oversized armor.

"You got them," the toad said with awe-inspired terror. "But how did you manage the haunted manor?"

Mathilde scoffed, "It's not haunted." Her voice was firm, but behind the strong outward appearance the mouse was presenting, Lore remembered the relief in her voice when she re-emerged on the back of the big shadowy horse.

Her mind also flashed back to the smiling creature who talked with her on the bench, and the way its golden eyes glittered with mischief. Did Lore think the manor grounds were haunted? No, she didn't. But that didn't mean she was going to share her encounter with the wayward creature, either. She bit her bottom lip and her hands gripped the dry rope off the boarding dock. *I don't know if I'd should tell anyone. And we need to keep moving forward.*

The first step onto the floating ferry stole her breath, and she didn't find it again until she reached her seat. Lore peered over the side and the ground below her moved farther and farther away, as if it were sinking, the longer she stared. The morning birds' song was a minor nuisance in comparison to the knots in her stomach.

"It'll be okay," Killmoore assured, sitting close beside her.

The toad's voice sounded over an intercom. "Thank you for choosing the *S.S. Clare* today. We know you didn't have any other choice, and no, we don't sell peanuts or fizzy drinks. Sit tight and enjoy the ride over Deadman's Chasm."

There was a buzz of static before the mic cut out entirely.

Lore's eyes drifted to Mathilde, who had her head craned out the window in front of them. Surely admiring the long, strong feathered wings that were part of some herculean bird—though Lore couldn't tell if the avian was living or dead.

The thought of how the ferry had been converted for the sky sent a shudder racing down Lore's spine.

Merlin's large triangle ears twitched as he silently sat in the seat in front of Killmoore.

"You don't have to sit by the window seat, ya know."

She whipped around to see that it was, in fact, Killmoore speaking. But it wasn't his voice. She closed her eyes, trying to remember where she recognized the voice from, and her effort pulled her away from her body and to another fuzzy memory.

Lore was standing on a bus full of children. The squeals and excitement pierced her ears. She turned, feeling like a ghost among the living, then she spotted a younger version of herself. Sitting quietly in a seat all alone, huddled up by the window. Lore's lip quivered as a tidal wave of sadness had hit her.

Before she could sink into the feeling, a kid with messy ink-spilled hair slid beside her younger self. "You know," he said with a welcoming smile. "You don't have to sit alone, or huddled by the window, ya know?"

Lore's vision cleared again as the memory melted away, revealing Killmoore was studying her face, his amber rimmed eyes full of worry. Lore didn't like how concern was becoming his default expression when he looked at her.

"Lore?" he whispered.

Despite Mathilde's *oohs* and *ahhs,* Lore still heard his question. *What was there to say?* So, she didn't say anything. Just gave a nod and quickly switched seats with him. When she faced front again, Merlin's gaze was already staring at her.

Not even a second later, the bat's attention flickered over to Killmoore. "So, I got us to the mountain, fox. Where exactly is this library?"

Killmoore averted his attention out the window. He was quiet as he watched the misty clouds go by.

Lore leaned forward herself, realizing she had hardly noticed they were moving.

"Well, technically, it's The Sanctuary." His voice was flat.

Merlin's expression twisted into a scowl. "You brought us from the Emerald Valley through the Blanch and up the mountains on the whim of a fairytale?!"

Killmoore winced from the harsh words. "It's not a fairytale."

Lore pursed her lips. By now, Mathilde's attention was brought to the thick tension that hung in the air like putrid smelling garbage in the alley from Dahl—Tansy's.

"You mean *The* Sanctuary?" Mathilde gasped. The excitement on her face and in her voice melted their hostility away like the spring sun against winter's last snowfall.

The fox's ears twitched. "Yes, *The* Sanctuary." His eyes didn't meet Mathilde's. He kept them fixed on the clouds passing by the window. "I've been sayin' 'library' because I knew yins wouldn't have come with me if I told you otherwise."

Merlin's face was still scrunched, and Lore couldn't hold her question further. "What is The Sanctuary?"

"Nothing more than the spinnings of nannies and dreamers," Merlin said, matter-of-factly.

Lore shifted to Mathilde, who rolled her eyes at the bat's dismissal.

It's nice to see her go against him from time to time.

Mathilde continued, "A place where everything is said to be documented that has ever happened in Thimbleton." The mouse paused for dramatic effect, but neither Merlin nor Killmoore seemed in the mood to feed her storytelling ego.

She huffed. "Anyway, it's also rumored to have tomes of other lands, histories of times lost, and spells to reach realms far beyond the normal scope." A smile spread across the mouse's face. "That's probably why Killmoore thought that was the best place to start our search for gettin' you home, Lore."

Merlin grumbled something inaudible under his breath as he turned and sat quietly in his seat.

Mathilde gave a nod before returning to peer out the window below.

Lore wondered if the bones of the creatures who lured so many to their deaths actually wound up at the north part of the island. *Did all things end up there someway or another?*

As if Killmoore could read her thoughts, he gave a gentle pat on her thigh. "All things in Thimbleton come from the north and when their time comes, they return to the north again."

Lore took the words and twisted them in her mind—trying to make sense of it. If there was a sense to be made of it, she didn't know, but how else would she have passed the time?

The ferry jerked and the sound of gears grinding echoed in the vast, empty sky.

Lore's stomach dropped as the ferry started losing altitude. She closed her eyes and bowed her head as she gripped the arms of the seat. Then let out a silent curse as the antlers on her head hit the back of Merlin's seat. Her stomach jolted and suddenly felt like it was in her throat and at any moment, it was going to fall out of her mouth as they fell from the misty skies over the chasm.

Lore glanced up through the loose pieces of hair that had fallen from her braid and she saw Mathilde clinging to the seat. Merlin was trying to chant some sort of incantation, but she didn't understand the language.

Before he could finish, a blur of orange swallowed up the four like some hungry heap of jello. It felt warm and like Lore was free floating in a toasty mug of cocoa on a bed of floating marshmallows. Her eyes glanced over to Killmoore, who didn't seem to find any relief in the warm jelly that cushioned the blow as the ferry crashed into the earth.

The windows that were once filled with the sight of gentle rolling clouds and golden setting sun rays were now broken and held nothing serene on the other side. Just pieces of earth enclosed around the cabin of the ferry. The sharp saw-toothed rocks punctured the wood like they were in the mud-filled jaws of a giant wolf. Luckily, whatever orange jelly Merlin summoned saved them from being pierced by any debris.

As the gelatinous substance slipped away from her skin, she heard the distinct sound of water lapping against a rocky shoreline through the broken wood planks of the ferry.

She walked past the sharp rock-like talons that bore into the ferry's haul, her fingers running along the sharp edges. She could barely see a few feet in front of her, let alone know where the shoreline started. Her hand gripped the stone and her knuckles whitened as Mathilde's words haunted her.

"Some say it was the murderous sprites that swam in the deep all those eons ago that chipped away at the earth and stone until one day they were so starved they died themselves."

"I'm not about to become fish food," she muttered to herself.

"I believe you mean Kelpie food," Killmoore said flatly.

Lore raised a brow at him. "Now what do we do?" Lore looked past him and saw Mathilde brushing some stray tangerine-tinged goop off Merlin. Her mind drifted south to Charmsend as she watched Mathilde fuss over Merlin the way she had watched Minifred fuss over her sisters.

Lore's stomach twinged. It was a kind of care and gentleness she wondered if she ever had before in her life—before falling into Thimbleton.

The faint images of the old woman whose reflection she had seen in the muddy puddles back in Charmsend came to the front of her mind. Did the woman wake early to make Lore breakfast? Did they enjoy cups of tea together by an open fire when the day was over? Did the white-haired woman, whose face was lined with wrinkles and smile lines, tuck her into bed at night?

The sound of the bat's leathery wings being fluttered, as if he were a dog shaking off the last bit of water from his fur after a bath, brought her away from the wellspring of her thoughts. "Well, the quicker we find a way back up, the better."

Cliffs of Wayward

As Merlin's words fell over Lore, the weight of them clung to the branches of the antlers that had sprouted from her head. She mindlessly brushed her hand against the velvet softness that was around the roots of her hair as she mulled over the Wielder's words. The bat's voice was different than normal.

Was that fear?

TWELVE

It didn't matter that Merlin was afraid, or if he wasn't. What was more concerning was the silence that clung to the thick fog sweeping over the wrecked ferry.

What would happen next? Lore's stomach felt like a restless ocean whose waves angrily crashed against the confines of her mostly human body. *What would happen to* them*?*

Mathilde's tail was as stiff as a board. "The frog and toad?"

"Why worry about them? They were with that Mordred guy." Killmoore's voice was dull as he searched in his bag for something to light. "Between the run in with the cat and lynx, and now the amphibians, the bear will know we're here." The fox steadied his breath. "It's only a matter of time before he makes himself known to who he considers intruders."

Small beads of sweat licked the back of her neck, and she absent-mindedly reached for the metal of the bracelet for comfort. But, of course, it wasn't there.

Her thoughts continued swirling. *Will my friends and I meet the same fate as the two guards? Bodies left to rot at the bottom of a chasm, only for their spirits to aimlessly wander the channels, never finding a way out?*

The sound of fire igniting shed light on Lore, and her dark thoughts fled from her mind as she watched Merlin exchange a smile with the fox's tart look. "While it is admirable you want to search for them," the bat began as he pushed past Lore, "I'm afraid the fox is right again. We should focus on getting ourselves out of the deadly chasm."

Lore's lips pressed into a thin line as she watched Mathilde's stiff tail flick like an angry cat's.

"Just because they may do bad things doesn't mean they're bad folk," the mouse muttered. "What if this was the only choice they had?"

"There's no such thing as only one choice," Killmoore interjected as the straps to his backpack slid over his ginger shoulders. "Besides, if the stories are true, better they be fodder for the angry spirits than us."

Mathilde's ears wilted. Then her small, gentle hands balled into tight fists. "I thought you were better than that, Killmoore."

Merlin stood still, looking at the clear wedge between the two, then his gaze pierced Lore. "What do you think?"

Her back straightened at the question. She understood the place Mathilde was coming from, but she also could read between the lines and understand the real danger they found themselves in.

She cleared her throat. "No one gets left behind."

Merlin's expression shifted, his brow pulled tight. "Are you certain?"

"Yes." No hesitation where he clearly thought there'd be. "Most likely they are injured." She gestured vaguely to the surrounding wreckage. "And I am sure if we found them, and you healed them…"

His caring, mad bat facade has crumbled away with every step up this mountain. And an ego driven wielder has surfaced in its place, but at least I can appeal to that.

The corners of Lore's face curled into a soft smile. "They would sing your praises from the high mountains of the north clear to the Romplands of the south."

Lore watched carefully as the gears in the bat's head began moving. The bounty hunter let out a scoff. "Well, you three heroes do whatever you decide. I'm gonna look for a way back to the top of the cliffs."

Mathilde stomped a foot. "And how will we find each other after everything is said and done?"

Killmoore let out a long, dramatic groan.

He's turning into a bit of a diva.

"Fine," he huffed as he slid his backpack off again and rummaged through it.

"What are you looking for, exactly?" Merlin asked, inquisitive fingers drumming on his chin.

The fox mumbled, "Something you'd have little interest in." A few more moments of his arm frantically shuffling in his bag passed before his face perked up. "Ah. Here it is." In Killmoore's palm, there was what appeared to be a simple spool of white thread.

"What is it?" Mathilde asked, voicing the question on everyone's mind.

"Lover's web," the fox said with a shrug, as if it were obvious.

"Where's it from?" Merlin's eyes gleamed like polished gold bars.

"I don't know. I—uh," the fox scratched behind an ear with his free hand, "bought it from a traveling salesfolk a few years back."

"You mean like that weird crow?" Mathilde had a teasing smile that hugged her face.

The white fur mask that adorned the fox's face seemed to hold a flustered, red hue. "N-no." He crossed his arms, "There's more than one traveling salesfolk in Thimbleton."

Mathilde's mind shifted from good fun to an expression puzzled with curiosity. "So, how's the Lover's Web work?"

Killmoore reached for her wrist and tied the thread around it loosely. "It works by keeping two parties connected, and lucky for us..." He plucked the thread and it let out a low hum like it was a guitar string. The white thread shimmered a brilliant silver. "It glows." His tone carried the false surprise, as if he had performed this trick before.

The hum continued to vibrate in the cavity of Lore's mind. The one where she often tried to pin down fleeting memories that washed onto empty shores.

This time, the melodic hum rattled her senses and shipped her off to a time before Thimbleton. She saw herself seated on a dusty wooden floor leaned against a rickety metal bed frame and across from her the raven haired man sat with his back against a wall and their legs crossing over each other. A guitar was in his hands and the two sat there, letting the melody fill the silence between them.

Lore felt like a ghost peering into a past life.

Her past self sat relaxed with her eyes closed, her head and shoulders moved along to the rhythm. The raven haired man's icy-blue eyes held nothing but warmth as he looked upon the freckles of Lore's cheeks and his gaze followed the freckled trail down her neck where they then speckled across her collarbones. He looked at her the way you look at the sky on a summer's night.

Something arose in Lore's stomach, like she ate a hive of buzzing bees.

The memory shifted.

The man seemed frozen in time and the freckles on her past self shone like stars. Glimmers of light floated around her and pulled her back to the empty shoreline of her mind, and the sight of shimmering orbs around the string twinkling like pale moonlight brought her back to the thick fog of the chasm.

"What else do you know about this web?" Merlin asked, rolling the illuminated thread back and forth between his fingertips, that hung between the fox and mouse.

"Listen, like I said, I bought it off a salesfolk, but—" The bounty hunter's face scrunched. "Oh, never mind."

"But what?" Merlin pushed, eyes greedy to know every word the fox was thinking.

Killmoore sat silent for a moment, then his whiskers twitched. "Fine." He let out a sigh and cast his eyes down to the rocky ground. "I like to imagine two lovers who were separated in a labyrinth of trees and smoke. Unable to find each other, a local spirit spun this special web, so future lovers would never truly be separated."

There was a sweet quiet that hung in the air between the fox and the mouse. It appeared to sour Merlin's curiosity.

"Well then," the bat replied, "I suppose you best be on your way and we will be on ours."

Lore watched as Killmoore's pointed expression fixed on Mathilde. His voice was hushed, like he was sharing a secret. "I'll unwind the spool as I walk. And after your little hero excursion, just follow the thread to me, okay?"

Mathilde nodded and pinched the glowing knot that held the thread gently around her wrist. The glow of the thread danced on the reflective surface of the mouse's curious eyes.

I wonder how it works. It's not like Killmoore is a Wielder or anything, Lore thought, hoping that it would halt the nerves gnawing in her stomach. Perhaps Mathilde was thinking the same thing as the gray mouse rubbed the glowing thread between her fingers. The little adventurer was always asking questions, always wondering.

Merlin turned without saying another word and Mathilde followed as the string unraveled itself from the spool in Killmoore's hand.

As Lore went to follow behind them, the fox's grip was on her forearm as he yanked her close. "Be quick. Stay alert. And keep an eye on what's in front of you."

Does this mean our chances of reaching the Sanctuary are significantly worse? Nerves twisted in her stomach. *Does this mean I won't ever reunite with the rest of my memories?* An unnatural groan echoed somewhere in the distance. *Will we even make it out of this cavern or will whatever crashed the ferry come crashing into us?*

Lore's eyebrows pulled together and just as quickly as he had grabbed her, Killmoore released her and disappeared into the fog. Lore's eyes drifted to the shimmering silver thread. She knelt down to pick it up and follow it to Mathilde and Merlin, though from the way the mouse's voice carried, she probably didn't need to.

The debris crunched under Lore's steps. The Lover's Web slid like silk between her fingertips as she neared her companions. She cursed under her breath every time the antlers on her head caught a piece of the sagging ferry ceiling. *If I didn't have these, walking wouldn't be such a problem.* The growing familiar ache in her calves radiated. *If I didn't have* deer legs, *walking wouldn't be a problem. Existing* wouldn't be such a damn problem.

As she followed the string that wove between the wreckage, the rolling fog greeted her once again. It seemed thicker this time, and the air smelled like fresh cherries.

She mindlessly gripped the thread tighter as she recalled Killmoore's warning to her. When she noticed the hole in the ferry had inky black feathers strewn along the splintered wood, her breath hitched. Her eyes fell to the ground where the large raven wing, which once kept them airborne, was severed from the wreckage.

The fog became thicker right before her eyes, consuming her surroundings. It suddenly had a sweet cherry aroma wafting from its wisps.

Lore stood still as the smell filled her lungs. It made her feel as if she were floating. Her eyes felt heavier, and through labored blinks she saw the fog shift and form into a creature whose eyes pulsated red and whose cloud-like body produced enormous wings that dripped ink spilt sludge from their feathers. A loud thudding filled Lore's ears. She tried to swallow down her fear, but her throat was dry.

Her footing wavered and her legs grew weaker and weaker with every passing moment.

The creature opened its newly formed birdlike beak, revealing rows of sharp needle sized teeth.

The tempo continued to beat against Lore's head, but it was slower than before. She leaned against the broken wood in the hole of the ferry and lazily aimed her gaze at the threat that was quickly shaping to be more dangerous by the second.

I need to run.

She tried to move her legs, but they felt like stone. Her head bobbed, and the antlers snagged a piece of wood as she fell to her knees.

The air swirled around her, and it felt like icy fingers grazing against her skin.

Her body shuddered, and the sleep that was beckoning her to give in became closer and closer, and the thudding slowed down so much Lore almost forgot about it. As her eyes shut and the darkness welcomed her with a cherry scented hug, she realized the sound echoing in her ears was her heartbeat.

THIRTEEN

Lore felt like she was floating off to what would have been the best sleep of her life, but then she felt her body weight shift. When she opened her eyes, it felt like she pried open a locked safe. As the pace quickened, she heard her rescuers jabbering and loose clanking metal.

"Where'd the others go?"

"Hard to say for sure."

"What do we do now?"

"Get as far away from that thing as possible."

As the last of the sweet cherry aroma that was filling Lore's lungs escaped her breath, it was easier to open her eyes, and when she did, her bouncing vision met with a very relieved frog.

"Oh, what a miracle this is. Put 'er down, she's awake." His words were rushed, and the toad let the human quickly slide from his shoulder onto the ground.

"Happy to see ya still in one piece, human."

Lore rubbed her antler and threw the few pieces of wood that were caught in the tangles of her hair to the ground. "I've a name, you know."

The frog drummed his slimy fingers on his chin. "Oh, humans do that too, aye?"

Lore felt heat rise to her cheeks as she looked around the empty area only filled with dense fog. "Where are we? Where were you two taking me, anyway?"

The frog puffed out his chest with a croak. "We saved you, miss."

"Yeah, from that weird monster," his companion added, confusion tinged his voice. "You should be happy you aren't in its belly."

Lore rubbed her temples. "But now we don't know where we are?!" She gestured to the surrounding emptiness with a flail of her arms. "How are we gonna get out of here, let alone find my friends?" She raked her fingers over her braid. "We were supposed to be saving *you*, and now I'm far away from my friends." Tears welled in her eyes. "And not only will they not find you among the wreckage, but they won't find *me*." Her voice cracked. "And the monster will find *them* instead."

Her hands were trembling at the thought. She knew Merlin was a strong Wielder, but all the beast had to do was be close enough to you, so you inhaled the sweet smelling gas. Then it'd consume you.

The amphibious pair looked at her, dumbfounded.

Oh, why did she expect they would understand the gravity of the situation? Her eyes darted around the clouded empty space. *I need to find a way back to them.* Killmoore was right. This really was a stupid idea.

"Yes, but you're alive," the frog's voice interrupted her thoughts.

"Yeah, we helped you," the toad protested. "You should be grateful." A gruff groan followed his words.

Lore felt her eyes grow with annoyance. As she fixed her gaze on them, she felt like she was taller. Stronger even. Maybe the antlers were some help after all. "And you're going to help me again." Her words were sharpened like the blades Killmoore kept holstered to him at all times. She dug her hands around in her flannel pockets, searching for something. Anything that could be of use. *What I wouldn't do to stumble upon the fox right now.*

The frog let out a raspy, chirp. "That isn't how you ask for help."

Lore let out a breath and rubbed her wrist where her bracelet used to be. The bracelet that tied her to her past, the bracelet that kept being plucked away from her. She let her jaw slacken as the reality of the situation settled into her mind.

"You're right, but let's be clear," her gray eyes bored into her two rescuers like serrated metal, "I'm not asking."

The toad gulped, but it was the frog's flinch that brought her away from her frustrations and anger.

She swallowed down a horse pill of guilt. "I—I'm sorry," she finally managed. Considering the frog's reaction to her intensity, it felt like she was looking at a reflection of herself. The distant sound of a man's shouts stirred in the attic of her memory.

It was like looking in a distorted mirror at herself.

Her eyes were still blinking back bitter tears, searching in the fog behind the two amphibians.

A version of herself at a different time.

A different place so familiar she could almost taste the scent of stale alcohol in the air. It caused her stomach to ache, thinking about how bad or not the life she was returning to could be won't fix what's happening right now. The thought pierced her heart more than any ounce of ice or fire magic could.

The dire circumstances of working with the two amphibians felt just as foggy as the day she fell down the well and first saw talking animals in Dina's Pub. She looked for any sign of her friends. Her focus fell back to her rescuers. "Lets not stray too far from each other as we try to find our way back to the wreckage." She tried not to wince as she walked. The ache in her calves made her wish for a stick to walk with. She must have lost hers when she inhaled the sweet smelling cherry smoke.

"Or ideally," the toad whispered.

"An exit," the frog said, finishing his friend's thought.

Lore rolled her eyes, then scanned the ground and the passing mist for anything to keep them together. *A stick?* She knelt down to grab it. *Yeah, this can work.* She picked up the stray branch that was about as tall as she, and whirled around, barely missing the top of the oversized helmet on the toad's head.

"Grab on and no matter what, don't take your hand off of it." Her words sounded a little too stern, even for her liking. It wasn't the way she wanted to use it. She'd much rather be taking pressure off her legs, but the three of them needed to stay together.

The frog and toad clumsily fought to see who'd grab the stick first like it was a competition of who was quicker—the frog eventually won. Lore ground her teeth together. *I* would *get stuck with two helpless damsels in a chasm filled with fog monsters.*

They had been walking for what felt like hours in the dense fog, and they still had yet to come across another sign of life. By now, Lore would have been happy to even come across another sentient fog monster who would sedate them all with a sweet smelling haze. But at least then it'd be quiet.

She was used to Mathilde prattling on and on with questions or pointing out something seemingly new and exciting, but the two amphibians did nothing but air their complaints as Lore did her best to navigate through the fog. She could only see about an arm's length in front of her.

To say it was a challenge would have been an understatement.

"It's a bit warm, innit?" one asked.

"Warm?!" the other squealed. "If anything, it's colder."

"All this steam makes it muggier."

"This ain't steam. It's monsters layin' in wait to gobble us up."

They often bickered about Lore's sense of direction, but never directly to her.

They'd announce things like, "Seen that rock before."

Not helpful. Another thing added to the list of unhelpfulness was the pain that radiated from her calves. It reached as high as her thighs and as low as her toes. Lore huffed in annoyance as the back and forth of the silly amphibians could have been something straight out of a wacky children's book.

"Been three times we've passed it now," the other would add.

Then why don't you suggest another way?

"Yep, you can tell it's the same by its jagged point."

Her cheeks were warm to the touch, and her fingers were nipped by the frosted air. With each painstaking step, her patience slipped away. "Do you have any other ideas about where we should be going?"

Both the toad and frog stayed silent. Only a hefty croak escaped the toad's mouth.

Lore grumbled to herself, but kept going. Every so often, she'd yank the branch they were holding onto just to halt the rambling, even though it only lasted brief seconds.

"'Course this happens to us when we finally get the treasures," one would groan.

"We were gonna make so many stews with that cauldron," the other would say, their voice full of enough pity to make a pit that the two could wallow in together.

"Oh, Lady Luck never grants us good fortune."

"First the invaders from the northern seas, now this."

"Then the blighted crops."

"Then the personality overhaul of ole Mordred."

"What'd we do to deserve such a deck of cards?"

Lore wiped a heavy hand over her face. She wondered which was worse. The vast emptiness of the chasm or the vast emptiness of the chasm with two bellyaching buffoons. She would welcome a looming fog creature at this point. Just anything besides these two groaning about how bad their luck is.

Then it happened, as if Lady Luck were near and heard her thoughts. She saw a shadow in the distance. It didn't appear to be moving, but that was okay, 'cause it also wasn't going anywhere the closer they got to it. *Yes, this could be something to set them on the right track.*

As the figure came into view, Lore's free hand grazed the cool stone and the intricate knots that were carved into its border.

"It's one of those there touch stones," the toad croaked out.

Lore's brow raised. "A touch stone?"

"Yeah," the frog replied. "Ya know, they are like little checkpoints."

Then, as if the stone were waiting for the frog to finish his explanation, the deep cuts that made the braided border emanated a green glow. In the center of the stone, the glowing green light trailed along what was an invisible symbol. A four-leaf clover.

"What's it doing?" Lore asked, the sound of footsteps tickling her ear.

The ferryman's oversized armor rattled as they jumped to hide behind the stone.

The clover cast a green beam of light, and Lore saw Killmoore. It's like she was watching his ghost, but her gut told her it couldn't be that.

Killmoore had the Lover's Web gripped in his palm and held close to his chest. When his eyes fell upon Lore, his worried expression melted. "So glad I stumbled upon one of these," he muttered. Relief wove like a ribbon between each word.

It was then she noticed it would have been foolish to think this version of Killmoore had seen her. This *version* had seen the stone behind her that the frog and toad were hiding behind. Even as the green light projecting Killmoore's image flickered and eventually disappeared, hope sparked within Lore once more.

"He can't be that far from here," she announced. "Come on, you two." She gestured the branch in her grip for the amphibians to grab hold of again. "Come on."

"What makes you so certain he isn't far?" the frog questioned as he gingerly took the branch in his miry grasp.

"Call it a gut feeling."

The toad leaned towards his comrade and whispered, "You think the human has the knowing?"

"Excuse me?" Lore said, jerking her head, looking them over, silently cursing the weight of the antlers on her head.

"Nothing, ma'am," the frog croaked. "Let's go find your friend."

Lore kept a suspicious look on them that Merlin would have approved of. "Fine," she grumbled. Turning, she realized she had no idea where to go next. But instead of admitting that aloud, she just went the way that felt natural. Where she felt like the fog was pulling her.

Towards Killmoore.

It wasn't much longer before she saw a figure moving in the dense vapor that covered the bottom of the chasm. The figure halted, and Lore and the amphibians drew nearer and nearer.

"Killmoore!" Lore called. She couldn't hide her excitement. She was ready for more company. *Familiar* company. Even if she thought Killmoore had been turning into a bit of a diva on this trip.

The fox turned quickly. "Lore?" his voice echoed through the space.

Her feet picked up her pace as she rushed to her friend. Yes, it hurt like hell, but she was so happy to see the fox. Lore, of course, dragged the frog and toad along for the ride.

The fox's excitement washed away with a wave of confusion as he looked behind her at the clanky, clumsy ferryman she had in tow. "Where are Mathilde and Merlin?"

Lore rested her free hand on her knee as she hunched over. "That's why I'm so glad to find you," she said, trying to catch her breath. I may not remember much, but sprinting feels like it wouldn't have been my thing. *Even more so now with her new deer shins.*

Killmoore offered her a skein of water from his pack, and the amphibians wasted no time claiming their gracious deed.

"We saved your friend here from the clutches of a rather angry fog spirit," the frog said, his throat ballooned out with pride.

"But where are the other two?" the fox demanded through his clenched, yellow-stained teeth.

The toad held out a trembling finger, "Well…we don't know."

Lore's head shot up. "That's why I'm so relieved to find you," she managed, handing back the skein.

Killmoore's gaze flickered over the items in his backpack as he put the empty water container away. "You were separated?"

"I never made it to them," Lore admitted.

"But she's lucky we made it to 'er. Am I right or what, toad?"

"Well, who knows where they are or if they found a way out," the fox said, his ears flattening against his head.

"Yeah, but you have the Lover's Web. So—"

"Woah, woah—the fox has *what,* now?" the toad interrupted with a mighty croak.

"Will you two just give us a moment?" the bounty hunter snapped.

The two amphibians' armor shuddered from the harshness of Killmoore's tone, but Lore tried not to give it much thought. They needed a moment to figure out some sort of plan.

"Well, good news is since I stumbled upon these touchstones, it'll be easier to find a way out," Killmoore said as he revealed a fish scale.

"What's that?"

"It's a scale from the all-knowing one." The fox gestured vaguely. "You know the salmon of knowledge?"

Lore shook her head no. "Bit large for a salmon scale," she remarked.

"The all-knowing one is up there along with the Great Spirits. So, I hope it'd be larger than your typical salmon."

"Well whys they got just a bag full of treasures?" the toad whined.

"Anyway," Killmoore continued over their complaints, "the touchstones produce a scale and you take the scale and it will lead you to the next stone. I believe the touchstones will lead us out of here." He then flipped the scale over his knuckles, much like she had seen him do with tael coins, and then the scale disappeared.

Somewhere up his sleeve, I'm sure.

"Oy, we didn't get one of those fish scales from the rock."

Killmoore shrugged. "You probably didn't wait the proper amount of time. Gotta be patient."

"Regardless, it doesn't matter because we are together so we can find a way out. Then we'll alert Merlin and Mathilde with the Lover's Web, which they'll be able to follow with no problems."

The bounty hunter nodded. "Yeah, that's the thought."

"So how's the scale work, anyway?" Lore asked, wondering where Killmoore would pull the scale from.

The fox flicked his wrist not once, not twice, but three times, and the scale appeared pinched between his index finger and thumb. "It glows stronger the closer you get to the next touchstone. If you go off the path it wants you to be on, it goes colorless," he explained.

Lore nodded, following along with his words. "Seems simple enough."

The smell of cherries permeated in the air.

The amphibians had gone *silent.*

Her heart dropped and her eyes met Killmoore's, which seemed fixed on a sight behind her.

She turned, and her heart dropped.

Their faces held blank expressions, their eyes were a milky white, as they stood engulfed in the sweet-smelling haze.

The fog creature shuddered and then let out a deafening croak as loud metal fell over its shapeless body, concealing the two ferrymen within it.

Her spiraling thoughts froze Lore in place. *Why can't I just summon the ice? What's the point of having the powers if I can't summon them?* Lore felt her hands trembling with frustration. *Would it make me a monster? Because I lack the ability to control it? Why am I so... so useless?*

Utterly useless.

"Quick, take this." Killmoore shoved something hard into Lore's mouth, jolting her out of her spiraling descent of self-loathing. "As long as you have this in your mouth, the smog's effects are negated."

"When did you get these?" Lore's question was muffled by Killmoore's hand on her face. The square candy coated the back of her throat with a bitter taste. *Gross.*

"We don't have time for a long story," he shot back, pushing Lore away from him as the armored creature hurled a rock. It landed right where they had just been standing. "But the short version is you learn to prepare for everything with the life I had led before."

Killmoore seems awfully familiar with the creatures up here. And multiple items from his life before are conveniently helpful now.

The fog beast let out another loud croak that made the earth tremble beneath Lore's feet. She tried to steady herself as her mind raced with what to do. The limited fighting experience she *did* have was against Crinkle. And even with the Crinkle battle, not only did she have a bounty hunter on her side, she also had a Wielder.

Another boulder hurled towards her and as quick as she could she darted to Killmoore's side.

"We need to put distance between us and that thing," Killmoore panted.

"We can't just leave them!" Lore pushed back.

Another deep ribbit from the beast had the human and fox bracing themselves.

The creature charged at them, its metal armor clanging so loud Lore thought her ears would bleed.

"They're with Mordred. And taking on anything to do with *him* is not part of our quest."

The rattling croak of the creature was interrupted by another stone flying through the air. Lore bolted from being squashed by the stone and slid in the dirt beside the fox. She didn't have to think about it, her legs just did it for her. Like a reflex.

"Listen, they didn't leave me behind. I won't leave them."

Killmoore groaned. "Between Mathilde's determination to follow in her dad's footsteps and your moral compass, it's a wonder we've survived so long."

"Well, at least we can rest easy knowing we probably met our demise doing the right thing," she joked, trying to lighten the mood. *I need a break. A nice sunset to look at, or a warm plate of food in my belly. For Pete's sake, give me some savory morsel of respite, before I blow a gasket.*

The beast opened its mouth, and murky water poured forth from it like some sort of putrid waterfall.

Killmoore rushed Lore and a flood of what she could only conclude was some bog water raced by the creatures' bugged eyes, blinking slowly until they finally shut.

"Great, it needs to recharge," the fox muttered as he fidgeted with the spool of silver glowing thread. He grabbed Lore's arm.

"What are you doing?!" she protested.

Ignoring her, the fox gently pricked the tip of her finger with his teeth.

"Ow!" Lore jerked her hand back from him, but not quick enough before he got her blood on the thread. The Lover's Web shimmered a vibrant red at the spool, then shot through the rest of the thread Lore watched as it traveled in the distance.

"And what's that gonna do?" she barked, babying the injured finger.

"Getting us reinforcements!" the fox spat, clearly irritated with the question. As if the answer was obvious.

"What?" Lore asked.

Killmoore ignored her and smiled when he saw the string had pulled tight. "Good. Good," he whispered, winding the thread back onto the spool. "They're coming."

Lore's eyes bounced between the resting fog beast and the spool of thread that was giving more slack than Killmoore could keep up with. "*Who* is coming?"

"They've gotta be close," he muttered to himself, still ignoring her as he looked out into the fog. He seemed disappointed at the nothingness he saw in the thick haze.

Lore looked behind him. "I think I see them," she said, her voice riddled with nerves. Looking clsoer, whatever courage she was able to muster up quickly vanished.

The fox looked over his shoulder as he had to do a double-take. "He let Mathilde get consumed by one of those things!" he growled. His fur stuck straight up in anger, and Lore gulped as the ground shook from another deafening croak.

The fog-morphed beast now sported mouse ears and chased a panicked Merlin closer and closer to them.

That wasn't good.

Merlin crashed into Lore. "We couldn't find the ferrymen, but we found that fog thing—and it took Mathilde."

Killmoore's amber eyes flickered with a fire that burned Lore when she looked at him. "You say that so casually, as if her life force isn't being drained as we speak!"

Lore and her companions tucked and rolled out of the way of the rampaging mouse-like fog beast and watched as the titan-sized creature with its stolen characteristics plowed into the other. When the monsters clashed again, the hazy fog got even thicker.

Had Mathilde been the best travel companion? *Not by any means.*

Her optimism was nauseating. Her ogling and aweing, yearning for tourism shenanigans were exhausting.

But she is my friend.

"They're territorial?" Merlin's question made Killmoore's hair stand straight like an alley cat fighting over food scraps.

She was my lifeline in Charmsend. I gotta be hers now. But how*? I can't call on the power of the Stag to bend to my will.*

"If we sit here doing nothing, they'll all die killing each other or they'll die from the beasts sapping their life. Stop gawking, and come up with something *useful* already, bat!" The serrated edge in the fox's tone softened to something more desperate.

Lore watched as he dropped to his knees and frantically started throwing items from his backpack searching for anything that he thought would help.

Pink chalk was tossed to the side so roughly, she assumed it would break in half. As if to confirm her suspicions, a little broken heart appeared in petal pink dust above the rolling haze. Then a ring of keys rattled against the stone covered shores of the chasm.

Her hand rested on the Stag's breath, the chill of deep winter emanated through the fabric of the bag that was clipped to her waist. *If I used it, though, there was also a chance it wouldn't just affect the fog monster, but also Mathilde.* Her hand dropped from the bag. *I am useless.*

Her eyes scanned the area, seeing nothing but the puffs of mist that engulfed them all. "Merlin," she faced the bat. "You said you can do three of the four types of magic?"

He brushed at nothing on his shoulder. "Well, actually three of five."

"Specifics don't matter." Lore stomped her foot. "Can you generate enough wind power to blow this," she flapped her arms, gesturing to the surrounding fog, "away?"

His head tilted. "What makes you think that'll work?"

The ground rumbled as the fog beast that had consumed the two amphibians roared.

"AH-HA!" Killmoore cried, elated.

Lore quickly turned to see the fox holding up a ring shaped like a perfectly puffed cloud. When he turned it in his hands, she realized it was a *locket* ring.

"What is that?" Lore demanded as the two fog beasts slashed at each other with metal armor and an iron mouse tail.

"Cloud storage!" The fox sounded much more reassured than earlier. Right as he was about to flip the lip open, another shake forced the delicate object from his hand.

It fell on the ground and was quickly covered by the white fog.

"For Warden's sake, Merlin—go do something about them!" the bounty hunter demanded as he examined the ground on all fours, his ears flattened in agitation. "Mighty Wielder my arse," the fox grumbled low enough that only Lore seemed to pick up on it.

Well, it was that or Merlin didn't care.

Killmoore's tail looked like it had been zapped by lightning as he continued searching. "Lore look over there!" he called.

Lore wasted no time and dropped to her knees and felt around the ground for the small metal ring. Her fingertips felt smooth stones, patches of moss, and not much else.

Shadows passed over her, making her look up. Her heart dropped, and she almost choked on the candy square Killmoore had given her when she spotted the two titans towering over her.

Time slowed when she spied a tiny Mathilde floating in the middle of the fog creature that had taken her. She looked so peaceful, almost like she was asleep. *The same can be said about the dead,* Lore reminded herself.

Suddenly, Merlin used her back as a springboard. As the sound of Merlin's crackling fireballs filled the air, Lore continued feeling around for the ring. Fighting back the what if's and tears welling in her eyes. *I can find this. I* will. *I will free Mathilde.*

She crawled to Killmoore and noticed the fog was spiraling into a small funnel. She moved toward it. Right as her fingertips touched the metal band of the ring, Killmoore's furred fingers took it away.

"Great job, Lore," he said, offering her a hand up.

The fox slid the ring on his finger and snapped the cloud shaped lid open. The fog immediately siphoned into the piece of jewelry, swirling from the air like water down the drain.

It kept going until the only remaining things on the river shores were the sounds of the ferryman collapsing on the ground, and Merlin's relieved breath when he caught the falling mouse.

Mathilde was safe.

Lore felt like her lungs were on fire from all the excitement, and the pain in her legs ached even more.

They were all safe.

"So…about those salmon scales?" Lore asked lightly, despite the fatigue she felt.

FOURTEEN

Lore's hand landed in the frog's as he heaved to assist her up the steep cliffs path.

"How much longer?" the toad bellyached loud enough so everyone heard him from the back of the neat line they were in as they snaked their way further and further up the cliff face.

The sweeping fog that once concealed all the secrets of the chasm was now as crystal clear as the narrow river that ran through it. The beautiful sights didn't help with Lore's aching legs though, and even if the whining toad was bothersome, she also wondered when the mountainous hike would end.

If only the ferry could have crashed on the other side.

Mathilde was close behind her. Every time Lore looked at the mouse, memories of her asleep in the core of the fog beast flashed in her mind and twisted her gut.

"You know, it was strange, really," the mouse said. "It's like I was having the best sleep of my life and I even got to see—well—" She changed gears. "It doesn't matter, really. But what does matter…" She trailed off, and the sound of her charcoal pencil scribbling in the green journal her father left behind was a sweet melodic sound Lore was happy to hear as they furthered their trek out of the Deadman's Chasm.

I wonder if they'd call it something else now. Her eyes flitted over the clear abyss once more. *Maybe the Rebirth Ravine,* she mused to herself. It was a clever name.

"We haven't said thank you yet," the frog said with a low *ribbit.*

Lore smiled. "Well, now I think we're even."

The frog laughed in front of her, making his loose armor rattle. "We are, yes."

When the winding path upward finally plateaued, Lore couldn't believe it, but her stinging lungs sure did. As she sat down on a nearby downed log to take a breath, she watched as the frog and toad shook the hands of Mathilde, Killmoore, and Merlin—vigorously making their arms undulate with the force.

Then they came over to Lore.

"You're not that bad, human," the toad mused as he offered a hand.

If I had a tael for every time I was told that...

"Well," she said, sheepishly running a hand along her braid, "we are all just trying our best."

"We're glad we made the right choice to save ya instead of runnin'."

The frog's statement made Lore think about what counted as *right.* Like if letting the cat and lynx go was really the correct choice.

Lore tried to brush off his statement. "Sometimes we do things because it seems like the only thing to do."

The croak of the toad sounded as the frog opened his thin mouth. The two exchanged a look, then the frog shifted his focus back to Lore. He bowed, and his oversized helmet leaned forward as he did.

The toad mimicked the taller and slender companion, and his helmet hit the ground.

"There's always a choice, milady human," the frog said in a whisper.

"What will you choose to do now?" she asked, offering a small smile.

She looked past the two ferrymen and studied her traveling companions. Killmoore and Merlin were looking at a map she didn't remember them having. Mathilde sat on the ground, scribbling more notes down in Gannon's green book.

Lore walked past the frog and toad, over behind the mouse, casually trying her best not to take the mouse's attention away from her drawings, scribblings, and writings. Lore rocked back and forth on her heels as she watched the mouse fervently put pen to paper. *She's so dedicated and thorough in what she does.*

A smile crept across her face as she watched the mouse put the finishing touches on the drawing of the monster made of mountain mist, then label it. The handwriting wasn't any better than the drawings, but that didn't matter.

Her attention carried back over to the babbling amphibians that now stood before them.

"Probably dessert," the frog said, answering her question as he rocked on his heels.

"Oh, dessert sounds lovely," the toad mused while rubbing his large, rotund stomach.

The frog's expression fell into a scowl. "No, no." He pinched the green skin between his bulbous eyes to really show his annoyance with his stout friend. "Like leaving Mordred's grunt ranks."

The toad said nothing, but thoughtfully rubbed his chin. "Then we'd have more time for desserts." He then snapped his fingers. "Maybe we could open up a pastry shop?"

The frog rolled his eyes and rubbed his moist chin. "Hey, I know!" His face lit up. "What if we start a mountain bed-and-breakfast?"

The toad clapped his hands together, sending the clangs of metal rattling in the air. Watching the two made Lore smile. The two ferrymen then looped arms and left the heroes.

"Tata!" the toad croaked to them without turning around.

"We're off on a new adventure!" the frog sang. "On the road again!"

Lore's eyes fell to the tea-stained paper bound tightly inside the green cloth cover. She watched Mathilde press hard on it as she colored in everything on the page but the fog shaped beast.

Then she noted the figure inside the belly of the monster. A small mouse. *Was Mathilde drawing what she saw from inside the beast?*

The fox's footsteps pulled her away from the disturbing sketch, and Lore watched as Killmoore collapsed on the ground beside her, resting his arms on the fallen tree.

He let out a groan and looked up at the clear sky. "Now maybe we can finally have some peace 'n quiet."

Lore laughed at the fox's hopeful statement. "So," Lore began as she slid from the log to the ground beside her friend. "Will we be under the stars tonight, or is the fabled Sanctuary nearby?"

Killmoore didn't open his eyes, just crossed his legs and lightly kicked her foot. "Under the stars."

FIFTEEN

Lore rolled up her sleeping sack while admiring the last glimmer of the stars before the sun greeted the sky with kisses of orange and pink.

"It isn't much farther," Killmoore said.

The human tilted her head, ignoring the weight of her antlers and their need for a level position. "Then why didn't we head there last night?" Lore's question wasn't higher than a whisper.

"Oh, don't try to be all hush hush. You know Mathilde is a heavy sleeper," the fox groaned. "'Sides, she'll have to wake up soon, anyway."

Lore shoved the sleeping roll into her backpack and stood up, despite the trembling from her calves. She chewed her lip and scanned around their camp sight. It wasn't for Mathilde's sake, but because she didn't know when Merlin would return.

Lore began an attempt to reason with her gut feeling.

He helped us in the fight against Crinkle. But he also seems to enjoy questioning Killmoore at every opportunity.

He seems to care for Mathilde.

But he seems more interested in Gannon's old journal.

Mathilde stirred and the mouse's rustling took Lore away from the silent battle she was having.

Mathilde stretched and, with a yawn, asked, "So, when do we leave?"

"Whenever the oh-so-self-important bat returns," the fox scoffed.

"Where did he go?" The mouse asked, rubbing sleep from her eye.

"Merlin wanted to scout ahead," Lore said.

Mathilde packed up her sleeping space. "Makes sense."

Killmoore groaned. "I told him I knew where we were going."

And as if those challenging words were a summoning spell, Merlin emerged from the frost covered shrubs. "*Did* you know where we were going, fox?"

Killmoore raised a brow at him.

Merlin continued to share his gripes. "We could have made it last night. Why make us sleep in the cold when it wasn't necessary?"

Killmoore scoffed and brushed the bat's steam off. "C'mon, it's just a bit further."

As Lore followed, she picked up a tinge of satisfaction in Killmoore's voice. Merlin *is* from the territory whose guardian is the season of summer—of fire. Did cold nights truly bother him? Did Killmoore *know* that?

The walk was maybe fifteen minutes, and Merlin grumbled the whole time. The air was thinner this high up the mountain, and it made Lore's lungs burn with desperation for more oxygen.

When they made it to the library that Merlin once wrote off as a fairytale, all she could think was that the large ash doors that welcomed them looked like they could have used a fresh coat of paint.

This is the place? Lore felt her face scrunch. She couldn't hide her disappointment. *How is a place that's so run down supposed to hold knowledge on restoring memories or a way to send me home?*

The entrance to the building, was a half-circle made of some sort of clay. A roof of dried grass and reeds, probably gathered from 'round the faery pools sprinkled throughout the mighty mountain pass, protruded from the mountainside. The door had similar braiding patterns that bordered it, and at the top of the arched entrance was a four-leaf clover. Each one was a different color of glass. A vivid blue, variegated green, vibrant orange, and velvety purple. But the obvious issue everyone was chewing on was the wooden letters that followed along the curved top of the door.

The Keeper's Library

Killmoore stood silent, his tail flicking side to side.

"This isn't the Sanctuary," Mathilde muttered.

"It is," the fox protested. At least it was at one point." He pointed to the emblem on the door. "Each leaf represents a Thimblish territory."

Merlin's leathery wings fluttered in the crisp breeze that insisted on steadily flowing. "But it is a library, and the librarian may have a book about Lore and her kind, and how to restore memories."

The tension that once rested on the shallow air had finally broken, and as Merlin opened the door for his traveling companions, a small bell rang. Almost a dozen Carrier crows flew out from a nearby small porthole window.

"Not ominous at all," Lore said, shoving her hands into her pockets.

When the door closed behind her, she had to admit whoever built this library was clever. By building it on the side of the mountain, the possibilities for expansion were endless. Even in the foyer, as the rising sun sent shimmering rays that kissed the clover shaped glass casting the colors on the pale floor stones of the entrance.

Fairly open corridors branched off in both directions. One was dimly lit, but Lore could see rows and rows of bookshelves that appeared to be untouched by any hands, but got some extra love from time and dust. To her right, there was a sweet lavender aroma tickling her nose, but the smell bled from an opening so narrow that the four would most definitely have to walk single-file in order to fit.

Merlin tapped his foot impatiently. "Well, if anything, you'd think we'd be greeted at the door." The bat had his back to the 'welcome desk' that walled the adventurers from a dark abyss that seemed to swallow all light. Where did the void lead to? If it led anywhere at all.

Killmoore adjusted his knapsack straps that seemed to get tighter and tighter with each quick breath. Lore watched as he fidgeted with the ends of the straps.

"Last I heard, it was hard to find a room without a face in it," the bounty hunter admitted.

Mathilde held the end of her charcoal pencil to her cheek. Lore knew the look. The mouse was trying to piece together all the reasons why such a place was empty. Lore went to her left, where the lines and lines of bookshelves were. She leaned against the doorframe and the antlers caught against its framing.

"Oh, for fuck's sake," she grumbled as she tilted her head properly so the antlers didn't catch against the ornate braided wood. The rafters were large enough that Petra would have had more than enough room to roam.

"Hello?!" Lore called. She cupped her hands around her mouth and tried once more. "Hello?!"

She squinted, her eyes fluttered from one corner of the eclipsed room of books to the other.

"Well, whoever runs this place must have some killer eyesight, because I couldn't imagine reading any book in this lighting."

Mathilde rested a hand on Lore's thigh, nodding her head in agreement, and Merlin held a quiet gaze into the book filled room. His eyes shined with a certain wonder, but Lore couldn't quite place her finger on what kind it was.

Killmoore shifted to face his companions and huffed, "Last time I was here, there were keepers everywhere you looked. It was like you were inside an anthill and the books were their queen."

Merlin made a clicking sound with his tongue. "Unless they've all gone invisible, I'd say this place looks rather abandoned."

Killmoore's grip tightened as he further explained, "Corvidfolk were here, wearing dreary color patchwork robes, and they all had funny haircuts. They'd walk around, asking if you needed help finding something."

Then a sharp voice pierced the conversation. "I quite like our haircut."

At once, the adventurers turned on their heels. Once again, Lore's antlers caught on the same door design as before. She muttered another curse under her breath as her eyes fell upon what seemed to be a balding raven in a long, drab gray robe with patches of chestnut brown sewn in.

It complimented the bird's pointed brown eyes as they flicked over the heroes. "Hmph," it said with its plumed brow raised. "What bring you up the mountain?" His feathery fingers gripped a small knife and slit open an envelope it had in its other wing. The corvid dropped the letter opener down on the wooden welcome desk as his gaze became rooted on the written words of the parchment. "I'll have you know most of our treasury has been emptied, if that's what you're after."

Lore's jaw tightened at the cold and cavalier greeting.

"It's a good thing we aren't after treasures. We are here for books," Mathilde chimed.

The raven's head lazily fell to the side as his sight was set on the red clad mouse. "To some, the secrets in those books," he nodded ahead to the dimly lit room they were about to venture into, "are worth more than the haul we had stored within the mountain."

Killmoore's hands landed firmly on his waist. "We're here to see if there are secrets about our friend here," the fox gestured to Lore. "We need to restore her memories before gettin' her home. Or, we think that's what we need to do."

The raven's head shifted position again, and his eyes followed after. Just watching him sent goosebumps up Lore's arms. Then his beady brown eyes looked down his long hooked beak at Lore. "Didn't figure a human wearing a pair of antlers was a common occurrence, even in these parts." Without tearing his gaze away from the rag-tag group in the foyer, he set the letter down to pick up another and slice open its envelope.

"We were hoping to check the archives to see what we could find to help get her home," Killmoore explained, anxiously rubbing the top of his paws over one another.

The balding raven scoffed. "And the next time I saw you, I was hoping it'd be the day these halls were filled with my brethren again."

The fox took two steps back. "I think you're confusing me with someone else."

The raven *tsked* as his eyes looked over another letter before sitting it down on the desk in a different pile.

"What's this guy talking 'bout Killmoore?" Mathilde asked. The confusion in her voice mirrored the heavy feeling pressing on Lore's chest.

The bounty hunter's ears drooped, and his eyes quickly looked back over to the raven sorting mail. "It's nothing. Just some keeper who thinks all foxes look the same." The nervous laughter that fell out after his words wasn't helping his case.

Merlin's eyes sharpened as he took a step toward the welcome desk. "Tell us what *he*," he pointed a finger at Killmoore, "won't."

Here we go again.

A smile cracked along the raven's hooked beak. "It was how long ago now?" He thought aloud as he dug the letter opener a little too hard in the wood, making the desk crack. "I think it has been at least one full cycle since the removal of my brethren. You were there that day, you were there with your axes, loading them up into a cart to go to Mordred's prison."

"I knew he wasn't to be trusted!" Merlin stomped a foot as Killmoore took another step away from the group.

Mathilde had tears in her eyes. "You said you were Thimbleton's best bounty hunter?"

The raven squealed out a laugh. "Thimbleton's best *schemer*."

Killmoore's fur was stiff as the truth he clearly worked so hard to tangle up, unraveled before his eyes.

Lore took another step towards him. "Killmoore, you can trust us." Her words were almost a whisper.

"But how can we trust *him*?" Merlin interjected.

I wish he would just shut up.

Lore chewed the inside of her lip as she felt Mathilde pull on her clothing behind her. It seemed the mouse was attempting to hide herself from the truth that was unwinding before her by getting lost in the criss-cross green pattern of her flannel.

Lore watched as the fox's chest heaved with labored breaths as he looked from his traveling companions to the floor.

"I'm so sorry," he uttered, then his sight set on the double doors they had just come through. "This was a mistake. A big mistake." Then he bolted, the slam of the heavy ash door which delivered the final blow.

Barely a moment passed before Mathilde's silent devastation became an audible muffle in Lore's flannel.

It shattered another piece of Lore's heart.

Merlin's golden rimmed eyes melted as he watched the human and the mouse. He turned and rested a hand on the welcome desk.

"You straighten him out, and bring back my friends and I'll see what we have on humans, memories, and portals," the raven said plainly.

"I don't know what to say to him." Mathilde's nose twitched as she rubbed her bleary eyes. "I feel so angry, but all I can do is cry."

The last part punched Lore in the gut. *I've felt that before.* She wrapped her arms around Mathilde and pulled the sniffling mouse into a hug, something she wished someone would do for her.

"That's okay," she whispered to the red-clad mouse. "You're allowed to be both angry and disappointed." The weight of the faceless humans that dance through her fuzzy memories haunted her, but all she could do was pull her friend in closer. At this point, it felt more to comfort her than the mouse.

Merlin huffed. "Well, I have a little idea how we could take care of him." The bat's gold rimmed eyes burned with a righteous rage. A flickering gilded flame danced over his clenched fists.

"I'll go." Lore's words echoed in the tiny foyer. The sound made her gulp. She had never spoken that loud before, but the awareness made her soften again as she knelt down to take Mathilde's hands in hers. "No matter what it was he did in his past, it doesn't change the fact he helped us back in Charmsend, and he's been helping us until now."

Mathilde nodded. "Yeah, you're right, Lore." Her ears didn't perk up.

"Charmsend?" The raven's interest piqued. "Haven't heard of news coming or going from there in some time."

Lore ignored the bird's comment and kept her focus on her friend.

"There is good in Killmoore, and I'm gonna make sure we let him know we see that, too."

Lore stood to leave, but Merlin stepped between the exit and her. "How do we know he won't turn on you and take you to some prison?"

Lore's throat felt dry, but she slackened her jaw. *This was Killmoore.* Someone who tried to put her wellbeing above his own back when the two of them were in Crinkle's house. "I guess we don't know that, but what I *do* know is we need him to get back the rest of the conspiracy of ravens that keep this library, so…" She held the Wielder's gaze even though she really wanted to look away. "If you don't mind, I'll be on my way. It's only gonna get darker out there, and I have a fox to find."

With that, Lore pushed past Merlin. Outside, frosted licks of the raw mountain air kissed her cheeks.

Lore didn't have to go far before she saw Killmoore's silhouette sitting on the edge of the cliff. He sat with his head hung lowered in shame. His feet dangling free above the chasm they fought so hard to escape.

As she neared him, the sounds of her footprints carried along the breeze. "Hey," she said as casually as she could, pretending the scene that played out didn't just happen. She plopped down beside him.

"I suppose I have some explaining to do." His voice was all but a pained whimper.

Lore leaned back on her elbows and looked at the stars that swirled into galaxies above them. "Not if you don't want to."

"Well, why else would you be here?"

Lore took a deep breath as she closed her eyes. "Because, my friend needs me."

"I don't deserve your friendship." The fox's voice cracked.

Lore's head tilted as she looked at the absolute mess he was. She studied the way his whiskers fluttered between each labored breath. The way his tears stained his fur as they traveled down his masked face.

"No one deserves to be alone." She tried to speak to him in the gentle way she wanted someone to speak to her when she first arrived in this peculiar world.

After another wave of tears from his eyes, his grip on the ledge eased. "It wasn't me. It was a friend of mine that I was trying to look out for." His words were gaining their balance again. "My friend, well—his chain of choices wasn't always the best."

The fox paused as if his eyes were searching over every smooth pebble at the bottom of the ravine. "But it wasn't his fault, he—we had it rough after our parents died in a looting from Northern Invaders. Well, technically, my mom was still alive, but you heard Molly."

Lore gave Killmoore an unsure look.

"Mordred came and took the healer. That was my mom. And I wasn't here to protect her."

Lore sat upright again, staring at the fox's expression. It was like she could see the memories of fire and blades play out on the surface of his sight, as if his amber rimmed eyes held the memory.

"I'm a good-for-nothin' coward."

She placed her hand. "No, you aren't. You didn't run away and abandon me and Mathilde."

"After my dad died and his parents died, it was hard because Mom never charged for her services or knowledge. So there wasn't much else for me to do other than beg on the street and hope strangers had a sympathetic bone in their body. The other option was to turn to Mordred and his growing clan where they appeared to be a family."

Lore's lips drew a thin line. "Were they?"

"No." The fox gulped. "It was anything but that."

The silence floated between them for a moment before the bounty hunter picked up again. "My friend chose that path and I saw how brutal it was to him. So, I took another." Tears welled in his eyes. "The raven wasn't lying. I *was* there, but only because I tried to talk some sense into my friend." He shuddered at what Lore assumed to be a returning memory of the events of that day. "We got into a physical altercation and I ended up taking these from him." The fox took the polished axes from their holsters.

Lore's eyes flickered over the familiar 'A' inscription on the handles.

"So they belonged to your friend? That's why there's an 'A' instead of a 'K'?"

Killmoore nodded, his hands tracing the letter. "I knew in returning here that there was a chance people would mistake me for him. They always did, even when we were kids, so I can't blame them."

Another long pause sat between the two.

"But—I knew getting you home was of the utmost importance to Mathilde, and you really grew on me for a human."

Lore smiled at the bounty hunter's confession. "Sounds to me this was all one big misunderstanding."

"I panicked and didn't know what to say back there," he murmured.

"Don't worry if you aren't ready to share the tale of you and your friend. You don't have to."

Killmoore's jaw slackened in surprise, and his eyes grew. "R-really?"

"Really," Lore said matter-of-factly. "You just got to agree to help us return the keepers to their library, and then the raven will let us look over those dusty books."

Killmoore's eyes returned to the fogless chasm. A new stillness settled over him. It was like looking at a stone statue.

It would be hard. He probably didn't want to face his friend again, especially after the last time they saw each other.

Right as Lore was about to reassure that Killmoore didn't have to decide tonight, he said, "I agree to your terms, Lore."

He shot up and offered her a hand, and they returned to The Keeper's Library. Upon returning through the double doors that looked paler than the twin light of the moons, they expected to see the surprised faces of Merlin and Mathilde, but what they got was a grim look from the balding raven who was still sorting mail on the desk.

"Where are our friends?" Lore asked.

"They retired to our guest chambers. Down that hall a ways then to the right."

Lore nodded. "Thanks. We'll be going to meet them now."

The raven tilted his head to one side, but didn't look at them. "Oh?"

"I think I have some explaining to do," Killmoore said, letting his shoulders drop a little.

The raven stood towering over the welcome desk, even dwarfing Lore, and that's with the antlers. "Yes. I believe you do."

Killmoore's eyes were downcast and something ravenous raised in Lore's chest.

"He doesn't have to. He said he'd help if he isn't forced to talk about his past," she said, raising her chin a little higher to meet the raven's gaze. The words and confidence alone made her stomach twist, but the action that followed made her hands tremble with adrenaline. She felt a frosted rush of power that itched her fingertips, ready to be used in defense of her friend.

"Lore, I want to share it," Killmoore assured her, with a gentle paw on her shoulder.

But you shouldn't have *to.*

The raven adjusted his focus back to the fox and in a swooping lunge, his beak was mere inches from Killmoore's face. "Sounds like a discussion to be had over some evening tea."

Lore's eyes bounced back and forth between them. *I don't wanna leave him alone with this creep.*

As if he could read her thoughts, the fox switched expressions like a mask. "I'll be fine." He beamed at her. The smile that revealed all his teeth.

Unconvinced, she sucked on the inside of her cheek. "Ok."

Lore turned on her heels and walked down the narrow hall to the right. Waves of lavender aroma welcomed her into an embrace. She glanced over her shoulder just to be sure the fox would be fine. She couldn't help it. But she only saw the two walking toward a dimly lit room filled with books that probably haven't seen a reader since they were shelved.

The farther she got from the entrance, the less she could hear, but it sounded like they were making small talk. Something about a bargain and a trade. Lore pursed her lips and continued walking. Cursing every step that her antlers grazed the low ceiling, and her fawn-like calves ached. Occasionally, she came across a porthole-sized window that looked out onto the mountain scape they trekked to get here.

It was surreal that they had only left Charmsend a mere four days ago.

By the time she reached the guest chamber area, she peeked inside the first room. To her relief, Mathilde was curled up on a bed, cocooned in the archaic quilts the keepers offered. "Mathilde," she murmured.

The mouse rolled over. "Hey, Lore."

Lore moved to sit on the foot of the child sized bed. "He's coming along, but…" She didn't know how to tell Mathilde about the fox's story. "But only if he gets the chance to tell his side at his own pace."

Mathilde said nothing. It was odd, the mouse never had been one for stoic silence before.

"You gonna be okay?" Lore asked.

Mathilde rolled back over and brought her knees to her chest. "I don't know. I feel—"

Lore waited, her brows pulled with apprehension as the mouse tried to find the words.

"It's complicated, but if it will deliver you a way home and keep my promise to you…" Mathilde let out a ragged breath of someone who had spent the last forty minutes crying alone. "Then I can put these feelings aside to do that."

Lore brushed the blanket and tucked the mouse in with a caring touch. "I understand. You should get some rest."

Mathilde's heavy eyelids closed without a fight, and Lore took the bed closest to the door. She laid there for what felt like hours.

Staring up, she counted exactly forty-two kinds of glistening gemstones buried in the ceiling, whose sparkle mimicked the stars outside. There were thirty-seven square patches on each quilt in the room, and two small circular windows on the outside. One door. And endless thoughts. *I don't think I'll be able to sleep until I know how that talk went.*

There were six beds in this room, but theirs were the only occupied ones. *Suppose Merlin still wants a room to himself. Silly ol' bat.*

Lore's fingers drummed on the wooden bedframe, then a passing light from the hall swept under the doorway, and Lore shot to her feet.

"It's about time," she muttered as she shot to her feet.But when Lore opened the door and craned her head out into the dimly lit halls, her friend wasn't on the other side.

SIXTEEN

An uneven, cawing cackle greeted Lore in the hall.

"What are you doing here?!" she demanded in an angry whisper, not wanting to wake Mathilde.

The crow hopped closer to the door and turned his head so Lore could see her reflection in his dilated bright yellow eye. "Crosby could ask you the same."

She went to close the door in his face, but the crow's bandaged foot shot out to wedge between the door and its frame.

"Crosby wants to know. Did those shinies work?" The feathers on his head shuddered as if someone had put ice down the back of his cloak.

Images of her ride on the nightmarish horse flashed in her eye as she muttered out a quick, "Yes."

His head bobbed low as he did a little hop. "Crosby is happy to hear." He tried to wedge himself into the room, but Lore planted her feet on the stone flooring.

"How did you even get here?" She tried to sound grounded, but she didn't know whether to trust her gut about the crow or feel sorry for the way he was struggling against her weight on the door.

The crow suddenly stopped trying, craned its head and flapped one wing. The sound echoed down the empty halls. "Crosby knows where all the doors are."

Now that he was no longer trying to enter the room, she tried to shut the door again.

"Crosby has something you may want," he pleaded, still not letting her close the barrier between them.

It took a moment for his words to register, but once they did, she stopped her efforts to block him. Mindlessly, her hand slipped from the wooden door and grazed her empty wrist.

The dim firelight poured into the room, casting Lore's shadow onto the bed where Mathilde was sleeping. She looked so peaceful. The mouse's breathing was steady, and her brows were relaxed. Her body seemed much less tense.

Is she dreaming? Lore wondered. *Dreaming of the cozy comforts of home? The one she had before I fell down the well into Thimbleton, forever changing any path the mouse had ahead of her?*

The crow quickly shuffled into the room and stopped inches away from Lore, bringing her attention back to him.

"Yes, yes," he mused as he clipped the clasp of her bracelet shut, securing it around her wrist. "See, I gave you back yours. Where is mine?" The crow looked at Lore with a winged hand held out expectedly.

"R-right," Lore said, then quickly unfastened the spurs from her boot. They fell into Crosby's hand with a clink and Lore even noticed the stray hairs still on the sharp bits of the spinning spur.

The crow gave a wide smile and slunk back out to the hall.

"Mr. Carver, I hope you aren't bothering our—" The raven came into view with Killmoore at his side and finished his statement as he cast a displeased look down onto Lore. "Guests."

"Crosby was doing no such thing," the crow squawked as his talons made a scratching sound as he moved away from the door and away from the towering raven.

Killmoore stood in the doorway. "Well, we will see you in a few hours."

Lore's gaze shifted to her friend. "Hours?"

"The bear and his lackeys tend to laze about when the moons first rise and the sun sets," the balding raven clarified.

"Ah," Lore said, shifting her weight from side to side. "Well, on that note, we better get some sleep."

"Quite a good idea indeed."

If there was one thing consistent, it was the raven's dour demeanor. Once the door closed and latched shut, Lore spun on her heels to see Killmoore already prepping the bed closest to the window.

"What are you doing?" she spat.

"I'm getting ready for bed?" the fox answered, though it came out more as a confused question than a statement.

She strode over, her arms crossing her chest. "I need to know what's the deal with that raven?"

"Everything is squared away, if that's what you're asking," Killmoore assured as he slid under the covers. He then placed his backpack beneath the thin pillow.

Lore chewed the inside of her cheek. "It wasn't."

The fox rolled to his side to face his back toward her. "Get some sleep, Lore. You'll need it."

Anger boiled in her stomach. *Deep breaths,* she reminded herself as she returned to her own bed of choice. They had just rested at camp, but somehow she was still drained. She absolutely could use the rest, but she also felt the threads of tension tighten between the fox and the mouse. It made her uneasy. But instead of bringing it up, she wrapped herself in the patchwork blanket and closed her eyes. *All in good time.*

That evening, the raven woke the heroes by a pounding on the door.

Mathilde groaned and pulled the pillow over her head. "Go away."

Their host peeked his head in. "Hope the dreams were pleasant." His brown eyes scanned the room. "Breakfast is ready in the mess hall."

Before Lore could ask exactly where the mess hall was, the door slammed shut. She sat up in bed and rubbed her neck. *I don't think I'll ever find a sleeping position that is comfortable as long as these damn things are on my head.*

As she massaged her muscles, Killmoore was already heading for the door, his knapsack slung over his shoulders.

"You're rather perky for only sleeping a few measly hours," she grumbled as she stretched.

The fox's hand hovered above the doorknob, but he didn't bother to look over his shoulder. "Just ready to get this over with."

He opened the door. "I'll wait for you guys outside. We had tea in the mess hall when we had our private talk, so I know where we are going."

The door latching made a small noise despite how gently he shut it.

The flimsy mattress gave way as Mathilde leaped onto Lore's bed. "Can you believe that?!" she called with a finger pointed at the door. "He didn't even check on me." She plopped down on the bed, her hands folded over her chest. Eyebrows pulled tight, the mouse's mind was fast at work knitting some sort of story to explain why he didn't wake her.

"Well," Lore sighed, clapping her hands against her own thighs. "As far as we were concerned, you were still asleep."

Mathilde grumbled something Lore couldn't quite make out.

She stood and wiped the remaining sleep from her eyes. "Listen, it's complicated, and sometimes things are like that, but what matters is he wants to help."

Silence.

"He wants to do the right thing, and I'm sure if you give him time he'll come back 'round," Lore assured as she buttoned the flannel over the cashmere sweater. While she was glad to be reunited with her bracelet, she could never think of parting with her green garment.

Mathilde leaped from the bed, her ears perked up. "Fine. I suppose I could try to approach it with your attitude."

Lore smiled and opened the door. *Whatever makes busting the keepers from the bear's prison easiest.*

"Great, because we have bigger fish to fry."

As they fell behind following Killmoore through the twisting halls, Mathilde finally pointed out, "I'd be careful where you say that, Lore. I don't think the fishfolk would like it much."

It earned a muffled laugh from Killmoore and Lore watched as the mouse hurried her pace to his side.

"Killmoore, I don't know how to feel about this mysterious past of yours—"

"I can—"

Mathilde grabbed his arm and interrupted. "You can tell me more about it when you're ready."

The fox breathed a sigh of relief. "Thank you, Mousey."

As they neared the mess hall, the sounds of their footsteps in the empty the Keeper's Library's empty halls were now rivaled by uneven, squawking laughter. The kind of laugh that scratched against their ears. It could only belong to one crow. *Crosby is still here?*

"We are so glad to have such esteemed guests in these hallowed halls." The raven opened his wings to their full span, revealing the corvid-kind was holding a long, pointed knife used to slice meat. The bird's feathers caressed the blade before he once again opened his onyx beak. "It's been so long since we've last had any visitors."

Merlin sat at a long table with his back to the entrance of the mess hall, perfect for seeing his large ears spasm at every little sound. The crow sat beside him.

The raven was interrupted by a sudden squawk from Crosby who couldn't contain his excitement.

Lore could imagine the dour look on the raven's face from the crow's birdbrained behavior.

Another caw from the crow rattled her bones. Crosby had such an earsplitting pitch to his every sound.

Mathilde stood close to Lore and grabbed the human's thigh as they watched. From the tight flatness the mouse held her ears, Lore could only assume she wasn't a fan of the random high pitched cawing either. *Was Mathilde's hearing that sensitive? Or was it something else? Fear?*

"As I was saying…" The velvet smoothness in the corvid's throat made the human shudder, and the bat's ears twitch.

"I do think we should wait for my companions," Merlin spoke quickly, his fingers tapping a bit impatiently on the table.

As the three rounded the corner, the sight that met them when they finally reached the others made Lore's stomach feel like it dropped into the chasm of death and splattered into mush at the bottom of the ravine. They could see three distorted shadows dance along the wall, and the silhouettes revealed something much more unsettling than the squawking laughter would have led them to believe. The looming shadow of the raven appeared. The way the flickering firelight warped the three figures sent an icy chill down the hall.

"Oh," The raven cooed, then pointed the knife at the sitting bat.

Again, Crosby let out another inappropriate amount of laughter.

"You're afraid there won't be any pieces left?"

The thought of the raven cutting Merlin quicker than he could hurl a spell terrified her.

"It's fine," Killmoore mouthed, paired with a shrug, as the fox went to take another step.

Mathilde's brow furrowed and as the mouse was about to march in to get to the bottom of whatever was happening, Lore quickly grabbed the mouse by her collar. *So much for the mouse being afraid.*

"No," Lore mouthed, but Mathilde's face became almost as red as the jacket she was wearing.

It might be selfish, but I can't risk Mathilde getting hurt. And Merlin is a Wielder. He'll be fine, right?

Lore's eyes drifted to Killmoore who had a hand at the hilt of an ax and moved both slowly and silently closer to the bat and birds. She was so focused on his progress, she hardly noticed the mouse wriggling against her hold.

Mathilde slid her arms free from the jacket and darted past the fox. Lore felt cold sweat bead on her forehead. *This is a bad idea.*

"Happy Unbirthday, Crosby," the raven said flatly. "I'm glad the room is a little more filled this time around."

The shadows on the wall quickly revealed the end of the story they were telling. The raven quickly brought the butcher knife down on the unsuspecting bat.

Without thinking, she trailed behind as she rounded the corner and supported herself on the doorframe as red confetti splattered her.

"WHAT!" Mathilde gasped, her heart surely still racing from what they thought they were witnessing.

Merlin turned in his seat, revealing in front of him was a round two tiered purple iced birthday cake that had yellow buttercream stars and key accents adorned on it.

The keeper looked unamused as he moved the slice of cake to Crosby. "First slice for the unbirthday bird."

Killmoore's brow raised and he gestured at the raven with his ax. "Who taught you to cut a cake like that?"

Lore let out a relieved breath, then proceeded to pick some confetti from the antlers as she moved to take a seat at the long wooden table. She was just happy the aches in her legs were more manageable today. Lore sat at the end so she could see Crosby straight on.

The crow seemed to savor every bite of his cake. His head craned back as he attempted to devour the whole slice in one go. He was doing a terrible job, really, it looked more like he was choking on it rather than eating it.

"What flavor is it?" Mathilde asked, her tail flicked from side to side.

Before someone could answer, Crosby sputtered out the half-eaten slice onto the wooden table's faded surface. The force of it sent some pieces flying in all directions.

Lore slowly brought up a finger and flicked the half eaten mush off her freckled cheek.

Crosby pounded his fork-holding wing against the wood surface, shaking the table, as he squealed loudly, "Crosby has only the best kind of cake."

"And what flavor is that?" Mathilde asked again.

"Honey," the raven said flatly as he, too, wiped purple icing from his face with the tip of a wing.

The scowl Mathilde was wearing melted away. "Oh," the mouse scampered over to take a seat next to Merlin.

Killmoore made an audible groan as he sheathed his weapons.

"Whatever did you think we were doing?" the raven asked pointedly.

The fox sat in between Crosby and Mathilde. "Not cutting an Unbirthday cake, that's for damn sure."

The raven shook his head. "Forget I asked."

Killmoore exchanged a 'can you believe this guy' look with Lore, who politely raised both her brows to tell him to behave.

"What is an Unbirthday?" *I've never felt like more of an outsider amongst Thimblish folk.* The weight of her antlers made her head tilt and the dull, but tolerable ache of her fawn legs poked her mind.

"You don't know?" There was surprise in the solemn raven's tone.

Lore shook her head.

Mathilde added, "I don't either. We don't have them in Charmsend."

"An Unbirthday is a special event that happens for keepers when the time comes that—" The raven brought a napkin to his beak. "Excuse me, I have been alone here for what feels like an eternity." He reached for the knife and cut himself a sliver of the cake. "I nearly shared Keeper secrets."

Merlin, who had been observing every interaction with a close eye till now, jumped in with, "Oh, well...what is the vague answer?"

The raven looked unenthused by Merlin's pushing.

"For the kids' curiosity," the bat amended with laugh, gesturing to Mathilde. His leathery wing caught the firelight, showing all the battle scars from the years of being an adventurer.

The raven took a bite and maintained eye contact with a smiling Merlin. Once he was finished chewing, he gave a casual flip of the wing. "It's a special day that happens once a year for a special someone who undergo a terrible fate for the greater good of keeping all things perfectly..." His tone was drier than Minifred's cooking. "Balanced."

It felt like a punch square in the chest. *Will Crosby...die?* Lore wondered.

Merlin shifted his gaze down to his plate and broke off another slice of cake. "Ah, I see." His gaze fluttered to Mathilde, and he smiled. "Better scribble that down in your book!" he mused. Then he finally took a bite.

Mathilde looked at the raven. "What *kind* of terrible fate?"

The Keeper's answer was simple. "It could be anything." Not a moment passed before he changed the subject. "Who wants the next slice?" He asked, leaning forward a bit too close for Lore's comfort.

"Me," the fox deadpanned.

The raven's face somehow, by a miraculous work of some fates, fell into an even gloomier state before he slid the chipped porcelain plate over to Killmoore.

Crosby's head bobbed unnaturally for someone whose body was sitting so still. "Do you like honey cake? Crosby *loves* honey cake."

Mathilde muffled a laugh with her hand.

What terrible fate is the crow tied to? Lore mindlessly fiddled with her bracelet. *Maybe I deserve an unbirthday, too.*

The raven continued to serving cake until everyone had a slice. Lastly, he pulled over another chair from a far corner of the room, ignoring how the legs scratched against the floor.

The sound echoed off off the walls, making Killmoore's ears flattened in response.

Perhaps the raven was doing it on purpose? Or did he not know how to read a room?

Crosby let out another ear splitting squawk and pulled his chair closer to the table. "Crosby would like more."

The raven slid his slice over to the crow, who happily began eating. He ate with such focus, Lore wondered if he forgot that the rest of them were there.

Lore finally forked out a bite of Crosby's unbirthday cake into her mouth. As the rich flavor of honey and lavender danced over her tongue, the fuzzy image of an old woman—an apparent stranger—with snow white hair trickled into the empty shores of her mind. Lore swallowed hard, she couldn't explain it, but somehow it gave her some sort of comfort. Everything would be okay.

SEVENTEEN

After the final bite had been consumed, Crosby ruffled his feathers. "Crosby has the loveliest of ideas!"

The raven grimaced. "And what might that be?"

The crow's head bobbed up and down and his yellow eyes grew to the size of saucers. "Crosby has traveled and discovered a new place. Crosby brings a story."

Killmoore's fork scratched against the plate. His brooding silence hung in the air, but it didn't seem to put a damper on Crosby, who shot suddenly to his feet. His chair landed on the ground behind him with a blaring thud. Lore, Mathilde, Merlin, and Killmoore all winced from the sudden sound bouncing off the walls of the empty room. The raven sat still, as if this happened every time Crosby visited.

Killmoore's mouth slightly opened, anticipating the words the crow was going to say.

"Crosby found a town."

Killmoore started mimicking the crow's gestures.

"A town in the valley of dead Emeralds," the bird said, only to suddenly stop moving and squint at Killmoore when the fox did as well.

Their friend wore his best shocked face, as if he wasn't playfully mimicking the bird. It made Mathilde giggle.

"But the valley and the pass are revived, and with their revival, it birthed a quiet little town." A brief pause filled the room before Crosby flapped his wings widely. "COZY!" he squawked.

Killmoore remained unchanged, but continued to silently and perfectly parrot the bird.

"Did you meet any mice?" Mathilde interrupted, putting a damper on Killmoore's perfect mime record.

The soured look on the fox's face put a smile on the Keeper's features.

Lore's eyes drifted back to the salescrow.

"Ah, Crosby did, indeed! She had purple eyes and was rather," The crow craned his neck to the side a bit too perverse for comfort, "tasty," the crow mused.

Mathilde leaped onto her chair. "You *ate* her?"

The crow let out his scratchy laughter, but no one else joined in.

"Crosby tells joke!" He laid his feathers on the table and let out a defeated sigh. "No one else thinks Crosby very funny?"

Mathilde huffed and plopped back down in her seat, her brow still knit in displeasure. "Who jokes about eating someone?"

Lore studied the crow. He seemed genuinely confused by Mathilde's upset reaction.

I have a hard time taking anything the crow says seriously, but Mathilde is probably on edge. She gave Mathilde a sympathetic glance. *She's never been away from her sisters—except from when Crinkle had imprisoned and then banished us. And making a joke about eating a mouse when there was a mouse in the audience wasn't very sensitive.*

"Anyway, Crosby helped them with a list of potential trade partners in other villages outside the valley." The crow paused as he realized he was the only one standing. He looked over his shoulder and noticed the fallen chair.

"Ah, just where Crosby left you," he mused to himself and everyone watched as the unbirthday bird stood it up and sat back down, ready for another bite.

"Then what?" Lore's voice broke the stillness.

"Well, then Crosby had to come here. I told you I'd see you again."

The memory of carrier crows holding lost jewelry, letters, and stringy pink tendrils that used to belong in someone's eye socket flitted across her mind. She shuddered as a familiar chill traveled down her spine.

"Crosby is always right," he said between bites.

Lore studied him closer. *This can't be the same crow.*

"Do you have carrier crows available?" Mathilde spoke up again. This time, her question was pointed at the raven.

"Yes."

"May I use one to deliver a letter?"

The raven took a deep drink from a tall chalice before delivering his dry answer. "Yes."

Dryer than the wine he's probably drinking.

Mathilde shifted her weight from side to side in the chair, wearing a soft smile.

Lore knew she was probably chomping at the bit to send her sisters a letter and regale them with all their misfortunes, but spin them as some grand adventure.

"Crosby told them a prime trading partner would be a town further east. In the owl's domain."

Lore raised a brow and looked at the raven. "Owl's domain?"

Merlin pats his face with a napkin and interjected, "The Great Owl spirit has domain over the entire east side of the Island."

Lore propped her elbows onto the table and rested her chin on the tops of her hands. "I didn't take Thimbleton to be its own island."

The crow flapped his wings once more, causing a bit of a whirlwind to dance around the table. "Her natural borders are what Crosby would call beautiful." He pulled his wings close to his body again and pulled his cloak around him with his beak then said, "It's the inside that has the messy parts."

The corners of Killmoore's mouth twitched, and the fox stood up, silently excusing himself.

"Finished already?" the raven asked. There was a curious twinkle in his chestnut-colored eye.

"As lovely as this little geography lesson is, we need to get moving soon, lest we want to meet the sharpened blade of Mordred's guards. I'll meet you at the front doors," Killmoore said, then left the dining hall.

Mathilde shot a look at Lore, who was already out of her seat following him.

Behind her, she could hear Mathilde and Merlin talking to the raven.

"So, this Mordred?" Merlin began. "Does he have any connection to a Guardian?"

She didn't stick around to hear the answer.

The torches on the walls flickered blue as the fox darted past, and the blue flames briefly grabbed Lore's attention as she set off on his heels.

The bounty hunter walked quickly down the twisty halls that might as well have been a labyrinth.

"Killmoore, wait!"

The fox didn't slow down. If anything, his pace sped up.

Lore jogged after him, only seeing the end of his tail as he rounded each corner of the corridors.

"Killmoore?!"

She clenched her jaw as the sound of her desperate footsteps echoed in her ears.

"You can't just leave like that!"

Still nothing from the fox.

"Was it something someone said?" she called.

As they came out into the room lined with bookshelves, she stopped. She looked up and saw a whole other floor.

Great.

She ran up the stairs, but was met with the large ash door slamming shut. It barely missed making contact with her face.

Rude.

She flung the door open and peered out from the library. Her eyes squinted in the growing night. *I can hardly see anything.* Looking harder, she could just make out silent trees and rocky grassland covered in a blanket of snow.

The wind delivered an almost inaudible whimper that she otherwise would have missed.

Her head whipped right, and she caught a piece of the doorframe on her antler. "Not now," she grumbled in frustration as she broke free, taking a chunk of the wattle doorframe with her. Her fingers worked quickly to brush the debris from the antlers as she followed the sound of silent suffering on the night breeze.

She spotted him sitting along the front of a rather large lake. Lore sat down on the stone bench beside him. She let out a sigh. "You know, it's rude to slam doors in people's faces."

Killmoore said nothing, just wrapped his tail around himself.

Lore let out a sigh, "I'm sorry, but–"

"There's always a but," he muttered.

"But what's been going on?" Lore asked as she searched Killmoore's face for any hint of whatever was weighing so heavily on him.

"I told you already."

Lore gripped the side of the stone bench and her fingers ran along the carved designs on the edge. Her eyes shifted from Killmoore to the lake. It looked like Thimbleton's sky was peering over a mirror.

"Do the stars tell stories where you're from?" His gaze stayed fixed on the sky.

Lore pursed her lips as she looked to her friend. She searched her foggy memories that came and went. She couldn't recall anything about the stars. It made her heart ache. Her answer was as hollow as a decaying tree. "I don't know."

The fox was silent as his amber eyes flicked from star to star.

Lore fiddled with her bracelet as she tried to go to the empty shoreline of her mind. Every time she wanted to remember something, she couldn't. She imagined herself sitting in the blank sand of her mind's beaches. Then, her head began to ache around her temple. She instinctively brought her hands up to rub the pain away, and there she saw it.

A book. She was sitting on a porch swing, flipping through a book.

Her eyes shot open and she grabbed Killmoore's hand that was resting in his lap.

He jumped at the contact.

"I remembered something."

The fox's bewilderment shifted to soft excitement. "Oh well, do share with the class, please." He gestured to the quiet lake. "We're all itching to hear it."

"We had stories, but they were in books."

The fox's smile faded, and with it, Lore's stomach knotted itself. *Is my memory wrong?*

"What?" she asked.

He gulped as if he were trying to swallow a dry streusel, then let out a ragged breath before meeting her gaze. "It's a damn shame."

He pointed to the sky, directing her attention to a constellation that was still visible even as the moon was on the verge of setting, and the sun was just starting to kiss the horizon of the jagged mountain peaks. "The best stories are written in stars, not books.

He picked at his claws and asked, "Do you want to hear the story about The Deceiver?"

Lore raised her chin to follow where he was pointing. There was one constellation left hanging in the sky, blue and black like a two-day-old bruise. *Sorta looks like a fox.*

She cast a glanced at her friend, who was laser-focused on the constellation. "Deceiver, eh?"

Killmoore nodded, removed his axes from their holster, and brushed something away from his cheek. "Everyone knows that for all the great qualities the fox holds, none shall outshine for that he is. A deceiver."

Lore reached for his hand, but he pulled it away from her as he began the tale.

"In the great forest of the celestial world, there were animals of all kinds that called it home. There were the otters who were well known for their friendly demeanor and protective nature."

Lore gave a soft hum. *I always thought otters were more fun and spontaneous than protective.*

"Then there was the bear, and everyone admired the bear's strength and stamina. Of course, I can't forget about the blackbirds that would sing lovely songs from the branches of the Mothertree that was said to be at the heart of this forest."

Wonder how pleasant the melody had been.

Lore noticed the way Killmoore slightly changed the tone of his voice as he told the story of each animal. *He was enjoying this.* Maybe spending time with the mice sisters gathered around the hearth had rubbed off on him. It made her smile. Or maybe he'd always had a knack for tales.

"When it came to courage, the boar had that covered." He paused and leaned over to Lore, "and then some."

The two laughed quietly together, then the fox continued.

"The cow was seen as a rich animal and everyone valued their company. The dog was a renowned tracker—no wolf could slink from it." He paused and grabbed the tip of his tail, "And they make pretty good friends, too..." His voice trailed off before he spoke again.

"The dragon had power over all the elements, and the observant eagle could see all hidden truths. The hedgehog," the fox puffed out a breath. "Well, ya look at em' and see they are naturally good defenders with their prickly needle spines, but they're soft-hearted and allow you to be..."

Lore watched as Killmoore's face softened with the pause.

His eyes blinked a few times too many as he collected himself. His gaze met Lore's. "Well, yourself, and they embrace you as is."

She nodded in agreement, thinking back to Sable, and how warm she felt in the hedgehog's presence.

"The cat protected the animals of the forest from the unseen. And we can't gloss over the mouse." The fox's fond feelings pulled at the corners of his lips, giving him his signature smirk, as the words were spoken with such admiration.

Lore smiled wide and Killmoore continued, "This mouse, in particular, was all about the little details. The other animals appreciated that trait. And we'd be doing a disservice if we overlooked the salmon. It's—"

"All knowing," Lore finished his sentence, remembering the scales from the ravine. She recalled the way they changed color in between Killmoore's fingers whenever they were heading in the right direction.

The fox nodded, then his perked ears drooped. He averted his gaze from Lore. "And then there was the fox."

"What was the fox known for?" Lore asks expectantly.

"For schemes, tricks, and mischief."

Lore bit the inside of her cheek.

"You see, when the day came that the mighty Mother, from which we're all born from would put the animals in the stars, they were all very excited. There were only twelve spots, though."

Lore counted to herself the animals on each finger, "But weren't there thirteen animals?"

Killmoore kept his gaze on the ground. "Yes, and the fox quickly noticed that, too. He left knowing he would be the one left out."

Lore went to place a sympathetic hand on his back, but Killmoore scooted down the bench.

His fingers fidgeted with his tail as he continued the story. "So, he decided he had to do something about it. He had to secure his spot in the stars. So that night when all the animals were asleep in their dens, the fox made a late-night visit to the mouse." He wrapped his tail around his palm like a rope.

"The mouse was confused as to why the fox was there so late, but the clever fox told the mouse that he knew the Mother would choose to exclude the animal that failed to bring her a proper gift. The mouse was puzzled by this as it didn't recall such requirements being stated. But the fox was very convincing, and the mouse realized it already items in its hovel that would combine into the most perfect gift."

Killmoore released his tail after giving it a final and gentle pat. "Happy with his work, the fox left the mouse to his very detailed gift making. The mouse stayed up all night and spent the following morning perfecting the item."

Lore sucked on her bottom lip as her brows knit in consideration. *I think I know where this is going.*

"When the time came to put the twelve animals into the stars, there were exactly twelve who showed up. The All Mother waited, but the mouse never showed. And so the fox got the mouse's spot." Killmoore's shoulders fell forward, and he turned away from Lore. "Everyone knows a fox is just a deceiver."

"Hey," Lore said gently, moving to close the distance between them. "What is it?"

The fox was silent. Every time he opened his mouth to reply, he would shake his head 'no' as if he couldn't find the words.

Lore rested her hand on his shoulder as he had done for her before.

"It's just you get told that you are something so many times that you actually start to believe them."

Lore tilted her head. "I don't know the fox in the story."

"Well, if you ask anyone in Cloch Chruinn, they'd say all foxes are–"

Lore cut in. "But I know you, and you aren't like that." She held his amber gaze, noting his eyes were welling with tears in the corners.

"You don't know me."

Lore scoffed as she reached down to pick up his axes and hand them back to him. "*You're* the one with the level head. The one who didn't look down on me because I'm a human. You were never scared..." Lore swallowed hard, then gave her best reassuring smile. "And you're the best bounty hunter Thimbleton has to offer."

Before Killmoore could protest her claims, a familiar voice called out to them.

"There you are! Let's go save the day, and free some birds." Mathilde seemed back to her usual adventure-seeking self.

The two stood up, and Lore watched as the fox chased behind the mouse—the story of The Deceiver still fresh in her mind.

EIGHTEEN

The late night fog rolled off the mountain cliffs like water, and falling thick snowflakes kissed the apples of Lore's cheeks.

Mathilde was right behind Merlin, buzzing with questions while Killmoore hung back to be the caboose to their little train of adventurers.

"What did you guys make of that raven?" The mouse asked, looking over her shoulder at Lore and Killmoore for a response.

"He was a raven," Lore said with a shrug, wrapping her arms around herself as a northern wind blew off the cliffs above them. Good thing I'm not in a dress.

The fox said nothing. His eyes held to the ground and the backs of Lore's feet. Maybe he was pretending not to hear the mouse's question at all.

"He was a bit peculiar," Merlin added, his large triangular ears still facing forward.

Mathilde's tail lifted higher and curled at the end. At least someone was giving her the speculation she was after, even if it wasn't an answer that dripped with intrigue she could use to spin a narrative.

"That's what I thought, too. Something just wasn't right about him. He was kinda creepy," Mathilde continued.

Lore bit back a sarcastic laugh. "His friends were snatched and all he had for a year was the company of Crosby. You may become a bit peculiar if that happened to you, too, Mathilde."

The mouse's tail stiffened defensively at the thought. "Yeah, but he seems like he is up to something."

Lore looked at the thick line of trees to their left and then to the steep cliffs to their right. She looked to the opening in the overcast sky and only a sliver of the moons' silver light pierced through. Her gaze drifted to the birds flying overhead, and she saw the constellation that caused her rust furred friend so much pain. "Sometimes folks aren't what they seem."

Mathilde tried again. "You guys didn't feel the weird energy that oozed off him?"

"No."

The bat's ears fluttered, and Lore could only assume he was listening for anything that may be approaching their band of misfit explorers.

"Mathilde, what do you make of the northern domain of Thimbleton?" Merlin inquired.

The mouse's head tilted. "Umm, I guess it's okay. A bit too foggy and cold for my liking."

"It is. You and your sisters are from the western region, yes?"

The question seemed to linger in her mind before she finally answered, "That's what I hear, but I grew up in the Emerald Valley, so that's where home is."

"Well, it doesn't matter where you're from because Thimbleton's boundaries have shifted with time and their names have changed just as many times."

"Oh I didn't know that," Mathilde chimed, her tail flicking with amusement. "Where do you call home, Merlin?"

"It doesn't matter where I'm from on the Isle. You're Thimblish, I'm Thimblish, even Killmoore is Thimblish." Lore eyed the bat, who was leading them through the mountain pass, following the directions the raven had given him.

"Thimblish?" A smile spread on Lore's features just saying the word. Killmoore had mentioned it when they first arrived at the Sanctuary, but she was curious.

"Thimblelonian was too long," the bat answered, turning around.

Lore raised a brow. "And what council decided that?" Her words were wrapped in subtle laughter.

"The council of the celestials," Killmoore said, melancholic behind her.

"Council of Celestials?" Lore asked.

Mathilde threw her hands up. "You know, the animals in the stars."

Lore swallowed hard, recalling the tale Killmoore shared with her just a few hours prior.

"The story of how they were placed there is quite fascinating," Merlin purred, ahead of the group. His back was to them, but Lore could imagine the grin on the bat's face to match the resonance of his voice.

She played dumb. "I haven't heard it before. Why don't you tell me?"

"The Great Deceiver," Merlin said, a little too satisfied.

The smugness was interrupted by Mathilde. "What you *mean,*" she spat, "is the Great *Giver.*"

Lore looked over her shoulder at Killmoore, who seemed just as confused as the bat. "Explain, Mathilde," Lore urged.

Of course, the mouse was tickled pink to share. She cleared her throat and channeled the theatrics that were well known in her home with her sisters. "Basically, long ago the celestial mother was planning to put twelve animals in the sky. Many, if not most, of the animals felt confident with their likely placement. But not the mouse."

Mathilde looked a little embarrassed at the next part. "The mouse was riddled with anxiety. But the clever fox swung by to give a gift to the mouse. A gift that would win the mouse a coveted spot in the stars. Which the gift delivered on, and when the Mother asked where the mouse found a gift so well crafted, the mouse was honorable and gave rightful credit to the fox." Mathilde gave a big smile to Killmoore. "And that's why the fox and mouse are together in the sky."

Lore smirked.

Merlin wrinkled his nose like he had just smelled a skunk. "Never heard that version. Must be regional."

"No, it's not. Look!" Mathilde pointed to the stars. "You can see the mouse is peeking out from behind the fox's tail."

"Can't say that I do," Killmoore said, a bit defeated.

"Well, come here and look at it from my point of view."

Lore shuffled beside the mouse with Killmoore.

"See?" Mathilde asked, gently pointing out the three stars protruding from the fox's tail. "The fox and mouse are together."

Lore caught Killmoore smiling as he held back tears. "Thanks for the perspective change, Mousey."

For a brief moment, Lore felt at ease—hope that everything was gonna work out.

Then, the wind blew.

Killmoore's nose twitched. "We're close," he whispered.

Merlin crossed his leathery wings. "The raven said we wouldn't be close to the camp until we passed the lightning-struck tree with a fire great enough to rival the eternal flame."

The fox shook his head. "No. It reeks of the ferrymen grunts and the bandits we met while leaving the village."

Mathilde scampered over to the side of the cliff and peered into the mist. "He's right," she murmured in agreement. "Come look!"

Killmoore rolled his eyes and grumbled. "I'll never understand why everyone's so surprised when I'm right about something."

Lore and Merlin joined the mouse in leaning over the cliff's edge. The fog that rolled off the peaks above them created a pool of mist that was too thin to hide the glowing embers of a campfire below.

The ground had varying rock features hooked into the ground, enclosing multiple fires.

Except, the rocks looked like *bones*.

The comparison sent a shiver down Lore's spine.

"They must have moved locations," Merlin muttered. "I wonder why."

Then Mathilde's large ears flicked to the side.

Lore heard the rustle, too, but it was too late to scream a warning.

What started with a rustle ended with Lore having a spear head poked between her shoulder blades. Between all of their shoulder blades. She looked ahead at her friends, Merlin seemed annoyed more than anything with the way his ears twitched as they walked down the winding cliff path. Mathilde kept as close as she could to the Wielder, most likely waiting for him to cast a fireball.

Lore's attention drifted to Killmoore, noting the way his whiskers twitched. The way his amber eyes that normally held a fire that couldn't be put out were now embers on the verge of fizzling out.

"Ya know, you seem familiar fox," the badger said, digging his spear deeper into the fox's muscles.

Before Killmoore could declare his innocence, Mathilde decided to declare that for him. "He would never run with the likes of you."

What a time to flip sides. Lore thought back to the mouse rejecting the fox. But it could have been that she was allowed to doubt him, but no one else was allowed to accuse him of a shady past. One that seemed shrouded in the thick gray fog of the Wayward Mountains.

The other badger let out a loud laugh that echoed off the ravine walls.

Lore glanced at Merlin, who was cuffed in iron shackles that swallowed his hands.

The badger holding the iron chain links pulled the bat along, seeming to take a bit too much pleasure in his rough treatment of the Wielder.

Lore looked at what she thought were rocks from the top of the cliff, but now she saw the area was scattered with weathered bones. They were being forced through some massive dead creature's ribs. Lore noticed every crack and splinter from what was most likely years of exposure to the elements. *Who did they belong to?*

"You just brought us back to your little camp?" Mathilde scoffed.

The badger holding Killmoore hostage huffed in annoyance. He leaned the spear on a stray bone and grabbed the much smaller fox by the scruff of the neck.

"Hey!" Mathilde snapped. "Don't handle him like that."

Killmoore gave her a warning glance to not aggravate them further.

The soldier ignored her and dragged Killmoore over to what Lore thought was a vertebra to the long dead creature's neck. With a mighty pull of his free hand, the badger grasped a long, thick chain attached to the bone. As he walked back toward them, the ground started shaking.

The closer the badger got to them, the wider the earth opened, revealing a cavern whose walls became lit by torchlight.

"What were ya on about, little mouse?" one of their captors chided, prodding them forward to march down the makeshift staircase that spiraled deeper and deeper into the earth. Into the mountain.

As the cave walls seemed to close in on them, the sound of rushing water roared through the cavern. The walls that were once engulfing them became hip high barriers and a grand curtain of water rolled off the stone above them.

Lore could see in the distance a little island whose shores kissed the water that circled it. At the center of the island sat a frozen heart the size of one of the houses back in Charmsend.

They continued to walk down, down, down the path until they were crossing a poorly crafted bridge made of stray logs woven together.

"This is a hazard, if I've ever seen one," Merlin muttered as they crossed it.

"No one asked you, bat," the badger growled.

As they walked around the frozen heart, Lore shuddered at the cold rolling off it. The movement only caused the spear at her back to press deeper.

With the frozen heart behind them, they were met with another flimsy bridge that led to yet another island. Lore noticed the small fires along the shore's edge. Each had a plump roast slowly being spun over it. The gazes and grunts of various animals were nothing compared to the bear in the center of the island. Lore felt like she was the size of Mathilde as the bear's eyes followed them.

He was seated on a throne of mismatched bones. Beneath him lay what looked like a pool of spilt ink.

"And what do we have here?" He hummed.

"Caught them snooping in the cliffs above, sir," one of their captors said, jabbing the spear against Killmoore's back to force the fox forward.

The bear—who she could only assume was Mordred—ran his tongue over his teeth, savoring the scene playing out in front of him.

"You've come crawling back to us?" Mordred joked, earning a laugh from his band of thieves sitting on the sidelines.

"What are you talking about?" Mathilde demanded, as if she were the one holding the bear by spear point.

Not now, Mathilde, Lore thought. *Killmoore was right.* Her desire to walk in Gannon's footsteps will wind up getting them killed. *I doubt Gannon would want Mathilde to be blazing into danger.*

The bear grabbed his rotund belly, and it jiggled a little as he laughed. "You mean he hasn't told you?"

Lore bit down on her lip, and a pit opened in her stomach. An abyss she felt like she was falling into. And she wasn't the only one troubled. She watched the mental spiral that Mathilde refused to go silently down.

Jaw tightened, Mathilde shifted her gaze to Killmoore, who was still quiet. "Killmoore," she said, a bit weaker than before.

"Quite clever moniker you gave yourself," the bear added as he adjusted himself in his self made throne. "Though I'd say it doesn't really suit you."

"Oh, enough with the pussy footing, just tell us whatever it is you find so humorous," Merlin seethed. The iron shackles around his hands glowed orange like the center of a fire flower.

"Okay, okay. Cool it, short stuff," the bear said with a casual flip of his paw that Lore noted could easily shred a face to ribbons.

Animalfolk snickered on the sidelines and consumed the air where there would have been silence. Mordred smiled. "Once upon a time there was a little fox that lived happily in the village at the foot of the mountain until Northern Invaders continued to hammer the town with their looting and capturing of locals. It wasn't long before the fox became fatherless. So, this fox did the smart thing and joined me and others who sought refuge further in the mountain with the hopes of sending dear ol' mom some goods."

Lore looked at Killmoore, searching for any twitch, subtle cue, or shift. But the fox stood still. Like the words from Mordred's story turned him to stone.

"The fox was decent among our ranks, but never really soared with the…" The bear paused, searching for the proper word. He laughed to himself and clasped his clawed paws together. "The *culture* we built here."

"I think you mean 'senseless brutality,'" Killmoore corrected under his breath.

The badger struck the back of the fox's legs. It made Lore's friend instantly drop to his knees.

Mordred continued. "So one day after we did what we had to do for survival," he side eyed Killmoore, then returned his gaze to the rest of the group. "He fled like a coward."

Lore looked to Merlin, who seemed less deep in thought and more steeped in frustration that not only at the fact they were captured, but also that their traveling companion had been a fraud the whole time.

So much for an experienced, level-headed leader. Lore held her head up a little higher, faking whatever she could so that Mordred wouldn't know the terror that trembled in her bones. "We didn't come here for dirt on our friend," she said through grit teeth, "We came for the library's keepers you wrongfully imprisoned."

The bear had a wash of amusement on his face as he rose from his throne. His footsteps sounded like thunder as he walked towards Lore, and the spilt ink beneath the throne puffed up into feather clouds.

Are we too late?

"What's a human doing with antlers, anyway?" the bear teased as he grabbed the rack protruding from her head and gave a hard, taunting pull.

Lore snapped free and her gray eyes hardened like the fine edge of a blade. "Don't put your damn hands on me," she spat. It felt like someone else had taken the wheel for her at that moment and she was just along for the ride.

Mordred put his paws up. "Ooh. A tough girl, eh?"

The onlookers laughed and squealed with delight.

"We will be leaving with the keepers," Lore asserted, ignoring what her gut told her about the feathery pile at the foot of Mordred's throne.

"You come to cover their unpaid fees for living in my territory?"

Fees for what? Keeping the mountain safe? Lore's face twisted into a scowl as the not-so-distant memory of the fog monsters found its way back to her.

"Fees that you pulled from your furry ass!" Merlin shouted.

The bear leaned forward and ran a long, icy claw along Lore's chin, bringing her eyes to his. "If ya ain't gonna pay their fees, then the only way I'll release them is if you bring me back the Moon Drop." Each word sounded like it was dipped into a bowl of honey.

One minute, Lore was listening to the demands of Mordred, then the next thing she knew she was in a garden holding a plant whose leaves were wide, flat, and a vivid green. There was an old woman there with her. No matter how long Lore looked at her face, it never shifted from a face that was fuzzy like TV static, but her words were clear.

"Put it in the ground, Moon Drop, but be gentle with the roots."

Then, Mathilde's shrill but exhausted voice penetrated the shattering sky of Lore's memory.

"Where is this Moon Drop?"

What is *a Moon Drop? Because surely what she remembered from her past didn't exist in this world. Right?*

The bear returned to sit upon his throne, then rested his snout on his paw. "Loch Luan."

Lore internally sighed. Clearly, they were supposed to know it when they found it. Hopefully Merlin would.

But the Wielder didn't seem happy at the news.

"Loch Luan?!" Merlin shouted. "Are you insane?!"

The bear shrugged. "Not insane enough to do it myself." A smile spread across his face as he patted the arms of his throne. "I've been sending the keepers one by one up to retrieve it for their freedom, but the only freedom they meet is that from their flesh."

Her imagination painted a vivid picture of skin and muscle ripped from the thin bones of the corvids' decayed corpses. Lore grit her teeth. *And the worst part is this bear doesn't seem to give a damn.*

"Their bodies always wound up washing back up here on our underground beaches."

"You know the artifact is protected by the Warden. You're setting yourself up for failure, sending ravens who have most likely only ever read about such dangers from the safety of the Sanctuary."

The bear's muzzle twitched in amusement. "Got the attention of a Wielder, didn't it?"

Merlin looked ready to shoot back another sarcastic answer, but Lore cut in.

No reason to poke the bear more than they already have.

"Why do you want this Moon Drop?" she asked.

The bear smirked. "Let's just say it has the power to restore what's been lost to the individual who possesses it."

"Deal," Lore said flatly. This was the only barter that could be agreed upon without the senseless slaughter of her and her friends. Her steeled gaze shifted to Merlin, whose ego was starting to pull at the frayed ends of his outward-facing self.

"Wonderful," Mordred replied. "Glad you see it my way." He gave a head tilt to one of their captors, who tossed the bag of weapons to Mordred. "I'll be keeping these, but you can have this." He laughed as he crumpled up a map and tossed it to Lore who caught it with the bitter taste of copper flooding her mouth from biting her cheek..

"Safe travels," Mordred mocked as the group turned to start their journey back up to the surface.

NINETEEN

Snowflakes continued to caress the tops of Lore's cheeks with frost laced kisses when they reached the surface again. She halted at the mouth of Mordred's entrance and watched as Killmoore whipped around on his heels. The nerves nipped at the back of her throat with the anticipation of a fight that was certain to unfold.

Did he stop because he feels he has to explain further on Mordred's story?

"Why didn't you do any magic there?" He pointed an accusatory finger at Merlin, who just raised his iron covered hands in annoyance.

I see we are walking right past that detail of confusion and straight to the gates of frustration. Why does this feel familiar?

"These shackles aren't your run of the mill. They must have had the keepers perform some sort of hallowed blessing on this to bind my abilities." Merlin's gold eyes glinted with a spark that revealed he would like to burn the whole mountain down if it meant Killmoore would be consumed in that fire. "Also, I don't think we need to be taking suggestions from a clear deceiver."

His magic could be bound? Why hadn't he done that to Crinkle years ago?

Soft, falling snowflakes filled the silence. If it were any other day, she would have marveled at the snow globe they were in.

"I still can't believe they expect us to go retrieve this artifact with your hands like that," Mathilde added, rubbing her chin.

Surely she was just searching for any other thoughts or concerns she could address before confronting the one that hurt the most.

"Well, you'd think a bat who likes to brag about how powerful his casting is could break a measly blessing," Killmoore spat, crossing his arms over his chest.

"I don't think arguing about what I can and can't do is what we really ought to be talking about here," Merlin growled. "You *lied* to us."

Mathilde's voice cracked as she nodded in agreement with Merlin. "You could have come clean at anytime."

Killmoore took a step back and let out a hesitant huff.

Lore recognized the fear in his amber eyes. It reminded her of the gut pulling feeling she had felt being the only human in Charmsend. She balled her fists at the thought of the fake story he told about his 'friend.' It played out in her mind again at a rapid speed.

"Killmoore," she took a breath and steadied herself. She needed her voice to be soft and gentle. He won't soften if we continue to attack him. "What really happened? We need to know, especially if we are going to be traveling together."

The fox's gaze was aimed at the ground as he rubbed his arm. "The flier, the one that brought me to Charmsend, was originally from someone that had been a victim to Mordred and his band of thieves. I thought it was my way out, and I could get a fresh start—that I could make myself my own kind of hero."

Silence feasted on the growing tension in the air. Killmoore continued, "Mordred was right about a few things. I was fatherless, but not because of the northern invaders. It was his greed and selfishness. He came from the Northern Lands and vowed to act as a guard for Cloch Chruinn. We didn't know much why we needed one. We'd never had threats before. But week after week, more of his lackeys came in until there were enough that he began to loot the town. The thing he said he'd keep us safe from, he turned around and did."

Lore's nails pulled away from her palms as she heard the fractures in the fox's pitch.

"Then it wasn't long before I was traded. My parents couldn't pay some ridiculous fee and Mordred requested they turn me over instead."

Tears welled in the corners of his eyes as the fox began to drown in his own memory. "They refused at first, but then, when Mordred said he could get me a warm meal and that no further harm would befall her or me, they both agreed."

Lore took a step towards Killmoore, who was still apologetically muttering out what happened.

"He lied, of course. As my father handed me over, one of his underlings cut him down from behind. That day, I felt my father's blood soak my fur." He brought an arm up to wipe away his stray tears. "Life with Mordred was hard and this…" He grabbed at the Soul of the Ocean beneath his shirt. "This was my way to a better life. And one day, maybe I'd come back to bag the bear."

Lore reached out to pull Killmoore in an embrace, but the fox stepped backward, away from her grasp.

"None of that changes that we still can't trust him, Lore," Merlin spat, rattling the chain links of his iron prison.

Killmoore's eyes glistened with heartbreak.

"Don't," she uttered.

But her words were too late as the fox turned and ran.

Lore's nails bit at her palms once again, as she turned to face Merlin, "What was that?!"

The bat's face stayed blank. "What I said was the truth," he insisted.

"He bared his bleeding heart, and you just stomped on it. He may have hid his past, but he was striving to be better," she shot back, feeling her head start to ache. The antlers seemed to weigh more the longer she spent looking down at the bat in anger. "He *left* them. He's expressed remorse. And he's *helped* us more than once!"

Merlin narrowed his eyes. "Nothing changes what we came to do."

We are only up here because Killmoore thought there was a way to help me, despite the risk of his past being dug up. A trickle of copper ebbed into her mouth as she punctured her skin. She'd bitten her lip again without realizing it.

Merlin walked around Lore. "Come on Mathilde, let's hold up our end and go get the damned artifact."

Lore's eyes shifted to the mouse, whose face was hidden behind the uncrumpled map.

Reddened eyes peeked over the flimsy atlas. "Come on, Lore," she whispered, reaching for the human's hand as she followed Merlin.

The soft snow crunched beneath Lore's feet the further up they traveled. The journey from the carcass in the ravine to the edges of Loch Luan passed in silence where there should have been Killmoore's sarcastic virtue that always easily made her and Mathilde laugh. Instead, they had walked in silence as the bat cursed at his hands, still held hostage by the enchanted iron. The warm pinks that painted the sky contrasted with the cool blue. *Wonder which divine artist thought that was an appropriate color choice.*

"We should be about there," Mathilde said, squinting at the map.

"Good. The quicker we get this, the better," Merlin huffed.

The snow continued to compress beneath their feet, and in the distance Lore thought she saw a figure. Her heartbeat picked up, but her pace felt slower. She felt like she was waist-deep in mud. It got harder and harder to move forward, but the fuzzy figure quickly got closer and closer, revealing it was a *pair* of kids seated on a sled.

A little boy with unkempt black hair. "We're going so fast, Lore!" he'd yelled with youthful vigor, holding onto what she could only imagine was a younger version of herself.

As that sled sped by, another slid into its place. Lore looked at an older version of herself and this friend. They had a fluffy black and white dog whose eyes were the color of icicles pulling them this time.

"This was one of the best ideas you've ever had!" he declared with a beaming smile. Then, as that memory slid down the snowy slope, the last one she walked by didn't have a sled at all. They were laying in the snow, looking at the sky.

"Pretty amazing, right?" he'd said.

The Lore from the memory laughed. "It's just a sky."

"A sky we get to look at together," he added with a grin Lore was starting to see as his signature go-to expression.

As their bodies laid in the snow an arm's length apart from each other, she thought how close they looked to adults.

Then, just as fast as the recollections erupted from a spring somewhere in the vast empty shores of her memory, they faded. She was walking beside Mathilde, who kept her eyes down on the map.

"I don't get it," the mouse said. "We should be there."

Merlin stopped in his tracks. The chain's links clanged in the gentle but biting breeze. "We are. But we aren't alone."

Lore couldn't tell where the reflection of the sky started or stopped. Then, she felt a cold spread through her bones as if the frost was lacing itself with her marrow. Her eyes adjusted, and she saw a ferry that was pulled onto the snow covered shore. Beside the boat stood a cloaked figure, hiding everything but a long beak behind its dark hood.

As Lore, Mathilde, and Merlin drew closer to the cryptic figure. It tilted its head with an audible snap, and a jingle of keys danced on the snow flurries gliding around.

"Warden, we've come for the Moon Drop," Merlin called out over the ongoing snowstorm.

The figure's beak opened and what started as a caw mutated into a meshed monstrosity of animal calls. It sent a wave of nausea through Lore. When the figure waved its staff, she felt like the stranger was willing the world to alter its center of gravity. The acid from her stomach bubbled in her throat.

The snow falling on Lore's cheeks, dissolving on her freckles, turned to pelting hail. Though none grazed her face, she heard the plops of the ice nuggets as they bounced off of Mathilde and Merlin and into the blanket of snow that covered the ground.

Lore felt the cold sensation prickle against her bones as she stepped toward the figure.

"Lore!" Mathilde shouted. "What are you doing?!"

She ignored the questioning calls of her mouse companion and, one foot after another, continued to inch closer to the strange ferryman. The chill that rested in her spread to her chest, where it felt like snowflakes had embedded themselves in her lungs. She was within arm's reach of the stranger, whose protruding beak began to recede. Where the figure's face should have been, Lore was left looking into a swirling sky of stars.

As Lore got lost in the abyss, she began to see faces fill the void. Faces she recalled like Petra's. And Crinkle's. Then faces she did not recall, but only knew from fuzzy recollection. The raven-haired man and the woman with white hair and wrinkles around her mouth and corners of her eyes. Evidence that she must have smiled a lot.

Her hand mindlessly reached out and her fingers grazed the smooth oak staff, and dozens of voices filled her ears. They were whispering, and their mumbles were spoken quickly. So quickly that Lore could hardly make out what they were saying. One thing was certain, though. Once she came into contact with the staff, the chill that had been haunting her bones left, and the whipping hail that pelted her companions, came to a silent stop.

The shifting faces she once looked upon faded into a swirling sea of stars on an abyssal canvas. The whispering that echoed in her ears was whittled down to nothing more than faint, distant murmurs.

Her eyes watched the cloud of her breath fill the space between her and the figure who craned its neck down to get a better look at her. Though with what eyes she couldn't fully be sure of.

"Take me to the Moon Drop."

The figure said nothing, but the ever-present murmuring whispers halted to silence. The stranger reached a feathered arm out for her charm bracelet, which happened to be catching glints of the sun's rays. As the quiet fed the growing dread, only Lore's thoughts were loud and clear.

We wouldn't be in this mess if I never tumbled down that damned well.

Who even says anyone is looking for me, anyway?

If I did the easy thing and just stayed here, then Killmoore wouldn't have run off. Mathilde and Merlin wouldn't be pelted with hail or at the mercy of some corrupt bear so they can finish a quest to get me home.

This is all because of me.

This is my fault.

Without giving it much thought, Lore pushed the canoe off the icy banks and into the frigid waters that bit her fingers with its splash against the wood. She turned to the figure, whose cloak fluttered like it had a mind of its own.

Lore's lungs quivered as she repeated herself to the curious stranger. "Take me to the Moon Drop." She held the figure's nothing-filled stare because a burst of wind erupted from its hood, carrying the sound of an eerie squawk.

Lore boarded the small boat with a clenched jaw. The figure did the same. She noticed the canoe didn't shift under the cloaked figure's added weight. *Strange.*

As it pushed away from the slush on the embankment, Mathilde darted forward, reaching for Lore.

"Wait!" she called, the exhausted desperation rang in her voice.

"I'll be back. It's something I must do alone," Lore called, chewing back any doubt of further breaking up the traveling party.

TWENTY

Lore let the tips of her fingers reach over and caress the top of the lake water. It cast a ripple in the flawless mimic of the winter sky. Her eyes drifted back up towards the cloaked figure who kept a steady stare on the seam of the reflection of clouds and water. *Not really one for talking.* The belly of nerves fluttered like a swarm of bees who erupted from a shaken nest. *I wish Mathilde could have come, but I want her safe.*

The cool breeze lifted off the water and with it Lore's eyes trailed to her left. The shape of the lake was clearly a circle but the closer they got to the islancd, the more it appeared to have a crescent-shaped appearance. An illusion depending on where you stood on the frozen shore.

The canoe scratched against the frozen shore and the figure lurched from the boat. Again, it gave no evidence of the stranger's weight ever leaving it. As the cloaked stranger tied the ferry to a stump, Lore noticed the beak materialize back into view. She carefully set foot onto frozen land again, the sound of the snow crunching beneath her step brought a strange sort of comfort. If the figure was ethereal, and somewhat of a ghost, at least the ground she walked on was surely there.

Her eyes gazed out to the line of sleeping trees whose bare branches held who knows how many pounds of snow. Ice crystals bloomed from the tree's crevices and crannies. Then, she spotted a tall upright stone that was covered in lace spun frost.

She eyed the cloaked being who didn't give much help as to whether or not to go.

Her legs began to carry her to the standing stone and the closer she got the more it felt like she was walking through jello. Time slowed and she couldn't hear anything other than her heartbeat that echoed in her ear. As she ran a hand along the stone the frost nipped at her fingertips, but the embossed knot work tempted her touch to not recoil from the frosted bite. She knelt down to look closer and behind the gauzed frost there were notches in the side of the stone that could have been put there from a kiss of a blade, or the persistent will of stone. The indentations sparked at her touch, and a faint blue light glimmered within them.

She stumbled back and looked over her shoulder at the figure who was leaning on his oak staff. She picked herself up and dusted off stray crumbles of snow. Over the tops of shrubbery she saw another stone, and so she followed. The human followed the stone path, stopping at each one to run her hands over it. They had long past succumbed to the cold, and she saw the tips of her fingers burn as the skin turned prickled pink.

Each time the phenomenon occurred, the sparks and faint light, then another stone would come into her line of sight where it wasn't before.

The final stone sank into the ground with a jarring shake. As it did, a stone table raised a few feet away.

I could only imagine Mathilde scribbling this chain of events in her notebook. She buried her nerves with a hard swallow as she approached the circular flat stone. I'll have to make sure I tell her every detail. At the stone were prints of all kinds of animals. Lore walked around the flat stone until she stopped at a pair of human handprints. She looked down to her hands, the tips of her fingers still burning from the bitter cold, and without a second thought slid them against the frigid stone. A ring of icicles burst from the center. Lore winced, not watching to see what else sprang from the stone table. After a few moments of silence, she took a look back to the table her hands were at, and behind the ring of spiked ice sat a glass orb with swirling white smoke.

Is this it? The Moon Drop?

She lifted a hand from the stone to reach for the orb, then she felt a warm light wash over her freckled cheeks. She was met with a beam of green that rushed into the sky. It soon began dancing with streams of deep blue and purple light. She lifted her other hand from the stone to grab the smoke filled orb and when she did the dancing light above her dwindled until it died. Then, all at once, she was swallowed by darkness.

She felt the ball in her hands when she looked down at it. It glowed with the colors of light that were dancing in the clouded sky. She looked around for any other sign of light, and then she was met with an eerie silver glow. Sparkling snow fell from its hindquarters.

"You again," Lore said through gritted teeth.

The Great Stag stopped only for a moment to cast a dismissive look at the human before continuing its walk through the abyss. From each step of the silver-hoofed stag, glittering trees and shrubs erupted from the murky shadows beneath. Lore's eyes grew in awe as she stared at the branches where shimmering stars hung like golden apples ready to be picked. Lore scrambled to stand. She noticed the lack of pain in her legs while she brushed away the darkness that clung to the fiber of her wool sweater.

"You can't just leave me here!" She called out, rushing after the spirit. Her hands firmly grasped on the glass sphere.

The Stag continued its walk to some unknown destination and continued to leave a silver forest in its path.

Lore caught herself as a thick, twisting tree root seemed to reach out and grab her legs. A ragged breath escaped her as she clutched the glass orb closer to her chest. "That was close," she uttered, her words shimmered with a metallic sheen to them as they floated from her mouth. Her eyes drifted back to the Stag who was weaving between the oaks, whose height would fool you into believing they had always been here and had seen so much pass by them.

"Wait!" Lore called out again.

Then it stopped, and Lore felt like Lady Luck may be on her side. The ethereal spirit knelt down next to a lone flower, whose petals twisted into a tight bud. Lore closed the distance between herself, the spirit, and the flower. She could feel beads of sweat line her palms.

"So, now what?" she asked in a whisper.

The Stag reached out and touched the closed bud with the tip of its nose and from it the petals unfurled into full blossom. When the soft yellow petals deepened to brown, Lore felt a cool rush to her fingertips. Looking up, she saw a young girl, whose freckles were scattered the same places as hers.

The child didn't seem to notice Lore, the Stag, or the otherworldly plane they were on. She was far too busy playing with a stuffed toy. With a closer look, it was what appeared to be an alligator from a claw machine.

Lore swallowed hard. She reached for the stuffed toy. When her hand met the soft fabric, she heard screaming nearby. She flinched and pulled her hand back quickly.

The girl's owl-sized gray eyes reflected an image of two adults screaming at each other. Their screams hung in the air, even after the picture faded. The only other sound she could hear was the frantic beat of her heart against her ribcage.

The Stag rose and mindlessly wandered off.

Lore scrambled to her feet, determined not to lose sight of the creature, and a little desperate to get away from the *ick* feeling of familiarity with that girl.

The Stag started moving again, and Lore attempted to follow.

Lore's legs ached as she pressed to catch up, jumping over silver roots and side-stepping the occasional sentient tree root and shrub.

The Stag finally came to a halt by a waterfall.

Lore doubled over and tried to catch her breath. When she looked at the spirit to give it a piece of her mind, her jaw slackened.

The waterfall was rushing starlight and poured into a creek filled with metallic glitter. In the center of the creek was the same girl, but this time the raven haired boy was with her.

She looked so different from the one who burst from the blooming flower. The one who had empty eyes filled with arguments. This little girl seemed happy and full of life.

They were standing together on a rock path to the other side of the river. A glowing red salamander sat on the smooth flat stone in front of the children

"Now, the trick to catchin' em lil' critters is ya gotta be quicker than them," the boy explained to the eager little girl.

The little boy squatted on a smooth rock that the glitter was rushing past. "'You watchin'?" he called with a grin. "Better take notes with your notebook if you have it." Then the boy lurched forward, and Lore's stomach dropped, worrying the silver waves would carry him away.

He emerged, black hair sticking to his face.

The little girl laughed and reached a hand down to help him out.

Lore shuddered as she buttoned the green flannel over the wool sweater. Her breaths were short and quick, and her eyes stung as if she opened them under water at a pool.

The Stag was quick to move over the stepping stones. The children dissipated like ghosts who were never there.

Lore quickly followed, but when she stepped on the first stone, the others drifted farther and farther from her. Her eyes met with the Stag who was already on the other side of what was once a small creek.

Lore sucked on the inside of her cheek, looking to where she just came. The trees were busy knotting themselves shut tight. Her only option was to go forward. Without thinking, she counted to three and jumped. The next thing she knew, she was being carried downstream in a river of stars.

She waved her arms frantically, "*HELP!*" she yelled, but the Stag didn't come. Lore felt her grip on the glass sphere loosen as the rushing waters tried to separate the two.

Then, her body jerked under a sudden strike against her antlers. They had caught a low hanging tree. *They were actually being helpful.*

Lore wriggled herself free and climb up on the branch. She held tight as the branch retracted into some unknown part of the cosmic forest.

Beneath her, she caught sight of the Stag, who didn't seem to notice her whizzing by.

When the tree branch finally met its trunk, Lore crashed to the ground. The sensation of falling into a dark pit was happening all over again. There was a *cracking* sound when she landed. She stood to see the cause and gasped.

The glass orb had shattered. In its pieces, the dancing lights formed faint reflections of the freckled-face girl. Swirling smoke started rising from the mess, forming a tall man. His face was not fully there, but his hands were all too comfortable as they traveled through the girl's long brown hair.

The back of Lore's neck itched, but no matter how much she scratched it, the feeling of his lips wouldn't leave her. Tears welled in her eyes. As she watched the light and smoke intertwine, a bright white light flashed nearby, and a gentle voice called out for her.

"Moon Drop?"

"Moon Drop, come here."

Lore ran as fast as her legs could carry her and suddenly the scene with the smoke and dancing lights seemed like another lifetime. A short and stout old woman greeted her. The stranger's wrinkled smile gave her a warm feeling. *As though she were home.*

The woman looped her arm through Lore's and led her to a cramped kitchen. "We were just about to ice the cookies. Your favorite part," the woman mused.

She then handed Lore a butter knife and a plain cookie. Lore's brain felt so scrambled from the whiplash that she could barely hold the items, but this was the same woman she had seen before. *If someone like this is waiting at home for me, then I need to get back soon.*

"What are you gawking at?" the old woman asked as she spread pale pink frosting over a heart-shaped cookie.

"N-nothing." She looked at her own cookie. The corners of her mouth pulled down into a frown when she realized she was holding only half of a heart.

Outside the kitchen window, Lore saw the Stag being swarmed by fresh powdery snow. Its icy stare bore into her, and even though she knew this place wasn't really her home, she wished she could stay and revel in it a bit longer.

She gulped and looked back at the woman, who was now icing her third cookie. *I don't want to go.*

She forced herself to say, "I have to go," and set her un-iced cookie on the green countertop.

"Well, when you change your mind, I'll be here," the woman replied.

Lore stepped away from the kitchen, and the whole scene transformed into puffs of white cotton that floated into the sky of nothingness.

Tears streamed down her cheeks, and she collapsed on the ground, bringing her knees up to her chest. The heaviness that usually weighed on her neck was now square on her chest as she choked back the cries that burned her throat. The pain normally surging through her calves ran rampant in her chest while she tried to navigate the waves of emotions.

The Stag knelt beside her and rested its head on her.

She flinched, then peeked through her fingers at the animal. "Why did you bring me here if you were going to take me away so soon?"

It said nothing, just stared at her with milky eyes.

Lore wiped the snot streaks away with the sleeve of her flannel. The echoes of the kids playing at the creek floated in the air.

Were all these things real? Things that happened? During life before the well?

Her hands began to tremble, and she clenched her jaw tight, bracing against the next thought. *Then that meant the image of the man in the smoke...* She caught herself before being pulled under by that riptide.

Her eyes burned, and she couldn't fight the scream that had been building in her throat. She threw her arms around the Stag's thick neck and sobbed into its silver fur. Until a blanket of frost enveloped around her and a steady beat filled her ears.

Thud. Thud. Thud.

Her lungs began to steady.

Thud. Thud.

Tension drained from her muscles, and her jaw unclenched.

Thud.

And as frost danced in her bones, she slipped away from the Celestial forest the Stag had brought to life with its every step.

Lore jolted awake. A bead of sweat dried down her forehead. She pushed aside the piles of blankets that she had been under. Her eyes scanned the room, desperate for Mathilde, but she instead met the gaze of a familiar raven.

"Oh, I see we're awake now," he noted in a rather bored tone.

"Where are my friends?"

Did they leave me?

The pace of her heart quickened.

Did they try to fight the cloaked figure?

Her breath felt shallow as she tried to find a steady pace.

Are their bodies gonna end up underground like Mordred said?

She blinked back tears.

They have to still be alive. They have to. Who else would have brought me here?

Lore felt the curious gaze of the raven dig into her.

Did I wash up back on the shores of the crescent moon lake?

The delicate lining of cold still clung to the surface of her skin and made her mindlessly reach in the bed, her eyes locked with the melancholic raven.

What happened to the Moon Drop?

The raven's standard long and sallow expression twisted. "Your friends?" He mused uncharacteristically. "Now that, that is exciting."

Lore moved out of the bed so she had something between them.

"They're off to take the Moon Drop to Mordred."

Lore's brow pulled tight. "That's impossible, I broke it."

The raven tilted his head to the side. "I saw it when Crosby brought you back."

"Crosby?!"

"Well, who else?"

How did Merlin and Mathilde make it back, then? Were they with Crosby? Or did they count their losses and leave me behind?!

Lore stomped a foot. "Oh, I don't know, maybe the bat or mouse I was traveling with?!"

The crow crossed his wings. "They came here worried because they said you'd been gone for hours with the *Warden* of all folk—you really must pick better company for yourself, child."

That cloaked figure was the Warden?

There was a more pressing issue, and Lore's heart raced at the thought. "We need to put The Moon Drop back." She didn't know how she knew that, but she *knew* it. Maybe her dream, vision—whatever—of it breaking was an *instruction*. Or a warning. Because why else would the only negative memory appear once it was *broken*? And if she couldn't recall more like *that*...maybe it was better *not* to restore them.

She still wanted to go home to the old woman, but Killmoore wasn't certain she'd get her memories back just by returning to her world. So, would it really be so bad if she aborted this part of their mission in order to do what needed to be done?

The raven's smile turned to a frown. "But then my brethren can't return home."

Before Lore could react, the large covid blocked the door. "I can't let you leave if it means the other keepers will stay imprisoned."

Lore glanced over her shoulder and saw the window on the far end of the sleeping quarters. *I told myself I'd never go crawling in or out of windows again.* At the sound of a *click,* her eyes snapped back to the door. The raven had left her. *Alone.*

She heard his voice call through the wood. "Don't take it personally."

Lore gritted her teeth in frustration.

"But you just have to stay put until your friends return with mine."

Lore whirled around on her heels and her hands thudded against the frame of the window. She could see trees and grass, so she couldn't be that far from the entrance. The window was a porthole. The kind of window you'd see on ships. *Oh, I'm never going to fit through this.* She let out a frustrated cry and covered her face with her hands.

Tap tap.

She spun on her heel and met the unnatural yellow eyes of Crosby through the glass.

"Human," he croaked. "The Lore human is awake."

She wiped her bitter tears off on her pants. "Crosby, do you have a way out of here?"

"Crosby has all the wares. What do you need?"

She tried to control the annoyance spreading over her face. "No, not wares," she began to explain. "a way out."

"No shiny ways. No shiny ways in Crosby's collection."

Lore groaned and turned her back to the window so her shoulders pressed against the wood. She then slid to the ground and pulled her knees to her chest. The smoke memory of the man played out again in her mind.

Stop that. She bit her lip to ground herself. *We need to be* here, *not lost in what may have happened.*

There was a small part of her deep down in her chest that knew those things *had* happened, but she wasn't ready to process that information.

Rocks falling through her antlers made her shoot up.

Oh, that damn crow—tossing in who knows what.

When she stood and looked back to the window, the crow's bright yellow eye was gone, but in his departure, a key fell from her antlers onto the floor.

She picked it up. The end of the iron key had a rusted fish figurine. Lore scrutinized the key, feeling the scales, looking at the way its mouth turned upward.

"The all-knowing salmon," she whispered. Running her finger along the smooth part where the teeth should have been. She bolted to the door and shoved the key in and after a brief moment, it subtly vibrated in her grasp, taking shape to the lock.

"How did Crosby get a hold of an all-knowing key?" she murmured to herself as she peeked out into the narrow hall.

Empty. She slowly closed the door behind her, the sound of it softly latching echoed in the corridor. Her chest began to rise and fall as she took a quiet step. Which way should I go? She looked to her left. The hall seemed to go on forever. Then glanced to her right, and the salmon key warmed in the palm of her hand.

Right, it is.

Her pace began to quicken as she rushed for a way out. The cavern spilled out into a room of bookshelves. *The library. The exit was close.*

"Oh, where was it now?" the raven hummed as he looked over the shelves lined with tomes whose spines appeared to be bound by cobwebs. "S," the raven murmured as he ran a long single feather along the spines.

Lore saw the empty welcome desk, and the door wasn't much further from it. Her heartbeat drummed a loud solo in her ears. She knelt by the bookshelf, watching the raven as he thoughtfully bobbed his head in between the shelves. As the keeper turned to the next chain of bookshelves, her feet slowly and quietly took her across the opening. The welcome desk was within reach, and the door. Not much farther than that. As Lore crossed the threshold to the foyer, she spilled from the inky dark void that Lore mistook for a wall when they first arrived. She brushed some shadow goop off her arm and shook some free of her antlers.

A flustered squawk materialized from behind her, sending static to her fingertips. She bolted for the door, her hands trembling as she tried to open it. *Locked.*

A stack of leather-bound books thumped against the welcome desk.

Her heart frosted over.

"And where do you think you're going?" the raven demanded.

With a quick movement she shoved the salmon key in the lock. As the crow stepped towards her, she pushed free and ran beneath a snow flurried sky.

"You mustn't interfere!" the raven called from the door.

If he left, no one would be there to keep all the precious books safe. He was bound by duty to the library until his friends returned.

The image of shimmering obsidian scales slipped through her mind. Her legs stopped, and as she pushed away the thoughts of Petra, it allowed her stinging lungs to gulp some of the thin mountain air.

Can't stop now, Moon Drop, a warm voice cooed in her ear.

She felt the embrace of the old woman around her, though the phantom of her was nowhere in sight.

Lore swallowed hard and took off running.

TWENTY-ONE

The cold lingered on the apples of her cheeks as she made her way under the ribs of the long dead creature. The secret opening was already agape. She swallowed hard, noticing the sleeping guards. Lore crept by them a bit stealthier than the raven back at the Keeper's Library.

Inching down the narrow stairwell, the wall eventually opened and she could safely peer below. Mathilde's voice carried up to where she was hiding. She felt a rush of relief wash over her as her companions were not maimed or dead, or worse, alive, but tortured.

But those fates could be just around the corner for them.

"The Moon Drop." Her voice was flatter than usual. Lore then rushed down the winding stairs and peered around the frozen heart.

A badger was busy freeing Merlin's hands from their iron prison, and Mathilde set the orb of dancing light at the bear's feet.

Seeing the Moon Drop again and intact sent a tingle through Lore's fingertips. She recalled how cold it was to touch. *Not even Merlin's golden flames could have warmed me.*

The remaining crowd of keepers flapped their wings with how close their freedom happened to be.

Mordred leaned down to pick up the fragile glass in his mighty paw, and Lore couldn't wait any longer.

It needed to be returned.

"Hey, you honey slurping son of a bitch!" she called as she rushed down the stairwell to the little island inside the cavern.

Mathilde's green eyes opened to the size of emeralds. "Lore!" she called and scampered toward the human.

"Lore, you're—" the bat rubbed over his free hands, "You're alive?"

She furrowed a brow, not liking his awe and surprise to see her standing before them. "Of course, I am."

Mathilde hugged her leg. "Then you'll get to bring the keepers back with us. How lovely," the mouse mused.

Lore rested a hand on her head. "Mathilde, we have to return the Moon Drop."

Mordred let out a gruff snarl. "Like hell you will. It's mine now."

The bear's grip on the glass ball tightened, and Lore's hand scratched at her chest like that would help free her heart from the icy grip. All it did was put a distorted smile on the bear's features.

Mordred squeezed the glass ball and Lore dropped to the ground as a tightness spread through her chest. The only thing echoing in her ears was the bear's sadistic laugh.

"I believe that's quite enough," Merlin spat as a purple flame left his hand and landed squarely on the bear.

When did his hands get free?

The lackeys surrounded the three. Right as they were going to charge, Merlin waved a hand, and a wall of purple flames danced around the trio. Each member of Mordred's army collapsed to the ground.

Mathilde helped Lore to her feet, and Merlin picked up the glass orb that rolled free from the sleeping bear's hand.

"And now it's back in trusted hands." Merlin smiled.

Mathilde furrowed her eyebrow. "You didn't have to kill them!"

He tilted his head, caressing the orb. "They're only asleep, child."

Lore rocked on her heels and shifted her gaze to the group of ravens behind the throne made of their dead brethren. "Why didn't you do that trick earlier?" Lore asked, a bit annoyed.

The bat rolled his eyes. "I know you hit your head when you fainted, but I was shackled with magic-blocking iron until now."

"And how did you get out of those, exactly?" Lore pressed.

Merlin had a sparkle in his eye. Clearly, he was ready to gloat about his greatness. "Salt, my dear! It has cleansing properties."

"Salt?" Lore crossed her arms. "How did you get hold of salt?"

"Well, we were betting on Mordred's cruelty—"

Mathilde cut in. "And the big ole bear gave us salt water when we said we were thirsty, which Merlin soaked his cuffs in after the guards left us."

That was actually pretty smart.

"Who's ready to return to some cobwebs and bookshelves?" the mouse asked the keepers.

Joyous murmurs spread through the crowd of corvids.

"Come on now, watch your step. Best not to wake them," Merlin cooed as the corvids followed behind Lore and Mathilde. "Though an eternal sleep would be hard to wake from," he muttered, following behind the group.

At the mouth of the entrance, Lore halted in her tracks and she forgot about the guards. She put a finger to her lips to signal the murder of ravens to be silent. As they did, she peeked out the narrow cavern and her heart felt lighter at the sight of an empty campfire.

She led the group out, and from behind the bones protruding from the ground at the entrance of Mordred's hideout, she heard a familiar voice gasp out.

"*Lore?!*"

She turned to meet the fox's worried eyes.

"I hid the guards over there. Where's Mathilde?!" His words fell from his mouth in a rush.

The tension left her shoulders. She was glad to see Killmoore again. A subtle grin pulled on her cheek as the mouse revealed herself from behind the towering conspiracy of ravens.

"I'm right here," she called, then her sweet tone soured. "The one who didn't leave."

Understandable reaction, I suppose.

The fox's tail drooped to the dirt. "Listen, I'm sorry. I shouldn't have left," he admitted sheepishly.

Merlin stood beside Lore, the glass orb cupped gently in his hand, "But you did, and it doesn't change anything now that you returned."

Killmoore's snout wrinkled at the bat's hard words.

"What brought you back?" Lore asked over the bat.

Amber eyes met hers. "I saw flames spiraling in the sky and I thought—"

"Well, as you can see, they are fine," Merlin cut in.

The fox's ears flattened.

Lore reached a hand out, and the fox reached for a shake.

She pulled him into a hug. "I've missed you, you sarcastic fox."

He hugged her back. "Glad to be back." He looked at Merlin from the corner of his eye. "I vow to look out for you and Mathilde."

Mathilde hesitantly drifted closer. Until the fox opened an arm, and she joined the hug. Anger rolled off the mouse's fur like water off a duck's back, and the tension that was previously on her shoulders melted away.

Merlin groaned. "Okay. Happy, happy, joy, joy all around. Let's get these corvids back to the library and move on to our real mission."

The ash colored doors opened and the stoic raven's demeanor dropped as a single tear escaped his chestnut eyes. "Welcome home."

The hugs were long, and the library smelled of sweet cinnamon and apples. Lore peeked in the library section searching for Crosby, but could not spot him. *He may have already left.*

"Thank you," the raven said. The relief in his voice washed away the cycle of stress and loneliness that he previously had lived through.

"Of course," Lore said.

"A deal's a deal, though," Killmoore added. "Did you find anything about Lore?"

The raven gave a nod and brushed off imaginary dust from his gray robes. "Are any of you familiar with the Crowned One Prophecy?"

Lore shrugged and looked at Mathilde, who was busy flipping through the pages of Gannon's entries. Killmoore shook his head, and Lore's brow scrunched as she watched Merlin's stare go blank.

Did he know something?

"Well, an old text coming from the Romplands reads:

> The forgotten one, the crowned one will be.
> Restore what has long been dead.
> In order to set Thimbleton free,
> The choice must be made.
> Prepare to be the one who fled,
> Or all humanity shall be shed."

Amidst the cheers of a coming home party, the band of adventurers remained silent. Lore felt like the frost of the Stag's breath was on the back of her neck. She shuddered from the chill.

"So," The raven continued, this time his plain face warmed, "Once you snuff out whatever evil is afoot that threatens Thimbleton and its Guardians, then you'd be sent home."

Lore nodded mindlessly.

"Well, thank you," Killmoore said, "though that tells us nothing in regards to her memories." Then he looped arms with Lore and cleared his throat to get Mathilde's attention away from the scribbling in Gannon's journal. She was certainly writing down the prophecy.

"We will be on our way, as the Moon Drop must be returned to Loch Luan," Killmoore added.

Lore watched as Merlin's face scrunched like a wet newspaper. *What was he thinking?* Her stomach turned over on itself while she watched the bat look over the Moon Drop, scrutinizing it with his golden eyes. Turning it over and over again within his fingers as if its essence could be unraveled in his hands like thread.

"Merlin," Lore said.

"Hm?" The bat didn't meet her eyes as he was focused solely on the Moon Drop.

"What do you make of this?" She paused, feeling as ridiculous as the antlers that adorned her head. "Prophecy?"

His golden eyes finally tore away from the silver light of the Moon Drop. "I think it's something to consider."

He swallowed hard. "There have been many who try to go against what the spirits whisper and it never winds up well. I suspect whatever perceived evil threatens Thimbleton, they must be powerful, strategic, and know that they are being closed in on. So we must act, when."

He paused and clicked his tongue. "When the opportity arises."

Mathilde nodded in agreement. "We know about the prophecy now, and that in itself is power. We know what to be on the lookout for."

"Precisely," Merlin muttered, his gaze being drawn back to the Moon Drop still in his hands.

TWENTY-TWO

The echoes of laughter and long reunited hugs played on repeat in Lore's mind as Killmoore rowed the canoe across the mirror of a lake. *When I complete this prophecy, will I be welcomed home like that?*

"It's beautiful," Mathilde murmured as she ran a hand over the water's surface, causing ripples like Lore had on her first trip over Loch Luan.

I guess I can only hope that's what is waiting for me.

"Still can't believe you guys saw the Warden," Killmoore sighed, "and I wasn't there for it."

"Well, maybe if you stuck around you'd get to experience the exciting bits, too," Mathilde teased.

"Well, the Warden has many things to protect. And since the Moon Drop was taken, I'm sure it's been decided another place needs his watchful eye," the fox added.

Lore's eyes drifted to Merlin, who was sitting on a thick book the raven had given him. The spine's letters were worn away to shadows. Lore chewed the inside of her cheek as she watched the bat surround the orb in a nest of frozen twigs he had collected on their way from the library.

"What are you doing?"

The bat raised his golden eyes to the human's. "Keeping it nice and cool," he said, as if it were obvious.

She felt a pull in her chest as she observed the bat, not quite the sharp pain that brought her to her knees when Mordred had squeezed the orb. But enough of a tug to notice.

A wave of nerves flooded Lore's gut, then the canoe scraped against the frozen shoreline. Her eyes fell back onto the frozen trees with the low hanging stars, the standing stones, that called out to her. "This way," she murmured as she left the boat.

The only sound was crunching snow as the animals followed her through the frozen maze. The island felt different somehow. Emptier than before. Lore let out a shaky breath as the stone table came into view.

"There." She brushed past the shrub and around the gaping hole where a standing stone sunk into the ground. "The orb goes here." She gestured to the middle.

The bat held the nest of frozen twigs, looking over the dancing light in the orb.

"Merlin," Mathilde chimed.

Lore's breath stung as she inhaled and exhaled. *Must be the frigid air.*

"Oh, sorry," the bat said, a bit flustered as she snapped off a few of the unruly branches. Then he sat the orb in the center of the stone.

A click sounded, and the green stream of light surged into the sky again. Followed by the deep purple and blue hues chasing after it.

Lore watched the lights dance in the sky. She felt it was a special moment she got to share with Mathilde and Killmoore. A flutter of butterflies danced in her chest as Mathilde watched with sparkling wide eyes. And that's when the pain started.

It was sudden and sharp. The hurt traveled up to her hips like frost spreading across a window. Lore's knees felt like they were cracked to the bone. Her body dropped with a thud in the soft powdery snow. Lore struggled to open her mouth. Her jaw muscles felt as if they were freezing shut. Her screams caught in her throat with a stinging ache.

Lore couldn't shift her focus off the shivers in her bones from the raw chill of whatever magic was currently breaking her. She felt hands holding onto her shoulders, and another pair rolling her onto her back.

She couldn't feel her legs. All she felt was numb. Her head plopped in Killmoore's lap, and through the pain of what felt like ice settling in her bones, she heard the fear in the fox's snarl.

"Hurry up, bat! Find whatever will make this go away!"

A gentle digit wiped a few tears from Lore's cheek. She locked eyes with Mathilde, who flicked the frozen tears off her fingers.

"We got you," she mouthed.

"*Ah-ha!*" Merlin shouted as he untied the Stag's breath from her side.

Merlin muttered something she couldn't make out. Blueish particles funneled into the orb, and the frost in her bones started to thaw.

Lore felt a weight off her chest. She could breathe easier again.

"Easy," Killmoore whispered while Lore tried to pick herself up.

The weight from her antlers felt heavier.

Did they grow?

Her legs trembled and begged her to sit back down.

Nope. I'm doing this.

Mathilde and Killmoore put themselves under her arms, and she felt the winter air flutter through her fur.

FUR?

She jerked her head down and sure enough, her pants busted at the seams and her waist down was that of a deer.

Shit.

"It's okay, Lore." Mathilde assured.

"We will reverse this before you go home," Killmoore said. As if it were that easy.

Why make promises he can't guarantee he can keep?

Then Merlin cleared his throat. The bat shifted his weight as he adjusted the thick book under his wing flap. *Why didn't he leave it in the boat?*

"Now what?" Mathilde sighed, kneeling down to pick up Gannon's journal from the snow. The green journal splayed out as she doodled down the dancing lights in the frosted night sky.

She must have dropped it when I was overtaken by...the transformation.

Merlin huffed. "Well, there was nothing at the library that was helpful for sending the human home."

"We did find a prophecy though, so I'd say that's better than *nothing,*" Lore added. Her legs ached, but were less shaky now.

"But it doesn't say how you'll get home," Merlin quickly shot back.

Lore looked at Killmoore who took out a flyer from his pack. "We could head south." His amber eyes drifted to Lore. "She can fulfill her role in the prophecy and we can all take note of what happens after in case any more humans decide to spawn into Thimbleton." His tail flicked back and forth. He was annoyed with the bat, but at this point it was a state of normal for their little group.

Mathilde's face lit up. "That would be a nice change of pace." She looked at Lore, hoping to find agreement. "I'm done with the cold."

Lore let a soft laugh slip from her chapped lips. "Maybe we'll find something along the way that can help me figure out whatever evil that prophecy was talking about that needs to be snuffed out."

Merlin eyed the trio and drummed his thin fingers against his chin. "The inhabitants of the Romplands have some access to ancient knowledge, and it is the origin of the prophecy."

Lore watched as the bat marched towards the frozen forest. "Let us go, then. The faster we put the Wayward Mountains behind us, the sooner we can get to the Romplands."

"This is going to be a great story!" Mathilde snapped the green journal shut.

"Maybe we should stop by Charmsend on the way?"

"We could get more supplies," Killmoore mused.

"It's settled, then," Merlin declared before walking off.

Mathilde followed, and as Lore went to follow her, the fox stopped her with a hand on her forearm.

"Lore." His tone scrounged the bottom of the pity barrel. The bat and mouse stopped in their tracks as they turned to see what the fox was going to say.

"I—There's something I need to tell you."

The human's eyes flicked over the bounty hunter. "And what's that?"

"My name," he said as he released her arm from his grip. He picked at the fur around his claws. "The truth is, my name is Arthur."

Lore looked the fox over.

The way his tail anxiously flicked from side to side, observing the way his ears were laid back flat. He was fussing with the fur that protruded between his claws.

She tilted her head, allowing herself to soften, then she smiled. "It's nice to meet you, Arthur."

The fox's amber eyes sparkled, as he scratched an itch behind his ear, not looking at his friends. "Maybe my friends could call me Artie."

Merlin narrowed his eyes. "'Artie'?"

Mathilde scampered over and took the fox's hand. "You look like Art to me."

A rosy glow flushed against the white fur that rimmed Arthur's face. "I can't change the past." The fox shifted as he folded the flier and safely placed it in his pack. "But I did learn a thing or two from it."

"Well, now that we see you, Arthur," the mouse reached for the fox's hand. "we believe in you." Mathilde whispered, the sound of hope echoing off each syllable.

"And I believe in you both, too," Arthur smiled, wiping a tear from his furred cheek.

"What?" Merlin scoffed. "Are we making bargains now?"

"Something like that." Arthur mused as he led Lore and Mathilde away from the stone table, and followed behind Merlin back to the boat. The chill in the air raised the hair on the back of Lore's neck, and she reached to brush her hand up to tousle her russet waves, and felt frost kissing her antlers. It was a relief her legs finally stopped aching, but each morning she felt like the fawn fur traveled further and further up. She met Arthur's gaze, observing her. "Thank you."

Lore raised a brow in question at his statement.

"For always letting compassion be louder than doubt," he clarified.

PART TWO

TWENTY-THREE

"And after we merely escaped with our lives through the fog-swept cavern, we saw a four-leafed clover shining in the moonlight. It was like a lighthouse drawing us in. Each color of the glass glimmered in the dark like they were thin slices of precious gems."

Mathilde peeked out of the corner of her eye to see her sisters still hanging on every word.

Arthur rocked back in his chair. "Oh, there was fog, yeah, but I don't remember it being swept."

Merlin was quick to add in a matter-of-fact tone, "I think Mathilde possesses her father's storytelling ability and really captures her audience with her regaling recollection."

The fox's tail snapped from side to side, but no words fell from his mouth. Lore shuddered from the annoyance radiating from her friend.

Mathilde snapped the green journal shut that once before, maybe Gannon had done in the same manner. "It most certainly *was*, Arthur. I have it written right here."

Minified set the tea tray down on the table and her eyes flicked over to the fox. "Is your name going to change every time you return from an outing?" She laughed at her own joke.

The wooden legs of the chair slammed down and the Fox's ears laid flat. "Arthur is my given name. Killmoore is my bounty hunter moniker." He folded his arms across his chest and gave a grumble. "Having two names isn't that unheard of."

Merlin's large, triangular ears wiggled. "Well, it'd be mighty hard to keep up with who knew you from which of your double lives."

A pause in the room as the fox's eyes drilled into the bat. It wasn't a secret that there was skepticism since their first meeting, and it hasn't improved over spending time together.

Mathilde cleared her throat and opened the book once again.

Lore sipped the warm golden liquid and ran her free hand over the long yellow wool skirt Mildred had sewn her since their return. *I can't believe we have only been back three days, and it felt like we never left.* Notes of honey tickled her taste buds. She watched as Mathilde waved her hand theatrically while reading from the book that was held open in the other.

"When we set foot in the ancient library, we met sprawling rooms and bookcases that towered up to the high ceilings large enough to hold a snake."

Lore recalled the golden-eyed shadow she met at the abandoned estate, just outside of Cloch Chruinn. Memories she wasn't sure would stay with her once she returned home.

The way the creature vanished just as suddenly as it appeared, didn't sit right with Lore. She tilted her head a little to the right, and the weight of her antlers pulled down. She rolled her shoulders back and readjusted as her thoughts spiraled deeper.

The sounds of Mathilde regaling her sisters faded to a soft whisper until the only sound she heard was the tempo of her own breathing.

Then a raspy, male voice echoed in the empty space.

Meet the shadow at the well, for he has secrets to tell.

It sent chills down her spine. Was he trying to warn her? Or was *he* the danger?

Lore drummed her fingers against the wood stained by years of tea spills. The shadow knew where she was from. Though he never said it outright, he seemed to know her. The kleptomaniac creature was definitely always down for a good conversation. The shadow also seemed to know about other planes. Lore took another sip of the tea that was no longer hot, but just right as it passed through her lips, and warmed her stomach. Clearly, he knew the plane she was from, and maybe if she could find him again. She paused at the thought.

I can't make him tell me a way home, but maybe I can cut a deal with him.

She nodded at the thought. Proud of herself for thinking about it. Now she'd just need to figure out what the shadow—that could move between realms—couldn't get himself.

The thoughts alone pulled her away from the quiet sanctity of her mind as the sound of Mathilde's dramatic retelling ensued, like butterflies fluttering around the room as if it were the first day of spring.

"And then, as the mighty bear squeezed the ball that held the very essence of winter itself, Lore fell to the ground. But with Merlin's powerful purple flames, the bear's lackeys were no match." She paused for dramatic effect, looking up, her eyes sparkling, still freshly high from the first adventure she ever went on. "And neither was the bear."

Maybel's eyes grew, and she looked at Arthur, who was quietly thinking to himself as he finished eating the breakfast the sisters had prepared for them the moment they arrived home that morning. "And where were you, exactly?"

"He thought it easier to run away," Merlin chimed in as he took a drink from his cup.

Lore's eyes drifted to the bat. "He came back."

Merlin shrugged. "Still left."

The sound of the chair slamming against the wood made Lore want to jump. Arthur slammed the door on his way out. Through the window, she saw him sit on the porch swing. The winter air rustled his orange fur with the occasional soft tiny snowflake that stopped to kiss his snout.

Lore bit her lip. "Tell us how things have been here? Surely there's been some changes."

Mildred's eyes lit up. "Oh, yes," she mused, tapping a silver shoulder that belonged to one of the twins. "Actually, there is a monthly market that takes place when the sun sets, and the moons rise."

"It happens when the little one is new," Maybel added.

"Moon. That is, the *little* moon," her twin clarified.

"It really is wonderful, though," Mildred continued as she pressed a paw up to her cinnamon cheek. "You'll all have to come with us!" she proclaimed, as if it was already decided.

Lore's gaze shifted to Merlin. Then to Mathilde, who acted like she hadn't spent a single day away from home. "Of course!" the red-clad mouse agreed.

As if a whirlwind blew through their house, the mice left the table and go for their jackets, hats, and gloves. Meanwhile, Lore helped Minifred pick up the mess left behind.

"Will you be joining us?" Lore asked in a whisper.

"'Fraid not," Minifred said, unfazed.

"It sounds like fun, though?" Lore added.

"Not as fun as a quiet house," Minifred said with a smile.

Then, the door blew open, bringing in a cold winter hello on its breeze.

"C'mon Lore," Mathilde called.

"I'll hold down the fort," Minifred teased, motioning for Lore to go.

Lore sat the last teacup on the silver serving tray.

"Okay," she mouthed. Then followed the mice and Merlin out of the yellow manor's warm, familiar embrace.

The old wood creaked as Arthur fell in step behind Lore.

"Where are we going?" he asked, his voice almost inaudible as the merry and cheer of the mice sisters flooded over his words.

"A special market," Lore answered.

The streetlights of Charmsend roamed the cobblestone streets in the chilled night. Moving like ants searching for folk who needed a light to get to the town's center. Lore watched as a light grew brighter and brighter, quickly rushing toward them.

"Grian!" Mathilde called.

The streetlamp circled around the group, its metal feet tapping with mirth. *Almost as if it were dancing.*

"Lead us," Mildred chimed in.

As the mice, bat, fox, and human trailed behind the living flame, the sounds of music and voices echoed down the empty streets.

Lore's breath hitched as she recalled the echoes that traveled through the caverns below the Wayward Mountain. Where Mordred had laid in wait for them.

Arthur's paw, not the breeze caressing her cheeks, brought Lore back to the present moment.

"Don't freak out, but I think I spotted a friend of ours," Arthur whispered in her ear.

Lore looked ahead, over the villagers chatting, and past the colorful banners of the booths, that marked where they had traveled from, to the familiar figure whose bright yellow eyes darted the crowd. Looking for the perfect specimens to hassle until his eyes landed on them. A squawk erupted from his throat as he flapped his wings frantically, calling them over. "Crosby is so happy to see you again."

Lore swallowed what felt like a frozen lump of ice down her throat. *Is he stalking me?*

His next words only chilled her more.

"Crosby knew he'd find you here."

"Oh, it's so good to see you again!" Mildred chimed to Crosby, whose head bobbed up and down, an unnatural thing for the animalfolk.

Lore couldn't place it, but there was a sense of unease around the crow. *It's odd how he's everywhere, and always with just the right item.*

"Crosby has brought you something very sparkly, very nice it is." The crow's voice cracked as he shuffled to behind his stand. He bent over so his tail feathers fanned out for the group to see.

"He brings only the best," Mildred mused as she tried to hide her excitement while rocking back and forth on her heels.

Items clinking and clanking onto the stone ground drew Lore and everyone else's attention back to Crosby.

Lore's hand instinctively reached for her charm bracelet. "And what will be the price for something so shiny?" she asked.

More metal hit the ground behind the crow as he squawked. "No trade, Crosby gives as gift."

Before Lore or Mathilde could question Crosby, the crow shot up, holding a small glass vial between his fore feathers.

"Come close to Crosby," the crow mouthed.

Mathilde, Lore, and Mildred—to Lore's surprise—did just that.

"Crosby holds the Essence of the Great Stag." Crosby then wiggled the small glass bottle in front of them. Inside the bottle, miniscule ice-blue and pulsing purple orbs floated around a single golden petal that seemed to be preserved by fresh frost.

Merlin leaned onto the counter, where Lore hadn't noticed him standing before. "And how is such power contained in something so fragile, like glass?"

Crosby didn't entertain the bat's skepticism, only focused his bulging, yellow eyes on Mildred. "Did you bring them for Crosby?"

The cinnamon-colored mouse nodded and presented a package that was wrapped in blue cloth. "Just as before," Mildred mused and sat the package down on the table.

The crow let out a shrill caw and quickly ripped a piece of yellow fabric from the cloth above his stall, then threaded the cloth through the small hole at the top of the bottle and gestured for Lore to lean down.

She was hesitant, but she did just that, trying to see what the crow wanted her to see behind his wooden stand. Crosby hung the Essence of The Great Stag on Lore's antler. Her face scrunched, and she pulled back. The yellow cloth above the stand got caught on the points of her antlers and her vision became only a brilliant shade of yellow.

Lore growled with frustration as she tried to pull the cloth off. As she fought with the cloth, she tripped over a stray stone in the cobblestone square and suddenly felt paws against her back. Then, as she tried to steady her breath, a sudden jerk on the cloth made her body fold forward.

"Don't worry, Lore. I got it," Mathilde assured.

"Oh, for Warden's sake," Merlin sighed.

Then the blinding yellow floated above Lore, revealing the glass bottle swinging in front of the faces of Charmsend's townsfolk staring blankly at her. Some faces smirked with amusement, and others looked horrified.

Lore's cheeks heated, and she grabbed the swinging glass pendant and yanked it free from the antlers.

"I can take that off your hands," Merlin offered.

Crosby flapped his wings furiously, "Crosby did not give it to tiny bat. Crosby gave it to the *human*!"

Mildred hummed a tune, hoping to calm the crow.

Human, Lore thought with a huff. *I'm not sure for how much longer.*

Merlin reached out an expectant hand, but Lore shoved the charm into her coat pocket.

"It's fine," she grumbled. *No reason to upset the bird again.*

Crosby relaxed at her agreement, but did not take the eyes of everyone at the market off of her.

The heat moved from her cheeks to her ears, and her stomach flipped. "I'm going back to the manor," she said through gritted teeth.

Then, without waiting for a reply from her friends, made her way through the crowd.

The sound of Lore's hoof steps filled the empty cold air as she walked toward the yellow manor. The larger of the two moons hung in the air. Full as the night she shot out from the well. She let out a sigh at the thought. *Still don't know how I am going to find a way home.*

The sound of footsteps that didn't match her pace pulled her away from the hopeless thought of being stuck in Thimbleton forever. Lore stopped, standing as still as a tree in the middle of the path.

"Who's there?" she called.

A warm voice called out to her from the shadows in front of her.

"Oh, human, is that you? My, my, look at how you have changed."

TWENTY-FOUR

From the frigid darkness, Sable emerged and slid her hood down. "How are you adjusting to those? I didn't realize they were at such growth."

"Eh, it's going." Lore sighed and averted her gaze from the hedgehog's kind, but curious, eyes. "The hooves are a bit hard to adjust to."

The hedgehog moved closer. "Here," she said as she dug around in a large brown satchel hanging from her round waist. Sable pulled out a pouch of herbs. The smell of mint seeped from the folded paper packaging and tickled Lore's nose. "This tea here should help relieve any soreness that the weight causes."

Lore gingerly took the tea from the hedgehog. The brown paper crinkled as her fingers gripped it.

"Are you headed to the market?" Lore asked as she shoved the herbs in her other pocket.

"I am, though it's nice to have so many travelers as customers," The hedgehog paused sighed. "Someone is taking business from me."

"Taking customers?" Lore asked as she raised a brow. "The Iron Rose is the best apothecary for miles."

"Well, apparently this salesbird travels beyond that and has prices I can't compete with." Sable let out a defeated sigh as she shook her head. "Tell me, though, how was The Library?"

Lore rocked on her heels as she thought about the journey the Wayward Mountains had required of her to get there. "It was—" Lore thought hard about what to say next. "Different from what I thought."

"Look who came to visit us," Sable mused as a light spilled from behind Lore, projecting her no-longer-fully-human shadow across the hedgehog's features.

Lore looked over her shoulder to see Grian.

"Well, it's good to see you," Sable said.

Grian took off the pointed metal hat that sat over its flame and bowed to the two.

"I better not keep you," Lore started. "I'm sure Grian is ready to escort you to the market square." Her voice sounded more hollow than she meant it to.

Sable smirked. "Oh no, dear." She then pulled a fire flower from her cloak and the small flames danced upward off the petals. "Grian is here for *you.*"

Lore looked up to the lamppost, who held its cold iron metal appendage, which was normally curled close to its thin body, out to Lore.

She then looped arms with the lamppost and turned to say farewell to Sable, but it was too late. The hedgehog had already walked away and the dancing flames' light was already dimming in the distance.

"Homeward, then." Grian escorted her through the door, and they walked to the yellow manor.

The stars glittered in the sky above, and the more they moved from Charmsend's town center, the quieter it got. And more beautiful. Colorful homes decorated the dim streets, creating the most breathtaking image one could ever paint.

"There's a certain stillness at night that makes even the most mundane thing…" She paused, searching for the right word to describe what she was feeling on the late night walk with Grian. Lore shook her head, not able to find it, but settled with, "Dazzling."

The lamp post nodded with a creak of its metal hinges.

"You know, Grian, I don't know if I am ever gonna get to go home."

Grian slowed its pace down and Lore matched the lamp post as her thoughts spilled from her mouth without filter like the waters that ran from the Infinite Run.

"What if fate says I *can't*?" Lore swallowed hard. "If there's no specific purpose my being here, then how can I expect there to be a specific reason I'd be sent back."

Lore's heart sank as the faint memories of people her heart knew, but remained nameless in her mind, played in her mind. The old woman, with eyes that made Lore feel warm hugs. The raven haired boy, whose smile she feels she had seen a thousand times. Not to mention the voices in her head that remained faceless. They were someone to her, too. Regardless of if they had an image.

"It seems hopeless."

The winter wind whipped Lore's braid behind her, and she couldn't find warmth in Grian's cold metal, so she picked up the pace once more and shoved her hands in the pockets of her skirt. Her fingertips touched the glass bottle that Crosby had hung on her antler. The bottle felt like it held a blizzard inside it. The cold that bit the tips of her fingers. Then, a blinding bright light clouded her vision, and suddenly she felt like she was floating. As she looked to her left, she saw rolling fields of green. To her right, she didn't spot Grian, but the old woman with a head full of white hair staring at the sky.

"Just look at that," she said, pointing to the sky Lore had sworn she had just fallen from.

"It's just an empty sky," Lore said as she sat up, and placed one hand on what appeared to be a checkered picnic blanket. The other hand stayed firmly wrapped around the glass bottle.

I hadn't even realized I fully grabbed it.

The Essence of The Great Stag felt like frost continued to trickle onto her hand. She swallowed and looked at the older woman. "Who *are* you?"

The creases in the woman's wrinkled face pulled upward as she smiled. "I am a part of you."

"Are you waiting for me back home?" She paused as she felt like ice punctured the skin of her hand. "Wherever home is."

The woman smiled and as she went to wrap her arms around Lore she said, "I wait no where for you, because I am always with you."

But before her arms could connect to Lore, the woman vanished, and Lore realized she had instinctively removed her hand from the Essence of The Great Stag to reach out to the old woman.

An earth shattering force pressed her back into her body. In the present. What had seemed to just be a daydream broke away and fragmented against the Charmsend sky like an icicle falling from a tree branch.

Grian had stopped, and Lore slowly let go of the lamp posts appendage as she walked toward the steps of the yellow manor. Soft glows of the fire inside beckoning her to feel their warmth.

She looked over her shoulder. "Thank you for seeing me here, Grian."

The lamp post took its metal hat off and bowed the same way it had done before Lore and it had parted ways with Sable. Then turned to walk the long stretch they had just covered.

"Walking back always seemed longer than walking toward," she muttered as she turned the great oak doorknob.

A voice called from under the looming shadow over Gannon's rocking chair. "Back so soon?"

TWENTY-FIVE

Lore walked closer to the hearth, and the dim dancing flames illuminated Minifred's face. The floorboards creaked under Lore's feet as she sat in the seat opposite of Mathilde's sister.

The coal-colored mouse was in a matching yellow sleeping set with pink flowers. Her silver eyes were soft. Minifred gestured to the tea tray on the coffee table between them, directly in front of the fireplace.

Lore nodded and reached for the teapot and poured the water into the daffodil cup. The steam rose as she did and the glass mushrooms on the mantelpiece slept soundly, as only the smallest snore could be heard.

She leaned back in the smaller rocker. Lore wondered if at any point it belonged to a partner of Gannon's. The thought passed by quickly when the groan of the solid beams above them were heard.

"Is," Lore paused, her fingers laced around her teacup. "Is that okay?"

Minifred nodded as she took a drink from her cup. Then brought her hands to her lap, still holding the cup for warmth. "The house speaks, but only when it is silent and empty can it be heard."

Lore reached up to itch a spot on her scalp around the base of the antlers. This had quickly become a new anxious quirk of hers. "So the manor is alive?"

She didn't mean the end of the question to be so shaky, but alas, it couldn't be helped. Her true feelings are becoming harder and harder to conceal as the reality set in with finality that she didn't belong in this place. In Thimbleton.

The sound of Minifred sitting her teacup on the table between them pulled Lore away from her spiraling thoughts. "No."

Lore let a sigh of relief escape. She had come to learn by now there was nothing that shouldn't be unexpected. But this was nice. The houses here were not alive.

"At least," Minfred began again, "not in the way you are thinking."

"What do you mean?"

"The house is alive, but does not live and breathe on its own." Minfred paused as she swallowed a lump that must have been building in her throat, "The bones of a house are brought to life by the ghosts of days past that lived in it."

Lore thought for a moment. Thought of the yellow manor, and all the lives it must have seen before the mice sisters and Gannon called it home.

Lore nodded in understanding, "I think that's beautiful, Minifred."

The mouse nodded. "Beautiful, but at times, torture."

Lore's peace shattered. "'Torture'?"

Minifred let out a sigh and the hearth's fire dwindled further, as if to match the oldest mouse sister. "It's torturous that the fond memories that the home whispers are the same memories that become the ones that haunt us."

Lore's jaw softened, and she searched for the right words to say. Minifred was a mouse of fortitude, who never hinted at needing to express deep thoughts in hope to receive another's comfort.

"Why are you sharing this?" Lore asked

Somewhere in the house, a grandfather clock chimed and Minifred's silver eyes looked Lore over as if she knew it would be for the last time. "Because you asked."

Lore pursed her lips and asked. "Do you enjoy your role?"

"What role would that be?" Minifred asked teasingly.

"Mother."

The mouse's smile faded and her eyes seemed flushed of their usual striking silver. "I will never forget the day our parents died. I could never be our mother."

Lore choked back the urge to back track. "Of course."

"Has Mathilde told you the story?"

Lore shook her head 'no' and the weight of the antlers atop her head made her neck ache. She began rubbing around her shoulders as Minifred cleared her throat.

"I was first born to George and Florence Nim. We called the town of Taper home. A small blink and you miss it kind of village." Her voice was rocky, but Minifred continued. "My favorite thing to do was be in my mother's shadow. I loved attempting to recreate every recipe. Mimic every way she moved when she organized our home. Then I went on to replicate and show similar love and care to my sisters that came after me."

"It sounds like you and your mother were close," Lore added.

"She was my very best friend," Minifred said, not hiding the tear that fell from her furred cheek. "But as closely as I followed her, it would not have prepared me for the day of such tragedy. The day we set out to seek a new start. The day we entered the Twisted Wood."

Then the door opened and, on the cold air that swirled through the warmth of the yellow house, drifted the voices of Arthur and Merlin bickering about something to do with the story of 'The Traveler.' And at the same moment, Minifred composed herself and shot up to welcome her sisters home. The quiet rest she got to herself, gone in the blink of an eye.

Lore stood up and looked at the fox and the bat. "You two fight like cats and dogs." She didn't bother to hide the annoyance that rang on every word from her mouth.

Merlin cocked his head to the side. "What an odd thing to say."

Arthur's ears were still flat as he added, "Yeah, wasn't that cat who owned the local bar and the white wolf lovers or something?"

Mathilde added, "Oh Lore, if you are gonna make a comparison, at least make it make sense."

Lore's jaw tensed as she folded her arms over her chest. "Well, it's just a saying in my world."

Merlin's gaze sharpened. "You remembered something?"

"No." *At least, not that.*

Her head ached as her frustration built. "Well, who is this traveler you both are going on about?"

Mathilde grinned as she pulled out Gannon's green book that had found a home snug inside Mathilde red jacket. "They are both wrong, and it doesn't matter because I know the right version."

Minifred was busy getting the other three sisters tea and cozy in front of the fire, but that didn't stop her from adding to the conversation. "There is no wrong way for a story to be told, Mathilde."

"Well, clearly there is." Mathilde gestured to Arthur and Merlin.

"There are multiple ways to tell a story, Sister. There are so many pieces of glass that must come together to create the picture that gets told. So there are multiple ways the same story could go."

Mathilde rolled her eyes and sat at the kitchen table. "Well, Lore." She cleared her throat. "If you would like to hear the best version, please sit." The gray mouse patted to the seat beside her, "and I will tell you the best version."

Lore watched as some mice made their way up to their rooms, how Arthur preferred to head back out into the cold air on the porch swing, and Merlin confidently went and took the seat in Gannon's rocker where Minifred had rightfully been sitting prior. Lore let out a breath, with it trying her best to let go of her annoyance, as she sat beside Mathilde. "Okay, one story before bed shouldn't hurt."

Mathilde's eyes grew wide with excitement as she flipped to the correct page in Gannon's green book. The gray mouse cleared her throat before starting. "Painted in the night sky, there is a constellation of stars that the old ones called The Traveler. This woman was said to go freely between the different planes."

"Planes?" Lore interrupted.

"Shhh," Mathilde chided. "Don't interrupt."

Lore rolled her eyes and rested her cheek on her hand.

"The woman could walk through planes," Mathilde continued, "and the ability was said to be a curse laid on her by the Mother Goddess. No one knows what the woman did to deserve such a fate, but she walked through the plane of mortals and roamed until she realized home was not there. The traveler walked through the Plane of Animals and again, did not find a home to return to.

"Then, with one final attempt, the traveler walked through to the plane of enchantment. Not even the magic that flowed freely in the air there could find the woman a home. Finally, she returned to the Plane of Celestial, where the Mother Goddess immortalized the wandering woman in the night sky, with stars, cursing the woman to wander the darkest depths of space searching for a place she might one day call home."

The skin between Lore's eyebrows wrinkled. "That's it?"

Mathilde sat the book flat on the table. "Yup!"

Minifred sat warm caramelized apples on the wooden surface between them and pulled out a chair facing both human and mouse.

"Not every story gets a happy ending," the older mouse explained.

"Well…" Lore bit her lip. "That's not fair."

Mathilde rested a paw on Lore's shoulder. "It's okay Lore, it's just a story. A bedtime fable, really."

Minifred, without missing a beat, in the softest voice, said. "It's a fairytale that mirrors life, because sometimes things just happen and we have no control. Life isn't fair."

Lore met the coal colored mouse's silver gaze. Her jaw tightened. "I think I'm going to call it a night."

She swiftly ascended up the stairs, her ears catching the way the steps whispered their creaks to her under each step. Blinking, she hoped the tears could stay contained. She quickly blew open the first door on the floor and kicked off her shoes and sunk into the purple blankets.

The familiar scent of warm spices filled her nose and her gaze fell onto the wallpaper where the pink flowers were shut tightly asleep.

She swallowed back a sob and stared out the window. The curtains were drawn back enough for her to see the stars stretching over the blue black sky.

Am I cursed? Did I do something so heinous and awful in my life before that I am also fated to travel and never find my home?

Her vision blurred and the images of the old woman with white hair and the raven haired boy circled her, but she was unable to reach out and ask for what she desperately needed at that moment.

A hug from someone who had known her and loved her.

TWENTY-SIX

The warmth of the winter sun greeted Lore when she opened her eyes. Still lying in the comfort and safety of the plum bedding, the rays of light danced on her face, and the pink blossoms on the walls of the room bloomed, taking in the morning sun. The scent of maple syrup and roasted pecans swept under the bedroom door, and roused Lore from bed.

The floorboards creaked and groaned under her steps as she made her way down the stairs. She recalled the way Minifred had spoken about the house being alive the night before.

The power our thoughts have.

"Good morning, Lore!" Mathilde called from the table, shoveling the waffles into her gullet.

"Mathilde, quiet please. You'll wake up our sisters," Minifred sighed as she poured hot kettle water into the cups on the round walnut table.

Lore took a seat by Arthur, who seemed stiff, even for the fox. Lore looked over her shoulder to see Merlin staring at the fire dwindling in the hearth. The glass mushrooms walked along the mantle with clinks and tinks of their stubby feet. Preparing to start their day, surely they would be busy doing… *Whatever sentient glass figurines did.*

Lore looked at her plate of breakfast and cut into her food. With each bite, she thought about the flavor of the cinnamon, and the sweetness of the syrup.

I need to get back home. To make sure my family knows how to prepare waffles like this... at the very least.

"What's bothering you, Lore?" Mathilde asked while she pushed her empty plate away from herself.

"Oh, just not a morning person."

Arthur's face scrunched, and Mathilde tilted her head.

Merlin rose from Gannon's rocker and cleared his throat. "We can't waste anymore time. Since we visited Loch Luan, the magic has been off balance. Let's get our supplies and go."

Lore let out a sigh. *Can I at least eat breakfast first?*

"There is too much magic surging through the air," Merlin continued. "I don't expect you, non-Wielders, to understand." He paused to sip his tea and probably revel in how he made the fox roll his eyes.

At that moment, the tenseness, silence, and awkwardness all overlapped each other like a three strand braid. Lore felt tempted to reach for her pocket for the Essence of The Great Stag.

If I could deal with the bone chilling pain that would come with it, I'd almost say enduring the frost covering my hand would be less painful than sitting here through whatever this situation is about to turn into.

Arthur cleared his throat and slid a piece of paper onto the table.

Lore's eyes recalled the paper. It was the same poster that wrangled Mathilde and her into helping the fox in the first place. The text was a bit more faded, but the coloring of the Soul of the Ocean—the gem from Crinkle's staff—was a mix of brilliant blue and green hues. "I technically have a job to finish."

Mathilde's eyes flicked over the paper. "Yes, well." She seemed to mull over her words. "No one is keeping you here."

Arthur ran a paw down his face. "I'm aware I am not a prisoner, but thanks for that clarification." His words danced on the line between exhaustion and sarcasm.

Merlin shrugged. "What are you getting at?"

"The queen of the Romplands is a very powerful Wielder," the fox said, as if that told the party everything they needed to know.

Minifred picked up the paper and scanned it over. "She was favored by the Great Owl, no?"

Arthur nodded. "Yes, she was, and she'll know more about that prophecy and Lore."

Merlin waved a hand. "Oh, the Great Owl can have awful taste from time to time."

"The stories of the queen's vast fortunes with the Great Owl spirit are well known in the southern lands. The tales of her favor even swept through Taper," Minifred added.

Lore locked eyes with Arthur. "You think this queen will be able to send me back home?"

The fox nodded. "Seeing as how I will be returning this gemstone to her…" Arthur paused and his ears drooped. "I'd even forgo the promised payment if she agrees to help."

Mathilde pushed her chair in. "That settles it then."

"Does it though?" Merlin pushed, "I mean, let's just look at what steps we've already followed that the fox has suggested."

Arthur groaned. "Here we go."

"We traveled all the way to the Wayward Mountains on the belief that the library there would hold the answers to send the human home, and we came back *empty-handed.*"

"That's not true. Technically, we saved the village at the foot of the mountain, and return the other corvids to the library," Mathilde said. "And got a prophecy."

"Lore *did* go to Loch Luan. And I think we all can agree that the Moon Drop showed her something," Arthur said, crossing his arms.

Merlin looked to be thinking about what the fox had said.

Lore felt like the wait for the Wielder's response was siphoning air from her lungs. *Was it really* that *obvious that I saw something? Surely if that's the case, as my friends, they would know I don't feel comfortable talking about it yet.* Lore tried to steady her trembling hands. *But then why would he point it out in front of everyone?*

With a sigh, she said, "You don't have to accompany us, Merlin. You are not chained to us like a prisoner."

It'll give me the chance to tell Mathilde and Arthur what happened.

Arthur smiled at her words. Though Mathilde clearly didn't like the idea of leaving without Merlin, given away by her glossed-over green eyes, she nodded in agreement.

Merlin finished the cup of tea Minifred had brewed that morning. The sun's rays flooded through the kitchen window and the quiet house stirred with life. Footsteps sounded above them. Lore saw the botanical wallpaper move with vigor. She imagined the deck of playing cards, now buried in Gannon's grave, speaking amongst themselves.

"If that is the plan," Merlin began, grabbing his purple wool cloak and heading to the manor's grand oak door, "then I suggest we leave now."

Arthur swiped the parchment from the tabletop, and Mathilde buttoned her red jacket and joined the bat at the door.

Lore scarfed down what food she could, for she didn't know when the next good meal would come. She stood and continued through the motions of getting ready to travel again.

She had her flannel, a heavier jacket, courtesy of Minifred. She stood in the entry of the yellow manor and took in the way the house looked. The dust particles that floated in the air, the chirping sounds of the mushrooms, and the exposed beams that had notches and scars upon them, if inspected close enough.

Minifred pushed in her chair and smiled at the group that was hovering around the doorway. "It was the greatest of pleasures, Lore, and I hope that when you return home, you will find it somewhere within you to not forget us."

Lore gave a nod that forced her welling tears back. Then the door opened, blowing in a winter breeze.

The town of Charmsend was bustling with animalfolk along the pathways and the group filed in with the crowd.

"No magic turnip this time," Arthur teased.

Merlin's eyes twinkled. "Oh no, I have a far better method of travel for this trip. But there is something we must retrieve first."

Before the gray mouse could ask what the item was, Merlin quickly filled in the blanks as they twisted and turned on the path that took them toward the graveyard and to the outskirts of town. "It's in my old cabin," the bat explained.

As they passed the iron fencing of the graveyard, Lore felt Mathilde slow down to stare at the headstones, knowing her father was there. Seeing them off in his own way beyond the final resting place, perhaps. At least that's what Lore liked to think.

Then the rundown cabin came into view. Down the fields of wheat that were sleeping for the winter, up the creaking stairs, and through the doorframe. The structure wasn't protecting really much of anything on the inside.

It was just as Arthur had left it, down to the papers nailed to the faded wallpaper and the red thread that connected them.

Merlin moved the dusty rug and leaped into the hole below, muttering something to himself that the others couldn't quite hear.

"It feels weird," Mathilde finally said.

"What's weird? Leaving so quickly, or the bat insisting on being vague and mysterious at all times?" Arthur stated as he crossed his arms and leaned in the doorframe.

"I can still hear you," Merlin chided beneath the floorboards.

"Is it returning to the place where we picked up an unexpected friend?" Lore questioned as she sat on the blanket covered couch.

"How this place has stayed the same," Mathilde replied. "Between being exiled, the fight with Crinkle, leaving Charmsend, and returning, the house still stands."

"Barely," Arthur added.

"Imagine all the events this house must have witnessed," the mouse mused aloud.

Then Merlin flew up from the hole with a small silver box in his grasp. "Got it," he said, holding up the box for all to see.

"A music box?" Arthur squinted.

The Wielder smiled. "Not just *any* music box."

"What's so special about it?" Lore asked, leaning forward a bit to admire the etched knotwork on the box.

"Come, I'll show you all," Merlin said, then he walked back out of the house, crumbling to time, and onto the porch.

The bat turned the key on the music box. The air was heavy with indifference as Merlin did this. Lore watched as Arthur took this time to admire his reflection in his polished ax, and Mathilde rocked on her heels, itching to start on the path toward the Romplands.

Then, as Merlin let the wind up free, music started playing. The stagnant winter air picked up, bringing on it dancing snowflakes. Dead wheat rustled, and the clouded sky parted, revealing a true blue atmosphere. From the blue heavens, a large bird descended.

As the beating of its large wings got closer to the ground, Lore noticed the sounds of steam whistling, and gears turning. The machine landed with a heavy thud on the ground. The field of wheat crunched beneath its large taloned feet, and the sun glittered off of its sharp wingspan.

"Everyone, this is Harpy," Merlin chimed as he walked toward the mechanical mount, music box in hand.

"And where was this mount when we traveled north?" Arthur questioned. "This would have been far quicker than an old dusty turnip." His orange fur stood up with annoyance.

Merlin answered back quicker than Mathilde could follow them. "Because Harpy would have had a hard time flying in such cold air, her gears and engines only work when the air isn't trying to kill you."

Arthur rolled his eyes. "The airship was fine up north."

"And Harpy's engine would have frozen to its core, because she doesn't run off fire," Merlin argued back. "Anyway, she will be fine flying south. Winter there is milder. So let's not waste anymore time and take the queen her oh-so-precious Soul of the Ocean back."

Lore was close behind Mathilde as they circled the winged metal mount. Steam hissed as it escaped from pipes that protruded under its chain mail-like feather pattern.

Lore stopped at the mechanical bird's face. Looking it over as it mimicked and inspected her. Merlin quickly diverted his attention to Harpy's chest. Lore watched as he peeled back the chain mail, and there in the center of the Harpy's chest was a beating heart. Well, the gears grinding together sounded like a heartbeat.

Merlin reached a hand further up the bird, who didn't seem to mind the very personal invasion of its cool metal parts.

"Ah ha," Merlin mused to himself.

Harpy opened its large hooked beak, and the same melodic melody that played sounded from the music box.

Mathilde was already on the bird's back in the large saddle that looked more like a boat than a saddle. Arthur begrudgingly climbed aboard.

Lore reached a hand up, and Harpy lowered its head. Her fingers touched the cool metal of its beak.

"Alright, time to go," Merlin called as he glided aboard the giant metal bird that could have easily crushed the small, rundown cabin behind her.

Lore couldn't shake the uneasy feeling she got from the machine. Though it was metal, it still looked like an animal—and also vaguely human, too.

TWENTY-SEVEN

The air gave Lore crisp kisses on her cheeks. With each flap of the mechanical bird's wings, they soared higher and higher until they were above the trees, and eventually above the clouds themselves. Only the very tops of mighty pines and oaks were in view now. The sun painted the tops of the puffy clouds with hues of golds and pinks.

"This is amazing," Lore stammered out.

"And much faster," Merlin added.

Arthur rolled his eyes. "I still think this would have been more convenient for our last trip instead of that stinking turnip."

And as if on cue, Harpy's gears hissed loudly, piercing the air, and the machine jerked a bit to the left.

"Regardless of when we sought this bird," Mathilde started saying as her gaze remained fixed on the horizon, "at least we get to enjoy it now."

Merlin seemed pleased that the mouse had continued to take and handle the fox's comments.

Lore's eyes drifted to Mathilde. The way her red jacket popped against the golden sky made her feel grateful for the friends she had been lucky to make while she was here, though Lore would have been lying if she said she didn't think about the friends she had in her life before.

How many friends do I have? Are they looking for me right now?

Or is that all just wishful thinking?

Lore pulled her knees close to her chest and wrapped her arms around herself like she was giving herself a warm hug. Of all the things to be worried about right now, she should consider how the queen of the Romplands will send her back home.

What magic does she have that Merlin doesn't have? And how did she get it?

Arthur scooted closer to Lore. He tapped her shoulder and pointed a finger at the darkening horizon in the distance. "Figures," he grumbled.

"Oh, you are always such a pessimist, fox," Merlin declared.

"He has a name," Lore interjected.

Merlin gave a nonchalant wave. "We will be fine, regardless," the bat assured as he tapped the metal feathers on the back of Harpy's neck. Those same feathers come loose from his touch. The Wielder shrugged. "It's all okay."

His smile almost made Lore feel at ease.

Almost.

Looking back on it, Lore couldn't recall what had happened first. The sheets of rain soaking them to the bone, or the rolling thunder. Regardless of what came first, it was for certain the lighting that struck them down, out of the sky. Luckily, injuries were minor and Merlin was able to magic away the pain and bruising, only leaving behind tiny scars.

She sat under the mechanical bird's large wing that malfunctioned due to the lightning strike, but Merlin was quick to use magic to position it as a makeshift shelter.

Arthur's dismay was clear as he spoke. "Why does it feel like the island is working against us?"

I agree. It sucks. There's always a greater force fighting us.

Merlin rolled his eyes. "Why does it feel like when there's an opportunity to see a silver lining, it's always *you* complaining?"

The fox's eyes sharpened, and his fur stood up in agitation. "Well, maybe I'd be less apt to complain if someone's self-proclaimed grand abilities actually helped."

Merlin scoffed. "Well, now you're being ridiculous. I can't control the weather, *Killmoore*."

Lore felt ice rush through her blood. "His name is Arthur."

Mathilde crossed her arms. "Yeah, Merlin. We've been through that already. We're his friends, so he allowed us to know his name. We should call him by it."

"Isn't it obvious? He's doing it on purpose, Mathilde." It sounded like he had chewed on his anger before it seeped out with every word.

"You're too *sensitive*, fox," the bat shot back. "And my abilities *are* helping. Don't you see the shelter above you?" Merlin's words boomed like the thunder in the rumbling sky as he marched toward the bounty hunter. "The healed scars from the crash? You're just ungrateful."

Lore wedged herself between the two, her hands stinging with a chill. "I think we all need to cool off."

Arthur's tail flicked back and forth with clear displeasure. "It'd be easier to cool off if *someone* could just admit he's a heinous little bastard."

Merlin crossed his arms. "You're so childish."

"I think instead of fanning the flames…" Lore knelt down to the bat's eye level, tilting her head so her antlers poked Merlin's ears. "You should share a silver lining if you have one instead of just preaching about finding them."

The Wielder's gaze narrowed on Lore. Then he spun in a pointless flourish and folded his hands behind his back. "The good news is," he said, addressing the whole group, "we can still get to where we are going by foot."

I'm so damn tired of walking everywhere. As if on cue, Lore's legs started burning in agony.

"Great," Mathilde said. The single word answer sounded like a heavy sigh that gave everyone permission to disperse.

The rain continued to pour down in the woods and Lore could hardly tell what was out there. Hell, the only indicator they were in a forest was the trunks of trees she kept running into after the initial crash.

Lore heard the fire *whoosh* to life and looked towards Mathilde, who was sitting quietly by the warmth Merlin cast into existence. Next, she glanced at Arthur, who was sitting far enough away from the group that the warmth of the fire most likely didn't reach him, but he was still sheltered under the metal wing of the Harpy. Merlin was looking out into the forest as if that would fix any problems that the group continued having.

Lore let out a sigh. All of this felt utterly and completely hopeless.

Eventually, Arthur joined the others by the warmth of the fire.

"I have a tale," the bat mused. "Though it's not from fairytale books, and it's not as short and sweet as others."

"Okay," Lore said, motioning her hand for the bat to continue.

"It really happened. And it happened many decades ago."

"Was Gannon with you when this happened?" Mathilde asked.

Merlin nodded. "Yes, he was. These were the earlier days of the Order of the Chimera, and I'd argue that these days were the group's glory days." The bat pushed up his sleeves.

"This was the third case after we had all first met at a tavern in a town called Mythvale. Locals were whispering some stories about the were-creature of Grand Caster Hill. Apparently, a few local officials went up and found nothing. But that didn't stop the stories from spreading like wildfire." Merlin added as he looked Arthur up and down. "So, naturally, high off of our previous victory, we took up a few of the leads."

The bat repositioned himself and fed another fireball to the campfire for dramatic effect. "The Umber Valley is littered with thickets and hiding places, so we figured the creature had to be taking cover there. But on the night of a full moon, we heard the most horrific howl. Lyudmilla was unbothered by this and explained that daywalkers were just a myth. There was no wolf that could actually turn human by the moon cycles. That didn't stop Crinkle from sniveling about the whole affair. Gannon and I suspected that a folkkind had used the superstition to fabricate a reason for passersby to leave the mansion on Grand Caster Hill alone."

"Were you right?" Mathilde asked.

Merlin smiled. "Naturally, after we walked the grounds of the abandoned mansion, it was clear someone was looting the place."

"Shame, I'm sure there were things in there now lost for good," Arthur spoke up.

Merlin nodded. "It seems we can agree on something, after all."

The fox smirked at the bat as he continued the story. "After we bagged the thief, our names spread further and our glory was growing at a quick rate. But from this story, we can take superstition at face value. There is always an answer. Most of the time it's just greed that is the issue, but other times, rarer times..." With another *whoosh,* the bat stole the fire from the logs. He held the fire in his hand, and the dancing flames cast shadows on his face. "There will be magic at play."

"Will there ever be another Grand Caster, you think?" Mathilde's voice was faint. The hope from the story now completely drained from her voice.

Arthur sighed. "Most likely not."

"Well, we may be surprised," Merlin chimed. "Maybe a Wielder with legendary ability may step up and claim the title for himself."

"Or herself," Lore added.

"Or herself," Merlin agreed.

"Maybe the otter queen," Mathilde threw in. "You know, the other night I overheard some folk at the marketplace talk about how she carries the Great Owl with her."

"When did I miss this conversation?" Merlin's interest piqued.

"What do you mean, 'carries'?" Lore asked. "Is she part owl?" Her voice sounded a bit more hopeful than she'd like. "Is she like me?"

"Not to burst any bubbles," Arthur interrupted. "But as someone who has met face to face with Her Majesty, she is in every way a normal otter."

Mathilde's brow scrunched as Arthur ruined the idea of what she had of the queen in her mind.

The fox waved a hand before continuing, "Anyway, the Grand Casters will probably end up being a tale we tell children at night or around campfires like this," Arthur added.

"What *is* a Grand Caster, by the way?" Lore asked.

Wasn't there something in Charmsend's library about it? Sabine...Something? But I can't remember the details clearly.

She expected Mathilde to whip out Gannon's book.

But it was Merlin who answered. "Think of it as a role chosen by the Great Spirits. The Grand Caster can wield all types of magic and is basically an extension of the spirit who chose them."

"With all that power," Arthur added, "the Grand Caster was the peacekeeper."

Interesting. Though I may have more questions.

And on that note the group decided to call it a night, and as Lore laid on the soft earth beneath her, she looked out into the forest that sheets of rain blanketed, and wondered what folktales she was told, or whose life stories she had. One thing for certain was, when she got home, she would share her adventures in Thimbleton with whoever would listen.

TWENTY-EIGHT

Amber leaves crunched under Lore's hooves as they continued their way south through the Umber Valley. The air was frigid as it rustled the treetops and overall traveling by foot wasn't unbearable. The most annoying thing Lore currently faced was managing the thin stray branches that seemed to bend in ways that were just close enough to catch her antlers as she walked under them, or by them. *But that was something bearable.* What was truly unbearable was how exaggeratedly Merlin told tales of his life's adventures.

From his tragic orphanhood to his estranged wealthy uncle, who mysteriously vanished…Lore was very pleased when Arthur halted the bat's self grandiose storytelling to point out the large footprint they had stepped into.

It had some stray feathers around it. Feathers large enough that if Mathilde held on tightly to one, and a gust of wind followed, the jet black feather would have caught the wind and carried Mathilde far—

Far

Far

Away.

Arthur checked behind the brush and found more footprints that led deeper into the darker corners of the Umber Valley. The group of adventurers expected to see items like strewn hay, yarn, and lots of fluff littering the forest ground like breadcrumbs.

However, all they saw were more foot impressions in the dirt and pile of golden and bronzed tinged leaves.

"Whatever made those prints will most certainly be back," Merlin pointed out.

"Back soon, by the look of it, too," Arthur added, guesstimating the sun's position on the other side of the thick canopy of trees above them.

Mathilde poked a digit into the soft earth. "Maybe it's friendly."

"Well, I don't want to stick around long enough to find out," Lore added, already walking in the opposite direction.

"Lore, you don't even know if that's the right way," Arthur called.

"Any direction away from those footprints—and whatever made them that could come back at any moment—is the 'right way,'" Lore huffed as she pushed a stray branch from her path. Her antlers getting snagged was truly testing her patience.

"At the very least, wait for us," Arthur pleaded, following her.

"I agree," Merlin said quickly. He tapped Mathilde's arm. "We should follow Lore. Humans were said to have good instincts with these things."

How much human of me is left? Lore thought as her fawn legs carried her nimbly across the forest floor. *And where was that instinct when the last humans of Thimbleton were killed?* Lore wondered to herself as she heard the animalfolk follow behind her.

"Arthur, do you have the map?" she asked, stopping to look at the fox.

He stopped dead in his tracks. "I thought Merlin did." He looked over his shoulder to the bat, who was walking side by side with Mathilde.

Merlin cleared his throat as he walked past Arthur and Lore. "I do indeed have the map," he assured.

Arthur and Lore sighed in relief in unison.

"In here," he added while tapping his temple.

Their sighs of relief quickly turned to groans of frustration.

"Oh, don't be like that." Merlin waved a hand. "Look, just a little more in this direction and we should come across the main travel path."

Mathilde tugged on Lore's arm. "It's okay. Just a bit farther and we will get to sleep in a warm bed."

Arthur's brow furrowed. "Do you know how much it is to stay a night in Silver Lining Landing?"

Mathilde frowned. "The cost of a hotel stay should be nothing for what the queen will pay you for returning her gemstone, surely."

Arthur ran a paw down his face. "Oh, Mathilde," he groaned. "Did you forget we are going to forgo the payment so we can instead secure passage for Lore to go home?"

Mathilde crossed her arms. "Well, no." She swallowed hard before continuing. "But I'd imagine we'd be in her good graces, and what kind of queen would have the returners of her precious gemstone sleep out in the woods?"

Lore watched as Merlin's brow seemed to twitch with annoyance as he spoke. "How about we worry about sleeping affairs after we return the gemstone? At the very least, after we set eyes on the cityscape. We still have a bit of walking to do."

Mathilde continued to grumble to Lore as Arthur and Merlin led the way, surprisingly not bickering about which way to take, or what path was right. "I can't wait till we reach the city and we can have some time away from them," she spat, clearly annoyed.

It would be nice to have a few moments away from the group's bickering divas.

"Think about it, Lore." Mathilde mused, like the idea she was about to throw out melted her nerves, "We will be in Silver Lining Landing. Imagine the shops, and libraries there we could check out. Oh, and the coffee shops!"

The open blue sky paired with the salty sea air was a welcomed sensation Lore never thought she needed. But there she was, enjoying it. They had stumbled onto the main path of travel the prior night and pushed on, and their grit was rewarded by the spectacular winter sunrise that was painting the Silver Lining Landing with light.

The colorful tapestries that flew just beyond the stone city walls caught the rays of dawn in such a way it made Lore feel a flutter of excitement. Now that she was here, in person, she hoped that she and Mathilde could go explore the nooks and crannies of the city. Lore pictured local shops that would have cozy fireplaces that roared with life, plush wool sweaters, and the whole shop would smell like warm leather and amber. The scent would wrap the entire experience up with a neat little bow. The thoughts soured as the pit in her stomach reminded her she was here to go home.

We're here on a mission. Not to explore the city. Her eyes lowered to the ground. *My connections here are only temporary.* That realization made her heart shatter, and her lashes held tightly onto the tears. *But does that make them any less important?* It was a question that she didn't know the answer to. *Come on Lore, get it together.*

"Ahem." Merlin cleared his throat as the group was preparing to cross the gate hidden within the stone wall. "I think it's best I sit this one out," the bat admitted sheepishly.

Mathilde tilted her head, her face scrunched up in confusion. "But Merlin," she gasped. "This is a city. A *royal* city."

As if that were reason enough for the old bat to be excited about exploring it.

Merlin laughed. "When you get my age, and have experienced many cities, they all start to blur and become the same."

Arthur shrugged. "You won't get an argument from me," the fox replied. "But if you would like to still do something, maybe stake out a nice campsite for us, so when we return, it's already taken care of."

Lore cocked a brow and watched as Merlin pursed his lips, the tips of his triangular ears folding over a bit at the request of Arthur. "That would be a good way to spend time."

Mathilde waved her hands, then quickly looped arms with Lore. "Whatever. Let's just get on with this so we can return the gem and Lore can explore a little before she goes home."

The harsh reality of their journey was finding a way for Lore to go home. A fact that had been so far in the back of her mind that she forgot the other half of the equation. *Once I leave, I probably can't return.* That thought alone broke her heart a little. The whole back and forth felt unreal. To be honest, perhaps most of it was denial, built from the fragments of hope that crumbled away to dust when the well that had brought her to Charmsend became rubble and ruin. When its ashes had blown away in the wind that day, it had taken all her hope of going home with it.

As the trio filed themselves among the other animalfolk coming and going from Silver Lining Landing, Lore looked over her shoulder to see Merlin's face empty as he shoved his hands into his pockets and turned to go find a proper camping spot.

Something was off with the bat. Though what, exactly, Lore couldn't be sure.

As the line moved and the animal continued checking what Lore could only assume was identification Arthur leaned over and whispered to her, "Don't worry they will only check you for identification if you are a merchant, which we are not."

Mathilde either paid no mind to Arthur's whispers or just didn't care. Lore thought the second option was more likely, since the small gray mouse hadn't stopped ogling the city with stars in her eyes since they had spotted it that morning when they emerged from the forest line of the Umber Valley.

When the individual checking merchant identification started pointing at others to come through the gate, the line shortened rather quickly. Lore expected some sort of examining gaze, but she didn't anticipate a big reaction from the officer, having forgotten she was a human...who was supposed to be extinct.

So, when the gasps came, Lore tried her best not to take it personally and put on the bravest face she could muster.

"Mornin'," the gate guard croaked out, its eyes still wide with dumbfounded shock. "And uh—what brings you lot here?"

"Visiting," Mathilde said, unbothered.

"Yes, visiting," Arthur agreed.

"Well, here I thought you had a living exhibit for the museum," the uniformed otter joked.

"Heh, nope." Lore admitted.

"It can *talk*?!"

You don't have to sound so surprised.

Arthur's ears flattened. "Yeah, and she also eats pesky annoyances."

Lore rolled her eyes at the comment, but it did get the otter to let them through without any further problems.

They had made it. Finally.

TWENTY-NINE

The moment the trio passed through the gate to the city, Lore's stomach dropped. She was used to animalfolk giving her a sideways glance from time to time, and of course it had become the normal that they gave her wide clearance when walking, but at this point in her adventures she didn't think she could make a whole bustling city freeze like they had seen a phantom. Lore stood frozen at the sudden halt of the street that appeared to curve itself as if it were the bottom of the letter 'U'.

Arthur shrugged and ran his hands through his orange fur, only to wave folks off. "Go on, get back to yer lives. Ain't nothin' to see here."

Mathilde looked at Lore with a smile on her face. *Odd.*

"Hey, Lore, I bet in a few years they'll be making jokes about us. A mouse, a fox, and a human all enter the capital and fill in the blank with whatever punchline ya like."

Lore felt her cheeks pull upward into a smile.

Arthur returned to their side, his face as flat as his ears. "What are you two smiling about?"

"Arthur, a mouse, a fox, and a human all walk into the capital and the city guard says—"

Arthur pinched the fur between his eyes. "Leave the jokes to the funny ones, Mousey," he teased before walking into the busy cobblestone seaside streets.

Mathilde rolled her eyes as she followed, waving a hand in the air. "What did I tell you about calling me that?!"

You don't seem to mind it when he's thanking you for something.

Lore let out a sigh and followed behind, taking in as much of the crashing waves as she could. The way the city was built on top of the water amazed her. Granted, most of the homes and shops seemed to be built right into the cliff sides on both sides of the 'U' layout of the city, which was smart. The way light linen fabric danced in the windows, which were being hit by the golden glow of the morning sun, paired with the gorgeous murals painted on the cliff faces, really seemed like something in a dream. The murals flowed into each other like a beautiful tapestry.

Unsurprisingly, it seemed to be the story of the four Guardians. The Great Salamander's flames burned down everything around it in the painting, only for the depiction of the aftermath of a forest fire to blend into the vivid greens and baby pinks of the Great Hare. On the right, beautiful gold, bronze, and umber of thick, woven trees braided into a breathtaking bitter winter landscape that showed the trees covered in a thick and warm blanket of snow.

"Where is the queen's court?" Lore asked as they continued to pass by animalfolk that were staring just a bit too long for Lore's comfort.

"Yeah, where are we walkin' to? Cause the city seems to end right up there." Mathilde pointed to the dead end that looked out onto the open sea. A stained wooden bench was there, most likely for sightseers.

The fox veered off to the edge of the stone wall where he promptly stopped, resting his black paws on the edge. When Lore touched the wall that was just high enough for Mathilde to see, Lore nodded when she saw at the bottom there appeared to be a cove, and that must have been where the queen's castle stood.

Mathilde was standing on her tiptoes and barely saw over the side of the four-foot wall. "I can't see it," the mouse grumbled. "Lore," she said, looking at the human rather seriously.

"Yes?"

"Pick me up," she muttered, crossing her arms.

Lore snorted back a laugh, only because if she burst into the laughter she wanted to, it might have wounded the mouse's pride more. So, silently, Lore picked Mathilde up, giving the red-clad mouse the view of a barely visible cove.

"Oh, for Warden's sake!" Mathilde shrieked and freed herself from the human's hands. She impatiently tapped her foot. "How do we get down there?" She sounded rather annoyed at the idea that they might have to scale down the cliff face of a rocky coast.

"Relax," Arthur said, walking back from the end of the street. Towards the dark stained wooden bench. Naturally Mathilde, and Lore followed and sat beside him.

"What is it?" Mathilde questioned, like she was back in Charmsend interrogating the fox for the first time.

"Would ya just look at that?" Arthur asked, pointing at the horizon.

Lore appreciated the watercolor sky and the way the golden light danced on the water. "Look, in the water." She pointed below.

"What about it?" Mathilde asked, her arms still crossed with skepticism.

"There're otters swimming," Lore said.

Mathilde moved toward the human to look over the side of the cliff. The mouse's green eyes widened in wonder.

"Otters swimming in the water aside, it's also just a beautiful morning. And I wanted to enjoy it a little with my two dearest friends," the fox said, with not a single trace of sarcasm in each word.

Mathilde's eyes widened, and she quickly clammed up. Lore watched as she uncrossed her arms and took in a deep breath, looking at the sunrise with her two closest friends.

The cloudless sky was vast, and the vastness reminded Lore about returning to her home. She wondered if there would be a hole in her heart the size of the Thimbleton sky that only Mathilde and Arthur would be able to fill. The feeling turned her stomach over on itself, but the void that grew after every memory she recalled also made her yearn for wherever home was. She chewed on the inside of her cheek. In that moment, she realized one common thing between both the magical world of Thimbleton and her home that she could barely put together with the fuzzy pieces she had.

They both required her to give up the other.

I can't have both.

Arthur gave his thighs a pat. "Well, I s'pose we better get on and get our audience with Her Majesty."

Another stab in the gut. Maybe I should tell them. Lore was struggling alone, and it hurt. "Wait." She said in an almost whisper. The two animals turned, tilting their heads to let her know to go on.

Lore froze. Her heart raced. *What if sharing my fears upset them? They've done so much to get me here.*

"I ... uhh." Lore was finding it hard to find a way out of this now.

Mathilde's whiskers twitched curiously. "You're not really one for losing words."

Arthur nodded in agreement. "Something bothering you?"

How could I have been so selfish to think of not accepting the actions Mathilde and Arthur are making to send me back? How ungrateful would they think I was if I told them I wasn't totally sure about going back? Especially now that we're so close.

"Lore?" Arthur pressed.

The human shook herself from her stormy ocean of thoughts and all that spilt out was, "I'll really miss you guys when I'm gone." She felt hot tears roll down her cheeks.

"We'll miss you, too," Mathilde squeaked out, rushing to hug Lore.

While embracing the mouse, Lore held an arm open, gesturing for Arthur to join. He did, of course.

The heroics of clawing my way back home can come later. Within their embrace, Lore felt a little bit of peace. Right now, they are here, and they are real, and they are my dearest friends.

The pug would not budge. "Sorry, mate. Can't letcha through." He leaned back, sitting on his hind legs, and crossed his furry, coal-colored arms over the iron armor covering the top half of his body. He stood in front of a narrow passage that led to brilliant blue hues glowing in the distance. *Probably some bioluminescent material.* Regardless, it was intriguing and made her want to see the palace hidden behind a crack in the stone.

She sighed as her gaze was brought back to the dog. The guard's armor had an emblem that matched the view the trio had just spent time admiring from on top of the cliffs. It was a detail Lore had missed initially.

Arthur ran a paw down his face. "Oh, come on." He pulled out his flier with the brilliant painting of the Soul of the Ocean. "She signed this, see?" He shoved the paper into the pug's face.

The guard put a paw on Arthur's arm and lowered it, his face unmoving. "Sir, the text on this is so faded I can barely see the letters, let alone see the words are supposed to say."

The fox let out a displeased groan, and Mathilde patted his back through his blue jacket.

The pug let out a low grumble. "Listen, I can let you and the mouse through to the royal courts, but I am not risking my job on the slight chance letting a human in is 'acceptable.'"

Mathilde's brow furrowed. "That human has a *name.*"

"And 'that human' helped get this stone back, so she should share in the reward." Arthur spoke with such certainty and confidence that it just must be so.

Just like him to speak with such conviction that he thinks that's enough to make others sway their opinions in his favor. But the guard didn't seem convinced.

Lore sucked on the inside of her cheek. "It's okay, guys. I can wait out here."

"NO!" both of her animal companions said in unison, turning to her. Then Lore watched as their eyes widened and they dropped to one knee.

She swallowed hard as she turned to see a carriage being carried on the shoulders of other otters dressed in robes that looked like sea foam. The sheer curtains were pulled back on the giant clam-shaped carriage.

Lore met the steely gaze of a large otter who wore a string of pink pearls around her neck and a thin strapped aquamarine gown that flowed from her body like gentle waves.

"So, the rumors are true." She sounded amused as she thumbed at her necklace. "There is a human that walks on the dirt of Thimbleton once more." Her eyes drifted over Lore's head to the dog guard. "What are you doing standing there?" she questioned, as if it was common knowledge the queen and this human were well-to-do friends. "Let them through."

THIRTY

The guard that was standing in front of the crevice darted over to assist the queen down from her luxurious ride. Then, the six otter guards sat the giant clam down and surrounded Her Majesty.

Looking between their shoulders, she gestured for the trio to follow them. "Right this way, heroes." A smile spread across her features as she walked over to the narrow split in the wall.

Three guards went before her, then three guards followed her, and finally the trio walked behind them down the narrow slit in the cove wall.

The pug returned to standing at the entrance.

As Lore walked, she felt the dampness from the jagged rock cling to her skin. It gave a shudder down her spine. Her eyes widened when she set her gaze on what was hidden under the city. Despite being subterranean, there was a soft, heavenly glow in the atmosphere that made Lore think of the snow and wind she met on the way to return the Moon Drop to Loch Luan.

To the left, there was a large bioluminescent waterfall that looked like a galaxy. It crashed into the river surrounding the main attraction like a moat. The castle was large and imposing. It didn't even appear to be made of stone, but ice. When they entered the halls, however, the castle was not cool to the touch.

"How curious," Lore mused.

"Stop that," Arthur whispered, and quickly swatted Lore's hand away from the walls.

"Sorry," she mouthed to the fox, but that didn't stop her from wondering what material built the castle. *Could it be glass? Was that practical?*

The question continued to eat through Lore's thoughts as they twisted and turned down the long, narrow corridors. There were portraits that decorated the walls. The one thing they all had in common, besides being otters, was the string of pink pearls around their neck.

Then they came to the end of the hall, and the queen's guards opened the double doors, letting the queen in first. The fox, the mouse, and the human followed close behind. When the doors shut loudly, Lore startled at the sound, which carried on the stagnant air of the mostly empty room.

Lore would say mostly because there was a large five-sided table. Aside from the two or three bookshelves that appeared to be covered in a blanket of dust, the others were filled with an assortment of small photos, trinkets, polished gemstones, and boxes and trunks.

The queen gestured to the table where the trio took their seats promptly, then walked to the only window in the room and stared outside at the cave that surrounded her. Lore could hear the waterfall crashing outside.

"So, the payment," Arthur started.

"Oh, yes, Killmoore. You will receive your payment." She looked over her shoulder. "Can I see it first?"

"Certainly," Arthur said, reaching for the satchel around his waist. He pulled out the glittering gemstone.

The blue and green shades lit up the room, and the otter queen's eyes shone back in response.

"Oh, thank you." She reached for the gemstone, which Arthur gingerly handed to her.

She turned quickly to return the Soul of the Ocean to a wire stand on one of the dusty shelves. "What a great bounty hunter you are."

Lore looked at Arthur. She'd forgotten that the fox was still going by the bounty hunter moniker to others, while those closest to him knew him and his true name.

"About the payment," Arthur began again, although his words sounded hesitant.

"Oh, of course," she mused. From one of the trunks, she pulled out a bag and tossed it on the table. Gold tael spilled out from the bag.

The fox swallowed hard. "That is very generous, your majesty, but..." He stopped trying to find his words as the tael sparkled in the soft glow of the castle light in front of him.

That is a lot *of tael.*

"We were hoping for a different kind of reward," Mathilde cut in.

The queen raised a brow. "That is all the tael I promised Killmoore when he originally took the job."

He could have used that to start a new life.

"Right," Arthur forced out. The fox let out a sigh as he took the tael spilling onto the table and plopped it back into its sack. Then he pushed it back towards the otter queen. "We were actually hoping since," Arthur looked at Lore. "Since Lore here played a big part in retrieving that gemstone for you, we were hoping that the payment could be sending her home instead."

I hate that he's sacrificing payment he's rightfully owed because of me.

The otter queen folded her hands over one another and tilted her head. "You helped retrieve my stone?"

Lore nodded. "We both did. Mathilde, too," she said, angling her head towards her friend, playing along with the angle Arthur was working from. *After all, if I push back now, then what? This may be my only chance to go home.* Her antlers felt heavy. *I just hate it has to be this way. Why not both?*

The otter queen nodded and brought a digit to her cheek. She appeared to be thinking some things over. "Are you enjoying Thimbleton?"

Lore scratched the back of her neck. "I would enjoy it more if I knew my place here, and in my own world." Nervous laughter escaped from her as she recalled the faint faces she sees from her own world that haunt her from time to time. *I wonder if Arthur and Mathilde will become faint faces that will haunt me when I go back.*

The queen nodded. "What do you think of Silver Lining Landing?"

Lore was quick to answer, "Oh, it's really quite beautiful."

The queen then walked over and rested her hands on the back of the chair across from Lore. "And how are you liking those antlers?"

It felt like a rock had caught in Lore's throat. "Oh—I, uh."

"With all due respect, Your Majesty, that is kinda personal," Mathilde cut in.

The queen chuckled a bit to herself. "You're right. Forgive me. I won't even ask about the hindquarters and hooves."

Lore waved it off.

The queen turned to the mouse. "And what is your name, darling?"

"Mathilde Nym, I'm from Charmsend." The answer had no hesitation.

"Oh, I've heard of that town. I have local merchants who travel to the monthly market there. It's such a quaint little place."

Mathilde nodded in agreement.

Then the queen focused on Lore again. "Have you heard of the prophecy about The Crowned One?"

The trio exchanged glances.

"Yes," Mathilde finally said.

"We heard it from the Keepers up north," Arther added. He scratched behind his ear. "Unless there's another iteration of it?"

The queen's eyes lit up. "Well, let me share with you how I was given the prophecy." She pushed the chair into the table. "It all started the night I myself was crowned."

Lore shifted from one side to the other as the otter queen started recounting the story.

"It was the night when both moons were full many, many, many years ago. My grandmother just stepped down as ruler and that night not only did I inherit these pearls, but I also inherited the prophecy that was given to my great, great, great grandmother. After the crowds cleared, and the halls of the castle were empty, with only the sound of footsteps of my kin. The footsteps of my kin as we came to this exact room, actually."

The queen's eyes seemed to drift backwards with the memory as she was recounting it. "My grandmother..." The queen moved back to the bookshelf that was not filled to the brim with stories bound with leather, but instead she reached for a different chest, beside where she had placed the Soul of the Ocean.

"First, she read this scroll to me when I was sitting in the chair you warm now, Lore," The queen turned on her heel presenting the small scroll in hand. "Ahem," she cleared her voice as she prepared to read from the paper that didn't seem to age with time.

Lore wondered if it was magical, or if the words themslves were charmed so powerfully that it affected the paper as a side effect.

"Revive what has long been dead.
In order to set Thimbleton free,
The sacrifice must be made.
Prepare to be the one who bled,
Or all humanity be shed."

The queen's gaze individually met each of theirs.

Arthur's teeth seemed to grind together a bit.

Based on the gleam of a new adventure in her emerald green eyes, Mathilde was very interested.

"Traditionally, it had only been known to the royal line, but once I became queen, I shared it. So my people would have the power of knowing when it was upon us. I didn't want them blindsided."

Lore's gut turned over on itself, and chewing the inside of her cheek would only do so much. Not only was the queen's version different, it also seemed so much darker.

She looked down at her hands and the table's reflective surface showed herself looking back. *Why were there always different versions of things in Thimbleton? Why couldn't there be a single answer?*

Lore had changed so much from the confused girl that some magic well belched her out of. The antlers looked more like a crown after hearing the prophecy from the otter queen's words.

If she were told the night she arrived in Thimbleton that she was the key to some prophecy, Lore would have died from laughter.

*But now...*Lore didn't think it was so ridiculous. Especially with all the adventures under her belt in Thimbleton.

This feeling of pride in my chest is new, but if antlers can grow on me, certainly so can self-confidence.

While Lore was still lost in the stranger that was looking back at her, the queen moved once more. The otter walked to another other bookshelf and began pushing it away from the wall.

Arthur shot to his feet. "Oh, Your Majesty, let me help you with that."

With Arthur's help, the furniture easily slid across the floor to sit beside its match.

The sound of a tapestry being pulled back and dropped to the floor echoed in Lore's ears. Mathilde let out an audible gasp, and Lore finally looked up to see what the queen had hidden.

Dark eyes stared back at her. They seemed to hold worlds of knowledge. The depicted creature's dark exterior covered its large, muscular body. She couldn't tell if they actually were feathers or scales. What was too obvious to miss were the spread wings that almost covered the whole painted sky.

"This is the Banewing."

Lore's heart felt like it froze all over again.

The queen continued. "The Banewing is said to guard an artifact known as the Warden's Warp."

Lore couldn't peel her attention away from the looming shadow currently staring her down. It felt like the Banewing was going to leap from the woven fabric and swallow her in an abyss of nothingness. While her eyes remained fixed, her ears listened.

"What exactly is a Warden's Warp?" Mathilde asked.

The otter queen took a moment before answering. "The Warden's Warp is how the Warden travels everywhere so quickly. It's how he can be at the exact place he is needed at the most opportune time."

Arthur snapped his fingers. "So because Lore is…" He looked her up and down. "She is *mostly* human, so the Warp will send her home, right? The exact place and precise time she needs to be at?"

The queen nodded. "That's the theory." She gestured to the tapestry again. "But it's guarded by the Banewing."

The mouse spoke up. "What does the Warden's Warp look like?"

The otter's voice was soft, almost a whisper. "No one knows."

"But the Warp will safely and most certainly send Lore home?" The mouse pushed back.

"There is a definite chance, I believe."

"Do you know how we can defeat the Banewing?" Lore murmured.

"Unfortunately, no," the queen responded, running a padded paw along the textile. "The Warden keeps the beast as a pet."

The Warden. It was so obvious in the name, but hearing it so clearly made it real.

"So, you're asking us to kill the pet of the most powerful guardian in all the realms?" the fox asked. His words were dripping with stress. "For a *chance* to send our friend home?"

"You're asking us to gamble quite a lot on a *chance*," Mathilde added.

The queen's voice was calm. Almost unsettlingly so. "Isn't that what all this has been? One big chance? Yet you two continue to pursue based on belief. The want to believe you can send your friend home?"

The exact place.

Jet black feathers brushed against her memory. She could practically hear the uneven squawks of the peculiar corvid.

At the most opportune time.

Lore's antlers cut the tension settling thick in the air.

Makes me feel as curious as a crow.

The otter spoke quietly but firmly. "What if chasing a chance is not so different from chasing belief?"

The trio didn't say a word.

"There are plenty of things that find their way into our life that make the impossible seem possible," the queen continued, "but none as powerful as friendship."

The otter's eyes had a certain softness to them as she smiled. "And it must be a depth of friendship you share if you are willing to travel from the far reaches of the North to the untamed lands of the South." The queen turned away from the trio, her hands folded behind her. "It's my belief that the Banewing may have met its match in you three."

THIRTY-ONE

As the trio exited the crevice, they could feel the eyes of the pug guard bore into their backs as they ascended the stairs that were carved out from the side of the cliff face. Many of the capital city's buildings seemed built right into the side of the rock face. *Work with the landscape instead of against it.*

The queen's advisor had gifted the trio with vouchers for a paid stay at a local inn.

Lore watched as Arthur gripped the vouchers so tight that the paper wrinkled around his digits.

"I don't think you have to worry about the ocean breeze stealing those," Lore said as she gestured to Arthur's hand.

"I know that," Arthur grumbled.

"Lore, leave him to his brooding," Mathilde joked as she bounded up each step with youthful vigor. That or just pleased that tonight she won't be laying her head on the muddy ground, or sleeping by a fire for warmth.

The stars glittered in the sky above the seaside town of Silver Lining Landing like little pearls that were plucked straight from the ocean, then carefully placed above the Capital of Thimbleton. *Did the Mother Goddess from the Thimblish stories connect all the magic and myths in this world? Or did everything simply fall in place to make it appear intentional?*

The queen had deemed the Mirrored Tides Inn the best the city had to offer. The inn's large sign in cursive writing flashed on and off as the trio stood looking at it. The neon sign also had a stop-motion wave animation.

Lore took in a deep breath as onlookers stopped. She thought she heard whispers of the 'Crowned One.' She swallowed the lump of nerves burning her throat. *Maybe I'm just hearing things.* But the otter *had* said she shared the prophecy with everyone once she became queen.

"We have to get Merlin," Lore sighed.

"Well, why don't you and Arthur go do that and I will take the vouchers, get our rooms, and try out each bed—I mean," Mathilde quickly corrected herself. "I mean check out each bed to make sure there aren't bed bugs or something else insidious lurking around."

Arthur laughed. "I doubt Her Majesty would send us somewhere with bedbugs."

"They don't discriminate. Poor, rich, the bugs don't care."

Arthur pinched the fur between his eyes, and his foot began tapping. "Okay, how about we check into the rooms and Lore fetches the bat?"

"By myself?" Lore whined, grabbing her arm uncomfortably as the stares from city goers bored into her. Their whispers intensifying loudly around her, like each hushed word was wrapping around her like a snake entangling its prey. Her mind twisted the words and Lore questioned if she could trust herself.

Arthur shifted on his feet and turned to face Lore fully. "I doubt anyone here would have the gall to do anything to the 'Crowned One,'" he said theatrically while his hands made quotations around the title.

Her brow pulled together. "You don't have to be such an ass."

"Do I have to accompany the literal child into a shiny hotel or go with the rare extinct human 'cause she's afraid of going alone?" He seemed exhausted, but that didn't take the sting out of his words.

"I am not a child!" Mathilde said with a stomp.

"*Extinct?!*" Lore's hands went to her hips. "What's your deal, Arthur?"

The fox dragged a paw down his face. "Nothing."

"You've been acting funny since we got those vouchers," Mathilde pointed out.

He shoved the vouchers into his coat pockets. "Okay, let's go get that damned Wielder," he seethed, marching off.

Mathilde and Lore exchanged glances and gave a shrug before following behind the flat-eared, tail-flicking fox.

Someone's moody. Lore thought as she rolled her eyes. With each stomp Arthur made, Lore was starting to think getting Merlin by herself would have been better.

As the guard at the gate let them exit the city more easily than they entered, Lore hoped getting back in would not be as attention drawing.

Arthur impatiently tapped his foot where they had parted ways from Merlin at the start of the day.

"Well, where in Warden's sake is he?" The fox was looking around the hill where they had last seen the bat. "I don't think he'd be hiding away in some bush."

Right as Lore was about to make a retort, the Wielder stepped out from the treeline. "Oh, quiet your complaints. I heard you just fine the first time."

"It's a loss cause, Merlin," Mathilde said. "The city has made Arthur absolutely unbearable."

Arthur pivoted on his heel. "Would you just cut that out?" His fur stood up, making him look bigger than he actually was.

Lore stepped in front of the mouse, staring the fox down. Her antlers towered over him.

"Either you tell us what your deal is, or you suck it up and sit this out instead of..." She gestured at him with her hands. "Whatever this *mess* is."

Arthur scoffed and shoved his hands into his pockets. "Fine."

Lore let out a breath, and backed away from him, now fixing her gaze onto a very intrigued Merlin. "The queen gave us some vouchers to pay for a night's stay at some fancy inn."

Merlin's eyes grew, and he rocked backwards on his heels. "My, how lovely. But I will have to decline."

"Why?" Mathilde asked, shocked at the bat's admission.

The bat shrugged. "I stay out of large cities as much as possible."

Lore pursed her lips. *Odd.* Then her gaze drifted to Arthur, who'd normally love a jump on the bat, but he was too busy dealing with whatever secrets he was carrying. *Again.* Lore stretched her aching legs. *I don't have the energy to pry, but I won't forget this.*

"Well, then I guess you enjoy the woods. We will rest and sniff out a lead. Then you'll rejoin us once the hard parts are out of the way." Arthur crossed his arms with a snort. "So, then you can be all 'back in my day, I journeyed there, and this nostalgic building should be the first place we look.' As if any of it was your idea to begin with."

Merlin raised a brow. "Are you finished?"

Lore and Mathilde both looked at Arthur.

The fox waved a hand in annoyance. "Here," he said, taking out the two of the four vouchers. He gave both of them one, then walked back down to the shining night lights of Silver Lining Landing.

"He acted as if you couldn't fill me in right now," Merlin said with a shake of his head, his large, triangular ears jiggling as he did. He put a hand on his chin and looked at them expectantly.

"Yeah," Mathilde said with her eyes narrowed, likely picking through her own thoughts.

"The queen was given some prophecy, and she thinks that I'm here to fulfill it. We need to get the Warden's Warp from some beast called the Banewing," Lore explained.

Merlin nodded along. "Oh, yes. What a simple task for us. Just slay the Banewing."

"You say it like it's so easy." Lore crossed her arms. "I saw what that thing looks like. It doesn't seem like a walk in the park."

The bat brushed some dirt from his cloak. "Sorry, did I not do the sarcasm well?"

"No."

"Feedback taken," Merlin said flatly.

"Well," Mathilde began. "That's basically it. If you want to sleep in the woods, that's fine, but I am opting for the bed. We'll meet you back here in the morning."

The bat nodded in agreement. "Sounds like a plan. Tonight, rest. Tomorrow. slay the Banewing and steal the Warden's Warp right from under his nose." He gave a thumbs up before returning to the darkening treeline of the Umber Valley woods.

"We have to figure out what's going on with Arthur," Mathilde pushed, as they walked through the streets that were teeming with animalfolk from seemingly all over Thimbleton.

"Yeah," Lore sighed, "I'm sure he's just stressed."

My concern is how weird Merlin *is acting.*

"Stressed?" The mouse laughed. "I think we are all a little stressed."

How can I explain it to her? She basically idolizes him.

Lore shrugged. "Well, whatever it is, let's try to not provoke him into lashing out."

And while Arthur would normally be on board, he's clearly already distressed.

The neon lights of the Mirrored Tides Inn glimmered in the night and drew Lore and Mathilde in like moths to a flame.

"Deal, let's just check in and get some rest." Lore said.

Why's everything feel like it's always up to me?

As soon as they opened the doors, music sounded through the walls. Lights were flashing from a room to the side. *There.* Lore spotted Arthur...having a conflict with the receptionist. *Oh, joy.*

As Mathilde and Lore approached, they just overheard the tail end of the conversation.

"Gonna bring someone else back to the room, only to leave by the time the sun breaks over the sea," she spat.

"Oh, save it, Vivian," Arthur seethed.

"Ahem," Lore cleared her throat.

The vixen behind the desk hesitated to peel her glower from Arthur. When she did, her eyes grew wide. She was snow white, with plush fur, and was probably better suited to living up toward the Wayward Mountains. How'd she find herself here?

"The–the Crowned One?" She stammered out.

"So a few have been saying," Lore sighed out as she slid both her and Mathilde's vouchers onto the desk.

The lights from the other room cast a dance of purple, pink, red, and blue over the receptionist's face.

"Here," the vixen said as she quickly pulled out the room keys and left them on the edge of the desk for the trio to take.

She wants nothing to do with us, does she?

Then from the other room someone called, "Vivian, get the bucket and mop! We had another incident!"

The vixen rolled her eyes and opened a door behind her that revealed what seemed to be a closed utility. As she wheeled the bucket around the desk, she glared at Arthur. "Our conversation isn't over, by the way."

Their friend raised a brow. "I think any entitlement to having a conversation with me ended when I left that morning."

Mathilde quietly got one of the room keys and gestured for Lore to follow her as the two foxes stared off. Before the voice called again for Vivian and the stare down ended with a growl of annoyance.

Arthur followed the two in silence up the stairs opposite of the room with flashing lights and music.

"What a day," Arthur sighed, "Had an audience with the queen and I am unlucky enough to have gotten tickets here only to run into an old." He paused. "Friend."

They unlocked the door to the room, and all Lore could think was, *All I want to do is sleep.*

THIRTY-TWO

The morning air drifted past the curtains and Lore's nose twitched to the smell of salt that danced upon it. The rays of dawn greeted Lore with the warmth of a summer's day, which was a nice change of pace.

It was definitely the warmest part of the island.

Lore rose from her bed and took in the hotel room. She hadn't really gotten all that good a look at it last night when they had finally made it up. The walls were a robin's egg shade of blue with white and brown speckles decorating it like stars in the Thimbleton sky.

There were ornate frames hanging, with intricate braided patterns going round the frame. Their bronze cast shone in the morning light. The frame was holding a photo of a cat that was wearing a shirt way too puffy for Lore's liking. The cat appeared to be in a stream with flowers floating round its head and the white cat was holding a paw out to a tree branch that was hanging a bit low. Another painting had a badger sitting staring straight at the painter with a solemn, albeit elegant, look on its face.

The stained dark brown bedside tables had knobs that matched the brass of the picture frames. Lore noticed a small detail she had seen somewhere else before. Each knob had an embossed little four-leaf clover.

Lore swung her legs over the bed and let her feet touch the plush carpeted floor. When she looked out the window she was met with a beautiful sight of the ocean crashing against the shores of Silver Lining Landing.

The folk that were out and about seemed to be a little older, and a smidge more quiet than the folk who enjoyed more of a nocturnal life.

Then Lore gasped when she saw a familiar set of large, pointed triangular ears walking about the cobblestone streets. Her eyes narrowed as she tried to identify the bat. *It has to be Merlin.* What other bat would wear a purple cloak like that? Lore turned and saw Arthur and Mathilde were still sound asleep in their beds.

As quietly as she could, she opened one of the side tables and found a notepad. She scribbled down a message and left it neatly on her pillow.

SAW SOMETHING—GONNA GO CHECK IT OUT. BE BACK IN TIME FOR BREAKFAST. - LORE

She chewed on the inside of her cheek as she debated leaving a description of what she saw, but she wanted to be sure it was Merlin before she got them riled up about it. With that, she slipped out of their room, down the carved stone stairs. She was hoping to walk straight past the receptionist's desk, but that flew out the window when the snow white fox with a gray muzzle and matching mask stopped her.

"Why is the Crowned One traveling with a sleazebag like Killmoore?"

Lore's shoulders tensed. She really hated when people referred to him by his moniker rather than true name, but it was his choice, she guessed. "He is a good friend."

"Well, he's a shitty lover."

Lore smiled awkwardly and made her way to the door. "Well, ya know, everyone gets different versions of someone."

"Don't trust a word he says," she spat, examining her freshly-filed nails. "He's nothing but a swindler."

"Noted," Lore grumbled as she walked out the door.

Why would I listen to a stranger I just met over someone I have been traveling with, and someone who has literally saved me multiple times? She shook off the interaction like a dog shakes off water, then continued with her mini-quest through the briskly cold and early morning.

The older folk didn't pay hardly any attention to her, or were just content giving her a wide berth, which was a nice change of pace seeing as how every time someone *did* make a big deal, it was either she shouldn't be living or something about the Crowned One. Which was getting old. Very quickly.

Lore spotted who she thought to be Merlin and followed at a safe distance. Luckily, it seemed the bat in question didn't bother to take notice. That didn't stop the whispers around her, though.

"The Crowned One is here? After ages of waiting?"

"Would ya look at that? Seein' the prophecy fulfilled in my lifetime."

"How much do you think those damn things get in the way?"

A lot. Far too often, and at the worst times possible, Lore wanted to answer, but she kept her eyes glued on the Wielder, who was now walking at a quicker pace. She noted the business he was getting ready to stroll into. The neon lights were off and the sign in the large window read, SORRY, WE'RE CLOSED. but that didn't stop the bat from knocking.

It was maybe five seconds later when a squirrel rocking an eye patch answered the door. It let the bat in, furtively looked left and right, then closed the door once again.

Lore watched as the squirrel drew the blinds shut and silently cursed under her breath. "Damn it."

She crossed her arms and seated herself on a bench nearby. Lore watched the neon sign whose lights weren't flickering. THE VELVET SIREN, it read. She pursed her lips and surveyed the building, seeing if there were any cracks or crevices she could slink through to overhear the conversation happening in the closed establishment. But alas, she couldn't spot anything out of the ordinary at first glance.

Then she saw it. A stairwell that led upward to another level. Maybe she could find something that would lead her to the top of the Velvet Siren. She moved quickly, though careful not to bump into any of the other folk that were out and about on their daily routine.

As Lore darted up the stones steps, she ended up running into a parent and child.

The goat parent's thick grey brow furrowed, but then softened after meeting her gaze.

"A human," they muttered as they gently guided their child behind them with an arm.

"Is it really a human with antlers like that?" the kid chimed.

Lore bit her lip, as she didn't know how to answer the situation that was unfolding before her. She laughed nervously and shimmied around the two goat folk before darting up the rest of the stairs.

Shake it off.

Once Lore got to the landing, she was pleased to see a slight crack in the wall that was large enough someone could get through it, but still slender enough that hardly anyone would want to walk through it.

As Lore side stepped through the split in the cave wall. The jagged rocks squeezed her as if she had asked them for a hug. Her antlers ground against the stone and the friction was frustrating, but she popped out on the other side okay, aside from a few scrapes on her hands and forearms.

The other side of the wall was open, large enough for Lore to stand, but there was only room for her to reach her arms out before touching each wall. The murmurs she heard put a smile on her face.

This was exactly what she had hoped for. Lore knelt down and put an ear to the ground. The voices were faint, but she could definitely hear Merlin. That was, without a doubt, him.

"—mad?" The voice had to belong to the owner of the Velvet Siren. An image of the eye patch-wearing squirrel passed through Lore's mind.

"—saw it—will be mine—signal," Merlin's voice replied coldly.

Lore's brow pulled tight together. Merlin didn't say he had friends in the area. Let alone that he would visit them. She returned to focusing on as many words as she could make out from the conversation happening below in the closed shop. Bar, brothel—*whatever it was.*

"—Larken Dreadway—"

Merlin's laugh sent chills down Lore's spine. "Larken Dreadway—'ave the key."

Lore's memory replayed the song she and Mathilde had stumbled upon Lyudmilla singing in the graveyard after their meeting with Arthur. The song traveled through her mind like she had it on repeat.

Larken Dreadway came down to the valley, and
he did declare,
'This is the day I'll put an end to that bonnie
white hare.

The conversation continued.

"—Queen—prophecy—Banewing," Merlin spat, sounding rather annoyed with his companion.

There was no response. The only sound Lore heard was water dripping in the small nook.

Me? He's talking about me. What do I have to do with Larken Dreadway?

Then the squirrel finally spoke. "—Mythvale—Banewing—under-prepared."

A bell sounded, making Lore's heart race.

That must mean Merlin is heading back to the hill now. She shot up and headed back to the crevice. She turned her head to look at the small nook she just eavesdropped through, then shimmied back through the jagged stones.

Suddenly, a hand wrapped around her forearm and yanked her out the other side.

THIRTY-THREE

Arthur's scowl was scathing. "And what were you doing?!"

"Getting some information," Lore's statement sounded more like a question than a statement.

He released his grip from her arm and took a step back. "Well, we need to go meet Mathilde."

Lore looked back at the crevice and back at the fox. "How did you find me?" she asked, ignoring his talking points.

Arthur let out a groan. "Your scent is strong."

"Are you saying I stink?"

Arthur's foot tapped impatiently. "Can we just go find Mathilde?"

Lore smirked and looked down the flight of stone stairs, and out into the plaza of the coastal city.

No Merlin in sight.

"Do you want to go find Mathilde or do you wanna hear what I found out?" The question fell out of Lore's mouth rather quickly, and rather clumsily. *Not as intriguing as I would have liked it to sound.*

Arthur's brow raised, and his tongue clicked. "Okay, you have a minute thirty."

Lore crossed her arms. "Why are you giving me a time limit?"

"Because Mathilde is somewhere down there." He pointed to the bustling capital streets. "So, spit it out before she finds us up here."

Lore groaned, "Fine." She let her jaw relax as she recalled everything she overheard just moments prior.

"Merlin met with some eye patch wearing squirrel before the shop opened," she began, but was quickly interrupted.

"What shop?" Arthur waited for the answer.

"Please hold your questions," Lore continued, but averted her gaze anywhere that wasn't Arthur's face. "Anyway, I could only hear parts of the conversation and I don't know what to make of it. They were talking about Larken Dreadway, being under-prepared, and the prophecy, and the something about the queen. There's a place called Mythvale—" Lore looked back at Arthur, who nodded along with all of her nonsense. "So, yeah. That's all I overheard."

Arthur brought a clawed paw up to his chin. "Hm, interesting indeed."

"What do you make of it? What does a long-dead bad buy have to do with anything happening right now? Merlin defeated him, didn't he?"

Arthur's eyes darted to the steps where Lore also saw Mathilde skipping up them with a tune on her breath.

"We keep an eye on Merlin," Arthur said before greeting Mathilde.

"Where did you find her?" she asked when she got to the top of the stairwell. She looked at Lore. "And don't go disappearing like that again."

Lore scratched the back of her neck and rocked on her heels. "I left a note."

"Note, smote," Mathilde insisted.

"Okay, fine. I'm sorry." Lore replied.

Mathilde pursed her lips. "It's fine. What were you doing, anyway?"

"She was just sightseeing before we went to meet up with the bat," Arthur explained.

Probably best not to say anything now. We will have to break it to Mathilde when we know Merlin's angle. She idolizes him and that could pose some...difficulties.

Mathilde narrowed her eyes on Lore after the fox spoke for her. "We could have done that together."

Lore exchanged looks with Arthur, then returned her line of sight to Mathilde, who now had her hands on her hips. "Next time."

The mouse nodded in agreement. "Alright, well, instead of standing around, let's go meet Merlin. I bet he's been waiting all morning for us."

Lore and Arthur exchanged looks again, but ultimately agreed. As the trio walked down the steps and headed toward the city exit, Lore couldn't help it. She looked over her shoulder at the Velvet Siren's sign that was getting smaller and smaller the closer they got to the exit.

Then she placed a hand over her stomach.

It doesn't feel right—not disclosing this information to Mathilde. But—

Lore watched as Mathilde excitedly ran up to the hill to greet Merlin, excitement ringing in her voice.

Would she believe me, though?

The question gnawed at her more than she'd like to admit. Merlin was a direct connection to Gannon, and herself? Well, I'm just some human who ended up in a world where I wasn't supposed to be.

"I was beginning to think you all slept in," Merlin mused.

"Nope, just a little sightseeing," Arthur said.

Mathilde shook her head. "Lore was out sightseeing before we agreed to meet, and we had to track her down," the mouse explained.

"Oh?" Merlin asked, his gaze drifting over to Lore. "See anything in particular that sparked your interest?"

Lore gave a faint smile. "You have no idea."

Merlin clasped his hands together and grinned. "Well, I have wonderful news."

"What is it?" Mathilde eagerly questioned. Her eyes darted around, looking for whatever the surprise news could be.

Lore watched Arthur give an eye roll, which, at this point, was normal when Merlin spoke.

Merlin removed his hat and bowed, then gave the pointed star embroidered cap a good shake. Out fell an array of gears, cogs, and other metal parts that look like they should have gone to a scrap pile long ago. But, instead, ended up stashed in the bat's hat somehow.

Merlin, always one for a good show, then with a snap, fire left his hand and drifted to the metal parts. The fire fell onto the scrap parts like glitter all at once, and it seemed to get everywhere. But the spark of life was enough. Merlin shooed the trio back to give the spell some space.

Lore watched as the gears contorted and grew larger and larger, until the gears locked, and the cogs fell into place and her brow furrowed with thought as she tried to take in what was before her. The thing roared with black smoke billowing out the back.

"And how long did you have that in there?" Arthur huffed.

"Not long at all, actually," Merlin was quick to point out.

Lore tried to control her expression. "Well certainly you didn't find it just lying around the Umber Forest?"

Arthur's eyes sparkled at Lore's question, but Mathilde only seemed puzzled by her skepticism.

Merlin gave a laugh and gestured to the vehicle. "I called in a favor, but anyway, come here." The bat walked over to the running vehicle. "It runs on magical energy, see?" He gestured to the lights that flashed and meters that lay still. "We'll get to Mythvale so much quicker and efficiently now."

"Mythvale?" Lore asked.

Merlin nodded. "The city is home to worshipers of the Great Owl. So, if we're gonna kill a Banewing, that's where the information will be. On how to do so."

While it danced around Lore's observation, if what he said was in fact true, then this could be very beneficial for completing the quest for the Warden's Warp. There were two seats in the front and a bench in the back. The vehicle's wheels were thin and solid metal. The hood of the car's black fabric looked similar to Merlin's leathery wings.

"Alright!" Merlin called. "Everyone aboard."

Mathilde leaped into the front seat. "Okay, let me at the wheel!"

"Oh, absolutely not," Arthur grumbled as he climbed onto the bench in the back.

"All this fuss over a car—can't wait till we try to best a Banewing." Merlin chuckled.

Lore's stomach felt hollow as she climbed in beside Arthur. The imagery of the beast taking flight in the pale blue sky that the Queen had shown them flashed in Lore's mind. She adjusted herself in the seat. Her antlers brushed against the leathery roof that was folded over head, and Lore thought if she wasn't slouching they would have punctured the roof.

"It's okay," Arthur assured her. "It's a rinky-dink contraption. I'm sure if you put a few holes in it, no one would even notice."

Merlin sat in front of Lore and looked at the trio. "Actually," the bat began. "Since there are no safety measures like doors and such." He paused. "I'd just feel awful if something happened to Mathilde. Lore, can you switch spots with her?"

Lore looked at the mouse, whose face was now shadowed by disappointment. "No," Lore said flatly, not bothering to turn towards the bat.

The cloud of disappointment lifted immediately.

"Arthur?" the bat asked, his voice cracked a little, probably at having to use the fox's real name.

Their friend crossed his arm and smiled. "You should know one of the greatest joys in my little world is telling you *no*."

Mathilde flipped back around in the metal seat and looked ahead. "Okay, onward!" she called, pointing her finger towards the dirt road in the distance.

Merlin groaned and shot a flame into the silver circle where she assumed a key would go.

The vehicle vibrated more, so much so that Lore swore her teeth were chattering. Then, with another roar and black smoke bursting from behind them, they drove off into the crisp air of the morning.

Oh, how I miss the temporary warmth from the sun this morning.

The ride was interesting, and luckily, no storms or lightning came and shorted out the magic. But the golden, bronze, and burnt copper scenery did get a bit mundane to Lore as the landscape remained unchanged as they drove. They occasionally passed other magical metal cars.

"They're called Magically Efficient Vehicles," Merlin explained. "Or M.E.V.'s for short."

Lore felt every bump in the road, and every jerk sent her sliding with the sharp turns that littered the Umber Valley. Sloping hills and wet valley roads proved to still be a hindrance, as their transportation became stuck in a mud hole.

The M.E.V. jerked suddenly before it came to a stop, and Mathilde went flying from her seat. Thankfully, she landed on the front hood. Lore quickly leaped out and helped the mouse down.

Merlin slid out, followed by Arthur, who huffed at the sight of the hole the contraption had found itself in.

A gentle rain started leaking through the tree's vibrant canopy and dripped onto Lore's freckled cheeks like butterfly kisses in the summer. Mathilde stood close by her as she watched their companions try to push the M.E.V. out of the pothole, which appeared to be consuming the front right wheel.

"I'm starting to think the Celestials are laughing at us," Mathilde grumbled before she pushed up her sleeves to go help push their ride free from its muddy captor.

Lore sighed. *It certainly seems that way.*

Just as she was about to join the other three, she heard steam and gears shifting in the foggy distance. She looked down the road they had just traveled and locked eyes with glowing yellow orbs. Ones that were approaching them rather quickly.

Her gut twisted, remembering the shadow spirit she had spoken with on the Wayward Mountains.

But *this* was far too big to be the talkative imp she had acquainted herself with.

"Guys," Lore said, moving closer to her friends. "We have company."

THIRTY-FOUR

Merlin's eyes grew wide. With shock or pleasant surprise, Lore couldn't tell. But the sight of a familiar albino wolf obviously shocked the Wielder.

Lyudmilla held the reins of a mechanical pony, which pulled the large wagon Dina and Lyudmilla had packed their lives into.

Silence hung in the air for a moment as everyone sized each other up.

Dina's fur coat appeared glossy in the sprinkling rain. The cat wore a smile on her face, and the love she had for Lyudmilla shone in her eyes.

The white wolf also appeared different. She didn't look as tense or on edge. Her shoulders were relaxed, and her pale eyes were warm with life and compassion. Then she laughed. Breaking the hardened silence that seemed to press on everyone's shoulder.

Mathilde laughed with the wolf, and it continued to be infectious to the rest of the party.

"Well, isn't this by the Celestial's grace?" Dina mused, climbing off the wagon to greet them.

"It's definitely something," Merlin replied.

"It's so good to see you both!" Mathilde called.

Lyudmilla flashed a smile. "And you—" Her gaze fell on Lore, "Here I thought you would have left us by now."

Lore shrugged. "Guess Thimbleton isn't tired of me yet."

"So, it seems you'll be camping beneath the stars tonight," Dina said.

"More or less, given how thick the canopy is," Arthur added.

"Well," Lyudmilla stretched her arms upward, "I suppose it wouldn't hurt if we crashed here, too. What do ya say, Di?"

"Sounds good to me. I'll get the tent," the calico cat agreed.

"I'll collect firewood," the wolf offered.

"I'll go with you," Merlin added.

"I'll search for something we can use to make a tent," Arthur said.

The animals scattered, leaving Lore and Mathilde alone.

Lore looked down at the mouse, who seemed to be glowing with excitement. "Whatcha thinkin' 'bout?"

"How proud Gannon would be that everyone seemed to have gotten a happy ending."

The admission stabbed Lore in the heart. The urge to tell Mathilde about the weird conversation she overheard pressed just behind her teeth.

"What about you, Lore?" the mouse asked, retracing her steps to their stuck ride. "What are you thinking about?"

Lore paused, thinking of an answer. She heard Dina grumbling as she moved one of her many, many boxes from the back of her wagon.

"I think Dina packed too much."

Mathilde burst into laughter.

"No, no," Dina insisted from her place next to the mechanical horse. "I packed *just* enough."

Lore shoved the uncomfortable feelings that were gnawing at her aside and went to see if the cat needed help. "Anything I can do?"

"Well, actually," she purred as she shoved boxes into Lore's arms. "Hold these." The calico proceeded to place even more on the ground. "Ah, there it is!" she chimed, promptly climbing into the back of the wagon. Wood creaked under her boots.

Lore remembered the first time she met Dina. The memory of the pub owner blowing smoke in Crinkle's face was something she hoped to never let slip from her mind. The thought that she might forget chipped away another piece of her heart.

Dina jumped down from the back of the wagon. "Mathilde!" she called loudly.

The mouse scampered over. "What is it?" Her green eyes flickered over Lore. "I am not a pack mule, Dina."

The cat smiled. "No, no, of course not. *But...*" She handed Mathilde the bag that was twice her size as she was tall. "Take that over there where it's dry, would ya?" Dina pointed to an open spot in the forest where fireflies glowed softly and the rain barely hit the dead, brown grass.

Mathilde sighed, but didn't object. Lore watched her do just that.

Dina took the boxes from Lore and slide them back into the wagon. When she took the first box, she suddenly made a silly face.

"Since when have you been you the type of cat to puff out her cheeks and cross her eyes?" Lore laughed.

"I've no idea what you're talking about, human. I am a *lady,*" the calico replied in an overly-dignified, clearly sarcastic tone. Once Lore slid the last box on top of the others, Dina lifted the wagon tailgate closed. She dusted her hands, "Alright, let's go see what Mathilde is up to."

Dina and Lore approached behind the mouse, who was sorting tent materials. In the distance, Arthur was returning with a fallen hollow tree in tow behind him.

"Alright, everything is organized, so now we just have to assemble stuff," Mathilde announced.

Arthur propped up the large hollow side of the log that looked about the size of the burrow the three of them had huddled in when Crinkle had banished them to the Twisted Wood. The wind blew, and the memory chilled her. It felt like such a long time ago.

"There," Arthur chimed, proudly looking at his makeshift shelter.

Mathilde giggled. "Afraid of a little water, Arthur?" the mouse teased.

Nearby, the ladies quickly got the cat and wolf's tent up.

"Well, look at that," Dina said, wiping her water-weighted fur out of her eyes.

"Looks great, kitten!" Lyudmilla praised.

The group looked over and saw the wolf and bat returning through the fog that was quickly thickening.

"Great timing," Mathilde added.

They made a pit and promptly threw logs into it. There was no need for kindling since Merlin's flame created a warm fire the instant it touched the dry bark. Eternal colors of fall painted the Umber Valley. The night air was crisp, but not biting. Regardless, they still appreciated the heat. Light danced on everyone's faces while they sat in silence around the bonfire. The sound of crackling embers and rustling leaves from the canopy filled the still air.

Merlin clearing his throat.

Killmoore shot her a disgruntled expression, and she could practically hear him saying, "Here we go again," as he retreated under his hollow log.

"This reminds me of the night we first journeyed away from Mythvale." Merlin's eyes darted to Lyudmilla, who seemed to be half-listening and half-asleep while Dina curled up in her lap.

"It was an interesting trip really," Merlin continued, not needing anyone to ask if they were interested because, like always, Mathilde sat there starry-eyed and eager to hear another story about Gannon. The thought alone reminded Lore that the mouse would likely choose the bat over her if and when she told her about the suspicious conversation.

The night continued, and as Merlin recounted his tale, Lyudmilla started grumbling about some inconsistencies.

In response to a story about the seasons corresponding with each cardinal direction, the wolf replied, "Being in the Twisted Wood all those years have clearly made you *touched* in the head."

After he described how he, Lyudmilla, Crinkle, and Gannon had met, she scoffed and said, "Your memory isn't what it used to be, old man."

His last story was about Larken Dreadway.

Merlin's fingers caught fire to cast a show on his face when he spoke. "The best for last, when ol' Larken Dreadway met his match…the Order of the Chimera."

His smile revealed two things. *An air of smugness. And obvious favoritism for this particular tale.*

"The Marten came from a land a ways east, and he had big plans. I know you've heard the songs sung, but what you may not know are the motives of the pine marten. Why would Larken Dreadway try to slay the Great Hare?"

Mathilde pointed out, "Something I always asked Gannon about, but he insisted it was too tragic to discuss."

The wolf nodded. "Gannon understands the weight stories hold."

Merlin gave a casual wave of his hand. "They do, but stories should be shared. Now…Where were we?"

"Larken's plans," Arthur replied flatly.

The bat rubbed his hands together right. "We had spent weeks tracking him, only to stumble upon him and the individual he kidnapped. The vessel of the Great Hare. It was deep in the Infinite Run. When the four of us cornered him, he spilled everything. His plan was simple. Kill the vessel, which by extension kills the Great Spirit, then he would ascend to that Spirit's spot in the Celestial heavens."

"How'd you get him to tell you his whole plan so quickly?" Lore asked.

Lyudmilla answered before Merlin could, "Because every villain is chomping at the chance to share their great plans, especially when they think they've already won."

Merlin cleared his throat. "Well, we had him cornered. The vessel was at a safe distance away, by the shrine of the Hare. Certainly calling upon the Spirit for help. But we had Larken sweating, second guessing his grand speech—"

"Hold on. I never knew he kidnapped anyone. Who was the vessel?" Arthur said a bit skeptically, looking at Lyudmilla for clarification.

The wolf mulled her words over before answering. "Things were a little different back then. And the individual taken at the time was a dying species." Her pink gaze glanced at Lore. "And as time moved forward and songs were written and stories shared…" The wolf's eyes softened, a look of pain etched itself in her features.

Lore felt like ice had spread through her chest. "You mean—?" She could hardly get her thoughts together to finish the question.

Dina rested a hand on Lydmilla's arm, and added, "Although it was only a little over fifty-five years ago, folk forget. Their memories are short and the true parts of a story...the hard to swallow parts—although important—get left out."

Merlin quickly grabbed the reins of the narrative again. "No, Lore, you aren't the first human brought back to Thimbleton, who was thought to be the Chosen One. In order for the prophecy to be fulfilled, each of the Guardians must have chosen their vessel, which is an extension of the Spirit. But it's dangerous. And in the case of Larken Dreadway, he discovered an ancient secret. That the Spirits could be killed if their vessel was." His tone gentled. "But let's hope you are the last."

"So The Great Stag chose to possess Lore?" Mathilde pushed.

"That's one way to look at it," Lyudmilla said.

"So, the battle?" Mathilde asked.

"Right," Merlin began with the clap of his hands. "The battle was intense, and the terrain was a bit difficult for some." He eyed the wolf as he said the last part..

Lyudmilla rolled her eyes. "D'you know how hard it is wielding an ax in a marsh?"

"How'd you defeat him?" Arthur pressed.

Merlin's smile curled with satisfaction. "I delivered the finishing blow. One well-aimed fire blast, and he was devoured by my flames."

"That most *definitely* didn't happen," Lyudmilla said with a scowl.

Lore watched as Merlin tried to play it off as nonchalant as he could, but Lore wasn't convinced. The doubt she had before continued to fester. And she didn't know how long she had before it fully spread, rotting all faith she had in the Wielder.

"What happened to the vessel?" Lore's voice asked with a crack in her tone. "Did the Hare help them?"

Lyudmilla's face darkened, but it was Merlin who beat her to the answer. "The Great Hare did what spirits do. Self-preservation. It broke the bond, and when two merged souls become severed, the weaker of them tends to not make it."

Time stopped for Lore. *Does this mean at any moment the Great Stag could sense it's in danger and just... sever the bond?* Her heart raced as the panic settled in. *Do I have any agency in this?* Lore felt like she was being pulled under a current of water she had no control over. *Will I die at its whim before I get home?*

The next morning, Lore roused from her sleep when the sun was only barely trickling through the treetops of the autumnal leaves. She'd heard Lydumilla, Dina, and Merlin stirring nearby. When Lore sat up, she looked around last night's campsite. Mathilde was still curled up, fast asleep, but Arthur had slipped off somewhere.

She pursed her lips, stood up, and joined the others by the M.E.V., finally free from the gunky, mud pothole.

"Mornin', Lore," Merlin greeted her.

Lyudmilla and Dina gave a nod of acknowledgement and continued their conversation.

"So as I was sayin', if you're goin' to Mythvale, a lot has changed since you had last been there," Lyudmilla said, matter-of-factly.

"Oh, did some gated communities pop up?" the bat asked.

"No, but it is a functioning city now. It's not some hole in the wall stop for folks who are tryna get their name written in the Warden's book anymore. There are still 'vendors.'" The wolf used air quotes at the end.

Merlin stroked his chin. "Ah, okay. Well, this time I don't anticipate buying anything like that."

Lore raised a brow. "Like what?"

Dina laughed to herself. "Oh, you didn't know?"

Lore's eyes darted to Merlin for an explanation, annoyance radiated in her cheeks. "Know what?"

"The city used to be more of Thimbleton's 'underbelly,' so to speak," Merlin explained. "It was beautiful. Homes and markets popped up everywhere you looked, built by the island's less-than-desirables."

Lore raised a brow. "So, a city of thieves?"

Merlin shook his head. "It was a city not bound by the rigid rules hanging over the rest of the island. The streets were loud, the metropolis was as colorful as a kaleidoscope, and magic buzzed in the air." He laughed. "Anything could happen. A brawl in a bar, uncovering long buried secrets, finding a bounty to score, or even meeting folks to start an adventuring group with." The bat looked at the wolf. "Maybe in honor of Gannon and …the Crinkle we knew…we should stop by Stabby's Pub."

The wolf crossed her arms. "Stabby is out of business, Merlin. Like I said, a lot has changed. It's not the same as before."

Before another word could be said, the M.E.V.'s horn sounded. "Let's get this show on the road!" Mathilde called from the driver's seat.

The engine roared, and everyone halted. Except Merlin, who promptly took the spot behind the wheel, and regained control of the contraption. Lore and Arthur huddled together, waiting to board the vehicle.

He'd clearly returned and packed up while Merlin had been talking.

"Alright, let's go," the bat in question announced, waiting for her to climb onto the bench behind the first two seats.

Lore climbed up, but the antlers on her head scraped against the leather. She anxiously bounced her leg up and down. The sound of her hooves on the floor of the vehicle still felt odd to her.

As Dina and Lyudmilla walked past them to return to their wagon, Arthur cleared his throat. "Are you two also going to Mythvale?"

"Yes," Lyudmilla said flatly.

"Great. mind if I join?" Arthur asked. "That *thing* makes me nauseous."

Lore bit her lip. *He must have felt uncomfortable to ask to ride with them.*

Lyudmilla furrowed her brow for a moment until finally saying, "You sit in the back, and don't make a peep."

"Can do," Arthur chimed as he gave Lore a wave, then followed the two lovers.

The scent of the smothered campfire served as a last goodbye as they took off.

This was gonna be a long ride.

THIRTY-FIVE

The ride was long, but Lore at least enjoyed looking at the trees painted in hues of amber and gold on the way to Mythvale. She was admiring the colorful shingled roofs in the distance when Merlin pulled off the road. Leaves and fallen branches crunched under the wheels. The engine rattled as it turned off and Merlin insisted, "Better leave this somewhere we know no one will tamper with it."

The group walked back up to the main road, where a familiar mechanical horse pulled a packed wagon.

The little horse that could, Lore thought to herself.

"Merlin." Lyudmilla sighed. "I told you it's different now."

Merlin gave a theatrical gasp. "You're asking me to *chance* someone swiping the converter? I think not."

The wolf rolled her eyes. "Just jump on the back already."

Mathilde, Lore, and the Wielder did without further comment.

The wagon rocked from side to side as they passed under a large metal sign that had 'Mythvale' written in a font that was almost as sharp as where the corners of the metal met.

"Well, that's new," the bat muttered.

The streets of the town were busy and colorful. The folk of Mythvale radiated a certain aura. Despite the vivid banners and clothes strung around, there was not a smile in sight. *I wonder why that is.*

All the same, It was nice. For once, the animalfolk didn't pay Lore any mind. She was just like the rest of her party—in everybody's way.

They took turns saying goodbye to Lyudmilla, who was taking their carriage to the residential sector of the city. Dina's farewell was short-lived, but Mathilde's lingered the longest of the group.

"I'm so glad you get to live a quiet life now," the mouse told the wolf.

Lyudmilla cracked a grin. "And I'm glad your adventure is just beginning." The wolf's gaze shifted to Lore. "Safe travels. Wherever home may be."

She nodded. "Thank you."

Lore's stomach ached at the realization that this might be the last time she ever saw the white wolf.

Lyudmilla was a bit of a brute, who reserved her words for preference of letting her axe talk for her, but deep down Lore saw the heart she fiercely guarded. The one of someone broken over the loss of a dear friend. Someone who had sung through tears in a graveyard when she thought she was alone. Someone who had tried to desperately hang onto another friend, who had long been gone thanks to the corrupting influence of absolute power.

Lore flexed her hand and hoped that even if she forgot Lyudmilla's face, she'd always hear the wolf's singing.

"So, where is this special library with hidden knowledge?" Arthur asked, his face dropping to a frown to blend in with the locals.

"Just a bit ahead," Dina said before she took off, weaving through the crowd with speed and ease.

They had walked for a block or two before Lore suddenly bumped into Arthur's back and Mathilde into hers.

"This is it," Dina mused, with her hands on her hips. Her tail swayed back and forth as she looked at the long-abandoned library.

The animalfolk crowding the streets gave the building a wide berth, as if it were the center of some plague. Boards covered the windows, and seemed to expand under their gaze. As if the building itself was exhaling a sigh of relief at seeing patrons for the first time in who knew how long.

"Does every town in Thimbleton have a dilapidated library?" Lore muttered under her breath.

Merlin's ears twitched at Lore's passing comment. "This one isn't supposed to be as enchanted as the others. But, to a degree, I suppose all libraries are magical."

I'll have to take his word for it. Because it doesn't look like I'll get to see for myself.

The group stared at the sparkling silver chains locking the front door.

Lore rocked on her hooves. She winced at a random pain that felt like an ice shard rammed its way up to her knee. *Just another day of living, I s'pose.*

Then Lore watched Merlin give the door a good shake. His frustration could have smoked from his ears. "Damn metal is charmed," he grumbled in frustration.

"Who would wanna lock up the library?" Mathilde whined.

Arthur scoffed. "Many folks, actually."

Dina nodded in agreement. "Some see knowledge being spread and get scared of things they can't comprehend."

Mathilde crossed her arms. "What makes libraries so wonderful is that everyone can go in and pick up whatever book they want."

"So, now what?" Lore asked. "We break in?"

Merlin's laugh was strained. "I'm sure I could crack the enchantment, but that could take days."

Arthur's face lit up with a new idea. "Isn't this the city where the Great Owl has her temple?"

The bat answered flatly. "Yes."

The fox beamed. "Owls are all about knowledge, so I bet we can find out who locked this up from the temple dwellers."

Mathilde caught Arthur's optimism like it was a contagious bug spreading through a school. "And, if we're lucky, maybe they'll give us a key to get inside!"

Dina tucked her paws into her bomber styled jacket. "The plot thickens." She smiled, her green eyes gleaming in the morning sun. "However, I must be off. After all, I've a story all my own to get back to." She gave the group a playful salute and disappeared down the street casually, as if she knew they'd be seeing each other again.

Lore tilted her head. "Wouldn't be a bad idea, I guess."

Merlin shrugged. "Fine. I know where the temple is. I doubt that had changed since I was last here."

Lore felt frozen in her tracks as she looked up at the temple spires towering over the other buildings. *Or perhaps it just looks that way cause it's also at the top of a hill.*

Large, white columns reached high to the single pitched ceiling. Orange and deep plum tiles lined the roof. A white marble circle, featuring a carved great-horned owl, hung in the center of the entryway.

What if that fell on someone? Lore wondered. But the likelihood of that was low. Because the temple was almost as empty as the library. *At least it isn't boarded up and enchanted shut.*

The marble owl's eyes pierced Lore, pinning her in place. It felt like she couldn't breathe.

"Come on, Lore," Arthur whispered, gently nudging her.

Mathilde was already darting up the polished steps with glittering violet sparkles. Merlin was not much farther behind her.

"Let's stick together, please!" the Wielder called over his shoulder.

Lore climbed the staircase until she stood on a black stone tiled floor. It was so pristinely polished, she could see her reflection as if it were a true mirror.

A single cloaked temple attendant stood on the other side of the hall. Mathilde eagerly approached them. "Hello, we have a question, if you don't mind?"

Merlin chased after the mouse. "Hold on!"

Arthur pursued the bat. "Calm down. She's just asking a question."

Lore stayed close to the fox's side. Her stomach flipped as the floor beneath them vanished. The drop was short but sudden. It was only moments before the opening in the floor above closed.

"I hate how frequently this happens to us," Mathilde grumbled.

"So, now what?" Lore asked as she picked herself up from the ground.

"We keep moving," Merlin said, holding his hand aloft and thankfully keep his fireball alive.

Cliffs of Wayward

The descent made the Wielder's magic their only lifeline.

Merlin's crackling fire almost distracted her from her own thudding steps. Lore took a breath and thought how ridiculous they must have looked. *That's what hooves will do to you.*

Without warning, a light appeared at the end of the tunnel. Almost like the silver lining of a star-filled sky. And there was now a breeze blowing through the tunnel, refreshing and warm.

Odd. Especially since the atmosphere that morning seemed more like a permanent late autumn, flirting with frost.

Silver, puffy clouds and hanging mist immediately surrounded them when they finally emerged from the tunnel. But it was an oversized owl of starlight and purple that grabbed Lore's attention. Its enormous round eyes appeared to have swirling galaxies in them.

The party of adventurers froze, and she felt like ice rushed through her veins from the top of her antlers, through her tightening chest and her trembling furred legs—stopping at the bottoms of her hooves.

The Owl stretched her wings, and the feathers gleamed like shooting stars. A gentle hoot conjured another warm breeze to kiss their cheeks.

Arthur immediately dropped to his knees. Mathilde did the same. Though the mouse was undoubtedly exhilarated, Lore saw the way the gray mouse's ears quivered.

When Merlin remained standing, Lore hesitated. Even if she wanted to copy her friends, her knees were locked in awe and fear.

The sparkle in Merlin's eye told her he was feeling anything but.

The mighty bird took flight from what appeared to be her nest, flapping her powerful wings to launch herself into the sky above. The downdraft dissipated the puffy silver clouds, revealing a floor of dying stars and moonlight. In the nest, three large eggs began to wiggle and crack.

Mathilde and Arthur shot to their feet, and they all watched as stone statues cracked from the eggs like baby birds.

Lore locked eyes with a large stone alligator. Her eyes darted to Mathilde, whose face was pale as if she saw a ghost. Merlin, for once, looked absolutely frozen in fear.

The second egg produced a bear. One she thought was dead. Seeing how perfectly it depicted Mordred made a shudder travel down her spine.

Arthur reached for a throwing ax, but Lore placed a hand on his arm and shook her head. "It's not him." She addressed Mathilde and Merlin next. "And that's not Gannon."

Mathilde pointed to the last one. "Then who is that supposed to be?"

For the first time since she had been in Thimbleton, Lore met the eyes of another human. *Another human.* One she felt deep in her gut that she may have seen before.

The carved wrinkled lines on the stone seemed just a little too real for her liking, but she couldn't stop staring. The old stone woman stood hunched over balancing her weight on a walking stick. Her hair was swept up into a bun atop her head. *It's her. It's really her.*

Her heart felt like it was close to bursting, only being held together by invisible threads. *It's the old woman from my memories.*

Lore looked back to the stone figures, who were now crawling from the nest of branches, roots, and lost things down to the ground where the adventurers were standing.

With a jump, the statues landed with a hardy *thud.* The woman didn't seem as old now that she was closer. Her wrinkles faded to mere laugh lines and the alligator's top hat matched the one Mathilde had stowed away for safekeeping back in her room at the yellow manor. And the bear seemed less ragged with anger, now more soft and stoic.

But Lore was busy staring at a bracelet around the old woman's wrist. It looked just like *hers.*

Had the old woman also visited Thimbleton?

"What is this?" Merlin demanded in a booming voice.

The alligator spoke with a deep voice, "To know what has been concealed, you will have to answer—"

The bear's voice bellowed out, cutting off and simultaneously completing the alligator's sentence, "The riddle of three."

"Solve it, and unlock a treasure beyond measure," the elderly woman chimed in.

"Is that part of the riddle?" Mathilde asked.

Before anyone could answer, the stone reptile spoke again, "I come in all shapes and sizes—"

"Well, what a great start," the mouse interrupted. "I'm sure this will be easy to narrow down."

"Shh," Merlin whispered.

Mathilde quieted, but wore the face of a child who thought a parent's rule was stupid.

Then the bear spoke next. "I make the bad more palatable and the good even sweeter—"

"Oh, an apple!" Arthur cut in.

"Quiet, fox," the bat chided, sharper than what he'd said to Mathilde.

"Without me, life is a sour endeavor, indeed." The woman's voice felt like a hug to Lore.

The statues went quiet, giving the adventurers time to think.

Merlin did his best thinking aloud, or he simply loved hearing himself talk. Because he was speaking loudly enough for them all to hear as he paced the floor. "It may not be an apple because while it seems culinary inspired, we shouldn't take it too literally to only mean fruit. We should also consider herbs, cuts of meat, and maybe even desserts."

Lore crossed her arms and mulled over the riddle from start to finish.

I come in all shapes and sizes.

She took a step back and looked at her companions where they stood. Arthur was the tallest of them all, if one didn't count her own antlers. Merlin was perhaps the sturdiest of the non-stone animals. And Mathilde's large, round ears offered quite the silhouette. *Hmmm.*

I make the bad palatable and the good even sweeter.

Lore thought back to the food shared with her in Charmsend around a dinner table with mice. Then her mind flashed to making cookies with the same old woman represented before her in stone. There hadn't been any time to frost them before the Great Stag had called her away and back to Loch Luan.

Without me, life is a sour endeavor, indeed.

The bat, fox, and mouse were still bickering amongst themselves when Lore had an idea. She cleared her throat to get their attention, but they didn't hear her.

"Ahem," she said, louder this time. "I think I may have the answer."

Merlin tapped his foot impatiently. "Well, don't keep it to yourself." He gestured to the statues, who stood in a neat row.

"The power of love?" Lore felt stupid for saying the words, but what else could it be?

An oppressive silence hung in the air, smothering any optimism the longer it stretched.

"Isn't something supposed to happen?" Mathilde asked, tilted her head expectantly.

"Not if that wasn't the right answer," Merlin replied, frowning.

"Let's not leave Lore to do all the heavy lifting," Arthur chimed in.

"Well, what do you suggest?" Merlin asked pointedly.

Mathilde blurted, "Family."

Nothing.

"Forgiveness," Arthur offered.

Merlin scoffed, earning a scowl from the fox.

"Do you have anything better, bat?" Arthur asked.

"The answer is obviously *power,*" the Wielder replied.

He was proved wrong when nothing happened at his proclamation.

"We've all had multiple guesses," Mathilde cut in. "Maybe Lore has another one?"

Lore felt a warmth blanket around her. A sensation she had thought she forgot since being plagued by the Great Stag's frost. She looked down at her green flannel. One of the few things she still had from her world in this new one. It felt important. *Was it a gift from a friend?* She fiddled with the hole near one of the buttons.

"The power of friendship," she whispered to no one in particular.

The ground beneath them shook, prompting the stone statues to crumble and revealing a way out.

Merlin bolted towards the exit without hesitation.

"C'mon, Lore!" the fox urged.

"Let's get out of here," Mathilde yelled, pulling on Lore's arm.

In the rubble of the monuments that immortalized their journey so far, a glint of gold caught Lore's eye. "There's something there." She rushed to sift through the stone fragments, eventually snagging something that felt cool to the touch. Her fingers tightened around the object, then the trio bolted up the stairs that had magically appeared upon solving the riddle.

At the end of the tunnel, she could see the blinding light of the midday sky that poured in looking like a river of white rushing water. When the group landed on the black tile floor of the temple's entrance, a title slid back into place over the stairwell.

The horned owl carving seemed to glow, and from the open columns, the autumnal crisp air rushed past them.

"Let's get out of here," Arthur said through gritted teeth. "The quicker we find the information about the Banewing, the better."

He was clearly shaken after seeing the Mordred statue. He descended the stairs quickly, as if he were running from the real bear himself.

Lore and Mathilde followed him.

Merlin stood at the base of the temple. "I see you made it out."

Arthur's expression was flat. "No thanks to you."

Mathilde shook her head. "Can the lover's quarrel wait? Lore has something important."

Their attention fell on her like a spotlight, and she opened her hand, revealing a golden key.

"Let's go see if this unlocks the library."

THIRTY-SIX

Mathilde held the mended gold key in her hands, looking it over. She had asked to carry it, and Lore had easily agreed. Lore thought surely the mouse was admiring her own reflection in the polished gold, but then her quiet footsteps made came closer.

"Here," Mathilde said as if she were just handing her another cup of tea on an afternoon spent in front of the fireplace. A soft smile spread across Lore's face as she felt the weight of the key in her palm.

She walked up to the chain-covered door and inserted the key. After a single turn to the right, she heard a definitive *click*. She expected a magical ray of energy to radiate from the library, or the spirit of the Great Owl to appear. Instead, the chains simply fell to the ground with a clang along with the lock.

Arthur gestured to the doorknob. "Well, open it."

Lore's hand on the metal felt cool to the touch. It made her think of the Moon Drop. She shuddered as the memory of the hooded Warden on the crescent lake came to mind.

She opened the door, releasing a scent of musky, old paper into the streets of Mythvale.

She turned when a *whoosh* sounded behind her.

Merlin already held a flame in his hand. "Let's hope we can find a power switch for this old place," the bat muttered.

Arthur clicked his tongue. "If it doesn't, I'm sure lighting the empty fireplaces wouldn't be too much of a task for you."

Lore held the door open for her three companions to enter, and none of the passerby seemed to care the library was now open. She pursed her lips. *Peculiar.* Inside, there was a wooden sign that faintly read, "Welcome to Thieves' Library." On either side of the phrase were carved serpents.

The others dispersed into the library, already hot on the trail of anything on the Banewing and what weakness it could have.

But Lore was stuck staring at the sign, feeling hollow. *Will I never recall Petra when I step through the door of a library at home? Will I forget those glowing orange, pumpkin-sized eyes?*

"Lore!" Arthur called, "What are ya doin'? Start lookin'. We've got a time limit, ya know."

That was news to her. "Uhh—since when?"

"Well, we certainly can't keep a queen waiting," the fox replied.

Lore got to work.

Day quickly turned to night as they continued searching.

Lore didn't know who found the book. But she joined the others in time to see a rather plain looking tome plop on a table, prompting a cloud of dust to spiral into the air.

"Hmm," Merlin grumbled. "Let's see," he murmured, flipping through the pages.

"Not what I imagined holding the Banewing's weakness," Lore noted.

"Sometimes things aren't as they appear," the Wielder replied.

Mathilde and Arthur huddled closer to Lore. The three of them peered over the bat's shoulders.

Lore's gaze landed on a diagram of the Banewing.

"It looks like a field guide," Arthur commented.

"Like Gannon's book?" Lore asked.

Mathilde cleared her throat as her fingers ran across the lines of text connected to the drawing with a line. "Gannon's book is more of a journal with the occasional drawing."

The human nodded and Arthur asked. "So, whose field guide is this?"

The bat took the book and flipped back to the front of the book. Merlin stopped. He clicked his tongue. "This may also prove useful." He turned the book to face the trio, showing off a sketch of a scale-like stone that almost resembled a scale. Beneath it, faded text spelled out the words, "Memory Stone."

"You think it's another treasure protected by the beast?" Lore asked.

"I believe so," Merlin said flatly.

Arthur leaned forward. "We got another shot at restoring your memories Lore!" The fox sounded more like Mathilde with unbridled excitement rather than his carefully-collected self. Arthur seemed a little embarrassed, so he reached over Merlin and flipped back to the Banewing diagram. "Its chest may hold some sort of weakness."

Merlin nodded in silence and snapped the book shut. "We shouldn't spend too much longer here now that we have what we came for."

"Are you kidding me?!" Mathilde shrieked. "We just got here!"

Merlin was already halfway to the door. He spun on his heel and gestured to Lore. "We have a human who could pass as a deer," he drummed his fingers on his chin. "A few more days, hours—we don't know—until the transformation completes, so we should stay focused on our mission."

Mathilde's ears drooped. Then her big green eyes shimmered with regretful tears. "Sorry, Lore. I hadn't thought of that."

She shrugged. "Don't worry about it." She put her arm around Mathilde and they departed the dusty library.

Under the cover of night, they headed back up the hill to the temple. The adventurers remained quiet as they considered how dangerous the Banewing was. The only sound during the trek was the creaking wagon.

Eventually, Merlin spoke up. "Leave most of the work to me." He addressed Mathilde and Arthur next. "The two of you would serve best as distractions." His tone was was graver than when they prepared to battle Crinkle and when they fought Mordred.

If I'm to forget any moment of my time in Thimbleton, I hope it's this one, Lore thought. *Because I don't want to remember the Wielder's fear.*

The edge of the forest was quiet. It had taken them a whole day to travel, and Lore would rather not linger on the back and forth between Arthur and Merlin. Just thinking about it made her motion-sick again, like when they had been in the turnip carriage.

"So, how do we find it?" Arthur asked.

Merlin was busy flipping through the field guide they'd found. "Should be somewhere in here."

Arthur walked towards the tree line. "While you do that, something tells me we'd be doing well to find its den."

Lore raised a brow, expecting resistance from Merlin, but none came.

"Fine."

The glimmering leaves of the trees felt like they were purposely entangling to block out the sunrise.

"Creepy," Mathilde whispered.

Lore agreed. "Yeah, but Crinkle's house was much creepier."

"You're right," the mouse chimed in.

Merlin was still flipping through the field guide.

The group stopped behind Arthur, who was kneeling on the ground with a hand in the dirt. "I'd say we're pretty close," the fox mused.

Lore ran her hand over the same footprint they had seen coming into Silver Lining Landing.

"Ah-ha!" The bat cried with a sense of victory.

The trio watched as the bat ignited a fireball. "Hope you all are ready." Then he threw it at a tree.

Lore watched as the apparently sentient fire traveled upward, consuming the flesh of the tree. "Are you crazy?!" she yelled.

The answer to her outburst didn't come from Merlin. It came from the forest in the form of a ghastly yowl.

"Just got to smoke the creature out," Merlin said in a hushed tone. His flames danced from his hands up his arms.

She swallowed hard as the tops of the burning umber trees leaned away with the powerful roar that echoed between the trunks. Lore glanced at Mathilde, who was behind Arthur, her bow drawn.

She rolled her eyes. *Of course*, Merlin had a bottomless bag for their fight, but not for their traveling needs.

Trying to stay calm, Lore swore tiny snowflakes exited her mouth with each exhale. But with each ground-shaking, tree-felling step, Lore's heart rose higher and higher in her throat.

Trees fell before them, groaning as they did, and the deafening screech of the dragon-like bird filled the air a just before the Banewing appeared.

Just like in the image the otter queen had shown them, and the illustration in the field guide, its feathers were so densely gathered, they looked more like scales. Its large head resembled a diamond with flat angles connecting at sharp points. Two ears sat atop its skull, but the surrounding feathers could be mistaken for horns. When its short snout opened, a gust of wind pushed the group of adventurers back.

Merlin muttered an incantation under his breath.

Void-like dark eyes drew her forward, and she felt ice crystals dance on her fingertips. *Now or never,* Lore told herself, even though her legs shook with panic. She widened her stance, bracing for another breath from the creature.

The bat launched what looked to be a spear of fire at the Banewing, officially kicking off the battle.

Now or never, she silently repeated.

An image of the Great Stag flashed in her mind. Lore pulled from her nerve-shaking fear, and a javelin of ice glided through the center of Merlin's flames.

Unmelted.

It crashed into the creature. In response, the Banewing spewed a projectile of green acid at where she stood. Luckily, Mathilde and Arthur knocked her out of the way just in time.

She landed on the ground with an oomph. Looking up, Lore expected to see the angry face of the Banewing, but all she saw was Merlin scowling down at her.

"For the queen!" Arthur yelled.

"For Thimbleton!" Mathilde cried out, raining arrows upon their foe.

"For home," Lore muttered under her breath just before her vision took on a blue hue.

Between the blades, fire, and ice, the Banewing tired quickly. Its vicious roars died down, and its sharp flying feathers slowed. Eventually, the beast was a panting dog who had run too much.

Rain started falling from the sky as if the heavens themselves were sad to see the creature defeated. As the Banewing let out another mighty roar, thunder cracked across the dark clouds.

And then Lore saw it. A gleam shone deep in the void-like eyes. Her stomach sank. *The true battle was just beginning.*

Pulling her gaze away from the creature, she finally spotted the true treasure. A thread stuck on the tree's bark, no wider than a hairbreadth, fluttered in the air. And next to it, there was a small split in the tree. But she didn't see broken bark around it. The edges made it look like a *tear.*

The tear was small, but just enough shadows leaked out of seemingly thin air. As quietly as she could, she snuck closer to it while the others dealt with the attention of Banewing. She pulled at the dark thread that seemed to be loose, and as she did, the tear grew, revealing something Lore would much rather hide away. *If only I could stitch this closed.*

The cloaked figure that had met her at the crescent lake of Loch Luan stepped out of the tree like it was a door, brief enough to be seen by the others. Before anyone could react, his feathered grip closed around Lore's arm too, vanishing the image of the Great Stag.

Without the Guardian clouding her vision, she could see clearly as the Warden pulled her through the fold of Thimbleton's reality.

THIRTY-SEVEN

It felt like she was passing through jello, but the sensation was short-lived. She collapsed on the other side of the tear and looked up at an endless sky of stars. Constellations she only vaguely remembered or had never seen before.

"The stars of lands far beyond the reach of Thimbleton," a familiar voice spoke.

Lore turned to look over her shoulder. Her eyes grew as confirmation settled in her gut.

Her kidnapper—if that was the appropriate term for the situation—was busy sewing up the rip in reality they had just walked through. The needle sparkled like the stars littering in the heavens, and the thread was as dark as the celestial backdrop. *Almost like the night sky, itself, composed the needle and thread.*

The Warden stepped toward her in the field of swaying plum-colored flowers. The crow smiled. "Crosby said he'd see you again." His yellow eyes were soft for once.

Lore felt like her mind swallowed her up as every memory that involved Crosby played out on a movie screen in her head. "I had my suspicions after talking to the otter queen." Her stomach felt at ease, and her hands steadied enough she could give herself a hug.

The crow nodded and offered her a wing up. "Come, Crosby has something for you," he chattered, leading Lore to a field that seemed to be littered with faint glowing embers.

"What kind of flower is that?" Lore asked.

"Not flowers, dying stars."

"Why would I want to see a star die?" Lore asked aloud as she pulled her hand back from the Warden. The being who seemed looming and all powerful, yet was somehow the same crow who she had sung an unbirthday song to. I don't think I'll ever understand Thimblish customs. *I swore he was gonna die.*

"Not the star dying. Crosby shows you what is in the star," the crow explained as he pulled a vial from the nearest purple flower. He gestured for Lore to take it. "Come now, we must make haste, or Crosby has fear Warden's guardian will eat your friends."

Lore gingerly took the vial from the crow. It weighed practically nothing. But somehow, the little thing was filled completely with liquid. *It looks like crushed violets mixed with broken pearls.*

"The things I do for my friends," she sighed. Popping off the top of the vile, she noticed a pinkish haze trail out along with a floral scent. She threw back the liquid like a shot. It was bitter, and the taste clung to her tongue like a lemon drop.

"Oh, wonderful," Crosby mused before picking her up. "Just this way," he said then carried her through the field of purple flowers and dying stars until they reached the star in the center.

"What is that thing?"

"Crosby lives here," the crow croaked as he sat her down beside the dying ember. She saw the faint markings of a door and as she looked back to see the towering crow, instead she was met with his face at her level. "Well, Crosby hasn't seen home for a long time now," he croaked as he pushed her toward the door. "You took the key when you broke through."

"Broke through?"

"Yes, Crosby saw you that night. You broke through with that mischievous mountain spirit. My key. Some call it a Warp. Crosby was using it to get to your world." The crow stroked a slender feather against her metal bracelet.

"Why were you trying to get to my world?" Lore asked blankly.

"Cro–Warden has business in every realm." The crow ruffled his feathers and Lore waited for him to elaborate. The corvid only motioned with his wings. "Go on now. Crosby wants you to unlock it." He gestured to the door.

"Was there really no other way in?" Lore asked as she gestured to the clear windows.

The crow shook his head. "Human girl expected Crosby to vandalize Crosby's own home." He shook a feather at her as if he were scolding a child. "No, no. Now hand it over. You won't open the door for Crosby."

Lore took a step back from him. "That's far enough, Crosby." She intoned. The crow's head bobbed up and down as he watched her for a moment. She took a deep breath and put the charm into the keyhole. A quick flash of light appeared, and then the door opened. Lore looked down, and the charm didn't seem to sparkle as it had before. She looked in the open door and saw a gleaming silver key.

"Made of stardust, the key is," the crow croaked as he happily danced into his home. "Ah, just as Crosby left it."

Lore nodded, still standing on the threshold.

Crosby turned to smile at her and gestured for her to walk inside. "Come now, Crosby has something for you, the other half of what you've been carrying."

Lore stepped in, the warmth of the fire warming her to the bone. As it did, she had a quick passing through as she mindlessly reached for the blue glass in her pocket.

Were all dying stars homes?

She pulled out the blue glass and showed it to the crow, who screeched with delight. And from behind his head, from thin air, he pulled out a bottle of blue liquid. It was similar in color to the Moon Drop she had seen on Loch Luan.

"Crosby has the memories."

Lore stood frozen, unsure of what to do. Should she take it right from him and run.

No.

That would never work. The Warden would catch her.

"Thank you," she stammered out as she reached for the bottle.

Crosby pulled it back quickly. "Ah ah ah," he waved a feather to her once again. "You must win it." Then he side stepped revealing a bookshelf full of board games.

"You want me to play a game with you?" Lore asked, still dumbfounded by the thought.

"No, you have to beat Crosby at the game," the crow mused as he searched the shelves for whatever he felt was just right for the occasion. After what felt like ages, he pulled a box from the shelf.

"Crosby would play this with friends back at the library in the mountains." He sat the game down and opened the box. Inside was a pegged game board and beads. "First to get stair steps to the celestial gates wins."

"I'm sorry what?" Lore sighed out as she sat crossed legged on the floor with the crow in front of the warm fireplace.

Crosby placed the blue beads in front of her, and kept the orange beads for himself. He then placed a blue bead at the center, then grabbed an orange one to place on the peg behind it. Then he placed the blue one down again on a random peg and another orange bead on top of the orange bead already placed. "Four in a row vertically, horizontally, or diagonally." He let out a squawk for emphasis. "Stair stepping wins." He then cleared the board and returned to Lore the two wooden beads that were painted blue.

They played for what felt like hours. The whole time, the blue liquid-filled bottle sat beside Crosby. Her memories being just out of reach gnawed at her, and the mental image of her friends tiring in their fight against the Banewing weighed on her shoulders.

Then she saw it. A blue stairway to the celestial gates on the pegboard. "I win," she muttered.

The crow gawked at the board with bulging yellow eyes before laughing out loud. "You did win," he agreed and picked up the glass vial gently within his feathers. "Before you get your memories back, Crosby requires a promise."

Lore gulped. "Anything."

"Swear on your memories, Warden's identity remains secret."

Lore thought about it for a moment. It made sense. She understood and grinned. "Not a problem. I hardly believe anyone would think I was sane if I said Crosby, the traveling salescrow, was the Warden."

The crow squealed with laughter, but held tight to the vial of memories. "Swear it," Crosby insisted gravely.

"I swear on my memories the Warden's identity will remain a secret."

Crosby smiled and held the bottle out to her.

Cold tears rushed down Lore's face as she saw the faces of people play out on the glass, and she swallowed the excitement that she would soon remember them. Though her mind worked against her, she reached out to take the vial. On it was a small white tag with the words, 'Drink me,' scribbled on them.

She looked back up at the yellow-eyed crow who was fidgeting with his feathers, nodding his head up and down.

Lore bit the inside of her cheek from the nerves as her fingers pulled at the tag. The faint reflection of her antlered self reminded her she was so far from home, but this was a step in the right direction.

Here goes nothing.

She pinched her nose and threw her head back, downing the drink in one go. Then a tingle traveled from the tips of her antlers to her fingers, then to her hooves.

Everything came crashing back to Lore, just as she had done when she crashed into the well's frigid waters.

Every smile with Maccon.

Every hard day at home.

Every fight.

Every drunken stupor her dad had.

But also, every summer she spent with Mamó.

Her tear-filled eyes locked with Crosby, who opened his wings for her, and she fell into the warmest hug she has had in a while. She let the tears flow as freely as the waters that brought her to Thimbleton.

This time, the veil didn't tear open. Instead, it blew open in the way a curtain does on a warm summer morning.

The Banewing skidded to a halt.

Arthur dropped his axes and darted over to Lore to pull her away from the Warden's grasp. As if she were a hostage.

Of course, the Warden let her go without a fight.

Relief washed over Mathilde's face when she and Lore locked eyes. The mouse rushed to her side, blinking back tears all the while.

The Banewing shyly returned to the Warden's side and wrapped around the floating cloaked being like a house cat would when its owner returned home after a long day out.

"Well, where is it? The Warden's Warp?" Merlin demanded.

Lore hesitated, but eventually answered, "I have always had the Warden's Warp." She held up her wrist. The silver charm caught the sunlight.

Arthur's jaw dropped. If it were possible, Lore was sure it would be on the ground next to his axes. "Would have been more convenient if they were a sparkly pair of slippers." He paused for a beat. "At least then it would have felt a bit more obvious."

"How do we use it?" Mathilde asked.

The Warden tilted his cloaked head and spoke clearly. "Water." He gave her the item the group of adventurers had come for.

Lore let out a shaky breath and held the empty bottle between her fingers to show Mathilde and Arthur she got something. "Killing the beast doesn't reveal the Memory Stone. There was no stone. Only memories trapped in a glass bottle. The Banewing only protects him." She gestured to the Warden, who was silently shrouded in the shadows.

"Well," Merlin cleared his throat. "We must be going then."

Arthur kept his sharpened eyes on the Warden and his beast circling below. "Looks like we can finally agree on something."

Lore looked back over her shoulder as Merlin led them away from the battle zone and back into the thicket of the Umber Valley. Lore watched as the Warden raised a wing. The fallen trees rose and were placed gently back into the ground to take root.

Mathilde's grip was tight on her forearm, and Arthur was eerily quiet.

"It's bad luck, ya know?" the fox finally muttered.

"What is?" Lore asked.

"Running into the Warden," Arthur answered.

Merlin's large, and normally upright, ears were flattened. He said nothing, just offered a gruff grunt in agreement.

And I've seen him twice, not to mention all the times he was just Crosby.

"Well, at least we can get Lore back to the queen."

"Yeah, but we didn't fulfill the prophecy," Arthur pointed out.

Lore carefully studied the way Merlin walked. Something was off with the bat, and not in the moon struck kinda way. Down to his stride, he seemed shaky. Lore's mind replayed what she overheard the morning before departing for Mythvale.

"Well, maybe the great evil and threat really didn't need to be removed." Mathilde ran through her thoughts aloud to the group. "Maybe the Warden and his pet just needed to be subdued."

Arthur shrugged.

"Well, at least Lore has her memories. Maybe the queen will still be able to send her home," the mouse mused. "This calls for celebration."

Lore bit her lip, as the same memories flashed over her mind, "The life I had before isn't one to celebrate," Her voice cracked, and she noticed that Merlin's ears perked as her voice did.

Mathilde stopped, her grip loosening on Lore's arm. "What'd ya mean?"

Arthur's tail swayed from side to side as his ears were standing straight. "Maybe this is a conversation best had at the hotel?"

Merlin stopped, turned on his heel, and looked Lore up and down. "I agree. Better save it for the hotel." He then turned again, leading them back to Silver Lining Landing. "I'm sure there's plenty you have to share."

THIRTY-EIGHT

Arthur closed the door and once it clinked shut, they all let out a collective sigh. He rested his back against the door and slid down to the floor. Mathilde collapsed in her bed. Lore stood in the center of the room, swaying slightly as she played with the memory stone in her pocket.

The silence was heavy on her shoulders.

She breathed through each echoing argument between her parents, each spontaneous adventure with Maccon, every summer with her grandmother, and each moment in between those when she felt entirely alone.

"You should sit down," Arthur suggested.

"No, I'm—" Lore sniffled, "I'm okay." Her eyes fixed on her friends. Despite the many close brushes with danger, she never felt alone.

"Well, tell us," Mathilde pleaded.

Lore swallowed hard. "Where to start." Her eyes stung as she held back tears. The person she'd want to see the most isn't even back home waiting for her. The ache in her chest left her entire being feeling hollow. *Was home even worth returning to?*

Arthur stretched his arms upward and rested his hands behind his head. "How about you start with how you ended up in Thimbleton?"

An ice cold tear trailed down Lore's cheek. "Right."

Another few passing moments of silence and Lore felt the gaze of her friends staring at her.

She cleared her throat and tried to steady her breath.

"It started at my Mamó's house."

Mathilde rested her chin on a hand. "What's a Mamó?"

Lore answered plainly, "My grandma."

Arthur leaned in. "So, it began at your grandma's house?"

Lore nodded, holding back tears, though her voice cracking may have given away the depth of her grief. "The day I was pulled down the well, was the day of her funeral…but a week before, I saw what I know to be the mountain spirit."

Lore let out a shaky breath. "The mischievous imp took my bracelet that she had gifted me before her passing, so naturally I chased it." Her hands trembled at the memory of plunging into the well's icy waters. "The spirit wouldn't let go of my bracelet, and instead pulled me down the well." Lore's eyes glazed over, recalling the burning in her lungs without air, fighting the spirit to swim up to safety, and the fear of drowning.

The mouse's paw on her hand pulled her from the fright-filled recollection. "I'm so sorry, Lore. I know what it's like to lose someone." Mathilde studied her friend's expression. "I can't imagine fighting a shadow and trying to mourn Gannon at the same time."

Lore swallowed past the lump in her throat. Unable to speak, she nodded at her friend, and patted the mouse's paw to comfort her in return.

"I'm really sorry that happened to your Lore." The fox's expression softened. "But I'm glad we got to meet you."

Lore felt tears sting her eyes as her vision became blurred. "I'm really glad I got to meet you all, too. Even if it was because of her…death." *If I forget them... when I return home, that'd be the real tragedy. A loss I couldn't mourn because I wouldn't have ever known they existed.*

Merlin cleared his throat. "I appreciate you sharing that with us, Lore, but I do think it'd be smart for us to get some rest."

THIRTY-NINE

The night was rough for Lore as she tossed and turned. The cold sweat on the back of her neck was making a damp layer and she couldn't close her eyes long enough to even attempt to sleep. Every time the darkness from the back of her eyelids closed, she saw flashes of a shadow out a bedroom window, cold hospitals, and a field of daffodils. Swaying gently in a warm spring breeze.

She sat up and let her legs hang freely off the bed. It still felt unreal that her once bare legs were now covered in fur. That from the waist down, she was a deer.

At dawn, they'd see the queen.

Lore raked a hand through her loose hair and her fingers briefly touched the base of the antlers. By now, she had barely remembered they were there. As the silver light of the moons that hung over Thimbleton poured into the hotel room, Lore's breath hitched as she saw an eerily familiar shadow darting through the empty streets. Her heart dropped, and her hands balled the bedding in her fists. She stood as quietly as she could and snuck out the door. She hoped the note on her pillow would be enough as she once again let her curiosity get the better of her. *Mathilde is going to be so annoyed, but better to ask forgiveness or whatever.*

After all, what else do they expect me to do?

Once the door latch shut behind her, she made her way down the flights of stairs, through the empty lobby, and out the door into the streets that were covered in a blanket of fog.

She spotted the long-eared shadow, but hid behind walls, trash cans, benches, and shrubs.

As she danced between her thoughts and what would have brought the creature down from the Wayward Mountains, she peeked back over the dormant shrub wall and saw she had lost the trail of what she *thought* to be the mountain spirit.

The street light flickered and storm clouds rolled overhead. The crashing sound of the ocean's waves below the cliffs that the city was built on echoed in her ears.

She then turned back to settle behind the shrub wall and swim in her thoughts, but she was met with gold eyes that were forged into a glower from fresh flames.

"Merlin?" she whispered.

FORTY

The small bat seemed larger than before. Perhaps it was the way the full moons cast a shadow behind him, or perhaps it was the fact that Lore was sitting down.

"Don't worry, I will make it painless." Fire engulfed his hands. "Well, as painless as fire can be." His eyes narrowed onto her, and as the first fireball left his palm, she instinctively rolled out of the way.

"Are you *crazy*?!" She screamed as she shot to her feet.

Merlin said nothing, just answered by throwing a fireball, burning with an angry heat.

Lore ran. *Back to the hotel or out of the city?* She didn't know where she just knew that she had to get as far away from Merlin as possible.

I had my suspicions he was up to something, but I was hoping I was hearing things out of context.

Nerves ate away at her gut.

That there'd be a reason.

Her body felt like it was trembling with every dash away from Merlin.

Not ending with me being hunted in the streets.

As Lore wove in between alley ways, around corners of buildings, she leaped out of her skin when she bumped into someone.

Her eyes met Arthur's and Mathilde's.

"Why do you keep disappearing?!" Mathilde questioned. Her brow pulled tight.

"How did you find me so quickly?" Lore questioned.

The fox pinched the skin in-between his eyes. "*Scent,* Lore, remember? You have a strong scent."

Lore's gaze hardened, which caused the fox's expression to soften. "Lore," he said lowly. "What's wrong?"

Then Merlin turned the corner and launched a fireball down the alley. Luckily, Arthur was quick to push everyone to safety, and avoided being burned to a crisp.

Mathilde's eyes grew wide as if she were seeing the Warden step from the veil again and mouthed, "No."

As the mouse struggled to find the words, Lore staggered to her feet and fought the frost that felt like it was creeping up her arms.

"Why?!" she shouted.

Merlin hurled another golden fireball, but with a swift movement of her arm, a wall of ice appeared in front of Lore. When the fire hit it, the flames sizzled into silence in the melted ice.

"Why do I always have to be right?" Arthur groaned, moving to stand next to Lore.

On the other side of the frosted barrier, Merlin seethed, "I thought it was already clear."

Lore tried to steady her breathing. *He knew the whole time that I overheard him in that run-down bar.*

As the bat spoke, flames spewed from his mouth. "I thought it was obvious once Gannon was out of the picture."

Lore looked at Mathilde, who seemed too frozen in shock to move at the sound of her father's name. But as she watched the mouse, frost started creeping into her vision.

"Long ago, there was one who thought he could take the place of the Great Hare. Simply by killing it."

"Larken Dreadway," Lore murmured.

Merlin continued his admission while pushing the trio back down the alley. "There was more to it. Once in a blue moon, a Great Spirit will put a fragment of themselves in a vessel. Normally, that individual would become the Grand Castor."

Mathilde and Arthur dispersed as the trio found themselves in the city circle and Merlin peppered them with fireballs. He continued his revelation. "And the only way to kill a Great Spirit and take their place is by killing its weakest spot. The vessel…"

Lore felt ice leave her fingertips as a protective wall shielded her from the blast of heat. Her heart felt like it was trying to claw its way from her chest. She jerked her head around, frantically searching for Mathilde and Arthur. The pit of her stomach only grew without an eye on her friends.

It only took a second for Merlin to break through the frosted wall.

"Make this easy for everyone," he growled, "and *stand still.*"

Lore couldn't tell if it was a sense of dread or magic, but in that moment it felt like winter made its home deep within her bones. She wasn't thinking. Instead, she did what felt natural, and that was shooting ice from her fingertips.

Heat from Merlin's flames rushed by her, and her fawn legs, which she had complained about thus far, moved her out of the way with a fine-tuned animal instinct.

Visions of the Great Stag disrupted her sight, but through her, the Stag launched a series of ice shards towards Merlin.

He evaded two, which shattered like glass when they hit the building behind the bat. One was all that was needed to slow the bat down. But that didn't stop him from sending another attack her way.

They exchanged shots at each other, left and right.

The constant battle, and lack of breaks, left Lore dazed. She didn't know this city like she had come to know Charmsend. Merlin continued to close the gap between the two. Her breath became more labored and her hooves caught an uneven brick in the path, sending her to the ground with a thud.

Merlin loomed over Lore, and just as the cool frost almost completely took over her field of vision, gray fur appeared.

Mathilde stood between Lore and Merlin.

"Why are you doing this?!" the mouse demanded.

The bat let flames dance on his fingertips. "This was *always* the goal."

Lore watched as the mouse's breathing became labored. She stood to her hooves, her furred legs trembling with adrenaline. "What about Gannon?" Her voice echoed in the empty streets covered by night.

The bat scoffed. "Gannon was a fool."

Lore swore she heard Mathilde's heart shatter on the cobblestone just a moment before she heard Arthur's snarling. Her eyes quickly locked onto the fox, who had pounced onto the bat from behind. Arthur's axes were locked around the wielder's neck, but Merlin only seemed annoyed.

He groaned and from the ground, two vines erupted to the surface.

Lore immediately knew from their bright blue thorns what they were.

Fire flower.

"Arthur!" Mathilde yelled.

Lore scrambled to cast a beam of ice that struck one of the green tendrils on a path to strike Arthur.

"You are such a stubborn thing," Merlin grumbled, waving an arm and sending a gust of wind to sweep Lore and Mathilde's feet out from under them.

Lore locked eyes with Arthur, who was on the other side of Merlin. Defiance steeled the fox's features.

"You three have proved to be much more problematic than useful." The bat turned to the fox. "You with your persistent skepticism." The bat shot a gaze toward Mathilde. "You with your abundant amount of questions and anecdotes."

Lore watched as the bat's face darkened.

"And you, human," he spat. "Your kind was said to be incredibly weak, but yet here you are, with the persistence of a cockroach."

Before Lore could think, Merlin made fire rain down upon the city.

She scooped up Mathilde and dashed for cover. Once in an alleyway, she scanned for any sign of Arthur. Panic rose in her chest when she couldn't spot the fox. Buildings became candle wicks and her vision clouded with swirls of charcoal clouds.

"He's out there," Mathilde coughed. "He's out there. I know it," the mouse insisted.

Thrumming bells echoed through the streets.

"I'll go," Lore said, dashing out into the Silver Lining Landing square. Lore didn't know where Merlin was with all the smoke and flame, but she didn't need to.

She felt the icy bottle of Stag's Essence call to her from her pocket. Her hand reached in and instantly Lore felt the burning licks of frost against her fingertips. She popped the cork off with her teeth, spit it out, and downed the swirling blue liquid. It tasted like a tingly mint was infused with the world's coldest water. When she inhaled, she was met with a sharp chill. And this time, the visions of the Great Stag were different. They now showed her and the Celestial Animal walking side by side.

She channeled the cold in her bones and directed it outward to encase her. A protective flurry of snow kept the heat at bay while she searched the area for Arthur.

"*ARTHUR!*" Lore called over the roaring blaze. "*WHERE ARE YOU?!*"

Instead of being met with a smart remark from her friend, a vine snaked around her ankle. It instantly shriveled and released her upon touching her frosty skin.

"Merlin!" She snapped, making the flurry of snow circling her grow to a howling blizzard as big as her. She shot a few shards of ice towards the bat's figure.

He moves like a shadow.

"You did all this for power?" Lore's voice faltered. She didn't understand how someone could only chase power above all else.

Power can't replace the comfort of a friend's listening ear.

The bat's laughter rivaled the city's ringing bells. However, now the bell's cries were accompanied by the screams of the locals. "You don't have to understand, in fact—" He hurled fire at her again, which was only smothered by her chilly powers. "I don't expect someone as simple as you to understand."

Power can't replace the belly aching laughter shared with loved ones.

Merlin stepped closer, and each step continued to add to the blaze of destruction around him. "I will be immortal in the stars. Everyone will know of me and my rise to greatness because the Stag's soul is tied to yours. I can kill it by killing *you.*"

Lore winced. She recalled all the warm ways in which Gannon was remembered. *After all, what is life after death if not living on through the stories told in your memory by loved ones?*

Her mind flashed to the sadness in Crosby's eyes when she crossed into the plane of the Warden's home.

"I don't think you know what you are asking for," she said.

The bird had clung to anything that reminded him of his prior companionships before being chosen for the responsibility of the Warden. The corvid didn't die.

Unbirthdays must be a sacrifice in exchange for the power he holds.

Her focus stayed on Crosby in his little house, made of a dying star.

"A permanent place in the stars sounds like such a lonely fate."

Merlin laughed at her statement. "Stupid human," he grumbled. A howling wind whipped up the flames behind him. "Now stand still and *die* already."

As golden fire licked her skin, she felt a sudden jolt.

Lore crashed and skid across the ground, Arthur at her side.

"You're welcome," he said quickly, already standing back to his feet. "Come on, I hear them coming," the fox said, pulling her along.

"Who's coming?" Lore asked in a strained breath.

"Water bearers," Arthur said, as if it were obvious. "Oh, where is Mathilde?" he demanded, rather than questioning.

"That way," Lore said, tugging against the fox's grasp. "We were in an alley."

The two maneuvered around fallen debris, making their way back to the mouse. "We need to get to—"

The fox was interrupted by a giant hug from Mathilde.

"Higher ground," Arthur finished, already eyeing some terraces that overlooked the square, even as he returned the mouse's embrace.

"I knew you were okay," Mathilde spoke through tears. "I'm glad you both came back."

"We aren't out of the fire yet," Arthur said. He gestured for Mathilde to step onto his hands, which were cupped together.

She did, and the fox boosted her up so she could climb up.

"Come on, Lore, you're next." His voice was growing frantic, and a faint stream of water was already pooling on the ground beneath them.

Lore could hear the rushing of ocean waves crashing through the streets. She didn't think twice and instinctively called the Stag in her mind. The season of winter howled in her and she knelt down to freeze the water beneath them. When she raised her arms, a tower of ice raised Arthur to the terrace.

The next thing she knew, she was pulled under a rush of water, her antlers collecting lifeless vines that once flowed with Merlin's magic. Being tossed in the current made fear rise in her chest at the memory of being pulled down the well by the mountain spirit. *She'd survived that, but would she survive this?*

She surfaced and gasped for breath as she looked around, her head bobbing just above the water. The gray waves of salt water were hard to navigate. She saw many animal folk on higher ground, but a few were successfully fighting the current.

A clawed hand snatched Lore from the turbulent current. "Hey, stranger," Lyudmilla said, gripping Lore's flannel, and the other firm on the hilt of her axe, which appeared to be jammed in the ground. "Gotcha."

"*Merlin,*" Lore stammered out. "The whole time."

"Ain't it something that two of the three blokes I knew turned out to be power-hungry monsters?" The water crashed against Lyudmilla as she spoke, but she seemed unfazed by the power.

As Lore got her bearings, she saw in the distance a small, unconscious figure floating.

"Lore, freeze the current," the wolf instructed.

"I can't."

"Yes, you can."

Lore knew water and ice were connected, but freezing some pooling water versus freezing the water of a rather angry ocean felt like a big leap.

Lore tried to concentrate on her breathing, but it was rather hard given the salty waves crashing against her lips.

"You can do this," the wolf whispered right in her ear, so she could still hear her over the roaring water rushing past the two.

Lore's fingertips tingled with numbness. She wasn't sure if it was because of the ice in her bones or the fear pulsing through her, but somehow, from that sensation, she centered herself.

Her vision iced over. The antlers atop her head felt like they were growing from winter's weight, and her hooves ached from the biting cold. Her mind drifted for a moment to the Great Stag. What it had meant to be its vessel, and if she was meant to become the Grand Castor, like Merlin had said when this fight began.

Would that mean I fully transform into an animal?

Ice spread from Lore like frost dancing across glass. The water froze around the wolf and human, and the water at their waist calmed. The two crawled from the hole onto the frozen sea water around them. Waves mid-crash, frozen in time.

Lyudmilla walked over to the small body slumped over, encased in Lore's magic. "Stop the show, you little rat with wings," the wolf growled as she tore the little Wielder from the ice and launched him across the way. "I've seen you survive worse."

"Lyudmilla," Lore said softly. "We should take him prisoner."

But it was too late. Merlin was already standing. A haunting laugh erupted from his body. When he looked at her, his eyes seemed to burn with a hatred she didn't understand.

Even now, as she stood as the primary target of Merlin's attacks, she couldn't bring herself to hate him.

The bottom—animal—half of her didn't fail her as she dipped and dodged the heat of Merlin's fire.

Her mind drifted to her father, the way his voice would boom like thunder, and even though the memory brought the faint smell of beer to her nose. She didn't hate her father, so how could she hate someone she saw once as a friend?

Each time Lyudmilla tried to close in on Merlin, he'd hit her with a vine that erupted from a nearby iced-over flower bed. The wolf howled with frustration, and Lore cast a few ice beams, but Merlin was able to neutralize them with a fireball.

She didn't know how he got there, but soon, she saw Arthur come in from the opposite side of Lyudmilla and get a strike on the bat before meeting a gnarled vine himself.

Lore searched frantically for Mathilde, and she met the emerald eyes of the mouse on a balcony. She had made a makeshift slingshot.

There were four of them and only one Merlin. *They could do this.*

The three on the ice struggled to move without slipping. Lore's ice beams became clumsy. And every time Lyudmilla or Arthur gained ground, twisting vines kept them at bay. Mathilde's ammo, from frozen ice shards to broken brick from buildings, was all swatted away on gusts of wind with a flick of Merlin's wrist.

As time passed and their struggle remained the same, Lore's breath became labored and she felt her strength start draining. Though her physical body was tiring, the winter that had settled deep within her flurried like she had a storm brewing inside her that at any point would break out. When her vision frosted over before, it had always felt like she was looking through a window with blueish glowing frost covering it.

But now, the layer of ice was getting thicker and all she felt was an intense cold surrounding her. The voices of her friends seemed to melt into the background, and her movements became pure instinct. The ice beams that shot from her hands earlier became unbridled blizzards.

Merlin's fire couldn't survive its sheer cold. Lore's hooves shattered the ice beneath her as she closed in on the bat. If she could take in his features, a different person may have reveled in his split panic. But Lore's heart ached a bit when she encased him in a tomb of bright blue ice.

His hands twitched with frost.

Arthur's paw rested on Lore's shoulder, and her vision defogged just enough to recognize her friend's face.

"You did it," Arthur said. "You nullified Thimbleton's greatest threat."

Lore felt Mathilde's embrace on her leg, though she didn't know when the mouse came down onto the icy battlefield. The warmth of her friends gave her a sense of comfort.

"Ahem." A familiar voice called their attention. "Thank you four for your service." Her voice felt like a warm spring breeze after a cold winter. The queen looked around her city that was damaged beyond belief. "It'll take time to rebuild and clean up, but better to rebuild something new then become buried under the rubble of what was."

She walked past the heroes with a guard close to her.

With a silent wave of her hand, she commanded the guard to secure a pair of iron shackles on the Wielder's wrists. "You're under arrest for attempted murder, and attempted ascension to the celestial kingdom."

The otter queen turned to look at the human, fox, and mouse. "When a city is destroyed, it always seems to come down to you three." Her voice attempted to carry a joke, but faltered at the end. "Story of the battle with Crinkle at Charmsend spread almost as quickly as the bat's fire." She let out a sigh. "Please come with me."

FORTY-ONE

The group recouped at the queen's palace. But even the glistening castle cave didn't raise their spirits.

"So, you can't send Lore home?" Arthur asked.

"No," the queen answered, her voice oozing disappointment.

Mathilde grabbed Lore's hand and squeezed as if to signal, "It's okay."

"Not until the prophecy is fulfilled," the otter added.

"So, she has to kill Merlin?" Arthur pressed.

Lore squeezed Mathilde's hand back.

"Most likely."

The two words hung heavily on Lore's shoulders. Her grip on Mathilde's paw loosened, and she walked out the double doors to a terrace where the blue waterfall glowed softly.

"What a way to start the day," a familiar voice teased.

Lore looked to her left and saw the mountain creature on the railing. "Long way from home for you, isn't it?"

The creature smirked. "No."

"Why are you here?" Lore asked. She looked at her friends, who appeared to be stuck in time. "They don't see you, do they?"

"No," the Puca said flatly.

"So, why are you here?"

The shadowy creature sat down and gestured for Lore to do the same.

She did.

"What troubles you?" The imp asked plainly.

Lore sighed, "Some stupid prophecy says I have to kill Merlin to be able to go home."

The creature's smile looked like a hooked crescent moon, "What was the prophecy?"

Lore wracked her brain. *There were two variations, but surely the spirit was asking about the otter's version.*

"Revive what has long been dead.
In order to set Thimbleton free,
The sacrifice must be made.
Prepare to be the one who bled,
Or all humanity shall be shed."

The Puca cackled. "Lucky for you one of my many talents happens to be loopholes." He rubbed his hands together. "Time spent away from the ones you love was the sacrifice."

Lore felt her jaw soften. "You're right, it was a sacrifice."

The imp gave out a hysterical laugh. "No need to separate someone's soul from their body."

*Separate. If a soul can be separated from a body then...*Lore felt so stupid for not thinking of that sooner. "You know—" she began, but Mathilde interrupted her.

"No, Lore. We don't know."

Lore let out a sigh and looked at the bat in the iron shackles. It seemed obvious now what she'd have to do. She took a step closer.

Arthur grabbed her arm. "Lore, are you sure you can end him?"

The human shook free from the fox. "I will not be like him. Killing isn't the answer. There is another end for folk like him."

A painful chill moved through her bones. Lore swallowed the nerves that felt like ice chips in her throat. The antlers atop her head felt heavy again with the weight of winter and her vision frosted over. Flashes of the Great Stag replayed in her mind as she reached forward and placed her hands on Merlin's shoulders.

The sensation of fire warmed her hands.

Followed by vines wrapping around her hooves. The chill within her core began to spread and while she heard her friends murmuring,

Lore couldn't fully make out what they said. Instead, she focused on her breathing. With every inhale, the metal taste of magic coated her tongue, and with every exhale, she felt the adrenaline rush of magic leaving Merlin through her.

His was a Wielder no more.

The only way to make dangerous folk not dangerous to others is by cutting them off from power.

FORTY-TWO

The water rushed down the side of the inner cave walls. The sounds of bells and low drums filled the cave.

"Are you certain?" the queen asked Lore. "Once you leave, you won't be able to come back."

Her chest radiated with hurt. Part of her didn't want to leave, but she knew deep down she didn't belong in Thimbleton.

"I'm certain," Lore said shakily.

The otter queen began her rite. Soft blue light filled the space like a moonrise on the first clear night of winter.

The water moved fluidly, almost as if it had a mind of its own, and snaked towards Lore. Arthur and Mathilde's grip on her hands tightened.

"I'm not ready to say goodbye," Mathilde admitted through tear-filled green eyes.

Lore pulled the mouse and fox into a hug as tears flowed down her freckled cheeks. Knowing what awaited her back in her world made it a bit harder to leave Thimbleton. To leave the magic. To leave her new-found friends.

Her mind flashed images of Maccon. Though she'd be returning to a world without her Mamó, that world was still hers, and she needed to return to it. Face her family and find magic wherever she could.

Arthur stepped back first, the water making its way closer to the three of them. Mathilde still held on tight to Lore. Arthur had to gently coax her away from Lore's embrace. "It's time Mathilde," he murmured.

His eyes looked like glass as he pulled the mouse from the human and watched as the water engulfed Lore.

It felt cold, cold like the water that brought her here. A blinding flash of light illuminated the darkness. And suddenly the antlers that were once atop her head floated in the surrounding water. The fur on her legs molted off, and the pain that was aching through her bones since the transformation began was washed away with the current.

She reached out and managed to grab one of the deer sheds as the water began to feel numb on her skin. She let out a breath, unable to hold it any longer, and that was when she felt like she was falling. This time she fell and landed in a field of purple flowers and saw constellations of worlds far away from Thimbleton.

"Hello, again," Crosby greeted her.

The crow helped her up, and the two began a walk through the field of endless plum-colored flowers.

"Crosby noticed the human is different," The Warden said gently as a soft warm breeze wove between them.

Lore gripped the single antler with both hands and fought back the bittersweet tears of parting with her friends. "Yeah, I suppose I was different when I saw you last. I was more animal-like."

Crosby shook his head in disagreement. "Silly human." He let out an abrupt squawk. "Not when you saw Crosby last, different from how you arrived in Thimbleton."

Lore tilted her head, a wave of confusion falling over her. "What'd you mean?"

"Less sad, more at peace."

Lore grinned as she wiped more tears from her cheeks. "I don't know about that. I'm going to miss Mathilde and Arthur. I'm broken up that I had to make the choice to leave them."

"You know," Crosby stopped and focused his gaze upward to the swirling galaxies and constellations, "Crosby knows a thing about true friends. True friends never really leave you—they just visit you in different forms."

Lore tried to control the trembling sadness in her hands as the crow kept talking.

"Because when one stares into the abyss for as long as Crosby has, one may see that everything is connected."

Lore didn't notice when Crosby opened the veil. She continued walking, letting Crosby's sentiment occupy her mind.

"Crosby," Lore began, "I don't think I can go back to who I was before Thimbleton."

Lore let out a breath as she focused on her words while her fingers ran over where she'd become accustomed to the familiar ridges of the antler. The weight no longer rested atop her head. Her legs felt as human as they used to be—she could even wiggle her toes again.

"But I think that's ok." Lore nodded to herself. "I was a different person then."

Then the sound of a crow cawing overhead drew her attention to the sky, where she saw a field of daffodils and she emerged from the treeline. Warm summer sun kissed her cheeks and an equally warm breeze hugged her as if to say 'welcome back.' The clear sky brought tears to her eyes and the sound of gravel beneath her feet sounded like home. She walked up the steps of the cabin, tears rushing down her face, and turned the doorknob.

It opened, and inside the house, the smell of her grandmother hung in the air. The cabin had been untouched, and she fell to her knees. Cradling the single shed that remained in her hand. The only physical remnant of her adventures in Thimbleton that made it back with her.

"*Lore*," Maccon's voice was raspy. "You're back."

She looked over her shoulder and saw her childhood best friend and nodded. Words couldn't capture what she felt to see him again.

He dropped to his knees beside her and hugged her. "You're ice cold."

She laughed through the tears.

"It's the hottest month of the year," he kept talking. He helped her up and walked toward the driveway, his eyes filled with worry. "Come on, we need to get you to the hospital."

"Then what?" she asked as he carried her to his truck.

"Then," He paused. "Then tell me where you've been?" he continued as he opened the truck door. "I've been here all summer waiting for you to come back." He paused, she could tell he was trying to find his words, "Lore, after the funeral we began going through her things. I thought you just ran off and needed to be alone and you'd show back up later that night, but I'm glad I stayed because I'm the one who found her will."

She fidgeted with the shed in her hands as he closed the door and ran around to the driver's side. "What was in it? Do I get at least one of her teacups?" she asked.

The corner of Maccon's mouth twitched as he fought the urge to smile. "Lore, you get the whole cabinet of cups. She left you the cabin, the land, everything. I've been taking care of it until you came back."

Everything? Lore's eyes found the blue brick well on the far side of the cabin as Maccon slowly backed down the dirt drive. Tears filled her eyes. They didn't sting with hurt, though. They poured over her cheeks with relief. *Not only do I get to live in the comforts of Mamó's home, but I also get the wishing well. The portal to Thimbleton. To my friends.* Her heart skipped a beat. *Could I go back?*

"I knew you'd come back home."

A sour thought crossed her mind. "What about my parents?" she whispered. *Surely, they're contesting the will.*

Maccon seemed hesitant, as his foot kept on the gas, "Well, your dad has been pretty consistently going to AA." He looked over at her and then back to the road, "And your mom has been going to therapy and taking a financial literacy class at the library."

Lore felt her eyes grow wide with disbelief and collapsed back in the seat. She had waves of mixed feelings that crashed into her. *It only took me falling down a well for them to get their shit together.* She was happy it was finally happening, but a sadness panged in her chest at what it took for it to happen. She looked out the window and caught a glimpse of her reflection. *Yep, still human.*

No Crowned One here.

"Lore, they were so worried when you vanished," his voice softened. "And I was, too." His ice-blue eyes seemed to melt when he brought his gaze to hers. "You're my best friend. I missed you so much."

Lore felt like her words were stuck in her throat.

"But tell me where you've been, Fire Flower."

Lore sighed. "You wouldn't believe what I went through."

"I might." Maccon slammed on the brakes at an empty four-way, put the truck in park, and cleared his throat. "I mean, I did just say your parents were getting their shit together, after all," he said, his voice shaking a bit.

She nodded and slid across the bench seat to give him a big hug.

"It's so nice you're back, Fire Flower," he said again, as if he had to keep reassuring himself that their reunion was real.

She felt a smile creep onto her face and returned to the passenger seat.

"So, tell me what happened." Her friend shifted the truck back in gear and began driving again. "At your own pace, of course. I can only imagine what you've been through."

"You'd have to be mad to believe it," Lore said breezily, picturing Mathilde and Killmoore back in Thimbleton. "Absolutely moonstruck."

"All the best people are," Maccon replied. His words engulfed her like the warm comforting light of a streetlamp.

EPILOGUE

ARTHUR'S POV

The cave was empty the moment she left. Mathilde continued to cry into my chest as the others silently left. We sat by the waterfall for I don't know how long.

Now what?

What will we do now?

What will life look like now?

"There, there," I whispered and patted Mathilde's back.

"What are we gonna do now, Arthur?"

My ears flattened. *It was true then. It was real.* I let out a breath and grabbed Mathilde's shoulders and knelt down to be eye level with her. "What'd she want us to do?"

The glossiness of her green eyes broke with more tears streaming down her gray furred cheeks.

"It's okay," I assured as I grabbed her paw and brushed away tears of my own with my free arm. "Come on, we got friends to see, a whole world to explore."

The mouse stopped dead in her tracks and the fox didn't have the heart to drag her along further.

"She will never be able to see my sisters again, never laugh at your terribly timed jokes, or squeeze my paw to let me know it's okay."

Then, right as I was going to bullshit some way around this very real, very soul crushing heartbreak, we crossed the river towards the queen's castle. A lone deer shed floated downstream, and I reached to grab it. I turned and handed it to Mathilde.

"Here. A piece of her is always with you."

The tears fell more, but she seemed pleased by the gesture. They left the caves and the two rising moons greeted them.

"She'll never get to see Taper now," the mouse sighed and held the antler closer to her chest.

"No, but you can take me there."

"She probably won't remember us." The mouse's realization made her already weak voice crack.

In the distance, the queen was talking to some familiar faces.

Lyudmilla and Dina waved them down, and reluctantly, I guided Mathilde over.

The wolf gave a solemn nod, but rested her hands on her hips and looked up at the sky. "We gave her a memorable goodbye, I say."

"It's not goodbye." Fell from my mouth quicker than anyone could reply. I squeezed Mathilde's hand and looked up to the same star filled sky. "It's until we meet again."

CROSBY'S CROSSING

HARDCOVER EXCLUSIVE SCENE

The water of the well washed away any remnants of Thimbleton's vivid magic from the crow's inky feathers. This was a cleanse the corvid became accustomed to through the eons. The crow's mind fluttered between thoughts.

Will the human be ok? Will she cross the thin plane of worlds or get lost in the Ether?

Crosby has seen many heroes through their stories, and he seldom thought of them after his purpose had been fulfilled in their tale.

Crosby's glowing yellow eyes snapped shut as his body began to transform. Lore was different. *Crosby and Lore had fun,* the crow thought to himself as embers of the universe fell around him. The sparks landed on his wings, warmth burning away at the form he took in Thimbleton.

Who needs Crosby's guidance next?

Shifting between realms was a painful process, but a necessary part of being the Warden.

What story will Crosby fall into?

Crosby wasn't sure when he'd return to the land of animals who could wield magic. The crow wasn't sure where he was headed. The only certain thing was the pull of agony in his hollow bones.

He, and he alone, must watch over the tales of the forgotten realms. A brilliant bright light that consumed his body now unwrapped the significantly smaller corvid.

Crosby's new form.

"Where you're heading next isn't like anywhere you've been before, my little pet," the dreamy voice of Crosby's overseer cooed. "You must lie low there, but your duty to keep our heroes on track remains."

ACKNOWLEDGMENTS

Whether you made it this far because you finished reading or if you just flipped to this page right after you got the book, thank you for picking up the conclusion to Lore's story. Thank you so much to the readers who made this book possible for your love of *Down The Well.* I'd like to think one day we can revisit the world of Thimbleton, but I guess only time will tell.

Adventures in Thimbleton was supposed to be a trilogy. If you have been following me online, you'll know Book 2 was suppose to have come out last year. But things happened on the back end, as they often do. So, instead, of just releasing that this year, I was eager to wrap up Lore's story. I had the idea of smashing books 2 & 3 together because I thought it would be better for the reading experience.

Big thanks to Zara for once again letting me have the control over the story in a way not every traditional published author gets to enjoy. And there's no one else I'd want to squeeze through tight deadlines with.

Speaking of tight deadlines, we couldn't have gotten this as clean as we did in the time frame we had if it wasn't for Inimitable Books' editorial interns, Rebecca and Tayler, sloshing through what ended up being dubbed "the Frankenstein draft." Thank you both for all the feedback and I hope the final product is something you both enjoy!

Big thanks for Keylin Rivers at Fantasy Cover Design! The dust jacket for *Cliffs of Wayward* is gorgeous, and I love the way the icy blues contrast the warm greens and golds of the first book.

And big thank you again to Gray for the maps! I know when we originally sat down way back when to talk cartography, I loved the idea that the book's map could act similarly to a video game map, where not everything is given away at once. It only reveals when the player—or in this case reader—gets to that new part.

Thank you to Nia for the illustrations in this book. Much like for *Down the Well,* your art added so much charm to the story. And now Loki gets to be immortalized in ink forever, a special easter egg for our little corner of the online author community.

Last, but never least, thank you to my Lilianna. Thank you for sharing what would be 'us time' with my writing. I know sometimes it feels like nothing more than a time-eater, but maybe one day it'll all pay off.

I love you.

ABOUT THE AUTHOR

Kelli (Veronica's true name) has a deep imagination, and a sail filled with ambition for the sea of opportunity ahead. As a teen, Kelli loved consuming all media about far-off magical worlds. As an adult, she enjoys using her own spellbinding creativity to spin whimsical worlds and charming characters from thin air.

She is a proud Appalachian, but you can't take the mountains out of the woman even if she resides in a coastal New England town. When she isn't crafting a story, she enjoys kitchen witchery, reading to her young daughters, and spending any moment of free time with her spouse.

SCAN ME

Loch Luan
Stormhelm Isle
Keepers' Library
The Cliffs of
Cloch Chruinn
The Emerald
Charmsend